Gingerbread Kisses

Hot in Magnolia

Gingerbread Kisses

Hot in Magnolia

Minette Lauren

Published Internationally by Minette Lauren
Magnolia, Texas, USA
minettelauren.com

Exclusive cover © 2021 Fiona Jayde Media
Interior Design by Tamara Cribley, The Deliberate Page

PRINT ISBN: 978-1-952387-03-6
EBOOK ISBN: 978-1-952387-04-3

This is a work of fiction. Names, characters, places and incidents are either the product of the author's imagination or are used fictitiously, and any resemblance to
any person or persons, living or dead, events or locales is entirely coincidental.

Acknowledgments

A sincere thank you to my editors Amy Sharp and Joanna D'Angelo. Your hard work is always appreciated.

A special thanks to Cristina Donoso for website design, book updates and your amazing friendship.

A kiss to my hubby for his endless belief and encouragement. I know I am not Isaac Asimov, but you still read every page I write, and that means the world to me. You are the best!

Not every story has a happy ending, but in Magnolia, all dreams come true…

Chapter 1

Ginger Lynn Harding pressed the accelerator and opened the sunroof of the sporty red car. The guy at the rental counter hadn't recognized her as the star of *Seducing Saturn*, but he said he wanted to give her a free upgrade because of her perfect smile. She didn't have a lot to smile about, and she sure didn't feel glamorous any more since coloring her golden copper hair a dull chestnut brown. Her symmetrical features and bright green eyes were still the trademarks of Dallas Derringer, but her new look felt drab. She missed her signature flame-colored hair that her mother named her for, but she didn't miss the name on her birth certificate. It sounded too much like a porn star. It was unfortunate that some Olympic ice-skating chick back in the '90s had also attached scandal to the name. So, for now, she preferred to go simply by Ginger.

Smiling as she took the curves of the winding backroads that led to Magnolia, Ginger turned up the jazzy Christmas music and let her hair down. It was only shoulder length now since she had cut off a good twelve inches after she was fired from the set. *Seducing Saturn* was axed after season two, and it was all because of her. She cringed at the memory of the director's harsh words. He'd actually called her a "stupid bitch" in front of everyone. And though his disrespect humiliated her and pissed her off, she felt like one. Why had she ever trusted her ex-boyfriend, Kirk McNeil, who had gotten her into this mess? He was a loser and a jerk, and even though she dumped him over a year ago, he was still haunting her like the evil demon he'd played in *Seducing Saturn's* pilot episode.

Ginger blew out a sigh, trying to let go of her thoughts, but images of Kirk and the video that leaked to the media wouldn't release her. Thoughts of what could have been, should have been, and "what ifs" made her miss the turn.

"In a quarter of a mile, make a U-turn," the navigation app nagged.

Ginger tapped her phone, trying to silence it. "Maybe I wanted to take the scenic route," she complained out loud. Great, now she was talking to herself. It wouldn't be the first sign of her losing it. She'd been having a bad month. First, she lost her acting career, then her new condo. Plus, she had to sell her car for less than she owed to get out of the payments, which left her flat broke.

It was nice of her cousin, Cecilia, to suggest a place to hide out until things cooled off and the media forgot about the scandal. She really couldn't face any more rag-magazine reporters sitting on her doorstep and asking questions she didn't want to hear, let alone answer.

Celia had run into a couple of issues herself. A few years back, she'd done some creative accounting with the taxes for a women's league she ran. Ginger hadn't asked her any questions because it was none of her business, and Ginger liked that Celia did the same don't-ask-don't-tell routine for her. Celia had invited her to hide out in Dallas at her parents' home, but there was no way she could face Uncle Todd and Aunt Brenda with all her baggage. The Lockwood side of the family was uber-wealthy, and her mother's brother was a stickler for social standards and propriety. Besides, it would be impossible to stay under the radar in the circles Celia ran in. People might recognize Ginger and talk about her embarrassing past. Maybe she should amend that to embarrassing present, since she couldn't seem to put it behind her. When she mentioned her concerns, Celia said she knew just the place. And now here Ginger was, stuck in Magnolia, Texas. It looked like the middle of nowhere, but the map showed it was just northwest of Houston. *Perfect.* She didn't know a soul here, and hopefully, no one would recognize her because of her new look.

Her cousin Hank lived in The Heights, but he was a pompous ass. She hoped she didn't have to fall back on that branch of her father's family for help.

"Continue straight for one mile, then…." She punched at her phone again, trying to shut off the volume. Red and blue lights flashed in her rearview mirror.

"Great, just great," Ginger complained as she pulled over.

Grabbing her driver's license from the Hertz envelope where she'd left it when picking up the car, she rolled down the window and waited for the officer to approach.

Annoyed by the five-minute wait and the blistering heat rolling into the vehicle, she tapped her hands on the wheel. Without as much as a hello, she stared straight ahead as she handed him the packet with her license visible on top.

The officer cleared his throat. "Ma'am, are you aware why I stopped you?"

Ginger tried to bite her tongue. She wanted to get this over with but being pulled over on top of everything else she'd been through was the straw that broke the camel's back. "Driving too fast in a one-horse town?" She craned her head to the side and arched a brow, though she realized he couldn't see her snarky wit through the dark-colored Tiffany sunglasses.

"Ma'am, can you step out of the vehicle?"

Oh shit. She forgot she was in Texas. This guy was probably riding on a testosterone high and didn't like sass coming from a lady. Of course, this irked her, too. She could say what she wanted. This was a free country, and besides going five miles over the speed limit, she hadn't done anything wrong.

"Officer, I object. I didn't do anything to have to get out of the car. Should we call the station to report this to your superior? I don't think I feel safe with you breathing down my neck and telling me what to do. Just give me the ticket, and let's get this over with." Ginger reached for her cellphone in the console.

That earned her a sharp, "Hands up where I can see them. Slowly remove yourself from the vehicle."

Chapter 2

Roland Karr started his day by stepping in a puddle of piss. His sister, Madalyn, had picked up a mangy dog off the side of the highway the day before, as she was known to do, and had unceremoniously left him for Roland to take care of.

"Don't be a scrooge," she'd tossed at him as she hurried out the door at 6AM.

It was almost Christmas, and it was eighty degrees outside at 9AM. *Bah humbug.*

His stomach rumbled. Maddie was working the early morning shift at the diner today, so he thought he'd kill two birds with one stone. Roland knew she needed the job since her recent divorce had left her a single mom, but he didn't have time to house-train someone else's mangy mutt.

Before going to the station, he drove to the diner to grab breakfast and tell Maddie that she needed to find other arrangements for her rescues, but she was busy. After she filled his coffee cup, Roland let her attend a few tables before trying to have a conversation. Her ESP must have alerted her to his intent because she kept pretending that she didn't see him. He tried waving as she returned to the kitchen, but Maddie darted left to avoid him. At the same time, Maria, the diner manager, rushed from the kitchen with a full tray of breakfast food above her shoulder. As Maddie crashed into her, Maria fell forward, catapulting the tray of pancakes, syrup and all straight into Roland's lap.

"Merry Christmas!" Maddie squeaked before apologizing to Maria and skating off to the back for a bus tub to clean up the mess.

His sister loved Christmas, and though Thanksgiving had just ended, she'd already strung up lights along Roland's front yard shrubs and the fireplace mantle in his living room. He hadn't protested because the one thing he enjoyed seeing most was his niece's face light up when she gazed at all the colorful lights. Kelsey had scribbled the day they were scheduled to get a fresh tree on the kitchen calendar. At exactly three weeks before Christmas Eve, they would go as a family to pick out the perfect noble fir. Kelsey assured him it had to be three weeks so that it was moist enough to last through the season. She'd heard her mother say anything earlier would be too dry before New Year's Day.

Roland shook the holiday thoughts away. The customers in the busy diner stared back at him with his crotch covered in hot pancakes and warm syrup dripping down his inner thigh. His disastrous morning just kept getting worse.

Picking off the discarded food from his lap, he made his way back to the cruiser. He would head to the house for a quick shower and change. The talk with Maddie would have to wait.

A car whizzed past him through a school zone and he made a U-turn. Besides the dog he'd dubbed Lucifer peeing on his floor, fertilizing his front lawn, and digging holes that must lead to China, he'd had food tossed down his pants, and now, he had to do a traffic stop. Roland hated ruining anyone's day, but the red rocket that zoomed through the stop sign in front of the school was asking for it. It was the elementary school where his niece attended second grade, and recently, there had been an accident between a parent anxious to pick up his kid and a student leaving on his bike.

Roland tried to reign in his temper as the brunette sassed him with her fancy sunglasses. Where did she think she was? Better yet, *who* did she think she was? He could tell by her bright red lipstick, perfectly pressed jeans, fancy top, and the gaudy purse in the seat next to her that she wasn't from around Magnolia.

He'd bet the money he'd won from the poker game last night with the guys at the new Hank's Honky-Tonk that she was from Dallas.

He'd felt bad about cleaning out Noah Harding's wallet after laying down a full house, but all was fair on poker night. Besides, Roland had done Noah a big favor when he connected him to the right people who helped expedite his liquor license and building permits for the new Hank's.

Plus, a few years ago, before Noah had left town, Roland had given Noah's gal, Alexa Nash, a warning instead of a ticket for crashing through the front window of the original Hank's. Back then, Noah had it bad for the pretty, single mom, but things had gone awry on the romantic front and Noah had jumped ship. Now the former military officer and entrepreneur had come back to Magnolia to re-open the new Hank's Honkey-Tonk. Roland hoped he would also try to repair the damaged relationship he'd left behind. He liked Noah and Lexi. They had both been dealt hard hands in life and could use a break.

Putting away his meandering thoughts, Roland watched the slim brunette slide out of her car. She probably wasn't packing a pistol in the glovebox, but you could never be too careful. After twenty years on the force, he'd seen and heard everything. Even if she wasn't drop dead gorgeous, with her quick temper, he would have watched her like a hawk.

"Turn around and put your hands on top of the vehicle where I can see them."

She raised her sunglasses to the top of her head, pushing back her sleek brown hair.

"Officer, I'm sure this isn't really necessary. Can't we do something to erase the sudden lapse in my ticket etiquette?"

Roland arched a brow and then raised his voice. "Now!"

He watched as she spun around, putting her hands on the car. Roland nodded with satisfaction, taking a moment to scan her ID. He said her name out loud, "Ginger Lynn Harding." He'd known a few Ginger Lynn's before. Most of them danced for dollars at the men's clubs in Houston. He'd feel sorry for her if she wasn't acting like one of the entitled members of the Magnolia Estates Country Club. She'd said, "…something to erase…." Was she propositioning him? It wouldn't be the first time a pretty woman had offered her services, but this lady looked as if she was more likely to eat nails than kiss up. On the other hand, he'd love to see her try to apologize her way out of this.

"Yes, sir. Is there a problem with my name?" Her tone was curt.

Roland tried not to grin. Yep, she was a tough cookie, and for reasons unknown to him, he liked her push-back attitude. Magnolia residents rarely showed disrespect. They might grumble over a ticket, but Roland had the reputation of being fair and honest. No one ever gave him lip.

"I have places to be today. Can you hurry it up? Whatever this is?" She gave her sleek hair a toss to the side, trying to get a look at him, but her wavy locks wouldn't cooperate. She reminded him of a 1940s film star. Her classic features were the stuff of Ava Gardner, but the hairstyle was all Lauren Bacall, and those green cat-eyes were cutting. He wondered how she would look at him if they had met under different circumstances.

Roland was torn between hauling her into the precinct for the moving violation, plus speeding in a school zone, or giving her a ticket and going home to change. A thought occurred to him. He could give her a warning and ask her to Hank's for a drink after his shift. Roland stared at her Texas driver's license while he tried to decide. As he'd guessed, she had a Dallas address. She'd probably fit in better at Bubbles, with its swank atmosphere and expensive cocktails, but he wasn't into the popular lounge scene. It was the sort of spot where the socialites of Magnolia liked to hang out. A lot of them were good people, like the mayor and his wife and the couple that owned the diner, but it wasn't Roland's thing.

Something about Ginger Harding piqued his interest, and he found himself simultaneously wanting to bring her down a peg or two and wanting to find out why she was so ticked off. If she was having a hard time, maybe he could help her. He didn't like to see anyone suffer. As he inspected her hourglass figure, telling himself it was for safety measures, he wondered if it was her sass that was making his pulse race. Women could be dangerous adversaries, too. He couldn't discount hidden weapons. She was on the thin side but with curves in all the right places. The way she craned her neck from side to side, accompanied by the small cracking sound, was a sure sign that she was losing her last bit of patience. Should he push her button or the kill switch? He decided he would leave his next move up to her.

"Wait here." The officer left her staring at the hood of the car and headed back to his vehicle. After what seemed like forever, he returned. She silently thanked God it was one of those amazing Texas fall days, with beautiful blue skies and sunny weather. At least the rental car had been washed when she picked it up, so her hands were pressed against the clean, smooth red surface. She was also happy that she'd never changed her driver's license from her mother's old address in Dallas.

"You can turn around now, Miss Harding," he said with his deep voice.

Ginger had done some voice-over gigs when she first moved to L.A. and worked with other aspiring actors, but she'd never heard a tone as rich as his. The officer might have angered her by pulling her over, but that voice—amazing. When she stared up into his intense brown eyes, his gaze never wavered. The flecks of gold looked like chiseled amber in the sun. His symmetrical features were punctuated by a straight nose and strong jawline. The constable's dark chocolate brown hair was cut a little on the short side for her taste, but he was law enforcement. They were known to have that military, type-A personality. She should know. She played one on *Seducing*

Saturn. Though her character was in the future and on a different planet, she'd studied police officers and their protocols to hone her acting skills. It was important that her character ring true on the screen. The show was a great success until she'd screwed it all up.

"I see you aren't from around Magnolia."

His tone seemed casual. Was he now playing good cop? Nothing pissed her off more than a man who couldn't stick to his role. Pulling her over and putting her through the wringer for going five miles over the speed limit made him a definite bad cop in her book. *Jerk!*

"What's it to you?" The words were out of her mouth before she could call them back. She needed to remind herself that this wasn't a movie script, and she wasn't running lines with her friend, Brendon. The officer's name tag glinted in the sun, reminding her to engage her better social skills. "I mean, Officer Karr, I don't plan on being in Magnolia long."

Ginger batted her lashes at him for effect. Maybe he would feel less inclined to give her a ticket if she played the damsel in distress. She was an actress, after all.

The officer pressed his lips together and blew out a sigh of what she could only figure was frustration or resignation. She took the opportunity to plead her case.

"Look, I am new in town, and I don't really know my way around. Maybe I could buy you a cup of coffee and a donut to make up for my bad behavior?"

Would he take that as a bribe? She really couldn't afford a ticket right now. Beside the fact that her bank account was near empty, she'd had two speeding tickets in the last year. Texas was strict about points, and she might lose her license.

The officer ripped the ticket from the board he was carrying and unceremoniously put it in her outstretched hand.

"Because you look like you aren't having the best day, I'm letting you off with a warning, Miss Harding. Next time you drive through a school zone going twice the speed limit and run a stop sign, I don't think you'll be so fortunate. Consider this your one and only warning."

As he turned toward his patrol car, he tossed over his shoulder, "Welcome to Magnolia."

Chapter 3

Seriously, she had to pull the donut card? Up until that moment, Roland thought he liked the sassy brunette. She made him want to break out a cigar, open a bottle of cognac and watch old black-and-white movies until dawn. She was a looker—rude, bitchy, and insulting, but she was also seductive, hot, and intriguing with that sultry Ava Gardner style. When she'd turned on her nice side, she had a pretty smile, and her emerald-colored eyes sparkled.

He knew in that instant that he should run. Right then, if she'd invited him to hell, he would have said yes, but when she'd offered him the classic coffee and donut, he'd been miffed. He should have written her the ticket, but knowing she was new in town and looking like she was having a bad day, he'd wanted to give her a break. The oak tree by the stop sign was overgrown, and he could see how someone who didn't know the area might miss the school zone. She was probably being harassed by one of those navigation apps while she was driving, telling her where to turn. He hated those damn things, but outside of Magnolia, he depended on them, too.

Roland drove home to change his uniform. The syrup had seeped into his pants and stuck to his unmentionables. He would have to take an extra ten minutes to shower, again.

As he pulled into the drive, he saw his younger brother's motorcycle parked out front. *What the hell is Luke doing here?* He lived in New Mexico with his girlfriend, Charlotte, and his adopted son, Kirin. There was no way Luke had driven all the way from Santa Fe on that hunk of junk. In a car, it was a thirteen-hour drive at best. *That knucklehead. I bet she threw him out.*

Luke was sitting on the porch, fiddling with his cell phone, when Roland walked up. His little brother's head shot up as Roland's boots clattered on the steps. The old chain on the porch swing clanged as Luke stood to greet him.

"Hey man, I was just texting you."

Roland's pocket vibrated as he reached out to clap his brother in a hug. Luke might be a pain in the ass sometimes, but he was the only brother Roland had. The last time he was in Magnolia, Roland ended up bailing him out of jail after a bar fight and putting him back on a plane to Charlotte. Between the small loans and airfare, Roland had been out a grand. He wondered why Luke was here now and how much it would cost him this time.

"Good to see ya, Luke. What brings you to town? How long you here for?"

The smile Luke wore faded, and he pushed back his overgrown bangs. He still had that surfer hair that all the girls were wild about back in high school. It was brown with streaks of honey-blond, and the back was trimmed shorter, but the front part had a way of falling across Luke's forehead and over his eyes. He still wore a hoop earring in one ear, and his irises were forest green like their mother's. Sometimes it was hard to look at his little brother since Luke looked so much like their mom.

When Charlotte first met him, she couldn't keep her hands out of his hair. Roland supposed it was why Luke never cut it, but at thirty-eight, the man needed to grow up and get a real job. Roland had warned Luke that an art degree wouldn't pay off. The art studio that Luke opened a couple of years ago was probably in trouble again.

"What, I can't drop in to see my family without getting the third degree? You're not glad to see me?"

Roland blew out a sigh. *Here we go.* "Of course, I'm glad to see you, Luke. You know, Maddie and Kelsey moved in a few weeks ago, and we sold Dad's place."

Luke pressed his lips into a sad, straight line. "She told me." Luke shrugged, giving a wan smile. "Don't worry. You still got a couch, don't you?"

Roland put his key in the lock and opened the front door to find the new stray eating said couch. The seventy-five-pound pit bull was a silver color that Maddie called blue. He was terrifying to look at with his golden tiger eyes and powerful jowls, but Kelsey treated him like her personal teddy bear. He'd advised Maddie that pit bulls were known to be aggressive, but she'd waved a hand at him, making a *psht* sound in response.

Roland had never had a dog in his adult life. They'd always had them as kids, but he'd been too busy playing ball after school or going around with his friends to pay much attention to the slobbering beasts. Now, he didn't have time, and if he did, he wasn't sure he was up to the work it entailed. After cleaning up dog pee this morning, he had to open the three cans of dog food Maddie had left on the counter for him.

The mangy mutt must have taken a swim in the water bowl and was now making himself quite at home in Roland's living room. Never mind that Roland had secured a baby gate in the kitchen doorway before he left that morning. The dog had chewed his way through the plastic and wood contraption and was currently gnawing on a hunk of the sofa. Alert now that the house had occupants, Lucifer dropped the fluff, but stuffing still clung to his muzzle. The stray's expression held no shame.

"Lucifer!" Roland growled. The pit bull growled back. Luke chuckled from behind him. Roland turned, giving his brother a sarcastic look. "Oh, you think that's funny, huh? Well, it's your bed that he's chewing up, and he's not potty trained, so you better hope chewing is all he's done."

Roland walked past the sofa and picked up the remnants of the gate lying on the kitchen floor. A splinter pierced his thumb, and he bit off a curse. He had half a mind to call the station and tell them he was sick—sick of picking up the loose ends of his siblings' lives. It wasn't Maddie's fault that her loser husband took off, but she had been the one to get pregnant and marry the jerk. Luke hadn't revealed his drama yet, but Roland was sure there was some class-five hurricane about to hit his cozy small-town life. Time would tell.

He opened the back door, and Lucifer bounced out into the backyard. Roland slammed the door after him. Pointing to the fridge, he motioned to Luke. "Make yourself at home. I gotta take a shower and rinse off the… never mind." He shook his head, not wanting to divulge the depths of his own terrible day. "Help yourself to a beer or whatever, and I'll be back."

Chapter 4

Ginger thanked her lucky stars for sliding out of the ticket. She hadn't been wild about the new mocha color she'd put in her hair, but it was necessary to change her appearance before leaving L.A. Evidently, it wasn't too hideous, judging by the way the cop had looked at her. He'd let her out of the ticket, even though she hadn't been very persuasive. In fact, she had to admit, she'd been downright bitchy. And besides the one moment where the corners of his lips turned up slightly, she thought he might haul her off to jail.

The officer frowned when she said donut, but he smelled like syrup, so she assumed he had a sweet tooth, though his body looked rock solid beneath his tailored uniform. The creases in his pants and sleeves and the shine on his shoes said he was OCD about his appearance, but it looked like he'd spilled coffee in his lap. Maybe that's why he was in a bad mood.

When he scowled at her, she tried to stay quiet and hoped for the best. Ginger reminded herself that this was a small town, and people were different in Texas. She needed to warm up and be friendlier. It was almost creepy how people waved and smiled all the time. It wasn't that way in Dallas when she'd been growing up. She guessed it was the small-town Texas thing. When she'd arrived in Magnolia, the guy at the gas station had never stopped talking, and when Ginger had fingered a pretty potholder by the register, his grandmother had offered to show her how to crochet—for free!

She looked down into the passenger-side floorboard at the plastic animal crate. "Don't worry, Igor. It's not forever. Hopefully, this whole sex tape thing will blow over after Christmas, and I can audition for another part. Maybe after we save some money, you and I can head to New York and do Broadway. No one would recognize me there, and at least I can sing. Maybe a musical would put us back on top." The thought of starting all over again made Ginger's stomach lurch.

A flip-flop sound came from the crate, and Ginger smiled. Igor was the only friend who understood her. The iguana had been a gift from Kirk right before they broke up. She'd wanted a dog, but her schedule and her condo didn't allow pets. Igor had been the perfect antidote for her lonely nights, and he was a great listener. Kirk had been a flash in the pan, and though he'd recently ruined her career, the one good thing out of it all was Igor. He might be a cold-blooded reptile, but he was warmer than Kirk, and Igor touched her heart. On occasion, the iguana crawled out of his terrarium and made his way into her bed. She'd been lucky that she didn't squish him in her sleep, but like a cat, he'd found his way onto her pillow and rested against her head like a sombrero.

Ginger was all alone in this world except for Igor. Her mother suffered from Alzheimer's and lived in a memory care facility in Plano. Her father died of a coronary at the young age of twenty-eight. Ginger was just a little kid when he passed and an only child. Her mother never remarried, and the extended family, including Celia, wasn't close, but Ginger supposed she could work on building relationships now that she'd returned to Texas. Feeling alone was foreign to her, but with the loss of her movie career—that had taken up almost every hour of every day—she felt alone and vulnerable. Hiding out in Magnolia was a new low.

Most of her Hollywood friends pretended not to know she existed after Kirk released the sex tape. Others were too afraid to be exiled by association. Even her favorite sushi restaurant seated her in a back corner and offered to make her order to-go. It was quickly revealed who was real and who was fake in the friend department. At least she still had Igor.

She looked at his crate with affection. "You'll never abandon me, huh, fella?"

Igor answered with another flip-flop from the crate.

Ginger sat in the parking lot of the Cupcake Diner and Dive, enjoying a breeze that swept through her open window. Scanning the text messages from Celia, she read out loud, "Ask for Melvina Banks."

"It's Melvina Nash now, honey. You must not be from around here. Melvina married celebrity Chef Riley Nash a few years ago."

Ginger's head whipped around as the thick southern drawl caught her off guard. The woman reached for the rental car's door latch and gave it a tug. "Come with me, sugar, and I'll find her for you." The skinny brunette with auburn highlights and a wide smile looked friendly enough, so Ginger nodded and followed her in. "I'm Mona, Mona Owens, the mayor's wife and president of the Magnolia Blossoms Ladies League. Are you staying in Magnolia? We could sure use more Blossoms."

Ginger was confused but followed the woman into the cute diner with its vintage look and modern flair. The checked tiles gleamed, and the display cases near the half-moon counter held delicious-looking baked goods. Her stomach grumbled. It had been ages since she'd consumed carbs. The high protein diet she'd been on since moving to L.A. had been hard, and half the time, she couldn't eat meat at all because of the vegan friends she hung out with. Most of L.A. was crazy about dieting. She'd once had an eight-course dinner of nothing but different variations of froth. She didn't even know exactly what the bubbly concoction was but figured it must be something with whipped egg whites.

Mona must have heard her tummy roar over the clatter of the busy diner. "You poor dear. It sounds like you're starving. Sit here and order, and I'll find Melvina. Get me an iced sweet-tea and a Caesar salad."

"Wait," Ginger said to Mona, but the twiggy lady was already through the swinging doors to the kitchen, calling out for Melvina.

Great, she was broke, and now she was possibly roped into buying a stranger's lunch. Ginger sat at the counter, and a pretty blonde with the name tag, Darcey, asked what she'd like to order. Ginger repeated the tea and salad Mona requested but didn't ask for anything else. Her budget was tight, and she needed to start working ASAP.

Mona returned with another pretty blonde who looked at her with a wide smile. "Ginger?" The lady was probably in her forties and full-figured, but her curves were in all the right places. Hollywood would have called her fat, but Ginger thought she was beautiful.

Now that she'd left L.A., she vowed to see people as they were and not tick off their shortcomings in her head. Before, she would have thought Melvina needed to lose twenty pounds, whiten her teeth and put highlights in her hair. Ginger hadn't always been so shallow, but it was the way of the industry she'd been immersed in.

Melvina hadn't used Ginger's last name, and that was great. Not many people knew Dallas Derringer's real name, but the less it was batted around in public, the better. "Yes, I'm Cecilia Lockwood's cousin."

Mona, who'd been super friendly before, now gave Ginger a quizzical, wide-eyed stare. "Celia's cousin?"

Melvina gave Mona a nudge. "Yes, I told you that Addy called me last week because she'd gone up to Dallas to visit her grandmother. She ran into Celia, who asked if Addy would talk to Pop about hiring Ginger."

Darcey put the salad and tea in front of Ginger.

"That's my order. Where's her food?" Mona pointed to Ginger and looked at Darcey accusingly.

Darcey's mouth gaped. "That's all she ordered."

"Aren't you hungry, gal? I swear I heard your stomach rumbling from the next county."

Ginger flushed, playing with the napkin holder as she shook her head. "I'm on a diet. I just came to talk to Melvina about the job."

Melvina nodded to Mona. "Could you eat your salad at booth eleven? I'll join you in five minutes." Her eyes roved over Ginger like she was assessing a stray dog. "Maybe I can talk you into trying one of our sugar-free selections."

Mona frowned, giving her a suspicious glance before picking up her salad and tea, then moving across the diner. Ginger could swear she heard the woman huff as she sashayed away.

Melvina smoothed her apron and poured a glass of water for a new customer who sat at the counter. "Sorry about that. Mona is harmless, but Celia has a history with the Magnolia Blossoms and…well, never mind. Let's step in the back, and I'll show you around."

Melvina gave Ginger a tour of the kitchen that ended in the break room. She pulled out two chairs and motioned for them to sit. "Addy didn't tell me much about you, only that you are Cecilia's cousin, and you need a job. Wanna tell me a little about yourself?"

Ginger's heart raced. She didn't like to lie, and yet, she didn't want to reveal her recent work history. She would stick to the basics and leave the rest in L.A.

"I—uh. I'm from Texas. My mom's up in Plano, but she lives in a memory care facility. I try to see her as often as I can, but it's hard. I don't have any siblings, and I'm not really close with any of my extended family. I lost my job recently, and I kind of need a fresh start. Something where I can come in, work, and not see anyone."

Melvina nodded as if she understood completely. "My brother's restaurant is called Fresh Start."

Ginger hoped Melvina was as nice and sincere as she seemed. Besides her pert ponytail and eyes that twinkled with empathy, she glowed with that wholesome, southern-lady charm—the kind seen on the Hallmark Channel Christmas Movies. Ginger couldn't help but like Melvina right away.

"What about Celia? You must be close to her, right?"

Ginger shook her head. She had to be honest, and by the way Mona looked at Melvina when Celia's name was mentioned, Ginger thought it best to be candid. "I haven't seen Celia since her brother Kenny got married ten years ago. We were still in college. I reached out to her now because I truly don't know anyone else." Ginger wasn't acting when her eyes filled with tears, and Melvina handed her a napkin from the dispenser on the table between them. "Sorry, I'm not usually emotional. I've—I've been through a lot lately, and I don't really want to talk about my personal life if it's okay with you."

Ginger dabbed underneath her eyes, thankful she hadn't used any mascara. "I'm not usually a mess, and I can promise that if you hire me, I'm dependable and a hard worker. I won't cause any problems, and I'll stay out of the way. In fact, I want to be invisible. I was hoping to bake, clean, or whatever you need in the kitchen."

Melvina gave her a reassuring smile. "Are you an experienced baker?"

Ginger frowned. She hadn't thought about references, but she was sure her friend, Jackson, from the coffee shop, would vouch for her. She had been a barista in L.A. her first year in California. "I worked in a coffee shop. I didn't bake, but I do make the best gingerbread cookies in the world." It sounded lame to her own ears. Geesh, what had she been thinking? Even small mom-and-pop restaurants wanted job histories, references, and experience.

Melvina tapped a pen on the table. "In the world, huh?"

Ginger stood up. She wasn't groveling to anyone for a lowly baking job. It was beneath her, anyway. She didn't know what she would do, but there had to be another job she could apply for. "I guess you're right. Maybe I don't fit the baker title, but I was hoping…." Ginger started backing toward the door. "Thanks anyway. It's a nice place you have here, and I appreciate your time."

She heard Melvina's chair scrape against the tile, and Ginger felt the woman's cool fingers on her elbow as she caught up to her.

"Hey, wait. I wasn't making fun of you. I'm competitive. You can ask my brother, Eli, or my husband, Riley. They know me better than anyone. You said you make the best, and my head is already whipping through recipes and planning a blind taste test. Now I have to hire you so I can taste your gingerbread cookies." Melvina's hand rested on her hip, and a cocky grin lifted her cheeks. Her eyes sparkled, and Ginger couldn't tell if she was teasing or if she really was challenged by the boast.

"I'm serious. I can't handle not being the best baker of anything, and every year a gingerbread house contest is held in Houston at the Galleria on Christmas Eve. Only the best chefs in the city enter, but I've tried to win for the last two years under my husband's restaurant, Braised. The first year I didn't even place, but last year we won second place."

Ginger was confused. Did Melvina think she could help her win? "So—," she drew out. "Does that mean I'm hired?"

Melvina looped her arm through Ginger's and walked her back into the dining room. "You were hired the moment Addy made the call. It's true that Celia and I don't see eye to eye, but you are your own person." She nabbed a clean apron from a box near the register and handed it to Ginger. "Show up tomorrow at 5AM, and we'll get started training. If you can make gingerbread cookies, you can make all the other kinds too. Thanksgiving is over, and now people will start buying for Christmas. If your cookies are as good as you say, I have a feeling we might win this year!"

Melvina turned, grabbed three large pink boxes and filled them with an assortment of treats. "I'm sending you home with homework. I want you to taste every one of these and write down what you think is in them. List your top three favorites and why, and I'll look at your list tomorrow."

Ginger didn't know what to say. It would take twenty people to finish all those treats.

Melvina stacked the boxes in her arms, then waved to Mona. "Okay then, Mona is waiting for me. See ya tomorrow."

Ginger turned toward the exit, but she couldn't see over the huge boxes she was holding. They smelled heavenly, and her stomach rumbled, echoing her thoughts. The door dinged, and a woosh of air assailed her. She muttered thanks as she tried to navigate through before it shut again. Her boot encountered a lump of what she presumed was the person who held the door with their foot, and she apologized.

"You again." The man's rich voice pricked her ears as she peered around the boxes. Before she could process the terse remark, he continued. "I guess you weren't joking about the donuts. Going to a police officer convention?"

"Geeze, Roland. You're so stereotypical." The man next to him chuckled. "Never mind my brother. His humor is too deadpan. Let me help you with those." The nice man had a toothpaste smile and sported a small, hooped earring in one ear. He lifted the boxes from her arms and turned toward the parking lot. "Which car is yours?"

Before she could answer, the same constable who'd pulled her over that morning replied. "The zippy red one that flies through stop signs and speeds through school zones." He stared at her without blinking. She didn't appreciate his announcing her traffic violations to the world, and she wanted to ask him who peed in his oatmeal but reminded herself that he'd let her off with a warning.

"I was going five miles over the speed limit. Everyone does it. That hardly counts as speeding." She smiled at the handsome man holding her boxes of treats. The cop's brother was gorgeous. He looked like he'd fallen off the audition bus in L.A. He was hot, but his looks were a dime a dozen back in Hollywood. The officer brother had the stuff of Al Pacino with a smidge of Robert De Niro back in the day. He even had a scar on his chin near the cleft, giving his almost perfectly symmetrical features a punctuation mark. He was wearing some type of vest underneath his uniform, which made his frame bulky, but his arms said he was more of a runner than a weightlifter. His tan face and perfectly toned physique said he was active and spent time outdoors. The sharp amber eyes and sculpted jawline made him look like a hard-ass, but there was intelligence there, too. If she were honest with herself, he was more her type than his Hollywood-looking brother. Pompous men with holier-than-thou attitudes were her Achilles heel. Wasn't that what had attracted her to Kirk? Begrudgingly, she admitted that Kirk couldn't hold a candle to the attractive constable. In comparison, Kirk was too pretty-boy handsome and shallow. Officer Karr emitted a masculine sense of strong capability, much like that of a Navy Seal.

The officer's sharp tone brought her mind back from its meandering. "It was ten miles over in a school zone. You failed to see the sign. And running a stop sign is a moving violation, Miss Harding. A misdemeanor in Texas could keep you from getting a concealed carry," he warned.

She tried not to cringe when he blurted out her last name for everyone to hear. Calming her beating heart, she reminded herself that most people wouldn't make the connection to Dallas Derringer. Brushing off his warning, she raised her eyebrows in mock surprise. "Do I really need to be locked and loaded in Magnolia?"

"Lady, I think—"

The actor-looking brother cut him off. "Roland, give the woman a break. Can't you see she's not from around here? And with you as the welcoming committee, she probably won't stay long."

Roland glared at his brother but didn't continue his sentence.

21

The brother with the sandy beach hair gave her a broad smile. "All right then, point me to your car, and I'll load 'em up for you. What's in here anyway? It smells like heaven!"

"It's my homework. Some people actually like donuts." Ginger gave the Hollywood brother a broad smile as she tossed her hair over her shoulder. Darting a smug look at the officer, she wondered if the hair toss had the same effect it used to have when it was a bright ginger-color. *What does it matter? That's not who you are anymore. And, while you are sentenced to Magnolia, nosy, hard-ass cops like Officer Karr are off-limits!*

Chapter 5

"Man, what is your problem? That lady was hot and nice." Luke looked over the rim of his coffee cup at Roland. "It's no wonder you're still single. You need to seriously work on your game."

Roland popped a French fry in his mouth, ignoring his younger brother. He drained his soda and fished in his wallet for his credit card. Darcey whizzed by, giving him a flirtatious smile along with their check. He handed her the card, and she bobbed on her toes before darting off to the register. Luke reached for his wallet, but Roland waved him off. "I got this one."

Luke relaxed. "Thanks. I'll catch the next one."

After their conversation this morning that was derailed by the Lucifer cleanup, he hated to ask his little brother again how long he was staying. It was obvious that Luke wasn't volunteering the reason he was in Magnolia. Roland supposed that whatever had happened between him and Charlotte needed time to work itself out. Maybe Luke's tongue would loosen up at the bar later.

Darcey returned with Roland's credit card, and he scrawled his signature across the bill. "Maddie's staying late until four o'clock, and she asked me to ask you if you could pick up Kelsey after school."

Roland let out a sigh. He never minded picking up Kelsey, but he was afraid poor Maddie was killing herself, trying to make ends meet. "Sure. Tell her no problem." He gave Darcey a reassuring smile.

"I can do it," Luke offered.

"Kelsey on a motorcycle? No way. Maddie would murder you if I didn't kill you first. Go on back to the house, and you can see her after I drop her off. Look, I gotta get back on patrol. I get off at five. The four of us can make dinner at the house tonight, then you and I can go up to Hank's and catch up. That will give Maddie time to help Kelsey with homework and get her into bed."

Luke looked toward the counter where Maddie was filling the pie case. She'd breezed out to say a quick hello while they ate lunch, but she was too busy to return. The diner was packed. "Yeah, she's got a full plate. If I ever see that loser ex-husband of hers...."

Roland nodded. "My thoughts exactly, but I doubt she'll ever see Ed again. Word has it he's married to some girl up in Dallas. She's nineteen and already pregnant. He's been behind on child support payments, but that's no surprise. Ed never could hold a job for long, and he drank up most of his paychecks before the divorce. If you ask me, Maddie is better off without him. Kelsey, too. She needs stability and better male role models."

Luke nodded, but he was looking at his empty coffee cup. "Yeah, but kids need their dad."

Roland chose his words carefully. He didn't know Luke's situation yet. "Yes, they do." He paused, waiting, but Luke's gaze never left the cup. Roland decided to put it back on Ed. "In situations like Maddie's, kids like Kelsey are better off without a dad."

At that moment, Luke looked older. The lines etched around his eyes and mouth were deeper. Roland's little brother was definitely going through something, and in time he would tell his big brother about it. If he'd learned anything from his years on the force, sometimes it was helpful to stay quiet. The best way to help or learn information was to listen.

After agreeing to meet Luke back at the house later, Roland slammed the door to his cruiser a little too hard. When he turned the key, the engine revved, and he put it in reverse without thinking. He'd barely tapped the gas when he heard and felt the crunch. Roland slammed on the brake as he searched the rearview mirror, pushing down images of Rosie Bush's walker beneath the back tires. He'd seen her sitting in her car before he got in his cruiser, so he was pretty sure she was safe. The cursory glance revealed a rusted-out pickup with the hood painted in primer. A young male was already out of the truck viewing the damage and pulling at his own dark head of hair.

The youth was none other than the night manager's kid, Maurice, though he was hardly a kid. He must be about seventeen by now. "Aw man, my mom's gonna kill me!"

Roland walked to the back of the car to look at the damage, rubbing his chin as he waited for Maurice to quit gesticulating with exaggerated worry. It was a small dent in the bumper.

"Your mom's not going to be mad at you. This was my fault." Roland shook his head, looking back at the café. At least he didn't see Luke or Maddie staring out at the parking lot to witness the embarrassing moment. Roland had never had an accident. He spoke at the high school about defensive driving every year. Rule number one, always be aware of your surroundings. Shaking his head, he thought about his speech to encourage young drivers to do a walk around their cars before backing out. It was the best way to ensure safety, even with today's back-up cameras. He'd been so caught up in thinking about the new gal in town with her feisty attitude and wavy brown hair that he completely forgot to look before reversing. It was lucky that Maurice's jalopy was all he ran into. Most newer cars had bumpers made of plastic. His own cruiser would have to have the rear panel replaced along with the bumper. He cringed at the thought of telling his boss. The chief would probably find it amusing but would not be happy about how it might affect the budget.

Roland knew his Dudley Do-Right reputation preceded him. He was a rule follower, but there was nothing wrong with that. The world needed order to function, and it's why he loved being an officer of the law. He didn't like arresting people or writing tickets, but it kept the rest of society safe. People like Maddie, Kelsey, Luke, and even feisty Ava Gardner lookalikes who would rather bite off his head than smile.

"Sorry, Maurice. Take it down to Mac's and have him fix it up. Tell him to send the bill to me at the station. I'll talk to your mom."

Maurice looked relieved. "Oh man, I thought maybe it was my fault. You being a cop and all."

Roland shook his head, blowing out a sigh. Admitting he was wrong didn't come easy, but teaching the law was his job. "I was backing up, and you were moving forward. If you saw me backing up, it's your duty to stop, but I know for a fact that I wasn't paying attention."

Maurice put a hand over his heart. "Man, what a relief. Eli got onto me for texting and driving, and now, I swear, I never touch my phone in the car. I saw you back up, but I couldn't reverse. Ms. Rosie was getting her walker out of the trunk."

Roland understood. He patted the kid on the shoulder, though the teen was as tall as he was. The kid's kind mother was an amazing cook, and though she didn't work in the kitchen as often as she used to, when she did, Roland could tell the difference in the fried chicken.

"Are you going in to see your mom?"

Maurice nodded.

"All right then. I'll go back in with you and explain."

Chapter 6

Ginger wanted to crow with satisfaction when Officer Karr backed his patrol car into the old truck. It served him right for being so grumpy and self-righteous. She'd been sitting in the parking lot, looking through apartment listings on her cell phone. But now what? She had the job. That was the most important order of business. She guessed she could check into a hotel next, but her funds wouldn't last for too many more days, and she needed money for a deposit on a new place. Her credit card was near the limit with the car rental, and she still needed to eat. Eyeing the boxes in the seat next to her, she flipped one of the lids up and grabbed a white cupcake. She hadn't consumed glutenous, sugary carbs in years. The icing melted in her mouth, and she moaned with guttural pleasure. "Um—um—um, this is better than sex," she said to herself through another moan.

"Oh, honey! You must be havin' a dry spell."

Ginger jumped in her seat as her head whipped around to the open window of the car. Damn, she needed to roll up the window and lock the door. People around here had no concept of personal space. An elderly woman with flame-orange hair and matching lipstick held onto a walker as she edged up to Ginger's car door.

Ginger tried to quiet her pulse after being startled. It wasn't like she was in danger of being mugged or anything. The old woman was at least eighty. A crumb went down the wrong pipe, and Ginger grabbed her bottle of water to wash it down. She wasn't sure she heard the woman right. "Excuse me?"

"Darlin', that Melvina does some good bakin', that's no lie, but better than sex? You must not be gettin' any. Or maybe you need to trade in your ol' ride for a newer model."

The woman revved the handles of her walker, making the sound of a motorcycle revving up. Ginger didn't know whether to laugh or cry. It was true. She hadn't had sex in a very long time, and the fact that she'd been immortalized by the stupid video that her ex released onto the internet was horrific and ironic. Her dilemma must have been evident.

"Oh, now, honey. Don't worry. We will find you a man…or woman, whatever your thing is. I don't judge. But, if you don't mind me sayin', we need to get you down to the Dipsey Doodle and fast. This hair color is all wrong for your complexion. You should do *Red in Bed*, like me."

"Is that the name of the color?" Ginger was flummoxed. The woman with flame-colored hair and tangerine lipstick was giving her beauty advice on how to get laid. *My, how the mighty have fallen.* A few months ago, she was dining at the top restaurants in L.A. and was sought after by every talent agent and director in the city. Today, she was being directed to a small-town hair salon for a beauty intervention.

"It's one of those designer brands, honey. Ask for Sharron, and she'll fix that godawful, dreary brown. You'll be gettin' better booty in no time."

"Well…." Ginger cleared her throat, trying to keep it together. "I'll consider it, but right now, I'm looking for a place to live. Know a good apartment finder?" She didn't really think the lady could be of help, but what else could she say to the nosy old woman?

It surprised Ginger when the lady piped up with, "As a matter of fact, I do!"

Ginger couldn't believe her luck. The brassy old broad, who called herself Rosie Bush, sent her to a beautiful ranch right outside of town. Ginger wasn't sure if the name was real or the lady had some odd sense of humor, but she didn't really care. The property was a gorgeous, sprawling expanse of pastures where horses grazed and woodlands surrounded what must be a hundred acres or more. It was owned by a single mom of three young boys. The lady introduced herself as Alexa but instructed Ginger to call her Lexi. Apparently, everyone else did. She turned out to be Melvina's sister-in-law, and Lexi was thrilled that Rosie had run into Ginger at the diner.

"I saw Rosie yesterday at the Dipsey Doodle and mentioned I might hire someone to help out. This place has gotten to be too much since I started my eBay store. Can you cook? Believe me, you don't need to be a chef or anything. The boys mostly want cereal, grilled cheese and tater tots, but I try to get them to eat a few veggies at least some of the time. The house is always a mess, but if you can run a vacuum, load the dishwasher, take out the trash and keep the counters wiped down, that would really help." Lexi bustled around the back garden as she talked, pulling weeds, digging up dead plants, and tossing them into a basket. She was full of energy and talked a mile a minute. Ginger liked the pretty blonde's warm appeal. What was up with all the blondes in Magnolia? Norwegians must have settled here. There was some confusion because she already had a job at the bakery, and that sounded easier than being someone else's babysitter and maid.

"There's a small house down by the creek. You'll have to walk down the trail for about five minutes to get there, but the place is really great. You could drive your car, but I don't recommend it. There's a four-wheeler you can use. It'll come in handy when you have to tote groceries. It has a basket on the back, but you may want to wrap your eggs in a blanket before strapping them in, or they'll be scrambled before you even crack them.

"The cabin's a small efficiency with an open floor plan, electricity, and running water. My mawmaw called it her *she-shed*. She used to go back there and garden, knit, and watch her soap operas. My grandpa used to say she was a witch and was down by the creek doing a bunch of hocus pocus, but I think they both liked a little alone time. Mawmaw was a little like Rosie Bush, if you know what I mean… not the pot or moonshine part but speaking her mind and all."

Ginger could only imagine. The candid old woman seemed like a handful. She didn't think anyone could keep that woman from saying what she wanted. Somebody married to a Rosie would definitely need a man-cave, she-shed, or bomb shelter—anywhere to get out of the line of fire.

Getting back to the subject, Ginger clung to what she needed. "So, you're offering room and board for some light housework and cooking?"

Lexi smiled. "Yes, and I'll pay you some cash. I can't afford a full salary or anything, but the boys go to school most of the day, and I wouldn't have a problem with you having another job after you drop them off at school. Ever since Gus took his pet rat on the bus and got kicked off, I've had to drive him, so now I take all three." She paused as if censoring what else she might have said. "Let's just say, it's safer that way."

Ginger weighed her options. She didn't have any siblings, so she didn't have any nieces or nephews, but she had been around kids in her lifetime, and she liked them okay. Children were usually more genuine than adults, and more than anything, Ginger needed a place to stay.

"How much is the salary, and when can I move in?"

Chapter 7

Lexi couldn't believe her good fortune. She'd mentioned to Rosie that she needed help around the ranch or that maybe she would rent out the cottage. Rosie suggested she kill two birds with one stone and hire someone to help and live on-site. The cabin was sitting empty, and it would save her from paying out more cash than she could afford. Ginger seemed perfect to help out with the boys, and she'd be good company, too. There were so many chores, and the new eBay shop added to her to-do list every day. Besides the ranch manager, John, the men he hired, and her three boys, it could be days before Lexi saw another living soul. She spent hours making stained glass and soldering windows with dried flowers pressed between the thin sheets of glass. With the ranch hands and her boys, she was surrounded and outnumbered. It'd be nice to have another gal around to talk to.

As she waited for Ginger to settle in and come back to the main house, she walked out to the barn to find an extra pair of gardening shears. They'd continue pulling some weeds in the courtyard garden before dinner and get to know each other.

As Lexi sifted through a drawer of old gardening tools, she heard the door hinges announce someone's arrival. When she looked up, John stood in the light of the setting sun. A yellow-orange glow surrounded him, and behind him the scattered stratus clouds were brushed with hues of pink and gold. Lexi gave him a beaming smile.

"Have you seen any gardening shears? I swear I had another pair out here."

John came to inspect the drawer, towering over her five-foot-two stature. He lingered there as she picked up a pair of tattered gardening gloves and moved a small trowel. He was close enough that she could smell the hay, horses and sun of his day. There was something else too. It was his scent, and it wasn't unpleasant. Lexi missed the way her husband, Jack, had smelled. She remembered when they were married, and he'd hug her. She would put her face against his chest, and the warmth of his body and the tangy scent of his skin would entice her senses. She fought the impulse to turn around now and inhale John's shirt.

John's hand brushed past hers, gripping something hidden in the back corner of the drawer. Lexi sucked in a large gulp of air. She'd thought for a moment he was going to hold her hand. There had been several instances like this over the past few months, and she'd wondered if she imagined it.

John held the shears in front of her. "If it was a snake, it would have bit you."

Lexi placed a hand over her heart as if indeed she thought it might have been a snake. "Thank you so much, John. I probably wouldn't have found them without you."

John's gaze locked with hers as she grasped the shears. Her fingers brushed against his in the exchange, and he continued looking at her. "Do you need a hand with anything up at the house? You know I'm happy to help any time."

Lexi appreciated John's work ethic. He was one of the hardest working men she knew, and she thanked her lucky stars that her brother had hired him. Without John, the ranch would be a mess. "Thanks. I'm good for now." She started toward the door of the barn, then turned, looking back at him before leaving. John was more than handsome with his golden-brown hair shot through with natural highlights from the sun. His perfect features made him look like one of those shirtless hunks seen on the cover of a romance novel.

It'd been years since Jack's death and three years since she'd had that night with Noah Harding. Should she let her mind go there? Putting a hand up to wave good-bye, she called back another thanks. The sun caught John's eyes, making them turn ice-blue. He tipped his hat to her with a soft grin. Lord, he was good-looking in a hot-cowboy way. Lexi made her boots move in the direction of the house. No good could come from mooning over the sexy ranch manager. She'd never thought of him that way before, and there wasn't any reason to now, except that lately, he'd been looking at her differently. Did she imagine the sidelong gazes, the shining spark of interest when he stared too long, the subtle smiles at every encounter, and the unnecessary nearness that had never occurred before now?

Shaking off a shiver of awareness, she pushed the thoughts of John away. It had obviously been too long since she'd been with a man, but there would be trouble if she started putting designs on her ranch manager. She should take Ginger up to the new Hank's and have a drink. It'd been too long since she'd been out without her kids. On the ranch, Lexi wore a lot of hats—cattle company owner, on-line crafts entrepreneur, and busy mother of three, but lately, she'd been nagged by a need to wear a different hat. She wanted to put on lipstick and style her hair. An urge to feel feminine washed over her, and she felt like she was suffocating by trying to suppress her basic needs. Maybe it was time to get out of the house.

Chapter 8

Roland had to admit that having family around felt good. Kelsey laughed more in one evening than he'd seen her do in the entire month she and Maddie had stayed with him. Luke might have some issues he was battling, but they were forgotten as Roland fired up the grill and whipped up his famous tomahawk ribeye. They had eaten all of one and most of the second before starting in on the peach pie that Maddie had brought home from the diner.

"I made this one myself," she said with a wide grin. Peach filling oozed out as she cut into the deep-dish pie and plated four slices. "Melvina taught me how to make pie crust today, and she told me I could take whatever I made home. I think she was worried that it wouldn't be up to diner standards, but she's such a sweet lady. I really like working for her and Pop."

"What about her husband, Riley? Doesn't he own half the place, too?" Luke asked.

"Yes, but he's in San Francisco, opening up a second location for Braised."

Roland rubbed his stomach. "What a waste. I hear those California people live off tofu and lettuce."

Maddie rolled her eyes at him. "San Francisco is amazing and has some of the best restaurants in the world. Ed and I drove through there once. We stopped in a little coastal town and had some of the best sushi I've ever tasted."

Roland chuckled. "Exactly my point. They won't know how to appreciate a great cut of beef."

Maddie gave him the sister-glare. "Roland, you are so…I don't know the word, but you are so that!"

Luke laughed. "Yeah, that's what I was telling him, too. This really beautiful lady breezed out of the diner today with a load of cakes and pies, and

Roland all but bit her head off. Apparently, she's an outlaw of the worst sort, going five miles over the Magnolia speed limit."

Maddie shared a knowing grin with Luke. Irritation vibrated through Roland, sparking a headache that he'd been trying to stop all day. It was at that moment that the dog jumped up and grabbed the remaining steak bone off Roland's plate.

"Lucifer!" Roland called out as he chased the dog through the kitchen and out the back door.

Kelsey was right behind him and then passed him when he tripped over the picnic table. "Rollo!" She caught the dog in her arms and hugged him tight. The pit bull was bigger than she was. Her little arms barely made their way around the dog's barrel chest. Roland's niece looked up at him with pleading eyes. Lucifer still held the steak bone tight in his jowls, but his tail thumped a mile a minute. It was all a game to the beast. "His name isn't Lucifer, Uncle Roland. I named him Rollo, after you." Her brown eyes were framed with thick dark lashes that she batted at him with perfect innocence.

Roland tried not to groan out loud. He somehow knew this mutt wasn't going anywhere. "Rollo" was going to be peeing on his floor, eating his couch, and stealing his food for however long Maddie and Kelsey stayed with him.

He looked back at the porch, where Luke and Maddie stood staring back at him. "Aren't you the least bit worried about this breed of dog, Maddie?" Roland pointed at the pit bull. "The beast is twice her size, and look at those jowls." Saliva dripped from one corner of Rollo's mouth, where he still held the bone clamped between his teeth.

His sister stood with a hand on her hip and a terse look on her face. "That dog is a bigger baby than you, Roland. The breed gets such a bad rap by the media, but at the end of the day, he's a sweet dog, and all he needs is food, shelter and love, just like the rest of us."

"I don't need love," Luke contested. Roland figured he was trying to distract his attention away from the dog, but it made him wonder again about the reason Luke had come to Magnolia.

"What about my couch?" Roland pointed toward the house, even though he knew it was a losing battle. Kelsey's eyes brimmed with worry, and guilt squeezed Roland's heart. "All right, all right, but someone needs to teach *Rollo* some manners. If he's going to stay here, we need to cover some ground rules."

Kelsey rolled her eyes, reminding him of Maddie. "Uncle Roland, why do there have to be so many rules? Rules are no fun."

Roland smiled, giving his niece an affectionate rub on the head before bending down and looking her in the eye. They'd had the discussion about why guidelines were important before, but hadn't he broken one of his own rules earlier, to always look before backing up? Two rules if he counted letting a lady out of a ticket because he thought she was pretty. "Okay. He can have the steak this time, but let's try not to make it a habit."

"Are you my brother? What a pushover!" Luke hooted.

Roland stood, giving his brother a pointed glare. "Only for Kelsey. No one else."

Maddie sidled up beside Luke, and both of them smiled at Roland. "That's not what Luke told me. He said a certain beautiful lady made you back into a truck today."

Roland glared at Luke before retorting, "Not true. There wasn't a lady around when I had an accident, except Ms. Rosie, and I hardly think she's the cause of my accident."

Luke chuckled. "Oh, she was around, all right. You should have seen the sparks flying when those two went at it. He was still smoldering when he got in his car."

"No one went at it," Roland protested. Kelsey squealed with a giggle. Rollo licked her, and she ran with him around the yard. Roland took a deep breath, trying to calm his agitation. "Luke is exaggerating. We had lunch after we ran into Miss Harding, so if there had been any 'going at it,' I would hardly say I was still smoldering after thirty minutes." He looked pointedly at Maddie, who was grinning like she had when they were young. He continued his defense, "The lady ran a stop sign in front of Kelsey's school. I think you would appreciate that I patrol the school perimeter."

Maddie's mouth opened, and she put a hand over her heart. "Was anyone hurt?"

Roland shook his head. "No, but she was also speeding."

"I hope you read her the riot act." It was then that he knew his sister was poking fun at him.

"He gave her a verbal warning," Luke chimed in.

"Did you kiss her?" Kelsey crossed her arms over her chest and started making kissy noises.

Roland looked at his niece with shock. "Who's teaching you this stuff?"

Maddie laughed. "She's in the second grade, Roland."

He threw his hands in the air. "All right, everyone. I think there has been enough teasing. Back in the house. Time to do dishes."

Kelsey groaned. "Aw, Mom. Can I stay outside with Rollo?"

Maddie looked at her daughter, then at Roland. "Another fifteen minutes and then homework, shower and bed."

Chapter 9

Ginger patted the top of Igor's scaled head and then placed him in the glass terrarium on the table near the window. He wasn't even two yet, and he seemed to be getting bigger every day. The little efficiency that had belonged to Lexi Nash's grandma was cozy and quaint. The kitchen had everything she needed, and Lexi had supplied her with fresh sheets, towels and bottled water, saying that the well water was safe to drink, but it didn't taste so good. The place needed a little dusting, but that would be easy. A pretty patchwork quilt lay across the back of the plush vintage sofa. The she-shed was chic and looked like something straight out of *Southern Living*. The pitched roof's exposed beams were painted white like the rest of the cottage's interior, and an antique light fixture hung from the center, giving the place a warm glow.

The cabin's proximity to the small stream that flowed through a clump of forest at the edge of the property enchanted Ginger, who felt like a character out of an English fairy-tale. Lexi had said she owned a bit over a hundred acres. The quiet atmosphere was exactly what Ginger needed, the perfect place to hide out until the world forgot about how far Dallas Derringer had fallen. She thanked her lucky stars that Nosy Rosie had overheard her complaints and directed her to the ranch. Ginger hadn't planned on taking up a second job babysitting and cleaning right away, but with room and board included, she now could afford to keep the rental car until she found other transportation.

Lexi hadn't minded that Ginger also held a job at the bakery and said they'd work something out with Melvina so she could help Lexi with the boys in the mornings. Ginger hadn't met the youngsters yet, since they were staying with their grandparents tonight, but according to Lexi, the boys were a hot handful. The light in the pretty mother's eyes and the smile on her face told Ginger they were also well-loved. She could only imagine growing up someplace so majestic. It might be light on entertainment, but the cottage had a TV and DVD player, so she could pick up a few movies when she was in town. The she-shed didn't have internet, so live streaming was out. She needed to catch up on her reading anyway. Ginger reminded herself to take her E-reader to the diner and download a few books for the weekend.

She'd never gardened before but agreed to meet Lexi at the house to help with cleaning up the weeds before dinner. The ATV was invigorating, and she thought she would like this part about living away from the main house. It put her in the center of nature. The tree canopy overhead was bereft of leaves, but the many branches and clumps of pine needles made an earthy, camouflaged kaleidoscope against the blue sky.

As Ginger entered the garden, Lexi handed her a pair of gloves. "These are new, and they are yours to keep. They'll get dirty, but they're washable." She pointed to the rows of dead vines and decayed growth left behind from the cool weather of fall. "I want to clear the brush in this section to make it look less macabre over the next few months. We'll till up the earth now, but we won't plant until spring. Make sure the weeds go in the black bin, so they stay out of the compost."

Ginger picked up a trowel and followed behind Lexi, who set a basket down between them. They worked on pulling up the dead vines and leaves and turned over the fresh dirt to fluff up the soil.

"So, what brings you to town? Ms. Rosie sending you over and Melvina hiring you gives me all the references I need for a tenant, but I'd like to know more about where you come from and why you chose Magnolia."

Ginger stiffened. She knew she couldn't be totally anonymous in a place as small and out of the way as Magnolia, but she hadn't wanted to dive into particulars yet. Just like she had done with Melvina, Ginger stuck to the basics. "I grew up in Dallas. I don't have any siblings, and my dad died when I was a kid. My mother lives in a memory care place, and I feel guilty because I couldn't take care of her all on my own." She looked at the soil as she talked. She saw Lexi's hands moving in her peripheral vision but felt the other woman's gaze flicker over her. She thought about the one relation she did have from Magnolia and the shocked look on Melvina's face when she mentioned Celia.

"I guess I should tell you Cecilia Lockwood's my cousin. That shouldn't be important, but I don't think that news made a grand impression at the diner today, though she is the one who referred me for the job." Ginger paused, waiting for a reaction.

Lexi shrugged, continuing to pull up vines. "Melvina mentioned that when I spoke to her on the phone earlier. Celia had her problems with the Blossoms, but it isn't any of my business, and you aren't Celia, so don't fret. People here will judge you on your actions, not your cousin's."

To avoid more questions about herself, Ginger asked one of her own. "How long have you been divorced?" Lexi stopped what she was doing, and Ginger realized that her distraction tactic probably sounded rude. "Oh God, I'm sorry. I didn't mean to sound nosy. It's none of my business." She shook her head as if trying to shake away the stupid question.

Lexi started to dig in the soil again, pulling at the wilted tomato vines. "It's okay. You have a right to know a little about us, too, since you're going to be living here." She took a deep breath and let it out slowly. "I'm a widow. The boys' father was a soldier in the Army. We married straight out of high school and had Gus right away. Bert came the year after and then, right after Damien was born, my husband got shipped off to Afghanistan. He was taken out by a sniper when his unit was out on patrol. My oldest barely remembers him and only stopped asking about his dad a year or so ago." She stopped, wiping the clean side of her glove across her forehead. A few crumbles of dirt fell to her jeans, and she swiped at them. "My husband's name was Jack. He was a great father, and the boys would have loved him." Lexi rested both hands on her knees and seemed to be contemplating what to say next. "Life's not fair. I guess that's why Gussy is always getting into trouble, and the others are a little spoiled, too. I find it hard to discipline them. My parents help out a lot, and my brothers are great role models for the kids. Admittedly, the boys spend too much time with my mother and father, but it's not the same as having their real dad around."

"You said your oldest is in fifth grade now?" Ginger waited, not wanting to ask how long it had been.

Lexi smiled at her, but it didn't quite reach her eyes. "Yes, he'll be eleven this month." There was a long silence.

"That's a long time." Ginger stopped herself. Who was she to say how long someone should or shouldn't wait to move on, but besides the kids, it didn't sound like there had been anyone in Lexi's life. If the boys were born close together, and the youngest was in second grade, it had been a while. That was a shame since Lexi was a beautiful lady. She seemed too nice to grow old raising kids and tending a farm all on her own.

"I know you're probably wondering. I have dated since, but it's been a while. I really liked this one guy, but I didn't know how to date after all the years with Jack. And I couldn't saddle the man with three kids and a ranch straight out of the gate. His life was taking off at the time."

Ginger watched Lexi as she continued digging. Were those tears in Lexi's eyes?

"Anyway, he wasn't officially divorced, and I wasn't ready to move on. Truth be told, I may never be. I kinda had my heart set on something special, and I think the moment has passed."

Ginger nodded. What was she supposed to say? It's not like she had any better luck at love, and she didn't have the responsibility of taking care of three boys. They worked in silence until the area was clean. They tossed the rubbish in plastic bins, and Lexi promised to show her where the main compost area was later.

"What about you? Have you ever been married? Kids?"

Ginger almost laughed but caught herself, remembering she didn't want to reveal too much of her past. "Let's just say, I haven't been lucky in love either." She thought about Kirk and how he'd screwed her in more ways than one. If there is a jerk out there, she had an internal homing device that would find them, even in the most unlikely places. Her pulse raced as she thought about the officer who was so rude to her earlier. She might have been pissed that he stopped her, but something made her thoughts keep returning to him, even now.

Ginger shook her head. "I don't know what it is, but I'm only attracted to type-A men, and I think the A stands for asshole." Surprised by the crass word she'd said, her gloved hand flew to her mouth before she remembered it was still caked in dirt. She sputtered and spit the small bits onto the ground.

Lexi chuckled. "It's a good thing it's not spring, or that'd be manure you're spitting out."

Ginger frowned at the thought. "I guess I'm lucky after all." They fell into hearty laughter. Each woman bent forward, leaned back and finally straightened with a sigh of relief.

"That felt good. I think we need to do that often."

Ginger smiled. "What, laugh?"

Lexi nodded as she removed a glove and rubbed her forehead. "Hey, let's get showered and head up to the new Hank's Honky-Tonk. I'm sure it's casual, but I haven't been in there yet. I didn't want to go by myself. The old Hank's had great hot wings and homemade chips, and I'm dying to see if they have the same menu. And, I don't know about you, but I don't feel like cooking or doing dishes tonight."

Ginger wasn't sure what she'd expected from a place called Hank's Honky-Tonk, but its intended shabby look, down to the peanut shells on the floor, was brand spanking new. Old diesel station signs hung from the wall, wide, flat-screen TVs were positioned everywhere, and the wood floors appeared hand scraped. It held a second-story loft that looked down on the main floor and featured a massive stage for a band. The building must have been half the size of a Super Walmart. Ginger's eyes widened at the thought, realizing that she was already thinking like a local. Only a gal from a small town would compare anything to a Walmart.

"Wow, this place is something. Did it just open?"

"Yep. If it's anything like the first Hank's, the food will be great. There's supposed to be a band tonight, but we don't have to stay long," Lexi rushed on as they took a seat near the bar.

"Stop. You had me at no dishes." Ginger held her hands up.

Lexi laughed. "You sure you want the job? With three boys, I assure you there are a lot of dishes."

Ginger knew Lexi was poking fun, but she was also sure it was true. "I can handle dishes, but it sounded good not having to wash them tonight. I should probably fess up now that I am not an experienced maid."

Lexi chuckled. "Don't worry. I'm not picky. I need some help. The boys are getting bigger, and there are a lot of things they can do on their own now, but with my virtual shop expanding and Christmas around the corner…." She sighed. "I feel overwhelmed. My parents and brothers are great, and I can get a babysitter when I need one, but it's time I get organized. Ever since Jack passed, my family is always around, trying to help."

Lexi shook her head. "And I appreciate it. I do. But I need to focus on growing my business so I can cushion the ranch through rough times. My rustic barn crafts are really popular, and I have more orders for the wildflower glass than I can keep up with. In the long run, I can't expect my parents to hold up the loose ends of my life forever. It's time for me to make money, and to do that, I need to invest in a domestic helper." She waved toward

Ginger. "That last drought about sank the cattle business, and I don't want to be the Nash who lost the family ranch."

Ginger remembered the name on the business card Lexi had given her to put in her purse. She saved it to remember her new address. "Burns Creek Cattle," Ginger repeated from memory.

Lexi shrugged. "Burns was my husband's name, and it will always be the boys' name, but my great-grandparents bought the land, and I'll always think of the property as Nash land." She chuckled, then sighed. "Sounds like a country singer's resort, Nashland."

Ginger smiled back at Lexi as a young woman in tight jeans and a low-cut t-shirt arrived to take their order. Ginger was surprised by Lexi's complaint. It would be nice to have family to look after you. The relatives Ginger had weren't bad or anything. Well, some of them were assholes, but mainly she'd been working on her acting career most of her adult life, and she'd never been around them long enough to develop a bond.

After signing her contract for the series, she hadn't had time to take extended vacations, including going home to see her mom. The first time she'd flown back to Texas after moving to L.A. was when her mother checked into a memory care facility. It was Uncle Todd who'd noticed things weren't right. Ginger's decade-long absence from Dallas still riddled her with guilt. She'd always meant to go back, but a part of her never wanted to see Texas again. The state offered nothing for her career, and all of her Hollywood friends were usually headed to Vegas, Cabo, or some other exotic destination that seemed like a much better time than sitting in her mother's living room. They'd never had anything in common, and her mother had been angry with her for running off to L.A. The short and skinny of it was their relationship had never been ideal.

Before memory care, her mother's small home had been located in a suburb, where most families settled down to carve out a simple life and grow old. Ginger had been young when she left Texas right out of junior college. Armed with an associate degree that wouldn't earn any money, she at least knew how to wait tables. It was enough to start in L.A. When she lived high on her *Seducing Saturn* life, she hadn't wanted to sit on the couch with her mother and watch reruns of old TV shows. With just the two of them, Christmases seemed too sad. Ginger hadn't realized that part of her mother's reclusiveness was a prelude to her Alzheimer's. She'd become forgetful and gotten lost going for groceries and to the post office. She was afraid people would notice, so she started having everything delivered. But, eventually, people did notice, and where had Ginger been? Maybe the loneliness caused her dementia.

Lexi waved a hand before Ginger's line of vision. Apparently, she'd gotten lost in the past. The waitress tapped her pen against the pad she held.

"You hungry? I'm buying. Get anything you want." Lexi gestured to the menu.

Ginger was embarrassed. Lexi thought her hesitance to order was a lack of funds. It was true that she didn't have a lot of money, but surely, she could afford whatever Hank's had on the menu.

It wasn't long after they ordered that the food was delivered. Lexi hadn't exaggerated. The new Hank's made the crispiest chicken wings, and the hot sauce bordered on volcanic. The homemade, paper-thin, crunchy potato chips were out of this world, and the draft beer was served in a tall, frosty glass. Ginger moaned as she bit into another crisp chip. If she kept consuming carbs like this, she'd be the size of Saturn. Lexi was driving, so Ginger indulged in a third beer. *What the hell.* In all the years she'd lived in California, she'd never once ordered a beer. On or off the set, she played a role, and her character only drank champagne or really expensive Bordeaux. Hank's didn't offer champagne, but the pear-flavored beer on tap that Lexi recommended was actually tasty. The hot wings left a slow burn that made her lips tingle.

"Was the old Hank's this good?"

Lexi nodded. "The food's the same, but the bar is a mite different. I didn't know what to expect, but after Hank Harding took over Bubbles, I imagined the Honky-Tonk would improve." She stared at her drink for a moment as if she remembered something unpleasant.

Ginger hated to interrupt her, but she couldn't hold back. "Hank Harding? I wonder if that's my cousin from Houston."

Lexi looked surprised. "You're cousins with Celia and Hank? I didn't know they were related."

"They aren't. Celia's my mother's brother's child, and Hank is from my father's mother's side. He's like a third cousin or something, but I remember playing with him when we visited my father's relatives during the summer growing up. Hank was a hellion back then, but I saw him ten years ago when Celia's brother, Kenny, got married. He was such a dick!" She covered her mouth and looked over her shoulder in case anyone should hear. "Sorry, I shouldn't have said that. It's just that he actually hit on me! When I pointed out that we were related, he said we were distant enough for it not to matter."

Lexi's mouth opened in shock, and then she shook her head with a chuckle. "I believe we *are* talking about the same Hank."

Ginger groaned. "Oh God, let's get out of here. He's the last person I want to run into." Most of her family knew about her Hollywood career.

Lexi held a hand up. "Hold on a minute, I concede that he used to be an ass, but he's come a long way since Bubbles opened a few years ago. You may like the new Hank, and I'm sure he'd like to see you."

Ginger wasn't sure if Lexi was teasing her or if she was serious. Didn't she hear the part where he tried to seduce his own cousin? Why would she want to see him? Hank had always been a good-looking man. A thought occurred to her and she couldn't restrain herself from asking, "Are you guys *friends?*" Her eyebrows rose as she emphasized "friends."

Lexi stared out at the other tables. She looked like she was weighing her answer. "Not that way, but we are friends of a sort now," she said simply. "Not besties or anything, but we've hung out. Believe it or not, Hank's grown into a nicer guy. He donates a lot of money to the school, the library, the Blossoms Ladies League, which also helps the community. I actually asked him to be my date for one of their charity balls. He was still a bit of the old Hank, but he did accompany me and acted like a gentleman when he took me home. The point is, he's trying real hard to change. If he does show up, you may want to give him a second chance."

"Well, none of us has a perfect past." Ginger leaned back against the booth's leather upholstery. "It's nice to hear he's trying to help others. I truly didn't think it was possible for a leopard to change spots, but it wouldn't hurt to have some family around. So, what is Bubbles?"

"Oh, you're gonna love it! It's a swanky champagne bar. Hank owns it, and he did a class-A job dressing it up. We'll have to do a girl's night out soon, so I can show you the place. I'll call Mona and the gals. It'll be fun."

Ginger's eyes widened. "Mona? The skinny lady with the thin lips?"

"Oh, you met her already?" Lexi shook her head, slapping her forehead. "I guess everyone knows the mayor's wife."

"She did mention she was married to the mayor. I met her at the café. She was waiting for Melvina, but I got the distinct impression that she didn't care for me."

Lexi frowned. "What do you mean? Mona likes everyone. She sometimes comes on strong, but she's a hoot and a real help to the community."

"Well, she doesn't really know me, but when I mentioned my cousin, Celia, she didn't seem too pleased."

"Oh." Lexi blinked. "Well, as I said earlier, you aren't Celia, so no one can judge you by that whole Blossom fiasco."

Ginger wanted to ask about the Blossom fiasco, but it was never in her character to gossip. At least, not after her own scandal. She reminded herself that there were two sides to every story and small towns enjoyed rumors like a dog with a bone. She was tired of being the media's juicy morsel, so she wouldn't let Celia be her gossip for the night.

Changing the subject, she reached for her credit card. "We better get our tab. I'm supposed to be at the diner early. You can show me the ropes around your place when I finish my shift at the bakery."

Lexi shook her head. "No, ma'am. I said I was buying tonight."

Ginger shook her head back at Lexi. "I can afford my share. I don't want to be a leech."

Lexi flagged down the waitress and handed over her credit card. "After you get your first check, I'll let you treat, and after that, we'll go Dutch. I don't want people to think I'm extorting you for free labor, and trust me, the boys will make you work." She gave Ginger a teasing wink. "But seriously, they are going to love you and your cute little lizard buddy. He won't eat Ann-Margret, will he?"

Ginger laughed. She'd been introduced to the cute pet rat with the rhinestone collar in Lexi's kitchen after they pulled weeds. She patted herself on the back for not squealing when Anne-Margret stood on the counter waiting to be noticed. Ginger reasoned that anything in a pink sparkly collar couldn't be too dangerous.

Lexi explained that the rat was a real Houdini and loved cheese. She also told her about Ann-Margret's field trip to the original Hank's, and how after the car wreck, Lexi was out of sorts and totally forgot the poor girl.

"Thank goodness when I remembered to go back for her, she was still there, sitting in the driver's seat like she was about to take a ride. I had already gone home, picked up my rental car and had lunch with my brother before it even dawned on me that she was still in the van." Lexi covered her mouth with one hand as she shook her head at the memory. "Lucky for the tow truck driver, I returned to Hank's before he arrived. Could you imagine his face if Ann-Margret had decided to make an appearance while he was in the car?" She chuckled.

Ginger enjoyed Lexi's warm nature and fun stories. If nothing else, living at the ranch would be entertaining. "Don't worry about cute little

Ann-Margret. Iguanas are herbivorous. Igor eats leaves mostly, but he likes flowers and vines too. I think Anne-Margret and Igor will co-exist just fine."

Chapter 10

Roland had never seen Luke drag his heels to the bar before, but he lolly-gagged around with Maddie and Kelsey until Roland thought he would give up and stay home. If Luke wanted to do second-grade homework with his niece, so be it. They had already washed the dishes, and there was no way he was taking Rollo on a walk. Maddie had rescued the mangy mongrel, so she could walk him. Roland wondered if his brother was trying to hold off telling why he was really in Magnolia.

It wasn't like him to come without Charlotte. Their son, Kirin, was half grown now. Roland couldn't remember the kid's exact age, but he was around eight when Luke met his girlfriend, and that was ten years ago. Kirin must be graduating high school this year, or maybe that was last year? Roland admitted that he wasn't great at keeping up. Time went by too fast.

The cool autumn air was crisp, and Roland welcomed the warmth of the many bodies inside Hank's. He saw his usual poker game going on at a corner table. Waving off their invitation, he made his way to the bar with his brother. They needed to talk. Maybe going to Hank's had been a bad idea. The bartender took their drink order, and Roland eased onto a vacant stool.

Luke turned his back to the bar, taking in the crowd. "Wow, it's early for a crowd like this."

"Christmas," Roland replied, taking a swig of his beer.

Luke gave him a blank look. "That's three weeks away."

Roland nodded. "Yes, but it's the season for parties, shopping, baking and celebrating with family. We're here, aren't we?"

Luke pressed his lips together, nodding. "Guess you're right. I never thought about Christmas as high season for the bar, but it's not like there is much else to do around here."

The comment irked Roland. "There is as much to do in Magnolia as there is in most city suburbs. Shopping, dining, sports, recreation. Plus, we're only a short way from Houston or The Woodlands."

Luke smirked. "Hm, there's the diner, Hank's, the golf course and the shooting range." He counted off on his fingers. "Did I miss anything?"

"Yeah, Mr. Know-It-All. Magnolia is growing. Bubbles is a high-end lounge, and there's a wine bar across the street where the old Hank's used to be. The Italian bistro opened up a few years ago. The neighborhood around the golf course has equestrian trails, and the Blossoms throw quite a few elegant parties throughout the year. In fact, the Snowflake Ball is coming up. If you're sticking around, you won't want to miss it. It's basically an all-white party in The Woodlands."

Now he had his in. Luke would have to fess up and at least tell him if he planned on staying a few weeks.

Instead of answering, Luke threw Roland's words back at him. "See what I mean? The party for Magnolia is being held somewhere else. Somewhere swankier than here."

Roland frowned. "That's not true. Magnolia is coming up in the world. And, though we have a very nice new hotel, the ballroom isn't big enough for all the attendees. In fact, the extensive guest list shows how much the area is growing."

"Are you going to ask the pretty lady from the diner?"

Roland frowned. "Who, the waitress?"

Luke pointed to a blonde and a brunette sitting at a table near the other end of the bar. Roland's pulse picked up. It was the Ava Gardner lookalike he'd pulled over that morning. As he studied her profile, he decided she was prettier. Her features were striking, and her defiant chin even had a small cleft that accentuated her heart-shaped face. He loved the soft wave of her dark, shoulder-length hair and wondered if she styled it on purpose to look 1940s. She was wearing a simple t-shirt and jeans, blending into the atmosphere, but her pert nose, high cheekbones and full lips were anything but ordinary. She had movie quality attributes, with perfect skin, straight teeth and shiny hair.

Roland recognized Lexi Nash sitting across from her and wondered how Lexi knew Miss Harding. The woman was definitely not from around here, and as his brother had mentioned, she didn't look like the type that would stay. The enticing brunette was the kind of gal that would go for Luke. Like his brother, she had model-quality looks with big-city interests, and it needled him that she would probably look better standing next to Luke.

Roland tried to relax. Maddie, Luke, and even Kelsey were constantly reminding him to let go and not be so uptight. He had a reputation for being strict, honest and fair, and he upheld the law to protect citizens. So, why should he relax? It was a serious job. If he let his guard down, someone might get hurt, like before. He mentally shook himself from journeying too far down memory lane. Now was not the time to rake himself over the coals. He was out with his brother to see how he could help Luke get his life back on track, not to be derailed by a sultry brunette with cat-green eyes and nice breasts. He wondered if they were real or the plastic kind bought from a fancy Dallas plastic surgeon.

"The pretty lady from the diner. The hottie you pulled over for speeding." Luke paused. "The woman you're staring at as if you would like Santa to wrap her up in lingerie and put her in your Christmas stocking."

Roland cleared his throat and looked at his beer, ignoring Luke's teasing. "No, I'm not going to the ball. I told Maddie she could go, and I'll watch Kelsey. I've already got the movie picked out, and I ordered a few bags of Moose Munch online."

Luke shook his head. "Roland, when are you ever going to get out there again?"

Roland scowled. He didn't want to talk about Claire, and he was tired of pussyfooting around his younger brother's feelings. Luke obviously didn't care about his privacy. "Enough, Luke. Why don't we cut to the chase, and you tell me why you're here?"

Luke scowled and took a drink of his beer before his eyes darted back to the ladies. Roland tried not to follow his gaze. The brunette had distracted him enough. Luke was silent, a contrast to the bustling happy hour crowd surrounding them. Finally, he looked Roland in the eye.

"Charlotte left me."

Roland made himself wait. He knew interrupting would only defer the answers to the many questions he had. Luke needed to tell his story in his own time, and Roland had come off as an insensitive ass.

"I'm sorry." Roland wasn't a total jerk. He'd learned over the years to be silent and listen. It helped in his role as a constable, but he'd learned it first at home. Luke might have been the most popular kid in school, but his emotions had always been locked in a cave. While the rest of the world blathered their complaints, it took a lot for him to reveal his true feelings.

"Turns out, she's been seeing someone for a while now. I had my suspicions, but I wasn't ready to face it." Luke looked down, studying the rail along the bar. "It's embarrassing. She had to ask me to leave." He shook his head and sighed, looking up at the ceiling as if he were trying to find the answers to his life written there.

"There's no shame in loving someone." Roland had never been in love. He'd thought he was once, but now, he believed it existed for other people. At forty, he was too old to "fall" into anything. Love was for people like Luke and women like Ginger Harding. He couldn't stop his gaze from darting her way. He tried to dissect what had gone wrong this morning. She'd been in a bad mood but had smiled at Luke, a man she'd just bumped into.

Luke traced the direction of Roland's gaze. He lit up with a smile. "You like Ginger?"

Roland scowled. "What? No. And, how do you know her name? Didn't you just get here?"

Luke looked at him like he was from outer space. "Duh, I took the cake boxes to her car. She told me her name, and she seems really cool. You should go talk to her. Buy her a drink."

Roland felt the muscles in his stomach tense. He hadn't forgotten about the casual encounter in the diner, but he had forgotten how fast Luke could work. Apparently, he was already on a first-name basis with the brunette—and now, Luke was single. Roland's stomach clenched again, and he chided himself. What did he care if his little brother was on a first-name basis with the new gal?

He avoided Luke's suggestion. "We were talking about you and Charlotte."

Luke drained his beer and signaled to the bartender to bring another round. "I guess therein lies the problem."

Roland again waited while the bartender delivered the drinks, and Luke scanned the bar. He wasn't in any hurry to explain, but when he looked at Roland again, he said, "We were in love back when we met. I think we were for a few years, but then our lives became old hat. We owned a house together, car notes, utility bills. I adopted Kirin, then he grew up and went off to college this fall. The house was finally empty, and when we sat there together in silence, we realized we didn't have anything in common to talk about."

"Were you seeing anyone?"

Luke gave him a look of suppressed anger. "Does it always have to be my fault with you?"

Roland didn't answer. It was his police training again that knew how to wait it out. People eventually revealed what he needed to know.

"That was years ago. When I came out here, and you sent me back. My head wasn't on right, and I'd quit my job. It was before the studio took off."

Roland lifted a brow. "The studio is doing okay?"

Luke shook his head as a dismal look crossed his features.

Roland decided it was a topic to shelve for later. "Does Charlotte know about the old affair?"

Luke put his hand up. "I don't want to talk about this right now. I should've known you were taking me out to give me the shake-down." He pushed away from the bar and started toward Lexi and Ginger's table.

Roland blew out the breath he'd been holding. *Great, just great.*

Chapter 11

Ginger was happy when Lexi asked for the check. She'd spotted Officer Karr and his nicer brother and didn't want to delve back into stilted conversation with her adversary—no, wait, she reminded herself that he wasn't her enemy. He had let her off with a warning, but he could have told her why he'd pulled her over before she'd lost her patience. The school zone wasn't well marked, and she'd been focused on finding her way. If she was speeding, he had every right to be angry, and the thought of running over a little kid made her shiver. Besides never being able to live with the guilt, the media would have a heyday with it. She could see the headlines now, *Porn Star Kills Child in High-Speed Chase.* If she were honest with herself, she should be thanking him for giving her a wake-up call. There were more important things in life than acting in Hollywood, and she needed to quit being angry at the world and focus on the present.

Before the waitress could return, Ginger saw the nice brother making his way toward their table. Earlier, he'd introduced himself as Luke. She remembered because she'd always liked that name, and the character she played opposite in *Seducing Saturn* had the same name. He approached their table wearing a friendly smile and emanating a casual demeanor that his brother didn't possess.

"Hi, Ginger. Did you get settled in?"

She nodded. "Hi, Luke. Yes, I'm staying with Lexi." She motioned across the table to her new boss, landlord, and hopefully, new friend.

Lexi smiled up at Luke, holding out her hand for a shake. "Nice to meet you. Aren't you Roland's little brother?"

Luke gave her a warm smile. "Lexi Nash. I wasn't sure you would remember me. I ran into Ginger at the diner today. I hope she shared whatever was in those boxes with you and your boys."

Lexi smiled. "I do love the diner's baked treats, but it's the icing that's my favorite."

Ginger noticed that Lexi didn't correct him on the last name. Instead, she scanned the bar. "Is Roland with you? Tell him to get over here and say hello. It's been ages since we've seen each other."

Luke turned, waving to Roland.

Ginger inwardly groaned. *Crap.* She'd almost gotten away.

Roland approached with a swagger that belonged in a Clint Eastwood movie. She begrudgingly admired his perfectly squared shoulders and narrow hips. She had an active imagination and imagined how he'd look with a leather gun belt slung across his hips and a couple of revolvers tucked inside the holsters.

He greeted them without mentioning their earlier meeting, which Ginger appreciated. She was sure Lexi would worry if she thought Ginger wasn't a safe driver. If Roland mentioned she'd been speeding in a school zone—wait, forget moving violations, what if her new boss found out about the sex tape? *What if Officer Karr saw the sex tape?* Ginger absently chewed one fingernail as she watched Roland and Lexi exchange pleasantries.

"The eBay store was a desperate attempt at keeping the ranch afloat, but who knew it would take off like that? My brother, Ran, just finished my new website, and Mom's trying to talk me into opening a real shop in town. She's a Realtor, and she says she's got the perfect location. It's tempting, but I don't know where I'd find the time. I just hired Ginger to help out at the ranch."

Roland smiled at Lexi, then his gaze swung to Ginger. There was something in his intense dark eyes that made her squirm under his scrutiny. When had she ever lacked confidence? She pushed her shoulders back and sat straighter. Working for Lexi and at the café was honest work. There was nothing to be ashamed of. Ginger mentally shook the defensive thoughts away. When had she become such a snob about manual labor? She'd worked as a barista in a coffee shop before becoming an actress, and she knew what it was to be broke. Fame would find her again. It was a matter of waiting out the paparazzi.

Roland grinned. "You'll love it out at the ranch. I've been there for one of Riley's famous fireman barbeques, and the place is beautiful."

Ginger didn't know if it was the warmth in his smile or the three pear-flavored beers she'd had, but her pulse quickened, and she felt a flush creeping up her neck. She had the sudden urge to pull her hair away from her face, and she wondered if her lipstick was still in place.

When she didn't say anything, he filled in the gap. "So, I take it you're staying on in Magnolia for a while?"

She nodded as he assessed her with those cool, amber-flecked eyes. A discussion of her exit plan wasn't on her list of things to chat about, but as soon as Ginger had enough money and another place to restart her career, she would be on her way. Guilt churned in her already unsettled stomach. Ginger didn't know how the pretty mother handled three boys, a hundred-acre farm, a virtual shop and who knew what else, and it wasn't any of her business. However, she didn't want to add to the single mom's struggles. She liked Lexi, and leaving her high and dry was the last thing she wanted. The officer's unwavering stare made her fidget. Ginger assured her conscience that when the time came to leave, she would try to give proper notice.

What if the tape got out before then? She wouldn't think about that. Her new look and different name was a good cover. All she needed was a few months to get back on her feet and save some cash. Room and board with Lexi was her best shot, and Ginger couldn't afford to screw up this opportunity. She had no other family or friends she could fall back on.

The five o'clock shadow Officer Karr sported, along with the out-of-style but woodsy-looking flannel shirt was appealing on him. Two buttons were undone at the collar, and his sleeves were rolled up, showing muscular forearms. Ginger had to admit, he filled it out nicely. His jeans were pressed, and his brushed leather boots were spotless. Fine, dark hair peeked from beneath his shirt and dusted the edge of his collarbone.

At this moment, he looked less uptight, smiling at Lexi and chuckling about someone they both knew. Something else now was tugging at the pit of her stomach. Did he like Lexi? Why did the thought bother Ginger? Was it that the smiling blonde was too nice for a hard-ass like him? Or was it that the sweet mother had three boys to think of? Officer Karr didn't seem right for an instant family scenario. Or was he? He would probably be too strict, and the boys might not take to a restrictive kind of life.

Ginger frowned as Lexi laughed harder, smiling up at him. Officer Karr had a dimple in his cheek that was sexy when he smiled. If she hadn't run into him the way she had earlier today, she might have taken an interest. Luke gave her a quizzical stare, then looked at his brother and back at her. He smiled, giving a knowing wink. *Wait! He doesn't think—.*

"Roland tells me a Christmas shindig is coming up that's sure to be the party of the year. I understand that my doubts about Magnolia's ability to be entertaining are soon to dissolve. Are you ladies going to the Snowflake

Ball?" Luke was making small talk, but the wink had alerted Ginger that he might be up to something.

Lexi blinked with what looked like confusion. "Oh, the Blossoms' all-white charity thing? I don't know. I'll probably be busy wrapping presents if the boys haven't already found their Santa Claus gifts."

Roland tilted his head with a reassuring grin. "I'm sure you can take time to enjoy yourself for one night. That's what grandparents are for."

Lexi shrugged. "I don't have anyone to go with anyway, and the last time I went to a Blossom fundraiser...." Her voice trailed off.

Ginger followed Lexi's blank stare. A man with a white Stetson and L.L.Bean catalog look made his way toward them.

"Noah Harding," Roland said under his breath, but loud enough for Ginger to hear.

Lexi glanced at Ginger with desperation in her eyes and stammered, "But—but, you should go. It'd give you a chance to meet some people."

Ginger shook her head, attempting to ignore the handsome stranger's approach. It was obvious that Lexi was trying to do the same. "No thanks. I'm not a party kinda girl anymore. I think I'll lay low. Besides, won't you need a babysitter if you're busy?"

The man shook hands with Roland and Luke, then tipped his hat to Ginger and Lexi. "Lexi." His voice was smooth and rich. His eyes held a look of wary concern, tinged with something intense as if everything was riding on the next move. Like a television drama, energy crackled in the silence, alerting Ginger that there was history between Lexi and this gorgeous stranger. Roland's sharp-eyed gaze said that he probably knew the story.

"Noah is the owner of Hank's," Roland said. "Noah, this is my brother, Luke, and Ginger Harding, who arrived in Magnolia today."

Noah's eyebrows raised in interest. His eyes were lit with curiosity. "Harding? My last name's Harding, too."

Ginger felt her hand flutter to her chest. "Oh geez, from what Lexi said, I thought my cousin Hank might own this place," she confessed.

Lexi's throat worked as if she were swallowing a lump of coal before she offered, "Noah is Hank's cousin. Maybe he's your cousin too?"

Ginger felt out of sorts. She didn't know what to say. "Um, maybe. It's a pleasure to meet you."

Noah reached for the hand she offered and gave her a genuine smile, lessening the tension at the table. "Don't worry, I'm nothing like Hank. The only thing we share in common is the grandfather who left us the original Hank's Honky-Tonk, and he passed away over seven years ago."

Ginger wanted to swipe her head and say what a relief it was to hear, but she didn't want to sound rude. Hank Harding didn't seem to have a favorable reputation at the table, but Lexi did say he was helping the community and trying to change. Ginger shouldn't throw stones in the current glass house she resided in. If Lexi found out about her past, Ginger might end up homeless.

Noah cleared his throat. "Lexi, can you spare a minute to um…."

Lexi's eyes were as big as saucers, and she looked ready to bolt, but Roland backed up, offering her his hand to help step out of the booth. It appeared she didn't seem to have much choice in the matter.

Ginger didn't know how Lexi could entertain saying no to a man that good looking, but maybe he had a *Hank* reputation after all. Noah said he wasn't like his cousin, but Lexi looked ill at ease, and Ginger started wondering if she might get left behind to find her own way home.

Lexi slid out of the booth and followed Noah somewhere out of sight. There they were, Roland, Luke and herself, staring at each other in silence.

Luke's eyebrows knitted together. Like Ginger, he seemed to be contemplating what had happened. It suddenly occurred to her that Luke might have been making a play for Lexi. He wasn't wearing a wedding band, and he seemed happy that she remembered him. For some reason, it made her feel better to think Luke was the one interested in her boss.

Roland's gaze fell on the credit card receipt the waitress had dropped off. "Can I buy you another drink? It looks like you might be here a little while longer."

Ginger had already consumed the pear ciders and didn't think they were strong but probably full of calories. "I'd better not. I have an early morning."

"I can get you a Coke or maybe a tea?"

Luke waved at someone across the bar. "Excuse me, Roland, Ginger." He nodded as he broke away.

Ginger smiled. "Maybe a diet soda would be nice." She motioned to the booth. "You want to sit down?"

Roland nodded, looking across the distance to where Lexi and Noah had disappeared. He waved down a waitress.

Ginger tried to relax, but there was something about his presence that felt overwhelming. It gave her a real chance to study his ruggedly handsome face. His strong chin, patrician nose and furrowed brow were all perfect together. She wanted to ask about the small scar, but she didn't want to be rude. "So the guy who owns this place, is he nice?"

Roland's eyebrows rose in thought. "Noah Harding is a good guy. He's had a rough patch of luck, but he looks like he's recovering."

It was a vague answer, but good enough for now. She didn't have to worry about Lexi being man-handled in the back of the restaurant. Not knowing what else to say, she continued with, "It's a nice place."

Roland nodded. "Yeah. I was telling my brother that a lot has changed since he left, and we have plenty of places to keep the residents of Magnolia entertained."

It was Ginger's turn to nod. A band struck up, and loud music muted the ambient chatter of the other diners.

Roland motioned toward the stage. "The Tomball Cats are playing tonight."

He said it like she should know who they were. "Ah, okay." She smiled.

Roland accepted the drinks from the waitress and thanked her, handing the young woman a credit card.

The pretty waitress stuck the card in her bustier and winked at him. "Thanks, Roland. I'll keep it warm for ya."

Ginger raised an eyebrow at Roland.

He looked caught out. "Um, Mindy, she knows me from…," Clearing his throat, he let his words drift into the music. He leaned closer, raising his voice above the thump of the base. "The band." he pointed. "It's Lexi's brother's band. They're kind of local celebrities." He motioned to a table near the stage. Ginger recognized the older lady with the walker and a pretty, young blonde. "That's his wife, Bonnie, and her aunt, Ms. Rosie."

The lady from the diner who took her inside to meet Melvina was suddenly at their table. "Why Roland Karr, you work fast! This lady just rolled into town today. What did you do, pull her over and threaten her with a ticket unless she came out dancin' tonight?"

Roland looked like he was at a loss for words, and was that a blush creeping up his neck? Ginger tried not to grin.

"Hi, Mona. I'm here with Lexi. She'll be back in a minute. Roland was keeping me company." Ginger decided not to share that he had pulled her over.

Roland stood, sweeping a hand at the booth. "Would you like to have a seat?"

60

Mona pressed her thin lips together in a wide smile, tilting her head down and looking up at Roland through dark false lashes. "Sorry, handsome, it's ladies' night. I'm with Ms. Rosie, Addie and Bonnie. We came to see Ran play, but I wanted to congratulate you. Manny tells me you will be the next mayor." She clapped her hands together with a small squeal then threw her arms around his neck.

"Oh, no, Mona. That's not a done deal. Manny only mentioned it to me—"

Mona waved off his protest and put her other hand on her hip. "Trust me, if my husband runs for Congress, and he wants you to be mayor, you will be the mayor." She looked back at the stage. "Ooh, this is my jam. I gotta go. Roland, take care of this new gal and watch her. She's related to Celia Lockwood." Mona gave Ginger a saucy wink and a wave as she sashayed off to the beat of the drums. Her skinny hips swayed a little offbeat, and the fancy hurricane glass in her hand that held only ice cubes said she was either tipsy or well on her way to being lit.

Ginger looked anxiously toward the door where Lexi and Noah had disappeared. It was her first day in Magnolia, and she was already sitting with the next candidate for mayor. If a reporter should show up, she might ruin this man's chances to be elected. Ginger needed to get out of here, quick.

Roland followed her gaze. "If they don't come out soon, and you want to leave, the ranch is on my way home. I'm happy to give you a ride."

Ginger's stomach was tying itself in knots. She decided it would be best for both parties to end this visit now. "I—I have to use the ladies' room. You don't have to wait for me. I'm sure she will be back soon, but thanks for the offer and the Diet Coke."

Chapter 12

Lexi Nash knew her share of heartache and had all but become a nun since her husband died in Afghanistan seven years ago. Except for Noah Harding. As she followed Noah through the crowded bar to his office, she remembered "the incident" that had brought them together. Gussy's pet rat had skittered over her foot while she was driving, and she'd quite literally parked her minivan in the front window of the original Hank's Honky-Tonk. The chemistry between her and the sexy bar owner had smoldered into a very happy ending on their first date. Admittedly, the affair turned into an awkward morning that felt like the worst hangover she'd ever had. More than guilt washed over her in the shower, and she couldn't handle the intimacy. Noah had been understanding about her hot and cold behavior, and he forgave her when she dropped by the bar to explain.

It had all happened three years ago, and they'd almost pieced things back together to make a real start, but then it all fell apart. Lexi was sitting in Hank's one night while Noah was busy tending customers. A beautiful blonde named Petra sidled up to her at the bar and revealed the ugly truth. The man Lexi was falling head-over-heels for was Petra's husband. Lexi was crushed. She didn't understand how the first man she'd given herself to since becoming a widow had lied to her about being single. She retaliated by leaving the bar with Hank Harding, Noah's cousin, who was up to his own shenanigans, trying to steal Noah's half of the bar. The whole thing ended in disaster, with Noah chasing after her to the ranch and seeing her wrapped in Hank's arms. She was guilty of kissing Hank, but it was a revenge kiss, plain and simple. A kiss she'd immediately regretted.

Little did she know that Noah left Magnolia that same night, leaving her and all his dreams behind. With the way things ended between them, it wasn't a surprise to her when he didn't say good-bye. Opening the swank new lounge, Bubbles, had been Noah's vision, but he'd handed it all to Hank. Months later, Lexi learned the truth—that Hank had orchestrated the entire setup with Petra to keep Noah from selling his part of the bar. By then, it was too late. Hank had admitted everything to her and genuinely seemed remorseful about the whole ordeal, but sometimes saying you were sorry didn't change things.

As Ginger liked to say, Lexi had been "off men" ever since, except for the Blossoms' last charity ball, when she'd decided to finally accept Hank's offer to take her out. If she were honest about it, she was the one who'd asked him since she'd needed a plus one and hadn't wanted to go alone. Petra left Magnolia when Hank ended their engagement, so Hank was officially single. Lexi hated to admit, she'd felt dejected and lonely after Noah left. But the night of the Blossoms' charity ball proved that she could never have feelings for Hank, despite his reformation. Hell, she doubted she could ever have feelings for any man while her fascination with Noah still haunted her.

Lexi's world did another tailspin as memories of the past shuffled through her mind at the speed of a Vegas blackjack dealer. Noah showing up at her table tonight—walking, talking, and breathing — was enough to make her hyperventilate. The last time she'd seen him was when she drove to Dallas to set the record straight. It had been shocking to find him in a wheelchair, but Noah didn't tell her anything about his accident or the woman he was staying with. Lexi didn't ask, but she needed to clear the slate from her end. Noah didn't say much in response to why she'd kissed Hank, and he certainly hadn't asked her to come in and work things out.

She'd said her good-byes and drove back to Magnolia in tears, believing it was truly the end of their affair. It was terrible, seeing Noah in a wheelchair, and it sickened her to know she couldn't help. If he'd been open to having a relationship, she would have been there for him throughout his recovery, even if he was permanently disabled. She would have done anything for Noah if he had been honest with her, told her he loved her, told her Petra was in his past. Anything besides the cold treatment he'd given her in Dallas.

Lexi didn't know why seeing him now made her want to hightail it out of there. She didn't have anything to run from, but she certainly didn't want to hash it out in a packed bar. What would she tell Ginger when she returned to the table? The new tenant seemed to have a past of her own, so maybe she wouldn't ask too many questions. Lexi wasn't the prying kind, either, but she had a good sense about people, and her gut instinct told her not to worry. Ginger just needed a friend.

Lexi followed Noah down a hallway, and he opened the door to his office. Motioning to a chair, he asked her to sit down.

It was better than the middle of the bar, but she didn't like being alone with him, either. She wanted to walk out. "It's too late for this, Noah. I don't know why I agreed to come back here, but you put me on the spot. If you wanted to talk, you should have done it in Dallas or at least reached out to me that first year." Lexi spun on her heel.

"Wait, you don't even know what I'm going to say," he contested, grabbing her hand and leading her back to the deep cowhide-covered chair. Despite the mood, its thick rolled arms and tufted back looked inviting.

She could feel the nerve in her cheek twitch, nagging her upper lip. *Hold it together, Lexi gal. You can do this. You can face him.*

Reluctantly, he let go of her hand. "First, I want to apologize." Sitting on the edge of his desk, he looked down at her, his silver-colored eyes pleading.

Lexi craned her neck, feeling disadvantaged and vulnerable at such an angle.

"I'm sorry. That can't be comfortable." Noah settled into the chair next to her, looking her directly in the eyes.

She stared at the light gray irises with flecks of white and navy-blue. They'd flashed silver when he used to kiss her, when he'd taken her to bed, and she would bet money on their color the night he'd seen her kissing Hank. Right now, they were begging her to hear him out.

"You came to Dallas to deliver a message, and I wasn't very hospitable."

Lexi breathed deep, catching the scent of his cologne and a tinge of whiskey. Did he have a shot of liquid courage before approaching her? Was he nervous? The thought bolstered her confidence. Maybe Noah still had feelings for her, or maybe he wanted to apologize for being an ass. Lexi knew that was a difficult thing to do for a Harding. It had taken Hank almost a lifetime to admit he was wrong… *but he had*, she reminded herself. She'd delivered the handwritten apology from Hank to Noah herself.

"I drove to Dallas because I wanted to clear up any misunderstanding. Don't worry. You don't owe me anything. We had fun, and then… we didn't," she finished simply, not knowing what else to say about the fallout. She wasn't even sure if it qualified as a relationship since they'd never made it as far as a second date.

Noah clasped her hand again. "It's not about what I owe. I know you aren't like that, Lexi. I should have told you what happened that night after I drove off, and I should have told you about my ex-wife, Petra, long before then. I owed you that much. I could say there hadn't been time. Our courtship was quick, but I should have told you my situation before falling into bed with you. I'm sorry. All the years in the military—I've never been one to talk much about the past."

Lexi understood. She remembered how Jack had been after a few tours overseas. "Hank told me about Petra. How you'd paid for her cancer treatment, and you didn't want her to lose any medical benefits. He said you were divorced in all ways except on paper. But I was hurt, and like I told you in Dallas, I only kissed Hank that night because I felt like a fool. For some strange reason, that foolishness made me want revenge." She put a hand over her forehead, remembering her own embarrassment. "Kissing Hank was stupid, and I shouldn't have done it, but that's all water under the bridge now."

Noah nodded. "I was the fool, in more ways than one. I should have told you everything, especially how I felt about you. If not before I left Magnolia, then when you drove to Dallas. Callie almost never let me live it down, but I used my injury to get her off my back and—"

Lexi shook her head and started to stand. "I don't need to hear about your recent love-life issues, Noah."

"What? Callie? She's my sister." He frowned and then sighed as if remembering. "Yeah, I guess I didn't say much about her while you were there. I figured you would think she was my girlfriend and be mad enough to never look back." He shook his head as his brows furrowed. "I'm sorry I felt like I needed to do that. It was wrong, and I know the accident isn't an excuse, but the doctors told me I'd never walk again. The thought of you trying to take care of me, when you already had so much to take care of…."

For the first time, she touched his forearm. Her heart clenched, thinking of what it must have been like to hear that you would never walk again. She also remembered the heartache she'd felt thinking that Callie was his girlfriend and how he'd embraced life with her and her children. "So, the kids I heard playing in your apartment?"

"Her apartment," he corrected. "I was staying with my sister and nieces near the VA Hospital. I'll admit. If it wasn't for her pull-yourself-up-by-the-bootstrap personality, I might never have recovered." He chuckled. "Callie is always good at giving gut-checks. Just ask Hank. Apparently, she called him out on the Petra bullshit, and it looks like her tearing him a new one resonated. She has that effect. My nieces are tough cookies, too."

Lexi couldn't help but smile back at him. "She sounds a little stubborn. I guess that runs in the family."

Noah nodded. "I know you have a friend waiting for you at your table, and I don't want to be rude and keep you locked in here, though it'll be tough to watch you leave." His eyes sparkled with light mischief. "I wish I had a cupcake to tempt you to stay."

Lexi remembered the box of cupcakes she'd taken to him after her guilty-widow-who-just-had-sex-for-the-first-time meltdown. She'd called him Doctor Icing as he'd teased her with promises of sexual exploits on their next encounter.

He grinned, and the gleam in his eye said he knew exactly what she was thinking. "We have a lot to talk about, and I'd really like the chance to take you on that second date if you'll let me. I want to make things up to you, and I'd like a second chance to start over if you're willing."

His smile was infectious, and Lexi was irritated with herself for smiling back at him. She was made of tougher stuff and should be more stern. "I'll think about it."

Noah nodded and walked her to the door, stealing a knee-bending kiss that nearly melted her panties off. As they broke from the kiss, he opened the door, and she stared dumbly back at him. Lexi guessed she could throw stern out the window. His devilish grin and intake of breath brought her back to reality.

"Do think about it, Lexi. I know I won't stop thinking about it until I see you again."

"That was weird," Ginger said.

Lexi glanced at her as they drove back to the ranch.

Ginger looked back at Lexi and then stared at the reflection in the side mirror as the streetlights faded into the distance.

"Was it?" Lexi sounded dazed.

Hell yes, it was, Ginger thought, but what part about this small town wasn't, with its nosy old ladies, judgmental women's league, and the town's holier-than-thou cop? To be fair, Lexi was very nice, and so was Melvina. Her friend Mona seemed friendly in the bar, but she was probably three sheets to the wind. Luke didn't live in Magnolia, but he said he'd be staying with his brother a while. Though Officer Karr had been a bit of a dick that morning, he did let her out of a ticket, bought her a soda and kept her company until the conversation got too uncomfortable. As she ticked off the good points of her day, she supposed the residents weren't all bad.

Lexi shook her head. "I almost thought Luke was trying to ask me out, but then I realized he was trying to get his brother to ask *you* out, but Roland didn't take the bait. I saw the way he kept looking at you, so I was kind of surprised he resisted. It was like he didn't want to like you, but trust me, he couldn't help it. I've known Roland for years. He's not the shy type, and he's picky. I never knew what his type was, but it makes sense. You've got that whole—," Lexi waved her hand around her face as she glanced at Ginger, "—movie star appeal. Sort of a modern-day Lauren Bacall with your hair like that."

Ginger's gut churned. Lexi's words fell too close to home. One of the reasons they hired Ginger for *Seducing Saturn* was her vintage film star look. She needed to redirect the conversation, and she might as well fess up. If Lexi knew Roland, he might tell her about the warning eventually. "I don't think Officer Karr cares that much for me. I was going a few miles over the speed limit today, and he pulled me over."

Before Lexi could react, Ginger quickly added, "It's okay. Thank God he let me off with a warning. I don't have time to take one of those Defensive Driving classes."

"That was sweet of him." Lexi opened her mouth to say something else and then shut it. Ginger waited, wondering what she was thinking. Lexi's brow furrowed as she continued driving.

"Hey, maybe you could go to the ball with Luke, and I could watch the boys. I'm really not much on socializing these days, and you could probably use a fun night out."

Lexi shook her head. "No way. You need to meet people, and there is no way I'm going by myself with Luke. It would seem too much like a date."

Ginger's eyebrows rose in a challenge. "So?"

Lexi bit her lower lip. "I'm not ready for that yet, and besides, he didn't ask me."

Ginger studied the pretty blonde's profile while she drove. "Lexi, you said yourself that you've been a widow for years and the boys are half grown. What are you waiting for? Maybe Luke didn't ask you directly but trust me, he looked interested."

Lexi's expression was hard to make out in the darkening sky. The dashboard light illuminated her tight lips and set jaw. "I can't. I tried to go on a few dates before, and it was… awkward."

Ginger didn't want to pry, but Lexi hadn't said a word about where she'd disappeared to or what the handsome Noah had wanted to talk to her about. Ginger barely knew Lexi, but in the short day they'd spent together, they seemed to connect. Tonight was fun, even with the run-in with Officer Karr and the mysterious Noah taking Lexi away for a secret rendezvous.

The car made its way down the long winding drive to the ranch. They both stepped out into the brisk night air, staring up into the inky blackness. Golden pinholes of light blinked back at them.

Lexi sighed. "I never get tired of its beauty."

Ginger was overwhelmed by the sight. "I never knew there were so many stars. I grew up in Dallas. I guess the city lights hid them all." She heard Lexi's boots crunch in the gravel.

"I know I'm not getting any younger. My kids will have their own lives one day, and I'll be here by myself. It's partly why I started making barn wood crafts and pressed flowers in old window frames. I can't live off of Jack's life insurance policy and the inheritance from my grandparents forever. I've invested most of it for the kids' college fund anyway. The eBay income kept things going around here when the cattle business was in a slump. I feel guilty about the time I spend selling my crafts, but I need the cash." She turned to Ginger and shrugged her shoulders. "The ranch has picked up since the drought, but if I don't continue to earn money from my shop, I'll have to sell this place."

Ginger didn't know what to say. "I'm sorry about what I said in the car. I didn't mean to be nosy. You just seemed like you needed a friend, is all."

Lexi smiled and linked arms with her as they walked toward the house. "I do need a friend, and I hope you and I will be good friends. But for now, you better get off to bed. Five o'clock comes early 'round here, and Melvina will want you there on time."

Ginger groaned, and Lexi chuckled. "I sure hope she likes my gingerbread cookies. I don't know how to make much else."

Lexi smiled, lifting an eyebrow. "Melvina is easy to work for, so don't fret."

As Ginger rummaged for the keys to the ATV, Lexi retrieved a flashlight from the car. "Here, you'll need this to go to the cottage and come back in the morning. The lights work, but it's kind of dark once you get there."

"Thanks." Ginger turned the key in the ignition, and the four-wheeler roared to life. It reminded her of a scene in *Seducing Saturn* where she'd pretended to ride a motorcycle in front of a green screen. When she'd watched the episode at a later date, she was in awe of the thick forest as the bike flew through the foliage and trees. She'd leaned left and right until she'd met a *crackarin*, a scaled, fire-breathing creature with wings. Goosebumps prickled down her arms and the back of her neck. This was the country, and it was pitch black. Ginger reminded herself that there were no such things as *crackarins*. Straddling the four-wheeler, she looked over her shoulder at Lexi. "Do bears live in Texas?"

Lexi chuckled, then gave her a concerned look. "Do you want me to drive you down there? I can come get you in the morning."

Ginger thought about saying yes, but she didn't want Lexi to have to wake up and escort her back in the dark. Ginger would have to go on her own eventually, so she took a deep breath and started the motor. "No. That's okay. It's not far."

Lexi nodded, then called out over the roar of the ATV. "Bobcats and coyotes, mostly, no bears. But be careful of the feral pigs. They can be mean, and they sure can tear up the land."

Ginger nodded and tried not to shake with fear. She rolled the throttle and moved slowly down the trail.

Lexi called out, "Oh and Ginger…."

Ginger stopped, craning her head back to see.

"If there is one thing I know about my sister-in-law, Melvina, it's that she is competitive. Word of advice, don't bake anything better than she does."

Chapter 13

Noah had to stay in his office for two reasons. One was the raging hard-on he had from kissing Lexi, and two was the fact that if he left his office now, he would run after her. Seeing Lexi again made him feel desperate. He'd wanted to see her before now, but he hadn't found the courage to seek her out. He'd needed two things first—the bar to be rebuilt and successful and to walk without his cane. After all this time, texting her out of the blue or making an unsolicited phone call seemed anticlimactic or even rude, but going by the ranch might surprise her. What if she'd recently started seeing someone and a man answered her door? What if her kids were there? What if she slammed the door in his face?

He was still in physical therapy, and he'd wanted to be stronger before walking down that road, literally. Over the last year, building the bar had consumed all of his time, and he'd somehow buried the urgency to make things right. Lack of confidence, fear of rejection or whatever else was stopping him had ceased tonight when he saw her. Noah hadn't hesitated. As if on auto pilot, he went after her without thinking. It was hard to contain his emotions and resist pulling her into his arms. He'd wanted to kiss her right there in front of her friends, constable and all.

Noah had forgotten the effect she had on him. He'd been in a funk for what felt like forever. After being in Dallas for so long, trying to recuperate, he'd thought he might never have the opportunity to make things right. Tonight, the sight of her made him feel as if he couldn't breathe without her. Noah didn't want to wait for all the apologies and courtship involved in having a serious relationship. He wanted Lexi to be his now.

When he finally cooled his thoughts enough to leave the sanctum of his office, Noah ventured behind the bar. Roland was still there with his brother, but Luke was playing a game of pool at the far corner of the room. Roland was staring at the vacant table where Lexi sat earlier. The hair on Noah's neck prickled. He hoped to God that the constable didn't have designs on Lexi. The only way to know for sure was to ask. "Can I get ya another beer?"

Roland's head whipped around, startled by the question. "Ah, no. I'm good. Driving tonight." He pushed an empty beer bottle that belonged to another patron and held up the glass of ice he'd been crunching on.

Noah held the soda gun above the glass. "Regular or unleaded?"

Roland grinned. "Regular. I'll run it off tomorrow."

Noah looked down at his own knee, thinking of how he missed that luxury. Running had been his exercise of choice before the accident.

Roland cleared his throat as if sensing Noah's disappointment. "How's the leg? You look well."

Noah didn't mind the question. He got asked all the time. "I do a lot of stationary biking these days, but my PT lady tells me I'll be good for the open road soon. I'm going to buy one of those fancy carbon fiber bikes, get one of those Styrofoam helmets and wear spandex shorts like those Tour de France riders."

Roland chuckled, "I can only imagine the expression on the cattle's faces as you make your way down FM1488."

Noah couldn't hold back his own hearty laugh. "Yeah, maybe I better keep it indoors for now."

Roland cleared his throat again. "Seriously, I'm glad you found your way back to Magnolia. It hasn't been the same without Hank's."

"That was one of the reasons I returned."

The constable looked toward the booth that was no longer empty. "And the other reason?"

Noah grinned. "I think that's obvious."

Roland took a large drink of his soda and set it back on the bar. "Good. Glad to see you came to your senses."

Noah breathed a sigh of relief. Roland wasn't after Lexi. "So, the new gal—." He paused. When Roland gave him a blank look, he continued. "You interested?"

Roland's brow furrowed. "She reminds me a little of Ava Gardner, don't you think?"

Noah didn't mind that he side-stepped the question. It was none of his business. "I thought Lauren Bacall." He motioned to his head. "The hair had that whole forties thing, but she's way prettier."

Roland nodded. "My thoughts exactly."

Ginger showered before bed, knowing she wouldn't dream of doing it at four in the morning. Instead, she woke up at four-thirty and made her way down the trail on the SUV, wishing she'd packed gloves to go with her lightweight down jacket and winter boots. She didn't know what to wear to the diner and should have asked Melvina yesterday. Most of the staff wore jeans and casual button-down shirts, so she hoped what she'd chosen would be acceptable. Wearing boots to ride the ATV, Ginger packed tennis shoes and her purse in a backpack. It would ensure that the extra gear was secure as she made it safely down the trail. It was nippy and still dark outside. The flashlight bobbed in her hand until she straddled the four-wheeler. The trees danced in the beacon of the ATV's headlights, like eerie ghosts beckoning her to join them. She shivered, thinking about the script she'd read for a movie, where the trees came to life and ate people in a dark forest. Could she do this bumpy, creepy trail ride every morning and night? *It's not forever. You survived L.A., girl, you can survive anything.*

Lucky for Ginger, the car ride to the café was less eventful and without traffic to interrupt her meandering thoughts. She was mindful of the speed limit on the off chance that Officer Karr was hiding in the bushes. It was important to start her day fresh, not bickering over traffic violations again, and most of all, she didn't want to be late.

The parking lot was empty, and the front door was locked. It occurred to Ginger that the diner hadn't opened for business yet, so she made her way around to the back. Sure enough, the door was unlocked, and she was able to enter into the warmth. Ginger stomped her boots on the rug to wipe off anything that might have stuck to them on the trail. Her hands felt frozen, and she rubbed them together vigorously as she shivered. Wasn't South Texas supposed to be warm? Yesterday felt like eighty degrees. What a difference a day could make.

Melvina rounded a corner with a bag of trash and gave Ginger a big smile. "Great! You're here. Let me throw this out, and I'll be right back. Did you remember your apron?"

Ginger nodded, pulling off her backpack. She felt like a kid on the first day of school and had no idea what to do. The only recipe she knew was her grandma's delicious cookie recipe, and Lexi warned her not to make it too good.

Besides baking cookies once a year at Christmas, Ginger's oven lived a quiet, cold existence. She lived off sushi from her favorite restaurant in L.A., salads from the coffee shop she frequented and occasionally, a grilled chicken breast from the place next to her condo. She'd given up eating when she moved to California, not that she'd ever had a weight problem, but five pounds could make or break an actress when competing for decent roles. *Seducing Saturn* had been the part of a lifetime. The series had taken off after the first season, and she hadn't thought she would have to worry for a few years about finding a new gig. In fact, she thought the show would inflate her resume and that she wouldn't have to scrounge for a job ever again. Thanks to her ex, she'd be lucky to get a role as a clown at a kid's party. Scratch that. They didn't hire people who were in sex videos for children's events. She shivered with the thought. How utterly humiliating. *If I ever see Kirk again, I will kill him.*

"Are you cold? I'll get you a cup of coffee." Melvina bustled past her and made her way to the front, where the smell of coffee percolating and the scent of fresh-ground beans wafted in the air. "We don't get many freezes here in Magnolia. Generally, one or two a year, but this one's come early."

Ginger nodded. "Thanks. I think I really need a hot cup of caffeine."

Melvina gave her a knowing smile. "I'm a tea drinker myself but an addict, all the same. I can't even think of starting my day without a cup or two of strong black tea to get me going."

Ginger ran her hand over the smooth, stainless-steel counter under the ticket wheel. A lone ticket with unreadable chicken scratch hung from one clip. "I like that you use hand-written tickets. Most people use computers for everything, but isn't it hard to tell what the orders are?"

Melvina sighed. "I know computers are more efficient, but what happens when the electricity goes out, or the system goes on the blink? Sometimes, it's okay to pause a minute and ask someone what they want or what comes first. Sometimes we miss a ticket, and that can cause chaos, but in general, we do fine."

Ginger took the cup of hot coffee from Melvina, murmuring, "Thanks."

"Sugar's on the counter, and I was about to go get the creamers out of the walk-in when you arrived. Give me a min, and I'll be right back."

"Walk-in?" Ginger repeated to the empty dining room. The kitchen really was a foreign place to her, but she would learn. She had no other choice. The bank app on her phone told her she needed to replenish her dwindling funds and fast.

After a tour of the kitchen, which included the walk-in refrigerator and freezer, Melvina put Ginger to work separating eggs for the cupcakes they were going to make. Ginger remembered standing on a step stool in her grandmother's kitchen doing the very same thing when she was eight. It was the last Christmas she'd shared with her grandma baking gingerbread. She supposed that was why it was the one thing she still baked every year. She never strayed from the recipe and made it exactly like the crumpled, yellowed paper said. She only took it out of her memory box once a year. The original recipe in her grandmother's handwriting was now in storage, but she took a pic with her cell phone before leaving L.A. A pang of regret assailed her as she thought about sharing the recipe, but Lexi's warning made her hesitate. Maybe she didn't have to share the exact recipe. She could add more vanilla and butter, maybe an extra egg or less nutmeg. She would figure out something. Ginger wasn't sure why, but she didn't want to share this particular memory with strangers, even if they were nice people like Melvina. It was the one gift from her gran that no one could take away.

As soon as the front door was unlocked, guests started to trail in, stomping their shoes as they entered. Many men removed their baseball hats, and women bundled in cardigans shivered as they removed their outer jackets. Melvina got busy taking orders, and the cook's line became a symphony of butter sizzling, eggs frying, and bacon crackling on the grill. Toast popped from the toaster with a swish into a long tray, and plates clanked together in the cook's window as a bell dinged with each completed order ready for pickup. Ginger didn't know how to continue with the cupcake mix, so she started cleaning up the cook's line for Maria, who was filling in for the morning chef. The scheduled cook had gotten sick, and it appeared they were shorthanded. Maria might be a manager, but she sure knew her way around the kitchen. Her dark braid, covered in a hairnet, was coiled in a thick rope at the base of her neck. Ginger was sure the braid would reach the pretty, thirty-something Latin woman's waist if she let it down. As if her thoughts had fingers, the braid came loose, unraveling down Maria's back. The thick braid swished back and forth like a whip in an Indiana Jones movie.

Her Spanish accent was thick, but Ginger understood her well enough when she said, "Can you watch this?" as she darted toward the back.

Ginger froze for a moment as she watched the eggs sizzle and pop. She slowly approached the grill as Melvina dinged the bell and added another check. Ginger looked over her shoulder for Maria, wondering exactly what she was supposed to do in her absence.

Melvina peered through the window. A look of desperation crossed her features as her mouth gaped. "Where's Maria?"

"I don't know. I think she went to pin up her hair."

Melvina shook her head. "Never mind." She pointed to the stack of clean plates. "Grab a plate, throw those two eggs on it and grab two slices of wheat toast from there." She pointed to the large toaster, shooting out an endless supply of sliced bread. "I'll be right back."

Sweat beaded on Ginger's forehead. Wasn't that what Maria had said? She scooped up the overturned eggs with a spatula, trying not to break the yolks and debated on buttering the bread as she placed it on the plate.

Melvina reappeared. "Use the knife on the cutting board to cut the toast in half. I've got the butter and jelly on this side. Don't worry, you're doing fine. Put two more eggs on the griddle and scramble them. Use extra butter," she added as she whizzed away again.

Ginger blinked, looking over her shoulder once more for the cook. *Where in the hell was Maria?* The only thing she knew how to cook, besides gingerbread cookies, was eggs and toast. What would she do if Maria didn't return? To Ginger's relief, Maria came back in time for the next order, and she stepped out of the way. Maria's hair was pinned up again, but she looked pale and worried. Ginger wanted to ask if everything was okay, but there wasn't time. Instead, she pointed to the scrambled eggs that were ready and picked up a clean plate.

Maria didn't waste time, plopping them onto the proffered plate with a soft, "Muchas gracias." Within a few minutes, they developed a system, with Maria pointing and Ginger fetching and to Ginger's relief, the orders seemed to fly out of the kitchen.

The pretty blonde she'd seen earlier introduced herself as Darcey while she punched a time clock and tied her apron strings. It wasn't long before she joined Melvina in the cook's window for what seemed like a thousand more orders.

When the breakfast rush finally slowed, Maria turned to her and grinned. "Bueno! You were very good today." She smiled as she enunciated carefully, "Thank you very much for your help."

Again, Ginger wanted to ask if Maria was feeling okay. The grill had heated the woman's cheeks to a hot pink, and sweat beaded on her brow. The Latin woman rubbed one hand over her stomach as she leaned heavily on the counter near the toaster, waiting for an order of toast. Suddenly turning, Maria dashed once more to the back. This time, Ginger heard the door of the employee restroom slam shut. Oh no! Was Maria sick? That was all Ginger needed right now. It was flu season, and something like that would put her out of commission for at least a week. She always got her flu shot, but this year, in the commotion of moving, she'd completely forgotten.

Melvina placed a ticket on the wheel and tapped the old-time bell. Ginger was new, and she didn't want to rat out Maria, but if the lady was sick, it was likely that the whole town would be, too, after the breakfast rush they'd served. The ticket was for three orders of hotcakes and three orders of bacon. That should be easy enough. Ginger had watched Maria make a dozen orders of pancakes on the grill. It couldn't be that hard. She doused the griddle with butter and poured the batter in nine mostly perfect circles and waited. All seemed well until she turned around and accidentally knocked the bottle of oil onto the gas grill. Massive flames shot up with a whoosh. The smell of burnt plastic permeated the kitchen air, and the chicken breasts Maria had been grilling for lunch roasted in flames. Ginger didn't know what to do, so she rushed out to find Melvina. Darcey was coming in while Ginger was running out, and the tray of dirty dishes went crashing to the checkered tile floor. The pretty young waitress glared at her before noticing the flashing flames shooting from the grill through the swinging kitchen door.

Darcey's mouth gaped with horror. "Lord, have mercy. Melvina's gonna have a hissy-fit." Stepping over the mess, the pretty waitress rushed to the grill and turned the dials until the flames finally petered out. She flipped the cakes that were now black on one side and gave Ginger a look of pity.

"It's all right honey, the diner has seen worse accidents than this. You should have seen when Raphe brought in Melvina's basset hound, Lulu, when she was in heat. Humphrey turned this place upside down, trying to get him some tail." Darcey broke into laughter as Ginger gazed at the colossal mess.

She didn't understand the joke and wasn't sure she even wanted to. The kitchen was in shambles. Between the broken dishes littering the floor, the crunchy, dark-brown cakes, and the burnt chicken and plastic burning a noxious odor throughout the kitchen, Ginger wanted to take off her apron and walk out. Earlier, she thought she had the hang of things and was even enjoying the work until it all got out of hand—mainly because of her clumsiness. Maybe she wasn't cut out for manual labor. Her arms were limp from working the cook's line, and her legs were wobbly from the adrenaline rush of the gas fire.

Maria came back to the cook's line with wide eyes and an open mouth of dismay. She made the sign of the cross. "Help me, Jesus."

Ginger held up her hands. "I am so sorry. I promise I'll clean it all up if you could fill that order." She pointed to the ticket with the three short-stacks of pancakes and bacon. "And, if you could point me to the cleaning supplies, I'd be grateful to get out of your hair." In truth, she had no idea how to clean a grill, especially one with melted plastic stuck to its metal tines.

Maria nodded. Directing Darcey to help Ginger find what she needed. The can of grill-cleaner and rags were thrown into a bucket and thrust at her as Darcey rushed off to tend tables. Ginger grabbed a washtub from the dishwasher area and went to pick up the broken dishes outside the kitchen door. Getting down on her hands and knees, she picked up the remnants of egg-sopped, greasy plates and coffee cups with lipstick-stamped rims. Thank God people weren't allowed to smoke inside the restaurant. Grossed out from touching the dirty dishes to begin with, she thought a cigarette in the middle of an egg would be enough to send her rushing to the bathroom, too. She didn't have time to be queasy. Ginger had to suck it up and help Darcey, who was behind now because of her clumsiness.

"It doesn't look like your days are getting any better. I didn't know you worked here, too."

Ginger froze, looking up into the amber-flecked eyes she remembered from yesterday. *Great, just great. On my knees, at his feet, cleaning. I bet he just loves this.* She released a frustrated sigh. "Hello, Officer Karr. I started this morning. Melvina hired me yesterday."

As she put the last broken plate in the tub, he bent down and picked up the dish bin. "This is heavy. Can I carry it somewhere for you?"

Ginger thought about his offer. Her arms shook from fatigue, but she declined. The kitchen was still a war zone, and she didn't think her boss would appreciate her letting the constable do her dirty work. His pressed uniform was too perfect looking. He could have been the poster model for a police academy advertisement. Solid pecs, squared shoulders, and firm biceps were visible beneath his creased uniform shirt. Ginger thought the seams to his trousers might rip when he squatted down to retrieve the overloaded bus tub. His intelligent brown eyes assessed her, but she couldn't tell what he was thinking. After yesterday's speeding incident and her running away to the restroom at Hank's, it couldn't be anything good.

With another drawn-out sigh, she said, "Thanks, but I've got it." Pushing through the door with too much force, she almost collided with Darcey again. The girl gave her a look of frustration. "Look through the window first. There is a mirror up there." She pointed to a round mirror on the wall that reflected the area surrounding the door. "Then you can see what's comin' and goin'."

Ginger frowned and looked back at the constable, who was still standing outside the door. Darcey noticed him, too, and smiled, patting Ginger on the shoulder. "It's okay. You'll get the hang of it."

It wasn't even ten in the morning yet, and Ginger felt dead on her feet. She used to grumble about getting to the studio on time or remembering lines. She complained that the writers hadn't captured her character the way they should have, or the many hours she had to spend in makeup before a shoot wasn't necessary. A stray wisp of hair escaped her ponytail, and she pushed it back, forgetting she'd picked up a bunch of dirty dishes. She felt something wet against her ear.

"Ick." She screwed up her face in disgust. Ginger didn't want to know what biohazard she had painted herself with. Was it the egg yolk, ketchup, or dreaded oatmeal? Her stomach lurched. *It's only the first day. Please, God, don't let me toss my cookies in public.*

Melvina came out of the office, bumping the door shut with her hip. One look at Ginger, and she shook her head. "You poor dear. This isn't the best first shift, is it?"

Ginger felt the urge to cry. She wanted to like her work. She really did, but there was nothing glamorous about it, and she hadn't counted on being a busboy.

"Give me those." Melvina stepped forward, taking the bus tub and dropping it at the dishwasher station. "I'm sorry the morning got away from us. We are often shorthanded, especially during this part of the year when everyone is out sick with a cold." She shrugged her shoulders. "Not much we can do about it. I wish I could say it's never like this, but the best I can do is tell you that it's not *always* like this." Melvina gave her a smile and patted her on the back. "You did great. I love the way you jumped in to help this morning. You're a hard worker, and I respect that in a person."

Ginger shook her head. "What a mess I made—"

"Oh, that's no big deal. When Maria was training, she set half the kitchen on fire. Good thing my husband's brother is a fireman. It was before the remodel, though, so let's try to keep those incidents to a minimum." Melvina winked and waved for Ginger to follow her.

As they entered the employee area, Melvina told her to grab herself something to drink and to take a thirty-minute break. "You deserve it, gal."

Ginger looked longingly at the back exit. She'd been there for almost five hours, and she was starving.

As if reading her mind, Melvina approached her with a green and white check pad. "Write up anything you want to eat, and I'll get Maria to whip it up fast for you."

Ginger glanced at her with trepidation. "You sure she won't poison me after I ruined the kitchen?"

Melvina chuckled. "She's seen worse. You'll get better. We all have to learn in our own time. You tried hard to help, and that's all that matters. Maria is a sweetheart, and the only thing you'll have to worry about with her is that she will mother you to death and try to make you fat. You got a boyfriend? If not, she'll be trying to find you a good man, too."

Ginger thought of her history with men and the constable who'd seen her at her worst. "I'll pass, thank you."

Melvina chuckled. "All wounds heal in time."

Ginger wasn't sure if she was talking about the kitchen fiasco of the morning or her past relationships. Deciding not to expand on the conversation, she responded, "Okay then. I'll take a garden salad and a cup of soup."

Melvina balked. "No wonder you're all skin and bones. You sure you don't want to try a monster burger with fries? It's my little brother's favorite."

Darcey breezed through the break room. "There ain't nothin' little about Eli." She winked at Ginger. "He's drop-dead gorgeous too, but he's taken. Some celebrity swooped into town and scooped him up."

Again, Ginger ignored the reference to available or unavailable men and returned to the conversation she was having with Melvina. She'd seen the massive burger and fries concoction and would love to try it, but after the cupcakes yesterday followed by the hot-wings and pear beer last night, she didn't think it was a good idea to keep indulging. "I better stick to the salad. I'm still full from the cupcakes yesterday." To be honest, she'd only taken a bite or two, but she didn't need to disclose every detail. Surely, Melvina had been joking about trying them all. There were at least three dozen.

"Great, I forgot to ask you for your notes. Which was your favorite?"

A dark-haired woman entered the back door and punched the time clock as she unrolled her apron in a hurry.

Melvina called out, "Maddie, you're late, gal. I need you up front ASAP. The lunch rush is starting soon."

It was the distraction Ginger needed. Lexi had warned her about Melvina's competitive nature. What if she admitted she hadn't tried all the cakes? Would Melvina be offended and think she didn't like them?

Maddie darted a glance at Ginger with a smile and a nod, then she sped off to the front. The woman's gray eyes were framed by thick lashes, and her hair was reminiscent of one of those sixties movies, like Annette Funicello or Sandra Dee.

Ginger couldn't imagine waiting tables like Maddie and Darcey, but the women seemed to know their way around a diner. Ginger hadn't wanted to be recognized, but who would ever think she was hiding out as a waitress in this small, southern town? She would study the other employees and try to learn the order of things. If she could make tips, it might get her out of Magnolia sooner. After she squirreled away enough money to feed herself for a couple months and lease a room from a reputable apartment building in the city, she could buy a one-way bus ticket to New York and never look back. *Work hard, focus on the future, make some damn-good, but not too-damn-good gingerbread cookies… next stop Broadway.*

Chapter 14

Roland felt sorry for Ginger, on her knees picking up broken dishes. His morning had had a similar start. When Rollo jumped at the table to greet him, hot coffee spilled onto his uniform. After cursing, changing, and cleaning up the mess, Roland hadn't had time to sit down to enjoy another cup.

Kelsey had been the most upset, begging him, "Please don't be mad at Rollo." Her big brown eyes pooled with unshed tears.

It made him angry at the dog and himself, but he smiled at his niece and told her not to worry. "Rollo will learn the rules in time. Once he understands what areas are off-limits, he will be able to stay inside again, but for now, why don't you take him outside and fill his water bowl. I think he needs a time-out to ponder what behaviors need practice."

"But Uncle Roland, he didn't mean to spill your coffee."

He smiled, nodding. "I know it wasn't on purpose, but how will he learn to act better if we don't teach him?" He didn't mention that his unmentionables had been nearly scalded. To the dog, he pointed toward the back door. "You, out!"

Kelsey followed Rollo to the door, letting the screen slam shut behind her. Roland released a sigh of frustration and counted to ten. He didn't like being the disciplinarian with his niece, and ever since Maddie had brought the mangy canine home, he found himself lecturing Kelsey more than he liked. It was just a dog, and the mutt had been excited to say hello to him. Had he been too stern?

"Sorry!" Kelsey called back to the house, interrupting his thoughts. She was such a good kid. Roland couldn't help but smile. He hated to admit it, but the dog was good for his niece. Rollo was teaching her responsibility. It was a little extra work to remind her to feed the dog and to keep his water bowl filled, but that's what uncles did. He had started taking the dog on his daily three-mile run to keep the mutt from bolting around the house like a loose cannon. The animal was becoming a part of his daily routine, and Roland had to admit, he liked the dog's company when the big oaf wasn't eating the sofa or sprawling on Roland's bed. It wasn't the dog hair on his sheets that bothered him, but the dog spent an abundant amount of time licking his own undercarriage.

When Roland dropped Maddie off at the diner, he decided to park and go in for his missed cup of coffee to restart his day. After Ginger scurried away with the bus tub full of broken dishes, looking embarrassed, he stood there staring dumbly at the swinging kitchen door. As the blonde waitress reprimanded her, Ginger's shoulders shrank, making him want to charge to her defense. The starlit beauty didn't look the type to work in a diner as a bus gal. She looked as if she were playing a role in a TMC movie that he hadn't seen yet, making him want to sit down and watch the rest of the story unfold. For a brief moment of insanity, he'd thought about dashing into the kitchen and tossing the bus tub aside, then taking her into his arms for one of those Hollywood kisses that the camera lingered over for half a scene. For unknown reasons, he felt like clasping her hand and leading her away from the toil of her day. Something about her gave off damsel-in-distress vibes, even though she resisted his generosity or assistance at every turn.

Last night, after Lexi disappeared with Noah, and not knowing how long she'd be, he'd offered to take Ginger home. He'd hoped she would accept his offer, but she'd scurried off to the ladies' room and then Lexi finally reappeared. Ginger had a strong chin that jutted into the air whenever he was around, but something in her eyes said she had a reason to be wary of men. He supposed it was his past experience with his high school girlfriend and then his ex, Claire, that sparked his chivalrous side whenever he laid eyes on her. Right now, there was nothing he wanted more than to blow off his shift and take her into the city somewhere for lunch. If he showed Ginger the spiffier side of the area, maybe she would finally smile. Right now, she looked miserable working in the diner. He didn't blame her. It was a thankless job that probably paid minimum wage.

Roland bet she was even more beautiful when she didn't look like the weight of the world was on her shoulders. Her pouty, full bottom lip and sorrowful emerald eyes made him think of a list of Hollywood actresses who'd graced the silver screen. Classic Hollywood movies were shown every Saturday evening in Magnolia's city park, but only outside during the summer. From October to April, they were shown in the annex of the

Cowboy Baptist Church, but it wasn't the same as watching them under the stars at night. Three hours away, in Austin, they showed old movies at the vintage Paramount during the summer and on winter holidays. The ambiance was perfect. It was almost Christmas, but he didn't know Ginger well enough to ask her to drive three hours away with him or to invite her to his home for a movie night. Damned if that wasn't what he wanted to do. He shook his head. His house was full with his sister, brother, niece, and Rollo running amuck. And what made him think she liked old films anyway? Ginger looked 1940s classic, but she seemed like the type to go in for the action-packed, shoot 'em up, badass movies. Or maybe she was a rom-com gal that liked hunky actors and the over-the-top storylines of unlikely characters falling in love—not that he had anything against modern movies. They were enjoyable enough, but there was something to be said about films that excelled at superb dialogue and intriguing plots. Movies that held the viewer's interest through the quality of the story rather than relying on big-budget special effects were rare today.

He knew where she worked, so there would be other opportunities to get to know her and ask her out. Since Maddie also worked at the diner, he had the perfect excuse to drop by, often. Now, if he could make the new gal like him enough to say yes to a date, but all bets were off if she didn't go in for *Casablanca*.

Chapter 15

Ginger decided Magnolia was having the weirdest December on record—eighty degrees yesterday, thirty-five this morning, and now it felt like a perfect seventy in the sun. She appreciated the mostly green landscape as she turned off the main road and made her way toward the ranch. This part of Texas was known for its mild temps and lots of sunny days. It wasn't L.A., but the town held a warmth and beauty that Ginger could appreciate—as long as it stayed warm. Winter wasn't her thing.

Lexi sat proudly on top of a white horse speckled with brown spots. The horse and the woman paused when they saw Ginger pulling into the gravel drive. They looked as if they were posing for Magnolia Magazine. The sun shone down over Lexi's glossy blonde hair, and the animal's long legs danced in place with its head held high. Lexi Nash was beautiful and nice, and that was something new to Ginger. Hollywood was filled with cut-throat beauties who would sell her out in three seconds flat for a bit role in a B movie. The only friends Ginger ever made in L.A. were gay men who weren't in the movie industry—unless they were behind the scenes in wardrobe or makeup, and even those men would sell her out for the right introduction to a good-looking actor or stuntman.

She waved, and Lexi waved back, turning the horse's head in the direction of the house. The pure white mane of the mount looked like a flag streaming in a battle charge. As Ginger parked and exited the car, a small herd of horses greeted her. Three young boys jumped from their mounts and clamored toward the car along with a baying basset hound. She backed up, lifting one leg as the long-eared pooch ran toward her at an alarming pace, yapping all the while.

"Chef!" they all called out in differing tones of authority.

The basset hopped up, placing both front paws on Ginger's jean-clad legs. She'd never had a dog of her own, though she loved all animals and wished she could have one. Chef was sniffing her shirt all over and pinning her to the rental car. Ginger was afraid to move. "Will he bite me?"

"He'll lick you to death," the tallest boy called out with a giggle.

Again, Lexi told the dog to get down. The basset gave Ginger's hand a lick and complied, bouncing off into the yard to play.

"Hi, Ginger. These are my boys. Gus, Bert and Damien." She smiled, pointing to the basset. "And that's Chef. He's a lover and very curious. I bet he smells the diner on you and is waiting for a steak bone. Riley and Melvina always bring him one when they visit."

"Oh." Ginger raised her empty hands. "I'll try to remember to bring him one next time."

Lexi waved. "It's okay. Next time, he'll know who you are and hopefully show some better manners." She hopped down from her horse, and the boys started to chase each other.

"So many animals," Ginger said with wonder. "How do you do it? I barely had time to feed Igor before I left this morning and turn his terrarium light on."

Lexi walked her horse as she answered. "I can't imagine life without them. My mawmaw and pap raised cattle until they were too old to manage the ranch. My dad's a lawyer, and my mom's a Realtor. My grandparents sold off most of what they owned, except the hundred acres they left to us kids. Jack and I bought out my siblings and decided to invest in cattle. It's been a family business for so long that I couldn't see it sold to anyone else. I've felt the calling to be around animals since I was old enough to sit at my grandma's knee while she sewed quilting squares. The cat, a rat, Chef, the donkeys, and my boys in the pasture are sometimes wilder than the rest of my cattle and horses combined. I have help. You'll eventually meet John.

"He's really nice, and I don't know what I'd do without his help, but I take care of feeding the horses myself. I love to see them fill their bellies." The speckled horse's tail swatted a ghostly fly, and Lexi rubbed its nose. She looked at Ginger with a warm smile. "To tell you the truth, I don't know what I would do without all of this. My life may be nonstop chores and nights filled with checking the boys' homework and making sure they've washed behind their ears, but it keeps me sane. I wouldn't trade it for the world."

Ginger nodded. "I can see you're really happy here. It would overwhelm me, but I have to say, the two days I've been here have been nice so far. I've never seen the sun come up so golden before, and the orange glow on the horizon this morning looked like a Monet."

They both watched the boys play with Chef, who chased them, baying, "A-roo-roo-roo." The horses clomped along behind Lexi as Ginger followed her to the barn. The white-washed structure was old but well cared for. The paint was recent, and it looked like some of the wood beams had been replaced. It had at least twelve stalls for horses and a large loft above filled with hay. Lexi removed the saddles and started brushing her white and auburn-speckled mount.

A man in tight jeans and a flannel shirt joined them. His dark blond hair bordered golden-brown. The crown of his head caught the light shining in from the open door as he hefted a sizeable bale of hay. His baby-blue eyes glimmered in the sunlight, and Ginger couldn't help thinking, *this man belongs in movies.* His broad shoulders filled out his soft cotton shirt, which was unbuttoned down the front. The white tank he wore underneath was soaked through with sweat and clung to his ab muscles, leaving no doubt of his washboard stomach. He was tall, fit, and a slight beard shaded his chiseled jawline and neck. He was a little rough around the edges, but a woman would have to be blind not to notice his raw, gorgeous-hunk-of-a-man potential.

The way Lexi barely looked at him said she must be blind, but her eyes finally glanced up and noticed his presence. A natural smile lit her sun-brushed face as she introduced them. "Hey John, this is Ginger Harding. Ginger, this is John Archer. If you want to ride, he'll help you find the saddles, bridles and such. He knows the ranch inside and out and is the best right-hand man I could ever ask for." She paused and added, "Ginger works for Melvina at the diner. She'll be staying down at Mawmaw's cottage."

The shy "How do you do" was barely audible. He took the reins and led the other horses to their individual stalls for Lexi.

"John will take care of the rest. You should get changed for dinner and come up to the house. We're making pizza tonight. It's the boys' favorite, and my famous chef brother made the crust from scratch. I'm so happy that he keeps my freezer stocked. It makes dinner a breeze on busy days, God bless him. All we have to do is add the toppings and throw it in the oven."

Ginger whispered to Lexi. "You have a romance novel cover-model in your barn, and you're asking me if I want pizza?"

Lexi chuckled. "Ah. John is a sweetheart, and he is handsome. I don't think of him that way. He is single, though. If you're interested, I can ask him up to the house for pizza." Lexi sounded sincere, then her features fell, and she put a hand on Ginger's arm. "No, wait! Don't even look at him. If you and John get together and things don't work out, I'll lose the best damn ranch hand I've ever had…or you, and I was just starting to think you and I were going to be lifelong friends."

Ginger smiled at Lexi's teasing tone, but her heart melted a little over the declaration. It warmed her to think she might have found a real friend. Ginger was supposed to be this woman's employee, but so far, she'd hardly lifted a finger to help. There was that hour or so in the garden pulling weeds, but she'd been at the diner all day, and now, Lexi was baking pizza for her and the boys. Eventually, she'd need to step up and earn her keep. Not many jobs included free room and board. It would be best to keep her eyes off the handsome ranch hand to ensure a roof over her head. "Don't worry. John Archer is safe from me. Remember, I'm off men for now." Following Lexi out of the barn, she called, "I'll join you for dinner, but I get to do all the dishes afterward. Deal?"

Lexi turned and nodded. "Okay then. Rest up. Dinner's at six."

Chapter 16

Roland opened his laptop and sipped the hot coffee Maddie had placed in front of him on the diner counter. He'd run his usual three miles with Rollo trotting at his side and missed his morning cup of caffeine at home. It was his day off, but he'd never been one for sleeping in. It was Saturday, and when he left the house that morning, Luke was watching cartoons with Kelsey, who was glued to his side, and Rollo, who sat on the other, was drooling on Luke's arm.

A quick internet search let him know that *North by Northwest* with Cary Grant and Eva Marie Saint was showing tonight at the Cowboy Baptist Church annex. It was one of his favorite classic movies, and he didn't want to miss it, even if the seats were hard metal chairs set too close together in a room with faux wood paneling and popcorn ceiling tiles. He'd ask Maddie, Kelsey and Luke if they wanted to join him. It would be a great way to spend some quality family time together and what they needed to ease some of the growing tensions from living in close quarters. Roland was sure his brother would appreciate a break from the couch, even if it was a hard metal church chair. The popcorn was made fresh by the senior ladies at the church, and some of the older men and young volunteers made cherry Cokes and Shirley Temples like they used to make at the old-style ice cream shop. It was unfortunate that the large fast-food places had moved into town and eventually forced the Magnolia Dairy Delight to close, but Roland still remembered the real cherry sodas and malts he and his siblings enjoyed when they were kids.

"Mornin', Constable Karr." Darcey gave him a broad wink and leaned on the counter with both hands, peeking over the top of his computer.

He leaned back and gave her a smile. "Mornin' Darcey. How's my omelet coming?"

Leaning down on one elbow, she whispered conspiratorially, "Maria is out sick. Word has it she's preggers, and Melvina's looking for another cook since the last one quit. Been training that new gal all morning, but...." Darcey straightened, shaking her head as she peered back at the cook's window. "I don't think Ginger is cut out to be a cook."

Roland glanced at the cook's window but couldn't see anyone. "No. I don't think she looks like she's cut out for cooking either, but give her a chance. You never know what people are capable of until they try."

Darcey came around to his side of the counter, leaning against the space next to him. She crossed her arms, making the material of her uniform stretch against the swell of her breasts. As she surveyed the diner, she let out a deep sigh. "I guess you're right. I suppose Ginger's not all bad. She doesn't complain about cleaning the cook's line or busing tables when Maurice is late, but it's only her first week. We'll see how long she lasts." Darcey bumped him with her hip as she sauntered off. "She's too damned pretty to work in the back. Melvina should put her out here with me. We'd clean up big-time," she called back over her shoulder.

Roland figured she was talking about tips. Darcey wasn't much for cleaning up anything. She took the orders and brought the food out. Mostly she chatted with customers and flirted shamelessly with the policemen and firefighters. It was all part of the draw to the diner. Darcey was a staple of Magnolia, and though she'd schmooze a stop sign, the ladies loved her, too. Roland knew about the few months she'd danced at the gentleman's club in Houston, but it wasn't long before she came back to the diner and started evening classes at the community college. He figured she must be near graduating, but he didn't want to be nosy.

Roland waited patiently for his breakfast, darting glances at the cook's window. He hoped to catch the eye of the gorgeous brunette. Thoughts of following her in her little red sports car and pulling her over to talk to her had crossed his mind more than once. It wasn't like there weren't other attractive and engaging women in Magnolia. He'd had his share of dates when he wanted them, but the fact was, no one sparked his interest like the sassy brunette behind the cook's window.

His attitude seemed bizarre, even to himself, because he barely knew the gal, and she hadn't put any vibes out that said she was interested. Her aura was the exact opposite of inviting. She'd stared daggers at him during the first two encounters and then seemed indifferent at their last meeting. He wasn't sure what it was that got under his skin or why he was so keen to ask her out, but he chalked it up to wanting what he couldn't have. Sure, she was a dead ringer for Ava Gardner, from the finely arched eyebrows and pouty bottom lip down to the adorable dimple in her chin. If he looked hard enough, he was sure there were other available women who had similar classic features, but it was Ginger's attitude that seeped into his awareness like the syrup soaking into his pancakes. He stared at the melting butter on top, longing for more than food.

From the first moment she'd huffed at him because he'd pulled her over, he'd felt the sharp zing of attraction. Then, when she looked up at him over the scattered broken dishes, with vulnerability shimmering through thick dark lashes, he knew he had it bad. Now he needed to take her on a date so he could meet the real Ginger Harding, which he was sure wasn't anything like the vintage celebrity he envisioned. It was the only solution he could think of to let go of the needling sensation that he needed to rescue her.

As Darcey dropped his check on the table, he saw Ginger fly from the kitchen with an apron in her hand. After flinging open the front door of the diner, she jogged toward her car. Roland dug in his back pocket, asking Darcey to wrap his breakfast to go. Cursing his cash-poor wallet, he handed her his credit card. With no other short-cut at his disposal, he'd have to wait. Through the diner window, he saw the red Infiniti zip out of the lot toward Nichols Sawmill Road. She was probably headed to Lexi's ranch. If he hurried, there was a good chance he'd catch her—speeding.

Chapter 17

Ginger was supposed to pick the boys up at soccer practice and now she was late. Melvina had asked her to stay through the breakfast rush and then showed her how to make biscuits and gravy. Ginger hadn't wanted to be a cook, but it was better than busing tables. Actually, she found she liked working in the kitchen. Sure, it was chaotic, and she wasn't sure she was all that good at it, but the waitresses pooled their tips and shared them with the rest of the diner staff. It padded her earnings for the day, and that was something she hadn't counted on.

The nonstop commotion of clanging pots and buzzing timers provided little time to obsess about her fall from Hollywood's grace. She was so deep into her work, filling orders for Darcey and Melvina, that she totally spaced on the time. Damien, Bert and Gus all stood in a line, waiting outside on the curb at the elementary school, where a few cars still waited to pick up kids from practice. Thank God! She was only ten minutes late, but luckily, she set her watch ten minutes fast, or it would have been a disaster. She'd never worn a watch before working at the diner, but cell phones weren't allowed past the break room. Melvina said they were a nuisance, and she didn't even bring her own onto the floor. Melvina's handsome hubby didn't seem to mind that he had to come rushing in on a few occasions to find her. Ginger had caught them in a lip lock behind the diner twice. Apparently, he'd been in San Francisco, opening another one of their restaurants. After being married for several years, Ginger thought their affection was sweet.

The three boys tromped toward her car with solemn faces. She gave them a worried frown. "What's the matter, guys?"

Damien, the youngest of Lexi's boys, was the first to look up, blowing out a very adult sigh. "Today is one of the few days we have free until we get off for Christmas break, and you're late. We shoulda been home ropin' Shrek and Donkey by now. I got a new Superman cape and everything."

Bert made a face at Damien. "That's baby stuff. I want to watch *The Avengers!*"

His arm shot into the air, and Damien cried out, "Ooh, ooh, me too!"

Ginger blinked in surprise, trying not to grin. It was only ten minutes past the hour. She gave them a nod in understanding. "I see. I'm sorry I was late. I'll try to do better."

The eldest boy returned her nod. "We'll let it slide this time. I got extra credit homework to do this weekend, so maybe you can help?" Gus was an industrious child. Ginger had him pegged to be a future politician or possible Hollywood actor. He knew how to lay it on thick. In the short time she'd known the little family, Gus was the deal maker. So far, he'd arranged extra gingerbread cookies for sweeping the kitchen floor and bargained staying up an hour past his bedtime for packing all their lunches. Her favorite haggle was when he negotiated his place in the front seat because he was the tallest and could appreciate the view. She still made him play rock, paper, scissors to ride shotgun, but he'd already earned a special place in her heart.

Ginger had practiced baking her soon-to-be-a-winner cookie recipe in Lexi's kitchen every evening to prepare for the upcoming competition. She'd brought samples to work and Melvina was wild about the taste, but Ginger couldn't bring herself to share her gran's secret ingredient, so for now, she only made them at the ranch. She thought about Lexi's warning to not make anything too good, but for Ginger's gran's sake, she made them like she always had, and they were the best. The boys were happy to eat their share and take the extras to school for their class. They'd even come home with a special request for orders from their teachers. Ginger had no doubt that The Cupcake Diner and Dive would take home first place this year at The Galleria Gingerbread Extravaganza. It was held on Christmas Eve day, and the Snowflake Ball would take place later that night.

Melvina had already shown her the blueprints for the gingerbread village they planned to build. It was a miniature replica of Magnolia's main street. The many ginger-citizens would be in an array of dress and Christmas cheer. As long as Ginger could let go of the original cookie recipe, they were a shoo-in. Sharing her gran's original ingredients might be worth it. Melvina promised Ginger the thousand-dollar cash prize if they won and offered to sign a sworn statement of secrecy not to share Ginger's recipe. All she wanted in return were the bragging rights and to put the trophy in the case at the diner. Between the prize money and another month or two working for Lexi and Melvina, Ginger would soon be Broadway-bound and onto another career doing what she was born to do—act.

Zipping along the old country road that led to the farm, she was careful to mind the speed limit. Lexi's boys were precious cargo, not only to their mom but to Ginger as well. She'd never wanted kids and had never seen herself as a nanny, but in a short amount of time she'd somehow grown very fond of their little cherub faces and their thoughtful conversations. It was hard not to smile as they debated the need for underwear on people versus animals and discussed why anyone would want to put mushrooms in eggs. They shared with her that their famous chef uncle, Riley, made a mushroom frittata that they had never forgotten or forgiven him for, and they warned her not to try it.

As the car topped the hill and made the curve, Gus screamed, "Stop!"

Ginger swerved, hitting the breaks. "What the hell?" As quick as the expletive was out, she looked in the rearview mirror at their stricken faces. "Sorry. I didn't mean to curse, but you scared me."

Gussy and the other two boys all pointed in unison. "Turtle!"

Sure enough, there was a cute little box turtle with a red head sticking out of his shell. He was strutting across the solid yellow line like he owned the highway. Ginger would have never run it over intentionally, even if Gus hadn't screamed, but the assault to her ears had scared her, and she'd almost skid off the road.

She took a deep breath and pulled the car safely to the side of the highway. "You boys stay in the car, and I'll move the turtle to a safer spot."

The turtle was in danger since oncoming traffic couldn't see past the curve until it was too late. People who didn't love reptiles like she did might smoosh it without a second thought. Jogging to the center of the road, she grabbed up the little fella, who promptly tucked his head and legs in and pulled his front flap shut. Just as she turned to run back to the car, another vehicle crested the hill and hit the brakes with a screech. The car swerved dangerously to one side and then overcompensated back in the opposite direction. Ginger danced right, then left, squeezed the turtle to her chest and closed her eyes as she braced for impact. The vehicle with Constable written along the side in big white letters sent a breeze over her still form as he crested the road and landed in the opposite ditch.

Feeling like the box turtle she still clasped in her hands, she slowly peeked her head out from between her arms. "Holy crap!"

The flap of the turtle shell lowered, and a little red head peeped out. Ginger looked at his cute little hooked beak. "Uh-oh, little guy. I think we're in big trouble now."

Gus opened the car door, but Ginger pointed her finger at him. "Do not leave that car!" Lexi was going to kill her when she heard about this tonight over tater tots and hotdogs. It would be all she would have time to make.

Holding tight to the turtle as she moved toward the wrecked vehicle, she held her breath until she saw Roland Karr's eyes staring back at her in the rearview mirror. She released the turtle in the direction it had been headed when she'd picked it up. "Run along, little man. I don't think you want to hear what the constable has to say about this rescue mission."

Roland admitted to himself that he'd been racing along, trying to catch the little red car. As Maddie would say, it was poetic karma. He'd been trying to catch the new gal speeding so he'd have a reason to pull her over and see her face to face. But who would have thought he would come around the bend and catch her standing in the middle of the road? Did she know he was following her? Was this some sort of sick prank? His car could have hit her. Luckily, his airbag hadn't deployed, and the ditch was barely a dip. He patted himself down, looked in his rearview mirror, and took a deep breath. His adrenalin spiked, and he shot out of the car, making his way toward her. She stood dumbstruck at the side of the road muttering to herself.

He grasped her arm. "Are you okay? Are you crazy? I almost hit you!"

She looked at him with lips pressed tightly together as she nodded. The woman wore an expression similar to Kelsey's after she'd done something she wasn't supposed to do and got caught red-handed. Surely, Ginger hadn't meant to make him crash his vehicle.

"I—I'm fine." She shifted, pulling her arm from his grasp. "Sorry. I didn't mean to make you run off the road. The turtle was going to get hit, and the boys were worried." She motioned to the car with the three boys staring out the windows.

Damien, in the front seat, called out. "Why'd you let it go? We wanted to keep it!"

Roland looked down, noticing the turtle a short distance away, making a rather fast escape for a little guy. "He seems pretty quick to me. Are you sure he needed help or were you getting him for the kids?"

Ginger shook her head. "No. I was making sure he didn't get squished. Some box turtles are endangered, and you're not supposed to pick them up unless it's to help them cross the road, preferably in the same direction they were headed."

"Please!" The boys called in unison through the car window. "Get 'im."

Roland smiled. It was the decent thing to do, stopping to help the creature get to safety, but *damn, she could've gotten killed in the process.* How would he have ever lived with himself if he'd run over her?

She waved at the boys to be quiet and looked back to his car. "I'm sorry about…." Her hands fluttered at her side as if she were at a loss for words.

"My car," he supplied with a grin.

She gave him a small smile, but it didn't reach her eyes. The fidgeting told him she was worried, and he wanted to see her smile again. Really smile, but right now, they weren't in a safe position to talk.

He squeezed her shoulder, this time with reassurance, and looked her in the eye. "The car will be fine. Metal bends. People don't. I know you wanted to do the right thing, but next time, please be more careful. I can't imagine if anyone else had crested that hill. They could've been texting or talking to someone on their phone. You could've ended up road-kill."

He watched as she nodded. Her emerald eyes were glazed over with contemplation. She was either thinking about her own good fortune or an alternate ending to the last five minutes. He felt empathy for her. The boys clearly had been set on saving and keeping the turtle. Sometimes children could overwhelm a person into forgetting good judgment. "Next time, I suggest walking to the highest bend in the road or wherever you can see the farthest and look for oncoming traffic first."

Ginger nodded again as if it had never occurred to her. "Sorry, but I didn't want anyone to crush the poor little guy."

Roland waited until her eyes met his. "Are you okay to drive? Why don't I follow you home?"

She shook her head adamantly. "Oh no! What would their mother think?"

Roland understood her concern. "I'll follow you home and turn off at the road before you enter the drive to the ranch."

"I'm okay. Really."

He noticed her hands were still shaking. "Humor me for the boys' sake."

Ginger nodded and started back to her car. "All right, but I'm okay, really."

Roland had an idea. "Maybe you can distract the boys from telling their mother all about it by bringing them to the movies. The Cowboy Baptist Church shows old movies on Saturday nights during the winter. Tonight, they're showing *North by Northwest*."

Ginger's face lit up. "With Cary Grant? Oh, that's one of my favorites."

Roland felt his heart skip a beat. It was her first genuine smile, and the way her eyes sparkled filled him with hope. Her glossy hair framed her face, and her perfect teeth bit at her full bottom lip. The air was motionless, and time stood still. It was the stuff of the silver screen, her looking at him and him wanting to kiss her senseless—for being senseless over saving a turtle.

Entranced by her beauty and rescue attempt, he reached into his wallet and handed her his card. "I'm taking my sister, my niece and my brother tonight. It's a nice family event. Everyone in town will be there. It'll give you a chance to meet people."

She hesitated as a concerned look furrowed her brows. "I—I'll have to ask Lexi."

"If they don't want to come, I can pick you up. Just give me a call, and I'll swing by. Movie's at seven."

She gave him another beautiful grin, her cat-green eyes peering up at him beneath dark lashes. This one said she knew he was hitting on her, and damn if he wasn't. Roland felt like a love-struck puppy drooling over an ice cream cone.

As she nodded and turned back to her car, tucking his card in her bra, the three little boys peered out of the window, giggling. As he returned to his own vehicle, he heard them chanting, "Ginger and the constable sitting in a tree, K-I-S-S-I-N-G...."

Chapter 18

Ginger looked in the hall mirror at her reflection, asking herself for the millionth time why in the world she was going to the movies with the constable at a church annex of all places. Lexi and the boys had declined, saying they already had plans. If Ginger wasn't mistaken, a look of relief had fallen over Lexi's face when Ginger told her about the movie with Officer Karr. Lexi had blushed prettily, explaining she was meeting a friend at the new Hank's. When Ginger returned to the house to wait for Roland, Lexi scurried out with all three boys, informing her that they were going to their grandparents for the night. Great. Ginger could sleep late tomorrow.

The sexy red cocktail dress and shiny lipstick Lexi wore said the *friend* she was meeting at Hank's was probably a hot date. Maybe it was the man who whisked her away the other night or Roland's surfer brother. Whoever Lexi was meeting, Ginger hoped he was a decent gambler because Lexi Nash Burns was bringing a royal flush to the table, and odds had it the *friend* might get lucky if he played his cards right.

The good-looking constable arrived on time, which didn't surprise Ginger. Roland seemed like he ran a tight ship. She supposed it was part of the appeal. A sudden urge assailed her to run her fingers through his perfectly combed hair and unbutton his pressed shirt. The man's strong jawline, along with the cords that moved in his neck when he looked at her with those serious, sherry-colored eyes, made her mouth dry and her pulse race. She had an affinity for bad boys, but something about this type-A, straight shooter made her want to be corrected in the worst way.

His eyes sparked with interest as he stared at her. "Wow, you look nice."

As she stood in the doorway and took in his attire, she smiled. His shirt was perfectly pressed with straight seams running down the arms. She wondered if he ironed his clothes himself or sent them to the dry cleaners.

The stiffness of the material said the shirt could probably stand up on its own. Even his jeans were pressed. His shiny leather cowboy boots looked expensive—the kind worn only on special occasions.

Am I a special occasion?

Ginger hadn't known what kind of off-duty car she'd expected him to drive, but the shiny red vintage convertible made sense. He had asked her to an old movie. That said there was something different about Officer Karr, so why not a classic car, too? She didn't know much about vintage automobiles, but she loved seeing them motoring around L.A. The city was home to a lot of enthusiasts, and she'd often saw cool classics cruising down the boulevard.

A small thrill went through her. Tonight, she would be the one riding around in a classic. "Wow! What kind is it?"

"It's my grandfather's 1953 Skylark. Beautiful, isn't she? Because she is a gorgeous red, I call her Lucille, after Lucille Ball."

If he knew who she really was, Ginger might have thought he was goading her, but he seemed genuine in his praise. "As in, *I Love Lucy?*"

He gave her a smile with a thoughtful nod. "Everyone always thinks of that show, but did you ever see her films? She was beautiful, so much more than the comedian she portrayed. I know there are other beautiful redheads, but Lucille was my favorite and this beauty here," he paused to open the passenger door, "is shiny red, curvy and as sexy as the actress herself."

"You have an affinity for redheads?" she inquired with a raised eyebrow and a teasing smile.

He cleared his throat as if checking himself for mooning over another woman while picking her up for a date. "Sorry, I get a little crazy about Lucille when I take her out for the night."

Ginger grinned as he shut the door. "Are we still talking about the woman or the car?"

"The car," he said with a chuckle. "Forgive me. I only take her out on movie night and to car shows when I can."

Ginger ran her hand over the dash. "I can see why you're in love with her. She's gorgeous. I think I'm green with envy."

His face lit up. "It shows in your eyes."

It was a little cheesy, but Ginger laughed anyway. "Those came from my father. My mom calls them kelly green."

"They are beautiful." The sincerity in his voice didn't come off as cheesy because he looked away like he hadn't meant to let the compliment slip. "So, do you like vintage cars?"

Ginger decided to turn things up a notch with the straightlaced constable. She'd been bored since leaving L.A. and a little lonely for a man's company. It was hard to recall the last time she'd been on a date, let alone had sex. Suddenly, she was having visions of doing it in the back seat of Roland's beautiful Lucille. "I don't know anything about cars, but I like what I see." Her eyes were on his face, and she watched his throat muscles flex as he swallowed. She liked that he was somewhat shy and conservative.

If she turned on Dallas Deringer, she could probably shock his socks off. Grabbing the seat belt, she pulled it slowly over her lap, lifting her hips to search for the buckle. The cream-colored leather seats felt wonderful against her hands as she straightened the folds of her skirt. Licking her lips, she continued their conversation. "Lucille is curvy, red, shiny—a very beautiful lady indeed, and I'm straight. Well, except for that time in college, and that was an experimental thing. It didn't really count." She batted her eyelashes at him as he stared wordlessly back at her. She couldn't help but wonder if he was picturing what she said or was he too straightlaced? It made her want to chuckle as his amber-flecked eyes assessed her. He was trying to figure her out. *Let him.*

A slow grin spread across his face as he put the car in reverse. Apparently, he wasn't going to comment on her flirtation, but as they started down the drive, he asked, "Top up or down?"

Roland arched a brow at her, and the shimmering interest in his eyes made her legs tremble. Butterflies did a tango in her stomach as she watched his hands grip the wheel. His bottom lip was slightly tucked between his perfect white teeth. The man hadn't missed a beat. He knew she was teasing him, and now he was up to bat. Maybe Roland would hit it out of the park tonight, end the evening with a home run, or possibly, lord help her—go into extra innings.

When she didn't answer right away, he gave her another devilish grin. "How about down for now. We aren't going far, and I think we could both use the cool air."

Chapter 19

Lexi walked into Hank's, where she'd agreed to meet Noah. It was early in the evening, and the place wasn't busy yet. She decided to avoid the hostess stand and went to the barstools bolted to the floor around the massive wood bar. The polished brass and cowhide leather seats were expensive-looking, and little gold purse hooks were fastened to the bar in front of each stool. The new Hank's was in a whole different class than the original, and though Bubbles had come out of the sale of the first Hank's, there really wasn't a comparison. The plush champagne lounge catered to an entirely different kind of crowd. Lexi bet the new Hank's probably cost twice as much to build, and who knew how much dough was spent each month to keep the lights on. It didn't have fancy chandeliers like Bubbles, but the new Honky-Tonk was a massive country bar and restaurant that was doing well all on its own.

Looking at the stack of postcards lying on the bar, Lexi could see there was a string of top-shelf musicians playing here through the holidays. Some of them she'd really like to see, but she didn't know how this meeting with Noah would play out. After their last conversation, the night Lexi was there with Ginger, things weren't exactly settled. Later that same night, Noah had texted her to ask when he could pick her up for a date. She'd declined to be picked up but agreed to meet him at the bar here tonight for two reasons—Lexi didn't want anyone in her family to know she was seeing Noah again, and she didn't trust herself not to fall into bed with him when he brought her home. She remembered their first date with too much clarity and didn't trust herself to say no.

So, tonight, as she tapped her fingernails nervously on the bar, Lexi wondered what the hell she was doing here. Her family might not be in the bar, but half of Magnolia frequented the new Hank's. It was hard enough to convince her mother she wasn't going on a date when she dropped off the boys. The place wasn't busy yet, but it was likely to pick up soon, and it wouldn't be unlikely to see one of her three brothers or their wives. "Crap," Lexi said to herself as she stood, turning to leave. She collided with a solid wall of muscle that smelled like summer laundry hanging on the line and sandalwood soap.

Noah smiled down at her. "You're not thinking of leaving, are you?"

She breathed in the scent of him like he was her only addiction in life. Hell, he might be. She could say no to anything else, but Noah's perfect smile, silvery irises that silently chided her, and his hard chest beneath her fingertips were enough to make her sit back down.

"No, I was going to the ladies' room," she lied.

Noah chuckled. "It's over there." He pointed. "Away from the exit."

"Oh, well then," she muttered, turning in the other direction.

Noah gave her a wide grin. "I'll be here when you get back."

Her heart pounded in her chest. Down, girl. If you keep breathing like this every time he smiles at you, you're going to pass out.

Noah watched Lexi as she crossed the bar to the ladies' room. The tight red cocktail dress stopped just above her knees and clung to her toned legs as she walked in the strappy, spiked heels. His pulse raced as the blood in his veins heated. If the urge to take her to bed was almost impossible to restrain the last time he saw her, tonight, the dress she wore would torture him and make it very hard to behave. He rubbed his fingers together as if he was trying to restrain their wayward notions.

"Boss, there's a problem with table thirty's order. Can you go talk to 'em?" Daisy's wide eyes and laced fingers implored him to help her out.

Smoothing over experiences for the guests was one of Noah's favorite things about the bar business. It was easy to make people happy. But, he'd told Lexi he would be here when she got back, and there was a needling fear that if he wasn't standing here, she might breeze right out the front door. He hated feeling desperate, but this was a chance he didn't care to take. "Daisy, you can do this. It is your moment to shine. Go back to the guests and tell them it's your mistake—regardless if it is or not—and express that you want them to enjoy themselves, so you are comping their desserts." He patted her shoulder. "Trust me, everyone loves getting something for free."

Daisy chewed on her bottom lip. "But they aren't havin' dessert. He's had five whiskeys, and she's on her fourth Mai Tai. They're gettin' sloppy and a little loud. I've tried to slow them down without telling them they're cut off, but the guy's having none of it, and the lady scares me."

Damn! That was an entirely different problem. Noah looked back toward the ladies' room door, but there was no sign of Lexi. Maybe he could settle this without too much issue. The waitress was new, and it wasn't a problem he wanted her to handle alone. Noah marched toward the table and waved for his bar-back to follow. Joey was on his heels before he reached the table. A grandmother and what must be her adult grandson both wore surly looks as he approached. The lady, who was every bit seventy, if not eighty, had bright orange hair with matching lipstick and a walker wrapped in Christmas ribbon parked next to her. She appeared to be arguing with the twenty-something kid in golf clothes but stopped mid-sentence at Noah's arrival.

Before he could ask them how they were enjoying their evening, and if he could do anything to make it more pleasant—like calling them a cab—the older woman pointed a bony finger at the kid and said, "I told him he was causing a scene and that you were going to throw him out. Plus, he won't be able to get it up later if he keeps drinking that damn whiskey!"

In all the years Noah had worked in the bar, he didn't have a ready response to this particular complaint. He could hear Joey's muffled laugh behind him.

The young "grandson" piped up and retorted, "Ah hell, Rosie. I told you I wasn't getting any tonight. Leave it be and let me have another whiskey."

Noah thought about the young man's request. If he was being pushed to perform with this old lady, Noah had half a mind to grant the man a couple of extra shots. He was about to interject in the ongoing argument when Lexi reappeared by his side.

"Hi there, Ms. Rosie. What a pleasure it is to see you tonight."

"Lexi, thank God! Would you tell my golf instructor that he needs to quit drinking and go home to his wife?"

Noah hadn't thought this could get any more bizarre, but the last statement almost made his jaw drop.

"Hi, Lance. How are things at the country club?"

Lance dropped his drunken-surly tone and beamed at Lexi like she was the free dessert. "Aw, it's all good, Lexi. Victoria's getting ready to have another baby, and Rosie offered to take me out fer a drinks," he slurred.

107

Lexi's smile was genuine, and she didn't miss a beat. "Congratulations! That's so nice. Is it a boy or a girl this time? Three kids in three years. You guys work fast."

The older woman Lexi had called Rosie scowled at Lance. "That's what I was telling him. He's got a baby on the way, and he needs to go home and pluck his wife while he still can. In another month or two, his balls will be as blue as the bluebonnets in spring, and then he won't be able to concentrate at the driving range." Rosie paused, then hooted as she slapped the table in front of Lance. "Pun intended. Get it? Drivin' range." She hooted again while wiggling her hips in her chair.

Lexi chuckled and nodded, like the conversation they were having was worthy of the Magnolia Blossoms Ladies League monthly luncheon. "I think you are right, Ms. Rosie, and if you want, I will use my phone app to get you a ride right now. Best Lance gets home and gets busy."

Noah tried to suppress a grin. Things, though still odd, were clearer now than before. Lexi handled it like a pro, and it made him want to kiss her even more. He squeezed her shoulder as she tapped at her phone. "Please, let me take care of this."

He turned to Joey. "Get Larry, the limo guy, to give this nice couple a ride to their respective homes—on us." To Lance and Rosie, Noah offered to comp their drinks. "Consider it our congratulations. With three kids, I'm sure we'll see you again soon. Next time, bring the wife. I'd love to meet her."

Lance and Rosie were all smiles as Joey escorted them out, though Daisy didn't look too happy.

"Well, there went my tip," she grumbled.

Noah pulled a wad of bills from his pocket and peeled off a fifty.

With a huge smile and a "Thanks, boss," Daisy quickly disappeared.

"At this rate, Hank's will be broke in a month," Lexi teased. "Free limousine rides with extra tip money to boot?"

"I guess I should thank you for mopping up that disaster. I don't think I could have handled it so easily or with a straight face."

Lexi chuckled. "I have plenty of experience with Ms. Rosie. Her niece married my brother, and now she's at every family brunch... as long as we serve mimosas."

"Well, if you ever want to be my bouncer, you're hired." Noah grinned. "The way the conversation was going, I thought the guy was...."

Lexi laughed. "Oh, he totally could have been. She likes them young, but I know Lance and his wife from high school." A frown creased her brow.

"What is it? What's wrong?"

Lexi shook her head. "Nothing, but I'll see Ms. Rosie at brunch, and now Lance will tell Victoria he saw me, and she'll tell her mother, Kate, who will tell—"

Noah held a hand up to stop her worrying. He took a deep breath, looking around the bar. Taking Lexi's arm, he steered her toward the exit. "Let's get out of here. I promised you low-key, and I want to deliver. Plus, I'm feeling kind of selfish. I want you all to myself."

Chapter 20

She wasn't his usual type. Roland had dated a lot of women, but most of them were nice gals who'd never been much farther than Laredo. The wholesome girl-next-door was fine by him, but most were too predictable, much like his life in Magnolia. He'd been envious when his brother, Luke, had moved to New Mexico, but Roland didn't feel a real attraction for the state, and he didn't know anyone anywhere outside of Texas. When he was young, he'd dreamed of running off to California and being a stuntman or another Clint Eastwood, but it wasn't realistic, and he knew it. Luke's decision to leave meant Roland had to stay. Who else would look after their aging father, sister and eventually, their niece?

Pushing his youthful dreams aside, he enrolled in the police academy, and volunteered for the fire department until he was elected constable. The job provided steady pay, and he was sure to keep his position as long as he didn't screw up.

There wasn't much crime in Magnolia, but things did happen from time to time, like when Lexi Nash crashed into the original Hank's Honky-Tonk in her minivan, or when Eli had that news reporter lady's head in his lap while he was at a stoplight. And that was after she'd had too much of Ms. Rosie Bush's pot brownies, but Roland believed Eli's plea of innocence.

As with most questionable stories in Magnolia, things had a way of working themselves out. It wasn't long before Eli married the pretty lady, who turned out to be the reporter's identical twin. The traffic incident, along with all the other gossip about the couple, was brushed under the rug.

Nothing *too* big ever happened in Magnolia, but the one tidbit of news he'd been keeping to himself was brought into the spotlight by Mona. Her husband was going to run for Congress, and he'd recently approached Roland about running for mayor to take his place. It was a huge boost to Roland's ego that Mayor Manny Owens thought he had half a chance at winning. He even offered to back Roland's campaign during the election, but the truth was, it was too public. He had succeeded in his position as constable, and the good folks of Magnolia had come to depend on his honest presence. There were plenty of other great candidates who could handle being mayor of Magnolia and leave Roland's simple life predictably the same.

He'd been a good guy all of his life. Good ol' dependable Roland Karr, always doing the right thing. But he had a small rebellious flame inside him that longed to break out of his comfort zone and go somewhere else, live another life. Maybe he could have been an actor, a stuntman or a race car driver. He'd never even tried. As he took the bend in the road, gripping Lucille's soft leather steering wheel and with Ginger by his side, the flame of possibility sizzled inside him. What was it about her that made him think about his present position in life and the choices he'd made in the past that got him here?

It was a short drive, but as he parked the car in the church lot and pulled the top up on Lucille, Roland felt the need to be reckless. He wasn't sure what prompted him to do it. Maybe it was the way she combed her fingers through her hair or smoothed the skirt of the dress she wore, but when she turned toward him, he was mesmerized. Her tongue swept across her bottom lip, and she looked invitingly at him, or at least that was his impression. Throwing his good-cop persona out the window, he leaned in without hesitating.

His fingers threaded through her chestnut hair as his head dipped to hers. The catch in her breath as his mouth roved over her full bottom lip, made his heart thump and his pulse race. She moaned, and his other hand clasped her waist, pulling her into a tight embrace. It reminded him of the scene in *From Here to Eternity*. Waves of heat crashed over them as Ginger met his tongue with her own, sucking at his bottom lip and twisting her hand in his shirt. He pulled her even closer to him. The full skirt she wore allowed her to lift her leg over his. He wasn't sure if she meant for her knee to massage his hard erection, but he was on fire with need. The slow burn that crept over his torso and down through his core wanted more than this moment, more than one stolen kiss. She'd unlocked a passion in him that would be too hard to put back inside.

Ginger moaned again, and his heart thudded in response. Her fingers tugged at his hair, silently demanding more. They wouldn't be the first to have sex in the Cowboy Baptist Church parking lot, but it was ten minutes until the movie started, and people were walking past the car—Magnolia residents who would recognize him. Everyone in town knew Lucille, and by this time tomorrow, they would be telling everyone he'd christened his car with the new gal at church. As much as he hated to end the moment—a moment that made him feel he'd been waiting for his entire life—Roland didn't want tongues wagging about Ginger. And he wanted her to like Magnolia.

With a deep sigh, Roland pulled away. "I'm sorry, I didn't intend to take advantage of you that way—I mean, here, now."

She sat back, giving him a cat-like grin. "I know. What a bad cop you are to ask a lady out to a movie and kiss her before the preview even begins."

He needed to think of baseball, the school crossing-guard Granny, Christmas carolers, anything that would make his body cool. *Down boy! Down.* Ginger's cheeky accusation made him chuckle. "Oh, I don't think that was all me."

She grinned at him again, giving him a challenging arch of her fine brow.

Roland took in a deep breath, trying to think. He loved old movies. He had wanted to meet his family here, but when Ginger called, he took a wad of bills from his sock drawer and handed them to Maddie, suggesting they go to dinner without him. Though Kelsey was disappointed he wasn't going with them, after a pause, she squealed with delight. She hadn't really been up for an old movie, and as his young niece twirled around, she chanted, "Ice cream!" to her mother and Luke. Now he felt the same excitement. Ginger was his ice cream, and the last thing he wanted to do was sit through a movie.

"You wanna get out of here?"

Ginger reached for her seatbelt. "I thought you'd never ask."

As Lucille picked up speed on the highway, he tried to think of where to go. *You got her to go out with you. Now what?* He knew what he wanted to do, but where? No matter what place his family went to for dinner and ice cream, he couldn't be sure when they would be home, and nothing was less sexy after casual sex than the whole family gathering around to meet the lady of the evening.

"I, um… I have a bit of a problem," he confessed.

She gave him another one of her signature sparkling cat-eyed-grins. "I didn't feel any problems."

He could become addicted to this woman. Roland gave her a tight smile. "No, no worries in that department. My sister Maddie, and her daughter, my niece, Kelsey, are staying with me while they find their footing, and my brother dropped in unannounced. As much as the idea of steaming up Lucille's windows appeals to me, I would like to spend some time getting to know you if it's not a total turn-off."

He couldn't see her clearly in the dark, but her head sank into her shoulders a little, revealing a possible shyness. He liked that Ginger was a firecracker. She was challenging, and he longed for that in a relationship, but she had a hidden side, too, and he was intrigued. The birthdate on her driver's license revealed she was thirty, which was ten years younger than him but old enough to make mature decisions.

"I don't want to offend you by asking you to go to a hotel with me, but my place isn't where you want to go. Trust me. And, with Magnolia being a small town, people won't leave us alone if we're seen out at the diner or somewhere local. I know too many people to get any privacy. Would you mind if we go out to The Woodlands? It's only about thirty or forty minutes from here, and the Gold Bar in The Grand Chateau Hotel is beautiful."

The streetlights streamed in across her white teeth as she smiled. "A hotel? Why, Constable, I never!" She drew the words out facetiously, batting her long, dark lashes.

In the car's dark interior, he couldn't see the mischief in her emerald irises, but he could feel her warm humor. Was she playing the vintage film actress for him, or was her performance because they had originally planned to see an old movie? She'd even dressed the part. Her skirt had a 1950s flare, and she wore a polka-dotted ribbon in her hair. The delicate pumps that graced her feet made her calves look long and sculpted. The wide belt enhanced her trim waist, and she'd been deliciously beautiful sitting in Lucille with her dark hair blowing in the wind. He'd raised the top when they were at the church. Now, they listened to the satellite radio that played big band music as they took the curves of the highway leading to the hotel.

"I wouldn't want to make any judgments about what you have or haven't done, Miss Harding. I'll tell you that I am an honorable man, and my intentions are—" He stole a glance at her, with her head tilted back against the headrest. She licked her shiny lips and passed a slender hand over the creamy skin of her long neck. He cleared his throat before finishing his sentence, "less than honorable." He paused, waiting for her to reply, but she stared straight ahead as if she hadn't heard him. He didn't know why he was so forward, but he couldn't help himself. She made him burn, wanting to know what it would be like to make love to her.

He thought he heard her moan. She was still teasing him. He decided to be direct. "Do you still want to join me at The Grand Chateau? Their breakfast is amazing."

Chapter 21

The Grand Chateau was fabulously chic. Ginger had never been to The Woodlands, and she was happy to find lively civilization so nearby—and sushi! She'd been to Houston before, so she knew she wasn't stuck on an island, and with the recent growth of Magnolia, there were plenty of places to hang out. Ginger reminded herself that her purpose in Magnolia was to keep a low profile. It was bad enough she was on a date with a straightlaced cop and possible candidate for mayor. She'd briefly worried that Roland might be onto her movie-star identity, but he seemed to be focused on the Hollywood of the past, and she doubted he was someone who went in for gossip shows or grocery store tabloids. His gentleman style was that of a modern-day Cary Grant. He was masculine, hot and his mannerism exuded confidence. Roland didn't seem afraid of her Dallas Derringer act when she'd turned it on. It was the persona she'd adopted after her big break in *Seducing Saturn* and quickly took over her previous, semi-shy disposition. It was one of the reasons she was accused of leaking the sex video. She wasn't a nun by any means. Who else at thirty could be that lonely? But that didn't make her a sex addict or a narcissist who wanted everyone to see her doing it on the internet.

Ginger was the one to suggest they get a room so they didn't have to worry about drinking and driving. She'd only been half-joking. They could have called a taxi or used a ride app, but Roland hadn't hesitated long enough for her to think it through. As she waited in the lounge for him to register, a seedy feeling crept over her. This was their first date. They hadn't even made it to the date part yet, since they'd ditched the movie they were supposed to see. Had he been planning to take her to bed all along? Anxiety climbed up from her gut and lodged in her throat. *Does he know who I really am and think I'll be an easy lay?*

He approached her with a slow grin, one hand loosely tucked into his front jeans' pocket. Roland walked like a tough cowboy in an old western, with his shoulders straight and his stride slow and deliberate. He was the right amount of ripped muscle and strong limbs, towering over her slight form. His thighs were thick and powerful for his six-foot stature. She'd felt their firmness while kissing him. Images of his legs tangling with hers in the starched, white hotel sheets flashed through her mind, stimulating the butterflies dancing between her legs. So, why was she upset that he was thinking of sex tonight? She was thinking the same thing.

As he approached the bar, his hand snaked out, and he massaged the tense muscles at the base of her neck. "You okay? We don't have to go to the room at all tonight. I can call a ride if you're having second thoughts. It's a suite, so there are plenty of sleeping options, and we can enjoy ourselves without worrying about a car later."

His soothing words were like a balm to her skittish nerves. She hadn't realized she'd been clutching her muscles so tight, but there were so many *what-ifs*. Roland was a great-looking guy, and he could be with anyone. Why had he chosen to ask her out? She didn't deny her good fortune to be pretty. It was what initially got her the role of a lifetime, but with mousy brown, shorter than usual hair, and a sex tape floating around the internet, exposing her at every unflattering angle, she was less assured than she used to be. Internet trolls and comments analyzing her body had dented her armor of confidence. Maybe it was poetic justice or simply the karma she deserved.

Ginger admitted she had been a little too big for her britches back in L.A. She remembered on a night out with the girls, she'd been rude to the men who approached their table, shutting them down with a razor-sharp tongue. She might have been overworked, tired, and irritated that fans couldn't leave her in peace to have a drink with friends, but it wasn't an excuse to be a bitch, and she had been. Later that same evening, she'd flipped off a photographer coming out of the bar. She'd been about to moon the irritating reporter, who kept asking her to "smile, baby, for the camera," but thank God, the security guard stopped her—she'd definitely had too much to drink.

Friends, she silently contemplated the word.

It was a week later that the video debuted. She'd wondered several times if there had been any connection between the gossip reporter and the sex tape's timely release. The Emmy she'd been nominated for and the new contract, making double what she'd previously earned from *Seducing Saturn*, was null and void once the tape went viral.

Sitting next to Roland, Ginger silently asked herself why she was analyzing the past. She was out on a date with a good guy, an officer of the law. Was she doubting her instincts because he'd gotten a hotel room? Were the strangers in the bar a reminder, that the people she thought were her friends in L.A. turned out to be strangers, too? What did she really know about Roland? He was a hunk with a strong personality that tempted her to test boundaries. He'd lived his whole life in Magnolia and was going to run for mayor. What if he was photographed or seen with her? Guilt gripped her conscience. It could ruin his career to be seen with a Hollywood tramp. How would small-town voters take seeing Dallas Derringer with their do-right constable. *I am not a tramp. I just always pick the wrong guy.*

It was unnerving to Ginger that she didn't know how the locals would react if her identity was discovered. After all the years she spent in L.A., Magnolia was like a foreign country to her, but the truth was, she didn't feel like she belonged anywhere.

Shaking away her doubts, she tried to focus on what Roland was saying. "Do you want to leave?"

Uh-oh, she'd been in Lala Land too long. The problem with his question was, she didn't know what she wanted. Their chemistry in the car was inferno hot. Just his hand on her neck, massaging her tight muscles, was sending a battalion of goose flesh marching over her body, down to her toes. She'd been aggressive in this, turning on her Dallas Derringer act as she rubbed her calf against his hard-on when they kissed. She was turned on by his sexy smile and his thick dark lashes over sherry-brown eyes.

It wasn't usual for Ginger to be so conflicted or indecisive, but her blood had pumped confusion to her brain, and her thoughts scattered with worry. Roland wasn't just any guy. He was the first guy she'd gone out with since Kirk. It had been too long since she'd had an orgasm, but that wasn't a reason to fall into bed with someone she barely knew. This wasn't L.A., and people were probably already talking about that kiss in the church parking lot. She didn't have many places to hide from the past. Did she really want to cause enough drama to have to leave here too?

Ginger reminded herself that she wasn't a horny teenager, though she'd been acting like one. She'd been acting like a lot of things tonight but admitted she hadn't really been herself in a long time. She was starting to wonder who that really was. There was more to her than Dallas Derringer. She hadn't been a straight A student as Ginger Lynn Harding or even a straight B student in school. Her idea of a good book was anything that made her laugh, and she hadn't had much time for reading anything besides scripts when she lived in L.A. Her motto used to be that life was too serious and too short not to have fun every moment that she could. At thirty, she was already tired of the Hollywood rat race, and after the scandal erupted, she was mentally, emotionally and physically exhausted.

Ginger had stayed thin, lived off slim tea and salads with no dressing for what seemed like an eternity. Judged for what she looked like, what she wore, what she ate, and what she'd done with her ex-boyfriend in the privacy of their own apartment, even though he'd taped her without her consent... she was sick of the endless drama. For once in her life, Ginger didn't want to act on impulse—to enjoy the moment with no strings attached. She admitted to herself that she was ultimately responsible for her actions. It may have been Kirk who taped and released the sex video, but she'd taken the Xanax before getting on a plane home instead of dealing with her fear of flying. That's why she hadn't noticed the camera's blinking red light in the corner of the room when they fell into bed.

Paranoia kicked in, and now she was wondering again if Roland knew her actress identity. Is that why he brought her straight to a hotel? Did he think she was easy because of the sex video? Ginger knew she was working herself into a confused mess.

Roland continued looking at her with concern. "I'm sorry, Ginger. I meant it when I said we could call a taxi or something. I didn't mean to be so forward or to upset you. Maybe we can hang out here for a while and get to know each other, then I'll take you home."

Chapter 22

"Where are we going?" Lexi clicked her seatbelt.

Noah shifted the car into drive, answering smoothly. "To the Grand Chateau."

"You're taking me to a hotel?" Lexi heard the annoyance in her exclamation, even though her body tingled with excitement at the thought. *No!* She would not succumb to her flaky hormones.

Use it or lose it, gal! Her body chanted back.

Noah shot her an open-mouthed stare. "Oh, no! I mean, yes. We are going to the hotel, but only because they have this kickass lounge I wanted to take you to, and they have a great champagne list. I knew you wanted to keep this evening on the down-low, and everyone in Magnolia knows us. After running into your old high-school chum and his…" He seemed to be searching for the correct name or maybe a description.

Lexi inserted, "and Ms. Rosie."

"Ah, yes, Ms. Rosie. What a lively—um—older gal. Anyway, I figured we wouldn't get any time to talk if we kept getting disturbed."

Lexi erupted in laughter. "Good thing Ms. Rosie isn't around to hear you say that." After regaining her composure, she agreed that the upscale lounge seemed perfectly safe. Her body was still doing a cheer. *Get it, get it, girl!* Her mind might be wary of falling for Noah again, but her body was ready to push her thoughts off a cliff. It was the exact reason she'd wanted to meet him at the bar and not be left alone in a car with him— *or at a hotel.*

He looked at her, his gaze compassionate. "Lexi, you don't have to be afraid to be alone with me. I'm not going to jump your bones. I promise." He paused and grinned sheepishly, "Not unless it's what you want."

His charm was infectious, and yes, she wanted to be ravished by him, but she steeled herself against his sex appeal. Maybe she should have worn her full-body Spanks. The thought of Noah seeing her in her granny panties would keep her in check. Lexi tried to focus. "How about you confirm a few facts before this meeting begins."

His brows rose in question. "Meeting? Are we going to a parent-teacher event?"

Lexi smirked. "Don't act smart. You owe me some honest answers."

"Now I feel like I'm in the principal's office." He chuckled. "But go ahead. It kinda turns me on."

Lexi couldn't hide her own grin. "Sorry. A life raising three boys trains a mother to be on the offensive *and* defensive line."

Noah laughed again. "Oh, I bet. How are the boys?"

"They're great, but you're changing the subject." She wagged a finger at him, and he leaned forward to nip at it.

"Caught me. What are the facts you want to know, Ms. Nash-Burns?"

"It's Lexi. I go by Lexi Nash now. I went back to my maiden name."

"Why? Isn't that confusing for the boys?"

It was a valid question. One she'd pondered herself after renewing her license and changing her name back. It wasn't something she sought to do on purpose. She'd lost her license and went to get another. It was inside the DMV where she was filling out the information card that she asked the clerk if she could go back to her maiden name. The clerk informed her it was as simple as filling out the card and notifying the Social Security Office of the change. She wasn't sure why she'd done it, except that it was after Noah had left, and maybe she realized she was ready to move on. Lexi would always love Jack Burns, her high school sweetheart, first love, and the father of her boys, but she couldn't move on as long as she carried his name everywhere she went. The name change had broken her heart a little more, but it had also loosened a tether to the past.

"People have been calling me Lexi Nash my whole life, even after I married Jack. It's what happens when you grow up in a small town, and everyone knows your family. Jack didn't move to Magnolia until high school, so…." She stopped and cocked her head. "Are you trying to avoid my questions?"

He put his hands up as if being held at gunpoint, then quickly returned them to the wheel as they took another bend in the road. "No, ma'am. Ask away." He held his right hand up. "I swear to tell the truth, the whole truth and nothing but…."

Lexi slapped at his shoulder. "All right. That's enough." She waited until his face took on a more serious expression before asking, "Are you still married?"

Chapter 23

The evening wasn't going the way he'd planned. Number one, Roland was missing one of his favorite classic movies, but he'd already admitted that he wanted more from this evening than watching an old film with Ginger. He didn't have to twist her arm, and she'd given him the impression she wanted to end this night in private. What had transpired between then and now was a mystery to him. As they sipped their cocktails and watched the live jazz band play, she seemed irritated. He'd apologized, but clearly that wasn't enough to save the date.

Maybe it was a test of some sort. Had he already failed? Undeniably, he should have waited before getting a room, but it was the weekend, and he thought the place might get booked. With his career, drinking and driving wasn't an option, and though he'd thought about the taxi from the very beginning, it was Ginger who suggested the room. She had met him halfway in the car, and if he hadn't interrupted their kiss, he wondered how far they would have gone.

Maddie had told him a thousand times that he was too honest, too straightforward. Maybe he ruined the moment of romance by stopping at the front desk. Damn, he wasn't good at dating. Constable work was so much easier. Everything was black and white. She said, let's get a room, and he did. People said that the color of love was red, but he disagreed. It was gray—murky, foggy, mysterious gray.

"I can order champagne if you prefer it."

Ginger stirred her rocks glass with dark rum and pineapple juice. "That's okay. I'm fine."

The music played, and the noise of the bar vibrated all around them, but the lively mood didn't seem to have a positive effect on Ginger. It was like someone let all the air out of her, and she was empty of things to say to him. SOS, this was definitely a date gone wrong. Roland wracked his brain, trying to think of how to turn things around. One look at the dance floor, and he felt hope breathe life back into his plan.

Ginger reminded him of a vintage diner advertisement with her drink straw clutched between her perfect full lips. Her delicate fingers held the straw that searched the bottom of the glass. He held out a hand to her and smiled. "Do you want to dance?"

She looked like she was contemplating saying no, then she gave him a nod and stood. It surprised him, but he was relieved. Maybe a little light entertainment would restore the mood.

As they stepped onto the parquet wood dance floor, the band struck up a slow song. Ginger stepped into his arms, and they joined the other dancers. Her scent and the feel of her soft skin were hypnotizing. Her skirt swirled as he spun her to the faster beat of the chorus, then he reeled her back in against his chest. He tried not to grin at the surprised look on her face. The two years of dance lessons with Claire had been fun and he felt confident in his ability to impress. Maybe he wasn't Fred Astaire, but his luck was definitely changing.

The stiffness in Ginger's shoulders dissipated as they went around the room with the other couples, locked in each other's arms. When she laid her cheek on his shoulder, relief flooded his system. Roland hadn't realized he'd been clenching his teeth, but as the slow song played, he relaxed the muscles in his jaw. Ginger's presence touched something inside him, and that something wasn't mere sexual desire. He wanted to help her. She'd arrived in Magnolia upset and wary of strangers. Out of her element, in a small town, he wanted to show her a good time—that life could be great here, and most of all, he wanted her to enjoy it with him.

Chapter 24

It'd been almost three years since Noah had met Lexi, and they'd been apart most of that time, except when she'd shown up at his sister's apartment to bring a message from his cousin. The letter had been an apology from Hank, describing in detail how he'd found Noah's ex-wife and paid her to come to Magnolia. Petra was supposed to tell Noah that she would take half of the money from the sale if Noah sold his half of Hank's to open Bubbles. But Lexi ran into Petra at the bar and upset Hank's plans. In the end, Noah saw Hank kissing Lexi in her driveway and stormed off to Dallas.

Shortly after, Noah sold out to his cousin, including the plans to make Bubbles everything it was today. He'd given it all to Hank because Noah thought he would be in a wheelchair for the rest of his life. Even though he'd given up on his dream, he couldn't live without seeing it built. Reaching deep inside himself to let go stung like hell, but it had been the chink in his cousin's armor. Noah selling the one thing that meant everything to him unlocked Hank's shallow shell and made him see the light.

It didn't hurt either, that Callie stepped in and gave Hank a piece of her mind. He paid Noah the asking price for Bubbles, but also in the letter was a contract giving Noah a thirty-five percent interest in the bar. He'd heard about Hank and Petra's engagement, but as Noah predicted, things quickly fell apart. Their upcoming nuptials hadn't mattered to him anyway because he'd never really loved Petra.

Noah didn't think Lexi really drove all the way to Dallas just to hand him Hank's letter, but receiving the contract and seeing her changed his life. After the accident, he'd given up on all his dreams, and he probably would have sat in that chair feeling sorry for himself for the rest of his life if she hadn't brought the letter.

Seeing her made him want more—for her, for himself, and for a chance that they might have something together if he got off his ass and tried. He cursed his way through two years of intense therapy, vowing not to give up. The determination paid off, and here he was, walking back into Lexi's world. Would she give him another chance?

She'd asked him if he was married, and now he could answer with a clean slate. "I am legally divorced. Petra wanted to marry Hank, but after Bubbles opened and he found out she was skimming the till, Hank put her on the first plane back to her family in Germany."

Lexi nodded. "I knew they'd broken up. Hank mentioned it when I saw him at Bubbles."

"Now, I have a question of my own. Is there something between you and Hank? It may seem selfish since I haven't been around, but I don't like sharing women with my cousin."

Lexi frowned. "God, no, there is nothing between Hank and me. I admit that I kissed him the night you left Magnolia, but that is all that happened. And as I explained before, it was a kiss that was supposed to make me feel like less of a loser for sleeping with a married man. I know it sounds stupid, but emotions were running high."

Noah nodded. "Yes, they were." He thought about that night and how he'd careened off the road and almost died.

Lexi's eyes shimmered in the lights of the hotel entrance as they pulled up to the valet. "What happened to you when you left? How'd you get injured?"

Noah wasn't ready to talk about that yet, and he was lucky that the valet was already reaching for the door handle. He patted her hand, which rested on the console.

"Let's go have a drink." He stood, tipped the valet, and smiled at Lexi as he looked across the hood of the silver Lexus. She smiled back, and her bluebonnet-colored eyes sparkled in the evening light. "I've really missed your smile."

The bar was crowded, but he tipped the hostess, who seated them at a reserved table in the back of the lounge away from the band. He loved the sophisticated ambiance of the place, but he wanted to enjoy talking to Lexi like they had the first time they'd gone out together. It amazed Noah that they'd only been out on one official date. Here it was, almost three years later and they were finally enjoying a second chance. Though technically, they hadn't spent much time together since that first fateful meeting at the old Hank's Honkey-Tonk, Noah felt like he knew the woman sitting next to him in all the ways that mattered. It was her warm heart, kind smile and determination to do all the right things that kindled a spark inside him, and it was that flame that made it impossible for him to put the past aside.

He could have stayed in Dallas. Hank's Honky-Tonk would have been successful in neighboring Fort Worth. There was plenty of money, and the city folks liked entertainment of all kinds. But he came back to Magnolia for Lexi. If she didn't forgive him for rejecting her when she drove to Dallas two years ago to make amends, he didn't know what he'd do. Would he give up on his dream again? It was a question he didn't want to ponder. Looking at the beautiful woman with him, he knew it was far too early to give up.

Noah decided to say what he was thinking. "Have I mentioned how beautiful you look tonight?"

She chuckled. "It helps that I left my Kotex at home this time."

He couldn't contain his laughter. Their first date had started with Lexi having a woman's sanitary napkin stuck to the back of her rump, and he'd politely removed it for her. She'd been embarrassed that her son had stuck one to the back of the dress, but he'd assured her that he understood. Her kids were young. At first, he'd thought she might cry or march back into her house, but she recovered, and the night ended with hot and heavy sex in her bed.

"I wouldn't have minded assisting you again. You didn't tell me how your boys are doing."

Her smile beamed bright and genuine. "Same as always, getting into trouble at every turn."

"Are the donkeys still sporting pajamas?"

Lexi laughed. "It was my underwear!"

Noah shook his head. "Now, I know your underwear is not big enough to fit on those donkeys. I've seen them."

Lexi sobered from laughing too hard. "The donkeys or my underwear?"

He felt the blood leave his brain and rush south as he thought about that first night, pulling the calico dress over her head. The only thing she wore underneath was a pair of lacy pink panties. She'd forgone the bra entirely, and her pert nipples had taunted him through the thin fabric of her dress all night. But tonight, the red cocktail dress she wore with those sexy heels put her little calico number to shame.

"Both." He sat back in the plush booth to allow his jeans to adjust. He'd need to think about something else besides Lexi's underwear if he was going to stand up anytime soon.

She gave him a knowing smile, her eyes sliding lower, then back to his. "Let's say that Victoria has lots of secrets, and one of my boys will become a textile engineer creating a new, stretchier spandex underwear to fit anyone who wants to wear them, donkeys included."

It was hard not to smile in this woman's presence. She was only thirty-three but held a world of experience in life already. From what he did know about Lexi, she'd survived losing someone she loved and was raising three high-strung boys on her own. He'd heard about her virtual shop and the hand-crafted stained-glass art she designed. Noah had anonymously ordered one of the large, salvaged frames for Hank's, and it hung above the center of the bar. He wondered if she'd noticed, yet. Her barn wood crafts were gaining popularity, and it would be hard to keep up with the ranch when things turned a corner for her new business. Magnolia was small, and it was easy to find out anything about anyone, but he'd Googled her during the time he was away. She didn't keep a personal social media page, but he was always looking for any announcement that might say she was getting remarried.

One day, he decided to quit looking and go back to Magnolia. If he was so worried that she might not be available, he needed to tell her that he wanted her for himself. The problem was, he'd only started walking without a cane a month ago, and he still had to concentrate on taking slow, solid steps. The intense therapy might be over, but he still had to do the exercises regularly to make progress.

His gaze took in the twirling couples on the dance floor, and he wished he could do the same with Lexi. When his eyes landed on Roland, he nudged her. "Hey, is that your friend with Roland Karr?"

Lexi's mouth opened in surprise. "Oh, hell. I thought Ginger was going to the movies with him at the church." Lexi grabbed her purse and stood. "Let's go before they see us."

Noah arched a brow as his hand darted out to catch hers. "Is there something wrong with them seeing us together?"

Lexi flushed. "No, but Ginger is my new tenant-slash-nanny-slash-friend, and I don't want to…." Her words trailed off, and a sheepish looked crossed her features as she sat back down.

"It's okay, Lexi. We're two grown adults, having a drink. I doubt anyone will stand up and argue that we shouldn't be here. She works for you, right?"

Lexi nodded. "Yes, but I don't want my family to know I'm out—." She shrugged and nodded toward him. "With you." She blew out a long sigh. "I think I could use a drink."

Noah motioned to a waitress, who brought a cocktail menu to their table. He waved it away. "Bring us your best bottle of champagne and two glasses."

Lexi smiled and gazed at him with a look that said she remembered their first night drinking champagne together. "I'll not be so easy this time, Noah Harding. If you plan on wooing me, you've got your work cut out for you."

Noah nodded, pressing his back against the booth. It was cozy and private, and lucky for him, his generous tip got him the best available, and the waitress would be happy with the tab.

The smiling lady returned with the bottle and two glasses. The cork made a slow hiss as a froth of bubbles ran over the rim of the bottle. She poured the glasses halfway and smiled before leaving them alone.

Noah held up his hand. "First of all, I don't have any expectations tonight, and second, it will be my pleasure to spend all my time spoiling you into submission."

Lexi's jaw dropped as if she were offended by his choice of words, but the slight tremble of her lower lip gave away her emotions. He remembered how she trembled with anticipation the first time they were together. She'd been alone for too long, and a woman this beautiful was not meant to sit on a shelf.

His heart thumped in his chest, and his pulse could be felt throughout other parts of his body. He couldn't help but stare at her beauty. The desire to lean closer and take her into his arms was overwhelming. He wanted to feel his lips pressed against hers and more. She'd been so shy their first night, but then she'd cried out with such intense pleasure that his body had reacted in kind. Lexi was untamed, unstoppable, and over the past many months, unforgettable.

"I didn't mean it like it sounded, Lex." He shook his head, unable to get his words to say what he felt. "I want to spoil you. I want you to trust me, and most of all, I want you to want to be with me."

The waitress returned with a plate of chocolate-covered strawberries and whipped cream. "How long have you two been married?"

Lexi jerked her head up in surprise, staring at Noah. He gave her a slow grin. "We've been together about three years."

"Newlyweds. So sweet! Well, I really hope you enjoy this. The manager had it reserved for a special occasion, but I told him you guys looked pretty special together." She winked as she poured more champagne into the crystal flutes.

"But we aren't married," Lexi corrected.

"Oh, well, I told him it was your anniversary, so if he comes around, play along with it, al-righty?"

Lexi looked like a deer in the headlights, so Noah nodded to the waitress as she flashed another bright smile, twirling around to help another guest.

"Newlyweds," She said with a slight snort.

"We could be." Noah reached across the table, placing his hand on Lexi's. He held up his glass and clinked it to hers. "If I hadn't been an idiot and run off to Dallas, this might have been our anniversary."

Lexi took a sip of her champagne, giving him a wary look over the rim.

He loved her blue eyes and the silky blonde hair that framed her perfect face.

"You don't have to talk wedding bells to win me over, Noah. We barely knew each other before you left, and you just came back to Magnolia."

Noah nodded. "You're right. I'm going too fast. I'll try to rein in my excitement. It's just been a long while since I've gotten to spend time with you. I want to get to know you better, and I hope you'll want to get to know me. What little time we spent together haunted me all those months in Dallas. What would have been, could have been—poking me while I tried to sleep at night. I thought I'd never be whole again, and now that...." He cleared his throat and paused to take a sip of champagne. "Now that I know I can be whole again, I don't want to waste another minute without you."

The band ended the jazzy tune they were playing and announced they were taking a break. Soft music filled the silence as it flowed through the speakers above. Guests exited the stage along with the constable and Lexi's new tenant. Noah noticed they were headed in their direction, but he didn't say anything to Lexi because he didn't want her jumping up and looking guilty again. He might understand her needing their reunion to be quiet for now, but he hoped she wouldn't hide being with him forever, like a dirty little secret. If people they knew saw them, there wasn't much they could do about it. Hell, he would like for all of Magnolia to see them together. He was ready to start their future as a couple tonight.

Chapter 25

Ginger tossed her head back and laughed as Roland twirled her off the dance floor and escorted her back to their table. She thought she saw Lexi Nash from the corner of her eye. With a subtle double take, she confirmed it and also noticed that her pretty landlord was accompanied by the handsome owner of Hank's. Ginger had been right about the hot date. The man sitting next to Lexi was smoking.

Roland's gaze followed hers. "Ah, I saw them come in when we were dancing, but they look like they might want some privacy."

Ginger nodded. "Yeah, probably, but you don't think she'll think we're rude by not saying hello, or that I was lying about going to the movies? I mean, we're in The Woodlands. That's pretty far from the Cowboy Baptist Church."

Roland grinned. "Exactly. I think they are trying to get away from the prying eyes of Magnolia, too."

Ginger looked at him curiously. "They have a history, don't they?"

He cleared his throat and tugged at his shirt collar. "Yep."

Ginger pulled his sleeve playfully, "And you're not gonna share the dirt?"

Roland frowned. "I don't do dirt."

Ginger thought about it. It was exactly the reason she hadn't asked Lexi, and she respected that Roland wasn't a gossip. It put him up a notch in her book. "Sorry. I was mostly joking. I don't like gossip either." Maybe she could share her past with him, and he might understand. Of course, he might also tell her that if she'd dealt with her fear of flying, she wouldn't have found herself the victim of a sex video in the first place.

"Good. Magnolia has enough fodder to keep the rumor mill burning until doomsday as it is. Alexa Nash has been through a lot, and so has Noah Harding. It'd be nice to see something work out for a change." He glanced at their empty glasses and waved to the cocktail waitress. It surprised her when he said, "Get your purse, and I'll close the tab. Let's pretend we never saw them."

It was hard not to hide her shock. Not only did they pay the bill and leave the lounge, but as they walked through the lobby of the hotel across the glittering tiles and fancy chandeliers, Roland didn't stop at the elevators. He led them out to the valet stand and handed his ticket to the attendant.

"Did I say something wrong?" She tried to hide her disappointment, but she could hear it in her voice, and it felt like she was deflating inside. The night had started with a bang, but then her hackles went up, and her insecurities cooled the mood. The dancing made her heart race and her pulse flutter, putting her in the mood to stay up all night. Roland had a firm, athletic build and a sexy swagger that turned him into a pro on the dance floor. She hadn't known what to think of this law enforcement officer who was so type-A. He might be a rule follower, but he had drop-dead sexy bedroom eyes that she wanted to see more of.

Ginger wanted to know what made him tick and, expressly, what turned him on. Sure, it had been her flippant suggestion to get a room, and she'd been riding on a Dallas Derringer high before she let herself get all worked up and wary. Roland was being the perfect gentleman, and now he was taking her home.

"It seemed like a good time to leave," was all he offered. She watched the muscle in his jaw work. He looked a million miles away as he stared at the row of cars, pulling in and leaving the valet.

Dallas Derringer had never been dropped off before midnight, not even on a work night. "I thought you got a room."

He turned to her, lifting an eyebrow. "And it turned out to be a mistake."

Ginger folded her arms across her chest as she stared at him. Was he telling her that her behavior put him in his place, or was he letting her know he'd changed his mind?

The car arrived, and the valet popped out of the driver's seat, leaving the door ajar as he rounded the shiny red Lucille to open the passenger side for Ginger.

She held out her hand to Roland, who mistook it for wanting assistance into the car. She arched an eyebrow at him. "Where's the key?"

He looked perplexed. "You want to drive?"

She shook her head. "To the room."

He put a hand inside his pocket and retrieved the plastic card, holding it out to her.

"Room number?"

"Tenth floor, ten-three-seventeen."

Ginger took the key card and returned to the lobby doors. She flipped her hair over her shoulder and glanced back at him with her famous Dallas Derringer cat-eyed, come-hither stare. In her sultry movie-star voice, she said, "Aren't you coming?"

Roland took a deep breath, trying to calm the erratic beating of his heart. Maybe this gal needed a kind of help that he couldn't give. Sure, she was slender, gorgeous, and had the kind of emerald eyes that would bring a simpler man to his knees, but she was hot and cold then burning to go upstairs. Maybe she needed a psychiatrist?

He ran a hand over his face, then took in a deep breath. He'd gotten the distinct impression she'd changed her mind about spending the night together, and for him, no meant no, not *maybe*, or *you could change my mind with persuasion*. As he stared at the lobby doors, his mind drifted back to Heidi Forester from high school. They'd gotten hot and heavy on their first date but hadn't gone all the way. Roland was too young and nervous at sixteen, and she'd said no. The next date, he'd done his homework, and Heidi had said yes to sneaking out of her house, even though she was grounded. After his dad had gone to bed, he pilfered the keys to the car.

They cruised around town, driving aimlessly for a while until they realized they might be seen. Roland parked at a secluded spot where things went further than either of them had planned. That night, they both lost their virginity. He hadn't used protection because he didn't have any, and teen hormones didn't care about warnings from parents concerning teen pregnancy or worse.

On the way back to Heidi's house, a car swerved into his lane, and Roland overcompensated, running headlong into a tree. He thanked his lucky stars that Heidi left the hospital with only a broken collarbone and a fractured wrist. He'd been shaken up, but nothing more than a few scratches and a threat of being grounded for life. The guardian angel who kept him alive that night breathed a sense of direction into him, and he swore to his parents that it would never happen again.

A few months passed with both of them grounded, and Heidi was forbidden to speak to him. Roland found out through a friend that she was pregnant, but by the time he got permission to go to her house, Heidi's parents refused to let him speak to her. They told him she'd already gotten an abortion, and she was never allowed to see him again. Shortly afterward, her family moved, and there hadn't been a damn thing he could do about it. Roland beat himself up for breaking the rules and getting them both into trouble, but most of all, because Heidi got hurt. He'd been lost in his own lust, and things went terribly wrong because of it.

Roland let out a deep sigh of resignation, pulled a twenty from his wallet, and gave it to the attendant, asking him to repark the car. His body was on a different alert now. The sexual desire that had made his groin ache earlier was being pushed aside by memories of the past. His brother and sister teased him about being a rule follower, but he doubted they knew why. Maddie had been too young to know what was going on with Roland and Heidi, and Luke was in his own world with his junior high friends, who skateboarded their free time away.

Claire came later. He'd thought they might have something more together, but she was a teller at a local bank and had found the money she managed to be too great a temptation. She'd let five or ten dollars find its way into her purse each day, and the bank let her do it until it was enough to convict her on a felony charge. Roland never had a clue. He never would have guessed sweet Claire would steal as much as a pen. If he'd known, he would have tried to help her. There were counselors for those who needed assistance staying on track. The rules were important to keep people out of trouble, and over the years Roland had learned to read the signs when someone was struggling.

Now here he was in another situation with Ginger. She was angry, then sweet, hot and then cold, and now she was boiling over. It was a warning sign that he knew he should heed. Roland silently wondered what Ginger was hiding and how he could help her get back on track. He wanted to get to know her, but he wanted more than tonight. *Rule number one, use your head.*

Chapter 26

Noah was saying all the right things, and Lexi's heart hung on every word that dripped from his silver tongue. Was he laying it on thick because he thought this is what she wanted to hear? She had to admit he wasn't wrong. Before he'd disappeared from Magnolia and her life, she'd fallen head over heels in love. It wasn't clear to her then, but the emptiness she'd felt in her heart during the months that followed his absence was like being widowed a second time. It was exactly why she didn't want her brothers or parents to find out she was seeing Noah again.

It had been difficult to hide the hurt, and after her run-in with Hank and the depression that hit hard after her trip to Dallas, Lexi's broken heart had been obvious to anyone who had eyes. She must have cried buckets of tears before she finally started to get back to living her life. Hell, she'd even thought that asking Hank to that Blossom dinner might be fun, but not because she was hoping for something more. Hank was still "Hank" even if he had turned over a new leaf. And despite being one of the best-looking men around, Lexi didn't have feelings for him or anyone else.

She confessed that when it came to Noah, in the back of her mind, she'd heard wedding bells ringing and saw a glossy photo of Noah, her, and her three boys all smiling brightly at the camera. In her dream of dreams, Lexi wanted happily ever after. But she knew better than to wish for a beautiful, perfect glass house made of love and contentment. They always shattered in the end, leaving her broken and bleeding her heart out in the shards.

Her hand flew up to stop the direction of their conversation. "Let's not talk about *us*, for now anyway." She held up her glass and clinked it to his. "This is nice champagne. Thank you."

Noah nodded, taking a sip. "You're right. I'm sorry. I'm like a bull in a china shop and—" He suddenly stopped what he was saying and pressed his lips together, making his fingers look like they were turning a key in a lock.

Lexi nodded. Glad he was listening.

"Tell me about how you've been. Tell me more about the boys, the ranch, the new business. I want to hear all about it."

"Thank God, it's all going fabulous at the moment. The boys are growing up too fast and can be a hot handful. They're into soccer, so that keeps them busy on Saturdays. And things are better since I have help, though Ginger works part-time at the diner, so we're still working out her schedule." Lexi searched the mostly empty dance floor. "I don't see them anymore. Do you think they left?"

"I did see them look our way, but I think they had their own agenda. Funny, I got the impression they didn't really know each other when I saw you at the bar the other night."

Lexi shrugged a shoulder. "I think it might have been one of those love at first sight things. Apparently, he pulled her over to give her a ticket but then he gave her a warning instead. The way she talked to me, it sounded as if she was miffed at men in general. I don't know what changed her tune, but she came in earlier and invited me and the boys to a movie with Roland and his family. Maddie has a little girl who knows my boys. But if Roland is here with Ginger, then I guess the plans changed."

Lexi twirled her glass on the table's slick wood surface. "Anyway, I was surprised to see them in the lounge, but they looked like they were having fun, and that's great. I want Ginger to like it here. She seems to have been wrung out by someone or something before she got to Magnolia."

Noah lay his hand over hers, stopping her from twirling the glass. "You didn't ask about her past before she moved in? Aren't you worried about her being around the boys?"

Lexi sat up straight, pushing her shoulders back. "Everybody's got a past. You should know that." She smirked.

He grimaced. "I guess you're right about that, but still. What if she's a bank robber or a kidnapper?"

Lexi batted his hand. "I can promise you, she's not on the FBI's most-wanted list. Sometimes, the skeletons in our closets are only scary to us. They don't hurt anyone but the owner. I think there is something there, but when, and if, Ginger decides to tell me, I'm sure it won't be anything that will hurt my boys or me. Besides, I really like her, and I think she could use a little family support right now."

"You want to share any of your skeletons with me?"

His tone was teasing, but Lexi's brows arched with mock candor. "Why Noah Harding, you are my only skeleton."

Noah thought about Lexi's teasing comment as they waited for the valet to bring the car. Was she hiding something? Maybe she hadn't been honest about an interest in his cousin Hank. Noah's ex-wife had almost married Hank, and there had been a slew of women who'd fallen for his better-looking, too-slick cousin. Was Lexi one of them? Until recently, Hank was never known for being a man of substance. Noah had to admit that his cousin had apologized and more than made up for any past financial hardships he'd caused. He'd also apologized for using Lexi and Petra to drive a wedge between them, but one of the few times they'd spoken over the last few months, Hank had surprised Noah by calling him out on his bullheaded ways.

As they pulled out onto the highway, he remembered the scowl on his cousin's face as he left the new Hank's. "You moved here and built the bar. You even beat all odds and walked again. Awesome. Good for you! Now, get your head out of your ass and go after her. I'm warning you, Noah, if you don't do something about Lexi Nash, she's going to be fair game."

Noah hadn't thought that Hank would make good on his threat after all the work they'd done together, repairing their relationship and managing both bars. There was a new camaraderie between them, and Noah hated to lose that. Hank finally felt like real family, but if he laid a finger on Lexi, Noah might have to kill him. Was Noah a fool to believe that any man who had a chance at Lexi would say no? Could he blame Hank if he did go after her, and could he blame Lexi if she fell for Hank? Hank had grown into a better man, and he had more than enough money. He could help her with the ranch and the boys. Noah mentally gave himself a shake. *So could you! And you're the one with her now. She's here with you, so stop doubting yourself.*

"You okay, Noah?" Lexi touched his cheek as he stopped at a red light.

He turned his face into her hand and smiled. She was the kind of woman who couldn't avoid feeling concerned about others. Lexi was warm, affectionate and caring. It's what he loved most about her. The innocent caress was feather-light, and it sent need coursing through his chest and lower. Silently, he reminded himself to keep it in his pants. *You are not allowed to push your way into her bedroom tonight, cowboy. You need to show her you are interested in a real relationship, not just taking her to bed.*

He cleared his throat, reaching up to touch her hand. He gave it a squeeze. "I'm fine. I was thinking that I don't want this night to end. I've really missed you. Why don't you let me drive you home, and we'll get your car tomorrow."

He darted a glance at her as she shot him a skeptical look but agreed. They drove in silence, each lost in their own contemplation.

As they turned onto the long dirt road that led to the ranch, he felt Lexi's eyes on him.

Her hand touched his arm and lingered there. "I know it's been forever for us, and I enjoyed tonight, too. But if you thought it would end like the first time we were together...." He heard her intake of breath. "I can't. Not tonight."

He could hear the quiver in her voice. Was she having as hard a time as he was, telling her body to stand down? The thought made his lower regions burn.

He parked the car in the drive and shook his head. "I wasn't going there. I promise. I meant what I said. I want to get to know you better. I want us to spend time together, and if that means seeing each other in secret until you're ready for the world to know, I'm okay with that, but Lexi—" he picked up her hand and held it to his lips. "—eventually, I'd like to meet your boys and then I want the world to know you're mine."

Chapter 27

Roland rapped lightly on the door. A few seconds passed, and he checked the room number again. Finally, the door opened. Ginger grabbed his hand and pulled him in.

She was wearing one of the room's fluffy white spa robes. "What took you so long? I was afraid you'd jumped in Lucille and left." She grabbed the material of his shirt and lifted up on her toes to kiss him. Roland didn't pull back, even though his head was running in a different direction. It didn't help that the king-size bed beckoned them from the center of the room. He could taste the toothpaste on her tongue and smell the scent of fresh soap on her skin.

"Did you take a shower?" Had he been lingering in the valet area, sifting through the past for that long?

Ginger giggled. "No, silly." She tugged at the material of his shirt, pulling it free from the waist of his jeans. "I washed my hands and face before I come, I did." She'd said it in a perfect Cockney accent. It was a line from *My Fair Lady*. Roland had seen it many times, but now he was thinking how much fun it would be to watch it with Ginger.

She snaked both hands around his neck, pulling him back down to her full lips. He didn't want to resist. Ginger was the one woman he'd met in what felt like forever who checked all of his physical boxes— fit, pretty, sexy, and her porcelain complexion didn't need any makeup. She was even more gorgeous now with it all wiped off. His gaze drifted to the puddle of clothes in front of the closet door. Roland's hands spanned her waist, brushing the tie that held her robe together. His fingers itched to untether it and bare her naked flesh to his hungry eyes. He wanted to rain kisses down her neck and shoulders, taking her breasts in his hands and teasing each erect nipple with his tongue. His heart thumped in his chest and his cock hardened at the thought of her naked beneath him, but he needed to focus. Though the incident with Heidi had happened so long ago, he honed in on the lesson learned. It never hurt to take your time in getting to know someone and playing it safe would save a world of hurt in the future. He was painfully aware that he didn't have a condom in his wallet, and he didn't want to ponder the contents of Ginger's purse. Would she have a packet hidden in the small pocket of her beaded bag?

She stepped back, looking up at him with concern in her eyes. "What's wrong? Did I kill the moment downstairs?"

Roland shook his head. "No. I thought we could order room service and enjoy a bite to eat. I didn't get the room assuming anything. I simply thought we could get to know each other."

Ginger smiled and nodded. "That sounds nice. I'll find a menu while you see what's in the minibar."

He could see the uncertainty in her eyes. She'd probably never been turned down in her life. He wasn't turning her down but pumping the brakes until he knew what she really wanted and until she understood what he was looking for.

This was a first. Ginger had never been put on ice before, so it was hard to hide her disappointment when Roland wanted to eat dinner instead of taking the hotel bed for a trial run. Admittedly, she was operating on empty, and if she was going to drink the half bottle of champagne from the minibar he had poured for them, she needed to put something substantial in her stomach.

Roland was a different breed of man. No one in L.A. that she knew said no to no-strings-attached, one-night-stand sex—with a celebrity, no less. Did he understand what she was offering? Magnolia was a small town, and maybe he had a few baby-mommas stashed away. She knew she shouldn't analyze it. Instead, she should appreciate that he wanted to take his time.

Reason told her that Roland wouldn't have asked her out if he wasn't attracted to her, and he definitely wouldn't have gotten a room with one bed if he didn't plan on having sex tonight—or would he? He'd said there were plenty of sleeping options. Maybe Roland really did have a full house, and he wanted some quiet time. He was a constable. He'd probably lose his career if he was caught drinking and driving.

Ginger shook her head, willing herself to stop over-thinking it. *Why does it have to be a one-night stand? What if he really wants to get to know the real you—Ginger Lynn Harding? He doesn't seem the type to watch sci-fi shows like Seducing Saturn or go in for modern-day action movies, and he certainly doesn't seem like the kind of guy who would secretly film the two of you having sex to exploit it long afterward. God, I probably need a shrink. Why can't I just get laid without picking everything apart?*

Ginger took a seat on the small sofa. It was a luxurious suite with a cozy sitting area, but nothing was overly large. The bed, nightstands, table, chairs, and loveseat offered little floor space to spread out. The faux balcony had a sliding glass door, but the built-in lock prevented it from opening more than a few inches. Roland opened it as far as it would go, and a light breeze blew in, making the sheer fabric of the gauzy drapes drift toward her.

Ginger reasoned they had to start somewhere getting to know each other. Feeling spontaneous, she asked, "What's your favorite movie?" You could tell a lot about a person by their book or film preferences.

He picked up his flute and eased in next to her on the loveseat. "That's too hard to answer. There are so many."

Ginger nodded. She didn't know if she had one favorite. There were unlimited movies she could watch over and over without tiring. "Okay then, what's your favorite recent movie?"

Roland's eyes crinkled as he scratched his head. "This is where I tell a secret about myself that you may find unattractive. Are you sure you want me to answer that question honestly and spoil the mood?"

Was there a mood? Should she let herself think about what would happen after room service? She nodded. The slow grin that spread across his face reminded her of a small boy caught eating the last Christmas cookie.

Roland cleared his throat before explaining. "I can't tell you the last time I saw a modern movie. I think I was born in the wrong era. I remember my mom watching old films on TMC or renting DVDs. I would stay up with her and my dad, past Luke or Maddie's bedtime. There was something about the classics that I connected with. Don't get me wrong, I've seen a lot of the blockbusters over the years when family was in town, and we went to the movies, but half of the time, I fell asleep. It's all shoot 'em up surround sound that makes your chair vibrate and your ears throb. I guess you could say that I get enough action in real life, and when I watch a movie, it's nice to go back to a safer time."

"Like World War II?" She was surprised, not that he thought old movies were from a safer time, but that he didn't care for modern action movies. "Wasn't that what half of the old movies were about—war?"

He chuckled. "Yeah, I suppose so, and I like those, too, but it's some of the not-so-popular films that I really get into, like *The Treasure of the Sierra Madre*, with Bogart, or *Marnie*, with Sean Connery. I also like *The Girl in Black*. It's a Greek film in black, and white, and it's a must see. *Cinema Paradiso* is one of the best classics ever made. Movies back then had a story to tell, and they didn't need special effects to do it."

Ginger was impressed. A man who looked all "Captain America" but didn't mind reading subtitles in foreign films. *Who is this guy?*

Seducing Saturn was all special effects, and sometimes she wondered if the writers were smoking something besides cigarettes and drinking more than coffee in the studio breakroom. There was a plot, but the script was jumbled. As she watched each season unfold, she wondered about sensationalism versus good storytelling. She wasn't a writer, so she really couldn't judge, but she had to say the lines, and sometimes they were difficult to pull off.

Ginger admired Roland's passion for movies of the past. "There aren't many men out there like you. Most people don't care for old films. They only want the latest and greatest. The bigger the explosion, the better."

"See, I told you that it might ruin the attraction."

She arched an eyebrow as she held the glass to her lips. After taking a drink, she leaned back and studied him. "Attraction?"

"Well, I mean…." Roland flushed, putting his hand to his collar. She adored the way he tugged at it when things got heated.

Ginger lifted her feet to his lap and settled back against the small sofa cushion. He cradled one foot in his hand as he sipped champagne with the other.

"Yes, I am very attracted." His sultry tone trickled over her.

Setting his champagne on the low glass table, he began to massage her feet. Ginger bent one leg and let him lift it higher onto his lap. The robe fell apart up to her mid-thigh. Everything she'd been wearing was sitting on the floor next to the closet. Trying to control her breathing as he looked at her through his thick black lashes, she wondered if he had Italian or Greek blood. Desire pooled in his sherry-colored eyes, and his bottom lip glistened with champagne droplets. His hands were still on her feet, but she pushed her leg toward him in invitation. The robe edged farther away from her flesh. Her breath caught as he leaned forward, running his strong fingers up each of her calves, hitting all the right muscles.

He wasn't taking things further than she offered, and she wasn't sure if she should be pleased or disappointed. It had been too long, and she wanted to have sex. A sizzle of anticipation streaked down her spine. His tanned face was a perfect arrangement of planes and angles, reminding her of Michelangelo's David. She trembled as his hand grazed the sensitive spot beneath her knee, and she couldn't stop wondering what he looked like naked. If she had to beg for it, she would. The tie to her robe was easily unwound, and she let the sides of the brushed-cotton fabric fall apart. He hadn't even kissed her yet, and she was baring all of herself to him. Room service be damned. Champagne and hot constable was all she wanted.

Chapter 28

They were standing at the door again. The same way they had three years ago on their first and only date. It was a tantalizing, torturous déjà vu. All Lexi had to do was open the door and invite him in, and she knew they would end up in her king-size bed.

Her body chanted, *open the damn door and go for it!*

Her mind screamed, *remember what happened last time after the fun!*

Noah leaned toward her, giving her lips a soft brush with his. It was polite, gentlemanly, the perfect ending to an evening of reconciliation. As promised, he was taking it slow and getting to know her. Lexi assured herself it was what she wanted and, more important, what she needed. She'd been around the block a few times and had made mistakes. If she really wanted this, she needed to be patient. Sometimes the right thing to do was the hardest. What if they said good night and he never called her again? Her heart ached at the thought. *Then it wasn't meant to be.*

A shotgun fired into the night and startled Lexi out of her worries. She jumped back and looked around Noah toward the barn. "That was close."

Noah squeezed her arm. "Stay here. I'll go take a look."

She followed close on his heel. "No way, Jose. It's my ranch. I'm coming, too. It sounded like it came from the barn."

As they reached the side of the house, she saw the outline of a man standing in the open doorway of the barn. The moon was full, and she recognized the golden hair of the ranch manager. "John? What's going on?"

He lowered the barrel of the shotgun and waited for them to approach. "Sorry, Ms. Burns. I heard some coyotes in the distance, and I thought they might be bothering the cattle. Snickers and Dora have been restless the last few nights, and I've had a few of the guys keeping a lookout. Tonight's my shift, and I didn't want to take any chances."

Lexi nodded. Though she'd legally changed her name back to Nash, she didn't correct anyone who still called her Burns. "Glad to know you're out here. I warned Ginger about the coyotes, but remind the men that she's staying in the cottage, so no one gets hurt. I'll give Ginger a heads-up again when I see her."

John held the shotgun barrel pointed toward the pasture, but his eyes seemed fixed on Noah. Lexi wasn't sure why she felt a sense of disquiet. She wasn't afraid of the coyotes. John was doing his job, and Lexi was saying goodnight to her date. There wasn't anything wrong with the scenario, but something about the three of them standing together made her uncomfortable. Was it because she'd been thinking, "what if" about John before she'd run into Noah at the new Hank's? Was it because she had felt John's interest grow over the past few months, at the same time as she'd thought about getting back out there?

Lexi looked out at the pasture, scanning the landscape. "Okay. Call me if anything else happens. I'll be in the house."

Noah escorted her back to the door. "Do you want me to stay? I can sleep on the couch and take you back to your car in the morning."

Lexi thought about his offer but knew inviting him in would be playing Russian Roulette. "I'm sure I'll be safe inside. Besides, John seems to have it under control, and Ginger won't mind taking me to fetch my car."

Noah nodded, repeating the name. "John."

Lexi looked back toward the side of the house where they'd come from. "Oh, sorry. I guess that was rude that I didn't introduce you. John's my ranch manager. He's great. I mean, he does a great job." She sounded flustered even to her own ears.

Noah smiled. "I would have introduced myself, but he was holding a shotgun, and by the way he was looking at you, I think he may have a bit of a crush. Of course, that red dress would stop any man who had a pulse."

Lexi felt heat rise to her cheeks, and the cool night air wasn't fanning her discomfort. "Oh, John has worked for me for years. I'm sure you're mistaken." She glanced down at the dress she'd bought after last Valentine's Day. It had been on sale, but she'd never had the courage to wear it out.

"If John was looking at me oddly, it's because I rarely ever get the chance to wear a dress."

"You look amazing, and I hope you have a few more like this one, because I plan on asking you out again. Often."

Lexi couldn't hide her smile. She wasn't sure why she felt shy, but it was awkward not knowing how to end the evening. There was nothing she wanted more than to invite him in, but as she'd already gone over her possibilities, she knew saying goodnight on the porch was the best option.

Noah gave her another soft brush of his lips against hers. She wrapped her hand around the back of his neck, drawing him closer and deepening the kiss. He enfolded her in his arms, and Lexi felt the thud of his heart beating against her chest. She wondered if he could feel hers. The invitation to come in for a night-cap danced on her tongue, but Noah ended the kiss and backed away.

"I'd better go before I find myself pushing my way into your living room. I vowed to behave, and I want to keep that promise. I hope to see you soon, Lexi. Night." He lifted a hand in the air as he reached for his car door. And with the rumble of his engine, he was gone.

Lexi sighed with wistful frustration. She'd fantasized about the dreamy Noah Harding for so long, and now he was here. Despite his cold dismissal in Dallas, she'd held onto the hope that he would return to Magnolia, wanting to share a future with her. She'd been angry at herself for clinging to such childish, romantic notions. And even though she'd tried to put Noah behind her, a yearning for him hovered over her until she felt like a horse being pestered by a horsefly. And now, Noah was back, and he wanted to be with her.

Lexi's previous thoughts of John were now wiped away, and she shuddered at the thought of how mucked up things might have been if Noah had waited another month or two. If she'd let herself try on another relationship, would she still be standing here, looking at her empty driveway and pining for a night in bed with Noah? That wouldn't have been fair to anyone. Lexi breathed another sigh of relief. *Noah Harding, you got here just in time.*

Noah drove the dark gravel road out to the highway with thoughts of Lexi on his mind and the taste of her lipstick on his lips. His fingers had itched to unzip the sexy red number she wore, and he'd fantasized about the dress and her panties puddled at her feet on her bedroom floor until he ached. He stretched his legs, trying to accommodate his rock-hard erection pushing against his jeans. Noah knew he needed a cold shower, but he wanted to make a U-turn and go back to the ranch instead. The thought of Lexi under him wearing only a smile was stamped on his brain from the memory of their first date. It was his own fault that he was driving home to an empty apartment and a lonely bed.

Noah tried to focus on something besides having hot sex with Lexi so he wouldn't chafe himself by continuously shifting in his seat. He thought of the ranch hand, who had all but glared at him. The man had it bad for her, and it was probably obvious to everyone but Lexi. Noah didn't like it, but he couldn't blame the guy. She was gorgeous, kind, smart and easy to make laugh. He honestly didn't know how she'd stayed single for so long, but he thanked his lucky stars that she was still available, and she seemed willing to make another go at a relationship.

Noah could admit when another man was good-looking, and the ranch manager wasn't hard on the eyes. It was dark out, but the guy looked fit from what he could see, and Lexi had looked almost guilty during the exchange. She denied that the guy had an interest in her, but did she have an interest in her ranch manager? The thought unsettled him. Noah had come back to Magnolia to make things work between him and Lexi, and tonight she seemed willing to hear him out.

Relief flooded his senses. She wasn't dating the ranch manager, yet, and Noah was here to make sure she didn't. He pulled into his parking spot and turned the engine off. He sat there for a moment going over the exchange, which led back to the parting kiss on the porch. Looking down at his hardened state, he breathed out a curse and muttered, "Ah, hell. Now I have to think of something else to get out of the damn car."

Chapter 29

Roland wanted Ginger bad, no question about that. The seam of his zipper was leaving an imprint against his erection. Then she put her feet in his lap, and he felt like he was about to explode.

He was sure she could feel his hardness. He rubbed her feet and calves without continuing their earlier conversation. Roland admitted it was hard to think when Ginger, clad only in a hotel robe, lay before him. He watched her as she took another sip of champagne, assessing him with her emerald eyes over the rim. She let out a moan of satisfaction as his fingers worked the arches of her feet and the curve of her long calf muscles. He felt mesmerized by her candid stare as she placed her flute on the glass tabletop and let her fingers unwind the ties of her robe.

In the glow of the room's soft lamp-light, he could see every curve of her body, but the trimmed ginger-colored hair at the juncture of her thighs was a surprise. She was a redhead, not a brunette. If her hair was such a beautiful shade of red, why would she ever color it?

He didn't ponder the question for too long because she was lifting one gorgeous long leg in what could only be taken as a direct invitation. He might have wanted to take things slow to make sure she was on board for some kind of future, but in the end, he was just a man. Flesh and blood, and right now, all of the blood from his brain had rushed south.

He kissed the instep of her foot and let his tongue trail its way to the back of her knee. He didn't want this evening to go too quickly, so he skated his way to her hip and up the flat plane of her stomach to her small pert breasts.

He'd never been a man who cared about the size of a woman's assets, but Ginger was perfect. Lean, fit, with the tone of a runner or someone who did yoga daily. She wrapped her thighs around his hips as his lips met hers. Toned legs squeezed him closer to her center, and it was almost his undoing.

Roland had to think of baseball, elephants, the pile of work waiting for him on his office desk. He tried not to move an inch until his thoughts cooled. If he wasn't careful, this could get embarrassing.

Her lips were warm, and her tongue was like velvet. The moan deep in her throat made electricity zip down his lower back, and he could feel his pulse racing as his heart skipped a beat. Suddenly, he wanted to touch all of her. His hands pushed at the robe, sliding it down both arms as he kissed and suckled her breasts. She arched for him, pushing her pelvis against his hard cock. Unable to stand any more torture, Roland pulled back, fumbling at his zipper. He felt her wetness on the rough material as he removed his shirt and shed his jeans.

He'd wanted to take his time getting to know her because he thought she was vulnerable. Ginger had seemed troubled when they'd met, and he wanted to find out why she was so defensive. Roland had never taken advantage of a woman, and he'd given Ginger every chance to take a rain check tonight. As she grabbed at his shoulders and tugged him back down on top of her, he erased all thoughts of taking it slow. He was overwhelmed with the desire to delve deep inside her and hear her call out in pleasure. The curve of her hip beneath his hand and the feel of her soft skin against his flesh was too much to deny.

Roland had always taken pride in staying on the right side of the law. He held himself to a strict moral code to help and never harm others, and he hoped tonight wouldn't damage their possible future together. But damn it, he was only human. There was one thing he was sure of right now. If Ginger was a drug, he was an addict who needed a fix. *Rules be damned.*

What was it about Roland that had her begging for sex? Seriously, the man was made of steel, and it bothered her. She'd all but thrown herself at him, and he still sat there, holding her feet and politely sipping champagne. She supposed it was the challenge that made her strip naked beneath his oh-so-cool gaze, and it had finally worked. She'd actually trembled, wondering if she'd made a fool of herself. What if he'd said no? Ginger pushed her doubts away, enjoying his big, warm hands as they stroked the undersides of her breasts. His hot tongue ran circles around her nipples in sweet, torturous revolutions, until she thought she couldn't take anymore.

Ginger arched into him, pulling at his shoulders. "Roland, I need you. We can go slow next time, but I need you inside me, now," she demanded, squeezing him with her thighs.

His hand slid between them, parting her folds, rubbing her sensitive nub in a mind-blowing rhythm before pushing his finger inside her with long, slow thrusts that made her whimper.

"Please," she begged. I want to come with you inside me. I need it."

Roland became very still, then cleared his throat. "I feel a little caught out. I didn't bring anything. I mean, I wasn't planning this." He stared at her, a pained expression mottling his gorgeous face.

Ginger let out a soft groan of frustration. It should make her happy to know he really hadn't planned this, but she didn't have any protection either. What were the odds? It had been over a year since she'd had sex, and though she had the reputation of a porno-making sex addict, she apparently was on a permanent cock-block from the universe.

"Oh crap! Neither do I," she confessed, lifting up on her elbows as Roland rolled to the side.

His chest was a living sculpture of cut muscle and warm bronzed flesh. The dusting of dark hair across his pecs highlighted his physique in the manliest way. He was daunting and sexy in his uniform, good-looking as hell in casual clothes—but naked, he was the stuff women dreamed of—*masculine, fit...* Her eyes trailed down to where his body showed undeniable interest in her. She licked her lips—*and well-hung. Thank you, God.*

Ginger grinned. "Well, I was hoping for the thirteen positions of the Kama Sutra, but there are other things we can do."

She almost giggled at his raised eyebrows and unblinking eyes. Was he worried he couldn't make it through thirteen positions or was he disappointed they wouldn't get to try? She didn't pause to ask. Looking up at him as she lowered her head to his lap, she touched the trail of fine hair that led to his happy place. Ginger had never felt one way or another about oral sex. She preferred intercourse. The feeling of being filled up inside was exhilarating, but admittedly, foreplay had its advantages. Taking him in her mouth, she rubbed her hand down his shaft to the base and up again, meeting her lips as she repeated the motions. She felt the grip of his hands on her shoulders as he moaned and then called out for her to stop.

"Wait," Roland said in a husky breath. "It humbles me to tell you that I won't last long if you keep doing that." He pulled her across his lap and settled her buttocks on his thighs. He kissed her gently as he stroked a tendril of her dark hair. He was buying time. "Why did you change the color?"

His eyes slid down to the juncture at her thighs.

Ginger realized that even though she'd lasered away most of the unwanted bikini hair, she'd left a small thatch of her natural ginger-colored curls. "I uh—" She covered the area with her hands, suddenly feeling exposed. "—I wanted a change."

Roland removed her hands, replacing them with his own. His fingers roved over the small thatch of trimmed hair, giving her a seductive smile. "It's perfect. I think you're beautiful just the way you are. You don't need to change anything."

She knew he'd probably say it to anyone in this particular position, but his words poured over her like hot scented oil and her feminine center tingled with each stroke of his fingers. She'd been hurt by previous relationships, especially the betrayal that had her running to Magnolia with her tail tucked. It was the worst time in her life. The sex video had ruined her career and simultaneously crushed her self-esteem.

Ginger had never let anyone get close enough for her to care about what they really thought, and here she was with a man she barely knew, ready to trust him with her body and possibly more. Something about his masculine touch, soothing voice and his willingness to wait set him aside from all the people who'd been pushing her in the past, herself included. Something was different about Roland. She didn't know exactly what it was, but she was open to finding out.

It was Roland who made the next move, lifting her from the couch, walking them to the bed, and pulling back the sheets with one hand as she slid down his torso. He pushed them both to the mattress and rained kisses down her body. There weren't any protests this time because she knew the confines of their evening together. She appreciated that Roland wasn't some guy willing to risk it all to get laid. It said she could trust him to take care of himself and, in turn, take care of her.

He pushed her leg up, lifting her calf over his shoulder as he dipped his head. The kiss he placed against her moist center made her gasp and arch in pleasure. He'd inspected her body and found one of her most important secrets. She was a ginger. As she pushed the past from her mind, Roland twirled his tongue around the bundle of nerves that sang with intense pleasure. She slipped her other leg over his shoulder and pushed her pelvis into his kiss. His tongue darted in and out of her wetness as she moaned with erotic elation. Her knees fell outward, and he buried himself deeper as he groped her hips with his hands. He held her to him as if he was starving, and she wanted nothing more than to nourish him. Unable to hold back any longer, Ginger cried out his name as she twirled her fingers in his hair, pulling at the tendrils and clawing at his shoulders so that she didn't slip from reality.

As Roland crawled up her body and laid himself to the side of her spent form, he stroked her long dark hair. "You taste amazing."

Ginger could barely catch her breath as her heart pounded in her chest. "Oh my God. *That* was amazing." She didn't mind stroking his ego before she went back to stroking his cock. He was good, and she would try to be even better.

Roland chuckled with what sounded like self-satisfaction and relief. "I'm glad you weren't disappointed about the Kama Sutra rain check, but if you're up for it, I'm willing to do the same moves twelve more times."

Ginger's heart skipped a beat and raced forward. A sizzle zipped down her spine and back to the place he'd kissed. Fresh need pulsed between her legs, and she straddled his thighs in an almost too crushing tease. It wasn't clear, even to herself, if she could be trusted. There was nothing she wanted more than to straddle his hardness and go for a ride, but instead, she placed one knee between his thighs and slid her breasts down over his cock, squeezing her flesh around his shaft. She felt power in the way his head fell back, and a soft moan escaped him. It was her intimate kiss that brought him to his first orgasm, and though it didn't take long, she applauded him for trying to hold onto the moment for as long as he did. The beauty of him arching to meet the thrust of her hungry mouth made her feel utterly in control. She wanted him, every inch of him, and when he called out her name, she shuddered with the pleasure of knowing how good it was between them.

Ginger was as hot in bed as the flame-colored hair between her legs. Roland couldn't quit thinking about the red thatch of hair that led to the sweetest foreplay he could ever remember, and he should remember it well, because true to his promise, he'd kissed Ginger to countless orgasms, making her eventually beg him to stop so they could actually call room service for sustenance.

The sun was up, and they hadn't slept a wink. In between long stretches of pleasuring each other in bed, Roland had held Ginger in his arms and they talked about movies, the best parts of motion picture history and the actors they loved best. Ginger told him about her father, who died when she was very young, and her mom, who lived in Plano at a memory care facility. She'd told him about the guilt she carried because she hadn't been able to take care of her mother when she should have, and how the remorse had multiplied when she could no longer afford the fancy place. In the early rays of dawn, she'd explained how her uncle had helped out, but she told Roland that she hoped to be able to pay her Uncle Todd back when she got on her feet.

It meant a lot to him that she'd shared her feelings. There was so much more to her than her beauty, and he wanted to know everything. Their conversation never touched the topic of previous relationships, but he could tell that she'd been hurt. The fact that she hadn't been with anyone in over a year spoke volumes. His insides clenched when she'd softly broached the subject after their third round of intercourse rain check.

Her fingers traced lazy circles along his chest. "Are you sure there aren't any condoms in the men's room downstairs?"

He looked at his watch. "Should I call the front desk and ask? The bar is long closed by now."

Letting out a breathy sigh that hitched a little, she slid her leg over his, pushing her pelvis into his hip. His erection pressed against the sheets, rising for the occasion. God, he wanted to touch her again and more. Roland wracked his brain, wondering if there was a sundry store in the lobby. He didn't remember one, and going down to the front desk just before dawn to ask if there were any condoms in the hotel was too much for his ego to handle. The embarrassment would rival his experience in high school, buying protection for the first time. Roland knew it was dumb to feel awkward with the purchase, but he knew a lot of people in the area because of his job—what if he ran into someone? Besides, it was enthralling watching her hips buck against him as his hands stroked up the flat plane of her stomach to the curves under her breasts.

Ginger moved on top of him, straddling his hips as she met his lips with hers. "It's been over a year for me. I'm not some sex addict or anything. I didn't know how much I missed sex until I met you. You're not like most guys I know."

He wanted to ask her why and who she'd been with that made her stay alone for so long, but she began sliding her breasts down his torso, and he could feel the moist trail of excitement against his thigh. Her kisses were gentle, and he didn't think he had anything left to give. He was forty, not eighteen, but someone needed to tell the lower half of his body as she massaged his already hard cock with her hands and took him into her gorgeous mouth. He was too entranced to think of anything else.

Chapter 30

Lexi arranged the dried flowers on the glass she'd cut for the vintage window frame. Using the old pull cords, she fastened a pretty hanger and laid another piece of glass over the flowers. This was a series of small frames that she could do on her own, but her latest commission was for a window salvaged from an old church. It had arrived on a semi-truck and took a crane and two men to take it into her metal building workshop. She usually bought her own salvaged barn wood and window frames, but someone in New York had come across a piece she'd done for a Houston customer. It hung over the mantle in a bed and breakfast, and she'd gotten several orders because of its beautiful array of bluebonnets. Now, she would work on gathering enough dried flowers to create something pretty for the massive structure. Her mind reeled with possibilities, and she couldn't wait to get started. The ranch she'd inherited had been the love of her life, but this new creative side of her had opened the door to something she didn't even know she'd been missing.

It was Monday evening now and she thought back to Saturday night with Noah as she worked. If there had been a panty-dropping moment the whole night, it was all the things Noah expressed about wanting to build something together and wanting to take it slowly. He'd checked all the responsible relationship boxes, including asking about her boys. Being a single mom, one of her biggest issues was finding a man who'd want half-grown kids. Three rowdy boys were a lot to take on for anybody, but Lexi had more baggage than an instant family. She had a ranch, a small internet business, and overly protective parents that tended to meddle in her life, even if it was unsolicited.

Telling Noah goodnight had been one of the hardest things she'd ever done, but relief and regret flooded her in equal parts as he'd kissed her and driven away. Lexi didn't know when she would see him again, but that was okay. She needed time to think, and she couldn't do that when he was near.

Ginger was a big help, taking the boys to school and bringing them back home. It would be Christmas before long, and Lexi needed to finish the rest of her gift shopping. She put away her cutting tools and covered the piece she was working on with a cloth. John entered, taking off his hat and holding it in both hands.

Lexi gave him a bright smile. "John, everything okay? I was wrapping up and about to go Christmas shopping." He'd been the best thing that had ever happened to Burns Creek Cattle, and she appreciated all of his hard work. She wondered when the best time would be to give him his Christmas bonus. Would he need it early to buy gifts?

"Everything is runnin' fine. I only wanted to tell you I was taking off and wanted to see if you needed help with anything before I left."

"You worked late Saturday night and all day yesterday and today. Don't you ever rest?"

John shrugged. "I get enough sleep and I'll catch up tonight. Can I help you with anything before I go?"

"That's awful kind of you. I think I'm all good, but I appreciate you stopping in to ask."

He lingered, and his intense blue eyes held a questioning stare. Nodding, he finally turned to leave.

Lexi felt like she needed to say or do something. She remembered the large frame from the church that was still in the crate. "Wait!"

John turned, hope clouding his clear blue eyes. "Ma'am."

"I actually will need your help getting this out tomorrow when some of the boys are around to help. I don't know if it's heavy, but it's awful big."

John walked back into the shop and followed Lexi to the crate. "Not a problem. I'll get Joey and Zeke to help first thing."

Lexi nodded, turned too quick and lost her footing.

John caught her and held her steady. "You all right, Lexi?"

Her eyes widened in surprise as she stared up at him. He had only ever called her Ms. Burns or ma'am for all the years that he'd worked there, no matter how many times she'd asked him to call her Lexi. She was holding onto his shirt, and she steadied herself before letting go and stepping back. "I'm fine. Sorry. I've been so clumsy lately. I guess I need to slow down, but there is still so much to do before Christmas."

160

John didn't step back. His eyes studied her face. "I'm here to help. If you tell me what you need, I'll do it."

He was close, too close, and the crate was behind her. Lexi shifted and studied her boots for a quick moment. "I've got it. I need a few more hours in the day, is all."

He cleared his throat as if sensing her discomfort and stepped back. "The boys must be some kind of excited about Santa. FYI, I caught them up in the hayloft, looking for gifts, so if you want the presents to be a surprise, you better hide them at the North Pole." His eyes crinkled with humor, and Lexi laughed.

"They are something." She shook her head with both wonder and pride at her mischievous minions. "Well, the joke's on them. I haven't bought anything yet, and then there is all the wrapping to do still." She sighed.

"Are you sure I can't help with anything else? I could drive you to town and help carry packages. I'd offer to wrap but trust me when I say you don't want me anywhere near your wrapping paper. My gifts usually look like Christmas gone wrong."

Lexi chuckled. "It's really nice of you to offer, and if I get too far behind, I may take you up on the drive, park, and carry. Those are the things I hate most about shopping during the holidays."

John reached out and touched her arm. His voice was quiet. "Let me help you, Lexi. You work so hard running this place and raising those boys." He tilted his head and gazed at her with an emotion she didn't want to name. She needed to get out of here before John did or said something they would both regret. He was handsome, strong, and kind. The boys loved following him around, and he was great at showing them the workings of the ranch. He didn't seem to mind their endless questions or squabbling over who got to do what first. It made her wonder about Noah. How would he be around her boys?

Noah and Lexi hadn't discussed when they'd see each other again, and she hadn't heard from him since Saturday night. A flicker of doubt nagged at her. *Maybe he's already changed his mind.* Until recently, Lexi had never thought of John as anything but a great helping hand that she could trust running the ranch. For the first time, she wondered why she hadn't thought of any romantic scenarios in all these years. He was handsome enough. She saw the way the women in the church looked at him on Sundays—the days she actually made it to service on time. Her effort to put in facetime with her parents was often foiled by unforeseeable events, like when the cattle gate was left open, and half of the herd tromped down Nichols Sawmill Road. She doubted John was responsible for that disaster, and the look on Gussy's face said he was quite possibly the guilty party.

If she had developed feelings for John, would he have fit in with her family? Every other Sunday, her parents made brunch, and the whole family was expected to attend. With all of her brothers married now and Raphe's new baby and her three boys, the actual meal was served in the long sunroom on several connected folding tables with pretty cloth covers that matched. Her real estate guru of a mother was threatening to buy Mona's mini-mansion at the golf course. Her parents didn't play golf, but they would soon need something the size of a castle to fit them all.

For a brief moment, Lexi tried to imagine John sitting next to her at one of those family brunches. He would fit in fabulously with her parents. They were pretty easy to get along with anyway, but all they would care about is if he loved her and the boys. Looking at John's expression, she had no doubt he would if she gave him a chance, and that made her back away. She didn't want to give him the impression she was thinking about it, even though she'd just pondered what it would be like. Noah had ruined any possibility of having a relationship with anyone else. Maybe if he hadn't come back and offered her a real chance, she could have had something with John, but now, she needed to tread carefully. She didn't want to lose her ranch manager, nor did she want to hurt his feelings. He was perfect, she trusted him, and she needed him now more than ever.

"John, you are the best help my big brother has ever given me." Riley had paid John's salary when he first hired him to help her. Since things had turned around and the ranch was paying for itself now, she'd taken on paying his salary without complaint. "I don't know what would become of the ranch without all that you do around here, but I think I can handle a little Christmas shopping on my own tonight. There won't be as many people out on a Monday evening, and my mom loves to wrap presents, so I'll drop them all at my parents' place when I'm done. They'll be safer there than here, especially now that I know the boys are on a covert gift-hunting mission." Lexi moved to the worktable to put space between John and her. Not knowing what else to say, she fiddled with the tarp covering the piece of glass.

He moved toward the door. "Okay, Ms. Burns. If you have no further need of me, I guess I'll see you in the morning."

Guilt washed over her. Was the disappointment that flickered in his eyes because of something she had said or done? Had he misinterpreted her actions or misread her feelings? She would never intentionally lead him on. If John did have feelings for her and she worked things out with Noah, how would that play out in the future? Lexi fiddled with the dried flowers on top of the workspace. Why did this have to come up now, after three years of lonely nights and solitary days when her boys were at school? Three years without any man in her life, and now she had two. *When it rains, it pours.*

The bar had been a mess when Noah opened that Monday morning, and even though it was a weekday, he'd been pulling triple duty through the afternoon and into the night. Lots of people were out holiday shopping, and the bar was booked solid for parties through New Year's Day. The main bartender who knew the ropes had called in sick, and when the cook and a hostess called in, too, Noah decided the flu must be going around.

He wanted to phone Lexi to hear her voice and find out when she would agree to see him again. She probably had no idea how hard it had been to kiss her goodnight and drive away after their date. He'd spent Sunday at the bar doing inventory, and though he couldn't stop thinking about her, he didn't call or text. Noah didn't want her to feel pressured, but hoped he'd given her a lot to think about.

That first time he'd taken her to dinner three years ago, they'd connected in a way that ended between the sheets. Maybe that was where he'd gone wrong. They'd hooked up so fast that he never had time to share his past. And then when she'd found out about his ex-wife, who wasn't legally his ex, things had unraveled from there. Everything good and bad that had happened led up to this moment, and he wanted to build a better future for them both.

It was late. He gripped his knee, massaging his leg as he fumbled with the top of the ibuprofen bottle. Noah wished he had something stronger, but he knew the dangers of addiction. If he'd taken a pill every time his leg felt like this, he'd certainly be an addict. Running a bar made him hyper-aware of the pitfalls that waited at the bottom of a bottle. He saw sensible men lose their shit after downing a few whiskeys. Some people were functional alcoholics. They'd come in after work every night and stay until close, but they never missed a day of labor. He mostly minded his business unless someone became unruly, but he'd sworn to himself long before the accident that he would handle his struggles without a crutch.

Thinking of crutches, Noah glared at his cane by the door. He hated that damn thing, but he still needed it at times. It was almost closing now, and Lexi would surely be in bed already. Noah stared longingly at his phone. He'd call her tomorrow and explain that today had been a nightmare. Hell, he'd have to come back extra early in the morning to get the bar restocked. As it was, he'd get the skeleton staff to clean up so they could all head home. Everyone had worked their tails off, and tonight had been as busy as Santa's sleigh on Christmas Eve. Though he wanted to see Lexi and hear her voice, what he needed most right now was sleep.

As Noah rose from the chair, he popped the two round tablets in his mouth and chased them with bottled water. Someone knocked on the thick wood door of his office.

"Come in!"

Hank's head poked around the door. "Thought I might catch you here."

Noah was more than surprised. "It's late."

Hank scratched his head. "Yeah, I do the closing most nights, too." He pointed his thumb behind him. "Over at Bubbles."

Noah grinned. "Sounds a little girly when you say it."

Hank chuckled. "Well, you came up with the name, so...."

"That's where you're wrong. Lexi came up with the name. And when she said it, it sounded sexy." Noah mused about the day she'd stopped by the vacant lot across from the old Hank's, and he'd told her his idea about the new bar. He'd been mesmerized by the sun shining down on her honey-gold hair and bluebonnet-colored eyes. Her smile had been infectious, and the way she'd talked about her love of champagne had sealed his fate. Though he didn't get the opportunity to build and open Bubbles, he was still a part of its creation.

Hank cleared his throat, looking uncomfortable as he approached the desk.

Noah waved at a chair. He still hadn't set foot in Bubbles, but he imagined Hank's office was a bit posher than the new Hank's.

Hank took a seat, leaned back in the chair, and propped one boot on his knee. "I was hoping to see you over at Bubbles one night. Is this place running you ragged?"

Noah sighed. His cousin had been more than fair, giving him a good percentage of the profits. Hank had invited him to see the place on several occasions, but Noah hadn't had the time—or the inclination to drop by. The apology and restitution for the money potentially lost should be enough to move on. With Hank's past record, the peace offering was not only unbelievable but about as good as it would ever get. Noah had forgiven him. Now it was time to truly let go. "The new Hank's keeps me busier than I'd like. When did Bubbles settle down and give you time to breathe?"

Hank laughed, slapping one knee. "It hasn't, but sometimes you gotta say, 'fuck it' and take time for yourself. Why don't you take Wednesday off next week and bring Alexa over? It's a little slower than the weekend, and it's classical night. We play nothing but symphony, opera, Baroque… hell, I don't know what they play, but it's soothing, and the ladies love it. Generally, it's a date night place on Wednesdays, but I think you'll like the atmosphere if you can tear yourself away from the sawdust."

Noah didn't know if that was a dig at the new Hank's Honky-Tonk's lack of refinement, but he wouldn't linger on it. His cousin had made an effort to make amends, and one day soon, Noah would have to step into Bubbles. What better time to do it than with Lexi on his arm—that is, if she said yes. The champagne lounge was a Magnolia hangout, and people would see them together. He had given her time to think, but he didn't plan on taking no for an answer. He'd seen the way she looked at him, and he knew she wanted to be with him as much as he wanted to be with her. Everything would be fine, as long as he didn't screw up. *Ready or not, Lexi gal, here I come.*

Chapter 31

Their one night together was hot enough to keep him burning for a lifetime, but he wasn't nearly satiated enough not to crave more. Roland was working in the office today, and as he reached for his coffee cup, he groaned to find it empty. Sitting behind his desk, thinking about his amazing night with Ginger had left him as erect as a flagpole, and now he would have to file another report before he could stand up to make his way to the coffeepot. It was almost lunchtime. Maybe he could catch Ginger at the café.

It had been a week since their hotel night together, and they hadn't exchanged more than a few texts. She'd been busy working two jobs and getting ready for the gingerbread competition. He didn't question the importance of her time at the diner. Anyone who lived in Magnolia knew that Melvina Nash, owner of the Cupcake Diner and Dive, was intensely competitive when it came to bake-offs. Her husband Riley had gone toe to toe with her a couple of times before they were married, and even a few times since. His wedding gift to her was the deed to the land next to the diner so she could build her dream bakery. It was hands down Roland's favorite place to go for food in Magnolia.

The Nash family were "good people," and Roland wouldn't dream of getting between Melvina and her new baker. Ginger had boasted to Melvina that her gingerbread was the best, and apparently, Melvina was willing to give her a chance to prove it. Cook, nanny, and now captain of the Cupcake Diner bake team, Ginger seemed to be a jack of all trades. Christmas was just around the corner, so he knew he needed to be patient with her schedule. Maddie was also working crazy hours at the diner, and she needed help with Kelsey, who kept both of her uncles busy. Besides, the holidays were always chaos at the station, with increased patrolling to keep drunk drivers off the roads.

"It's too bad you can't fetch coffee," he said to Rollo, who'd been accompanying him to work the past week. The cushiony, overstuffed bed he'd bought from Pet Land sat in the corner, but Rollo was belly up, twisted into a half-moon shape in the chair next to the windows. Roland had covered the ancient wingback chair with a blanket to keep the dog hair off it, but as Rollo hopped up and down, the blanket kept sliding to the floor, no matter how many times Roland tucked it around the chair.

"Damn, Karr, someone needs to buy that dog some underwear," the captain bellowed as he passed Roland's office.

Roland chuckled, looking at the pewter-colored dog that Kelsey referred to as blue. "Don't worry about him, Rollo. Captain Barnhart's just jealous."

"I heard that!" the captain called back from the break room.

Roland smiled and pointed at Rollo. "You da' man," he whispered.

Rollo woofed a loud affirmative.

"I heard that, too!" Barnhart bellowed again.

Roland took the dog on his daily three-mile runs, let him ride in the patrol car and took him to the diner when the weather was nice enough for Rollo to sit in the car. Roland had never thought he had time for a dog, but it was Rollo's boredom that led to chewing up things, and that had led to Roland taking the dog with him everywhere. In the presence of people, the dog was a perfect angel. He'd become the station's new mascot. Roland guessed it was true about a dog being a product of how you treated them—like people. The pit bull strutted through the station like he owned the place, and if Roland hadn't been so smitten with Ginger, he would have to admit that Rollo was a chick magnet.

Roland stood, grabbing his keys from the desk drawer. Without hesitation, the dog jumped to attention and hit the floor with four paws sliding in at his heel. Ears and tail up, he let Roland hook his leash to his fancy blue leather collar and trotted at his side. Rollo had an internal clock, and Roland didn't have to tell him it was lunchtime.

"Maria picked a fine time to get pregnant," Darcey muttered. "You'd think with Maurice in high school and his sister in junior high, that woman would be done with spittin' out babies."

Melvina shook her head. "Darcey Gallagher, don't you have silverware to wrap before your shift ends?"

The blonde waitress rolled her eyes at Ginger through the cook's window as she pushed another ticket under the wheel. The door dinged, and Darcey turned to check out the guest. "Damn, I know that man is old enough to be my daddy, but he is hot! I'd give him a lap dance for free, but watch this. I'm going to get him to give me a twenty." Darcey winked.

Ginger tried to see through the slot to the entrance, but she was too short. Darcey's five-ten stature wasn't her only physical asset. The girl was built like a Barbie doll, and Ginger knew there was no way those breasts were natural. She tried to avoid gossip, but it was impossible in a small town like Magnolia. Ginger overheard some of the older ladies talking about Darcey when she dropped off food at their tables. Apparently, the flirty blonde had taken a brief leave of absence after Melvina's brother-in-law, Raphe, broke up with her.

Rumor had it that the waitress did a little pole dancing for cash before finding her way back to the diner and community college. It was obvious the old tongue-wagging women wanted Ginger to tell Darcey they knew about her sordid past, but Ginger wasn't playing their game. Her mom and grandma used to do that with her aunt. Hell, it wasn't really gossip since Darcey often complained she should have kept stripping. Whipping her long blonde ponytail around, the young waitress said more than once that "The tips are way better, and I never had any complaints while walkin' around in a G-string." Ginger admired the waitress's sassy attitude about the town gossip. If she could let it roll off her back, could Ginger learn to do the same if word got out about her own sordid past?

Filling the next few orders was easy. It was the end of the lunch rush, and Ginger was ready to take a break. Darcey hadn't been at the cook's window in a while, so Ginger grabbed her drink and went out into the dining room. She paused at the soda fountain, filling her cup as she looked across the diner. Darcey was bent over the table with her boobs in a customer's face, or nearly. The blonde waitress's giggles rang out, and Ginger recognized the warm chuckle of the man being schmoozed. She couldn't stop herself. Within a few seconds, her feet found their way to the table. A crisp twenty-dollar bill lay on the ticket along with some change. Darcey had brought his change back with a to-go order, and it looked like he was getting up and leaving the twenty as an additional tip. Ginger tried to tamp down the burst of jealousy in her gut, wondering if Darcey had offered him a lap dance. The waitress couldn't be more than twenty, and Roland was twice her age.

"Ginger." He sounded surprised.

She plastered a smile on her face. "Roland." She tried to think of something else to say, but her mind was swirling with too many thoughts about him and Darcey playing patty-cake at the strip club. She picked up the dishes, and Darcey frowned at her.

"You don't have to bus tables. Maurice is here today."

"He went on break," Ginger shot back tersely.

Darcey's eyes narrowed. "I can get Officer Karr's dishes. If I were you, I'd take a break while you can. There'll be lots of work to prep for dinner."

Ginger didn't trust herself to speak, so she nodded and turned back toward the kitchen.

She heard Roland call after her. "Ginger, wait!"

She wanted to keep walking but figured the jealousy burning over her like jalapeno jelly-slime would be seen by everyone. It was irrational to feel this way about someone she'd just met, someone she'd only gone with on one date. *Someone I had seven orgasms with because his tongue and fingers must have written the Kama Sutra themselves.*

Turning back to him, she waited without walking back to the table. He closed the distance with his to-go order in hand, and Ginger noted the crisp twenty still sitting on the table. Darcey was already moving in to pick it up.

He reached out and touched Ginger's arm. "I was hoping to see you here, but Darcey said you were busy."

She wanted to roll her eyes and huff like a teenager, but she managed a look of indifference. "I *am* busy. I came out to help clean up the dining room while the order wheel was empty."

He nodded. "I understand, and I don't want to hold you up, but I wanted to see if we might get together when you get off work. I could pick you up at the ranch." His eyes glittered with hope. The rich brown irises were veiled by his thick lashes as he looked down to where his hand touched her arm still. He let his fingers slide down to her hand, where they squeezed her fingers gently.

He was asking her out. She needed to let this jealousy thing go. Maybe he was generous by nature and hadn't been flirting. He couldn't exactly control who hit on him, and no one could control Darcey's flirtatious nature. Besides, he was asking her out, not Darcey, and he was holding her hand in the middle of the dining room. "I can't. I promised Lexi I would watch the boys while she goes shopping again tonight. It's been hard filling the kid's lists this year. Apparently, the stores are all out of Space Ninja Heroes."

Melvina poked her head out of the kitchen door. "Ginger?"

Ginger looked at Roland with regret. She'd been looking forward to seeing him again, and she wanted to finish what they'd started in bed.

He was sexy standing there in his uniform, giving her a crooked grin. "Want some babysitting company? I'm good with kids. I can give them my Stranger Danger talk."

Ginger chuckled at the thought of Roland sitting Lexi's boys down at the kitchen table, telling them to be wary of strangers.

"Is that a yes?"

"Ginger!" Melvina's voice carried over the restaurant. "I've got four to-go orders I need help with, please."

"Gotta go." Ginger headed for the kitchen and was at the door before she turned back and looked at Roland, standing there with his take-out food in hand, looking bewildered. "Yes. Come by around seven. But I'll warn you. Dinner is hotdogs and tater tots."

He pressed his lips together, nodding. "Okay. I'll bring the wine."

Chapter 32

He wasn't sure what he expected when he asked to help babysit Lexi's three boys, but Roland had to admit he was having fun. It was dark when he'd arrived carrying two large pizzas and a bottle of red wine. The boys had been ecstatic about the pizza, and after dinner, they had begged Ginger to make them hot fudge sundaes, and like any good babysitter, she complied.

Ginger pointed the ice cream scoop at him. "You want one?"

He shook his head. "Naw, that's all right. I think I had one too many slices of pizza with tater tots."

"I told you I was making dinner." She cocked her hip to one side as she fussed, wearing a knowing smile.

He looked at the hotdogs swimming in the pot of water as he passed the stove. "I know. That's why I brought pizza."

She laughed. "I admit, I haven't had a hotdog since I saw the Padres."

Roland's eyes lit up. "You're a baseball fan?"

She waved a hand. "A friend gave me tickets."

"Were they playing the Astros?"

She put three glass bowls on the counter. "Dodgers."

"In L.A.?"

Ginger suddenly looked like she'd confessed a secret. There was a moment when the scoop hovered over the ice cream, then she continued to fill the bowls. "Yeah, in L.A."

"Were you visiting?"

She paused as she put the lid on the container and put it back in the freezer. He could hear the boys in the living room playing with their basset hound, Chef.

"I—um, was there, for a time," she said.

He nodded, getting the feeling she didn't want to talk about it. "Well, the Astros have been on fire. If you ever want to catch a game, my cousin has season tickets. I'm sure I could buy some of his seats. He never makes all the games."

She turned to him, smiling. "That'd be cool."

Was that relief in her eyes? What was hiding in L.A.? Had she dated a baseball player? God, how would he compete with that?

"I always wanted to go to California. My brother, Luke, made it out of Magnolia first and then Maddie ran off with that loser—." He stopped himself. There wasn't any reason for him to air his sister's dirty laundry. Besides, maybe Ginger was hiding out from some loser, too. He really didn't know much about her past.

"I mean, life sort of happened, and Dad needed me after we lost Mom to cancer. He had a few tough years and then some more. A couple months ago, we moved him into a senior living apartment. It's smaller, easier to manage and has caregivers to help, but Maddie and I make the rounds at least every other day."

Ginger balanced the three bowls in her hands like a practiced waitress. "What about your brother?"

"He fell in love and chased a gal to New Mexico. They opened up an art gallery, and he adopted her kid." Pausing, he thought about how much to share. "I think things fell apart recently, and Luke's here trying to figure it out."

Ginger scooted around him and set the bowls on the table. She called for the boys and returned to the kitchen. "What about the adopted kid?"

Roland eased onto the barstool, crooking one leg to rest his boot on the rail. "He's grown now. Went off to college, and, well, things changed between Luke and the kid's mother, but Kirin is still Luke's son. I'm sure they'll find a way to work it all out."

Ginger retrieved her glass of wine and sat at the island with him, watching the boys laugh and eat their dessert through the open alcove to the TV room. "It happens a lot."

Now was as good of a time as any. "So…what's your story? I mean, you're beautiful. Lots of guys must ask you out. Have you ever been married?"

Her eyes widened with surprise. "I—uh, I've never been married, and I'm too busy for relationships."

He couldn't figure her out. She didn't look like a cook or a baker. She didn't look like the kind of woman to be single, and most of all, she didn't look like the kind of gal that would stay in Magnolia.

His line of questioning was making her wine taste bitter, but Ginger couldn't put the glass down for fear of fidgeting if she didn't have something in her hand.

"Were you in the restaurant business before you moved to Magnolia?"

Ginger tried to stick to the truth as close as she could. "I was a barista."

Roland shook his head. "Don't take this the wrong way, but you don't look the part."

Ginger knew it was his lawman training that sent the questions marching out naturally, and he probably wasn't trying to nail her to the wall, but as the sweat beaded on her forehead, she felt trapped. The door off the kitchen was only three steps away, and she opened it to let some fresh air in. Ginger waved a dishtowel around, trying to create a breeze. It was a cool night, and the wind that rushed over her was a balm against the warmth of the kitchen.

"Ginger?" Roland's voice was quiet with concern.

She was irritated. "What is a waitress, cook, baker, barista person supposed to look like? I mean, are you embarrassed to date a woman who still hasn't figured it all out yet? Maybe I like cooking. It's relaxing."

He glanced at the boys, who had all finished their ice cream and were now staring at them.

Ginger flushed with embarrassment. "Is everyone finished?"

They nodded in unison.

"Then go brush your teeth and get ready for bed, and you guys can watch one more episode of that space cartoon thing you love." Every time Ginger babysat them, they always watched *Ninjas from Mars*. Thank goodness they hadn't discovered *Seducing Saturn*. It was too old for them, anyway, but Lexi limited their television time when she was home, so Ginger hoped her secret would stay safe.

The mere mention of their favorite cartoon was all the encouragement the boys needed to jump up and run to their rooms.

Roland approached her slowly. "I don't care what job you do as long as you're happy. I think that's what I was getting at. You don't look happy when I see you at the diner. I was asking because I care about you, and I want to help."

Ginger nodded but didn't trust herself to speak. She liked the bakery, but admittedly it wasn't where she belonged. She guessed her disappointment of recent events showed. Roland was kind, and it was natural to ask questions of anyone's past, especially when you were getting to know them in the biblical sense. Heat ran down her spine at the thought of having sex with Roland tonight. She'd bought a large box of condoms at the drugstore, and they were burning a hole in her nightstand. It was time to end the inquisition and save the mood. She wanted to get laid.

"I appreciate you wanting to help. I really do, but can we change the subject? I'm not ready to talk about my job right now."

The boys were in their pajamas in the TV room, and it made her smile to hear them giggle and make space noises from the couch. Roland smiled at her, moving in closer. As his lips brushed hers in a slow, chaste kiss, she could only think of one question to ask. "You want to sleep over?"

His voice was husky when he answered, "I thought you'd never ask."

Chapter 33

Lexi came home right after the boys went to bed. Ginger and Roland helped her bring in the bags, then headed out. It was a brisk evening but not freezing. Ginger held the key up to the four-wheeler. "You want to drive?"

Roland's eyes lit up. "Now that's what I'm talking about. Is the cottage far?"

She pointed at the tree-lined trail. "It's about a ten-minute walk or a two-minute ride."

He took the keys and hopped on the ATV, making room for her on the back. "Does the trail go farther? Can we extend the ride?"

Ginger smiled as she snaked her leg over the four-wheeler and snugged her hips against his backside. "The trails go all around the property, and it's pretty fun when the boys and I go out, but I was hoping you might be in the mood for a different sort of ride."

He glanced at her over his shoulder, his eyes glowing with excitement. "I'm so in the mood." He revved the engine, and in less than two minutes they were at the she-shed. Roland parked the vehicle and Ginger hopped off. Grabbing her hand, he tugged her to the front door and asked for the key. His quick work unlocking it made Ginger giggle.

She turned on the light, using the dimmer switch to adjust the mood. The place was so cozy and romantic. When she'd first arrived in Magnolia, she thought it was the perfect retreat to be alone. Standing there with Roland at her back, trailing kisses down her neck as his arms wound around her middle, she had an entirely different feeling about the place. She could hear the water from the creek trickling outside. The wood logs set in the fireplace were ready to light. Should she set the mood with a fire and ask him if he wanted a drink?

Roland turned her toward him, lifting her chin. He looked her in the eyes as his mouth dipped to hers, taking her lips in a gentle kiss. She pressed herself against him, and his hand slipped beneath her shirt, cupping one breast as the other pulled at the hem of her top. Relieved of her shirt, she started unbuttoning his, then pushed her hands over his strong, chiseled chest. The crisp hair beckoned her fingers to trace lazy circles around his nipples, and she couldn't resist placing kisses on each hardened pebble. Moaning with anticipation, he shrugged free of the sleeves and slid his hands down her torso to unfasten her jeans.

Pushing off her slip-on boots with her feet, she stepped out of them as he slid the soft material down her thighs. She stepped out of her pants and felt the cool air rush over her mostly naked form. A shiver ran down her spine as he gazed at her standing in the middle of the cottage. Wrapping his arms around her to keep them warm, Roland whispered into her ear. "Should I light the fire?"

Ginger nodded. They could start their evening on the couch and work their way to the bedroom after the cabin warmed up. As he lit the fire, Ginger found the remote to the mini-split unit that heated the place. It wouldn't take long. She spread the quilt over the couch and then grabbed the faux mink throw to cover them with. Roland returned to her, and she held the blanket up in invitation.

She bit her bottom lip as she stared up at him. "Uh-uh. No pants or boots allowed."

Roland gave her a devilish grin as he quickly shucked his boots and jeans before sliding under the blanket clad only in his boxer briefs. Taking up where he'd left off, he kissed her again, slowly at first and then deeper as they sank into the cushions. He kissed her neck and released the clip of her lacy bra, worshiping her breasts with his exquisite mouth and tongue. Memories of his expertise from the hotel made her pulse race with anticipation, and her thighs parted invitingly.

His hands trailed a heated path to her silk panties, pushing his fingers below the elastic band and brushing the thatch of hair he'd praised so many times. As he pressed against her nub, sparks erupted inside, and she lifted her hips to him for better access. The fire crackled and popped in the grate, mimicking the explosion she felt building within. His fingers parted her wet layers and thrust deep inside of her. At first, he used one long appendage before adding another, filling her almost to capacity and making her beg for what she really needed. She wanted all of him, but his hand moving against her as his fingers pulsed in and out, over and over, made her too weak to stop. The orgasm beat its way to the surface, breaking free as she let out a guttural squeal. The pleasure was just too intense to bite back.

"Oh God, yes," she called out, bucking into him. When he slid to his knees and took her in his mouth, she let him taste her with his tongue. Roland circled her bud and suckled at her center until she couldn't hold back any longer. As she cried out for all the world to hear a second time, she silently thanked God for making the cottage far away from any other structure on the ranch. As the sensation of his kiss became too much to bear in the wake of her satisfaction, she started to giggle with satiated euphoria. Roland Karr knew exactly how to ring her bell. *Kama Sutra, eat your heart out.*

It was well after midnight, and Roland knew he had to work tomorrow, but the woman was insatiable, and it turned him on. He had never made love with anyone for this length of time, ever. As he rolled the fourth condom over his hard shaft, he said a silent prayer to God that he could live up to expectations. Watching Ginger buck and moan beneath him was all it took to get in the saddle again. Her tight sheath gripped his cock, and he could feel her excitement dripping onto his fingers as he grasped her buttocks. Damn, she was wet. The rhythm had them both moaning with pleasure, and he drove himself into her until she cried out loud enough to wake the rooster in the hen house. He thrust once more, and the sizzle that had worked its way between his shoulder blades shot down his spine and pushed at his testicles for release. He exploded inside her. The orgasm was intense. As he hovered above her with his head craned back, he could only hope his expression looked as hot as it felt. Thinking about it, he couldn't help chuckling in the aftermath. It had nothing to do with the overstimulation of his cock or the way she flexed around his erection once more. He felt giddy, elated, on top of the world, and he didn't know if he could ever get enough of her.

Ginger played with the edges of his hair that fell across his forehead. The feathery light touch of her fingers made him push his cheek into her hand and kiss her palm. "You're amazing," he whispered. "Too good to be true. A superstar." He breathed heavily as he withdrew and rolled to the side so he didn't squish her. He couldn't help but chuckle at how loud they both had been.

The moonlight streamed in through the window across her face as she turned toward him. Her forehead furrowed, and he wondered what was suddenly worrying her.

"Then why are you laughing?" Her voice was unsure.

Roland rushed to explain as he sat up on one elbow, looking at her. He rubbed a hand over her exposed shoulder. "Oh no. I wasn't laughing at you. I had this image of Lexi's three boys rushing to their window to spy the coyote making all that noise tonight."

Ginger's mouth opened as her eyes widened. She took the small cushion from under her head and tossed it at him. "I do not sound like a coyote!"

Roland put a hand over his forehead as he shook his head. "That's not what I meant, either. How about a she-wolf, lioness, tigress...." He waited until she grinned at him. "They're a little young for the birds and the bees talk yet, and I'm pretty sure anyone within a mile from here could hear us." He gave her a lustful grin. "You are sexy as hell, lady."

Ginger put both hands over her face and fell back onto the pillows. "Sorry, I know I'm loud, but it felt like heaven. If I suppress the noise, the feeling isn't as good." She peeked at him through her parted fingers. "There was a point where I thought we might spontaneously combust." She began waving her hands in a fanning motion.

"I'm not complaining. You can make as much noise as you want. It's great for my ego." He took her hands and leaned closer to kiss her. As she relaxed and kissed him back, he moved on top of her, loving the way her body naturally arched into his, as if they were made to lie together like this for eternity. He hadn't planned on going another round, but his body was awake, and by the moist heat greeting him, Ginger was, too.

Roland awoke to Ginger licking the inside of his calf, and she was moving upward. They'd had another marathon night, but who was he to cry mercy. His shaft was at full mast, and there was nothing better than morning sex to start your day. Sunshine pooled across the bed, and he opened his thighs to allow her access to the family jewels. She was licking him with the bare tip of her tongue, darting out at him like she was licking tiny pieces of confetti off his body. Roland gave her an encouraging moan as he spread his legs wider, hoping she would climb up and take a ride. He knew Ginger was talented, but this light tongue touching experiment wasn't doing much to satisfy his raging hard-on.

"Come on, baby, you're killing me here. Higher, harder, faster." He groaned with frustration as she jabbed him with another light dart of her tongue.

"What was that?" Ginger came from the doorway that led to the small bathroom. As she stood in the doorway with her silk robe open and the ties dangling at the tops of her beautifully toned thighs, realization hit him hard where it counted. The light tongue tip that finally reached his ball area was not Ginger! He threw the covers back and leapt out of bed naked. "What the hell?"

Ginger burst out laughing, until Roland grabbed the broom next to the small refrigerator.

"Stop!" She put herself between him and the bed. "It's Igor, my pet." She still held both hands out to ward him off.

Roland was trying to process what she was saying, but the green thing with a horny back and long green tail was slowly turning around and giving him a mischievous, tongue-darting leer.

"Put the broom down, Roland. Igor is my friend. He only wanted to share your warmth." She started giggling again hysterically. Between great guffaws, she managed to squeak out, "Besides, I heard you give him specific instructions."

Roland was too busy inspecting his junk to laugh. He wondered if he could catch a disease from a lizard touching his balls. "What kind of person has a lizard as a pet?"

Ginger's laughter finally subsided as she sat on the bed, taking Igor in her arms to pet him. "He's not a lizard. He's an iguana, and he has feelings, so settle down. I want him to like you." She continued to hold the iguana and stroke his back as if he were a fluffy Siamese cat or a French bulldog.

Roland knew that people were afraid of pit bulls like Rollo, but he'd grown fond of the sleek brute of a dog. The truth was, there wasn't a bigger baby in the whole world. That dog loved people and cried whenever he was left alone. Roland hadn't wanted a pet, but he admitted now that he really loved having a dog. It was hard to imagine what would have happened to the poor mutt if Maddie had taken him to the shelter. Roland cringed. Wasn't that what he'd originally suggested? So, Igor was a pet, like Rollo, and apparently, Ginger thought he was a dog. It pulled at his empathy strings, and he grabbed his boxer briefs from the floor. Once his manhood was secure, he sat on the bed next to Ginger.

"Does he bite?" He reached out tentatively to pet the green, scaly creature.

"Only the men I sleep with."

Roland pulled his hand back, and Ginger laughed again.

"I'm teasing. Igor hasn't met many of my friends, but Lexi's boys beg to visit him often. Apparently, Chef likes him too, but maybe a little too much. Igor gets tired of all the dog slobber." She held the reptile out to Roland. "He's safe. I promise. He's only a year-and-a-half old, so he's really still a baby, and he likes to give kisses, as you have recently learned."

Roland smirked, then grinned, reaching again for the iguana. "A baby? What is he, twenty-four inches long already? And I thought reptiles were all cold-blooded with no emotions."

"Some people say so, but Igor and I are best buds. He really gets me, and besides, my condo wouldn't allow me to have a cat or a dog. Igor was great at hiding out, sometimes too well. One time, my neighbor found him on the roof outside his window. Luckily, he was a zoologist, and he knew Igor was a pet who must have crawled out through another window."

Roland chuckled, watching Igor's tongue dart out, touching his hand in various places. "So, Houdini found his way home."

Ginger gave him an aha look. "That would have been a great name for him." She took Igor back to the large glass terrarium. Dropping him in, she shook a little ball with a bell. "He likes to play," she explained. "There's a treat inside."

Roland nodded. How had he missed the huge glass tank between the window and the bed? "You got plans today?"

"It's my day off from the diner, but I promised I'd watch the boys."

"Perfect. Mind if I join you? We can take them by the house to meet *my* pet. I have to work later, but we can hang out for a little bit."

Ginger nodded. "Let me guess. Big pit bull with a shiny blue collar."

He couldn't hide his surprise. "How'd you know?"

Ginger chuckled. "Maddie showed a picture to us when she was looking to find him a home. I guess she found one."

Roland nodded with a smile. "Yeah. He grew on me. Now, I should tell you before you see my place that it used to look nice before Rollo ate the couch, dug up the plants and stained my wood floors."

Ginger put her hands to her mouth. "Oh no, and you still kept him? That's sweet." She approached the bed, straddling him as she lowered herself onto his lap. "You're a good cop, Roland. The world could use more men like you."

He kissed her gently as he pushed her shoulder-length hair from her face. "You're pretty great yourself, Iguana Momma."

She laughed, and he rolled her over, pinning her to the bed. Her laughter was replaced with a small gasp as he nipped at an exposed nipple and raised his knee to press between the juncture of her thighs. She spread her legs, opening to him. It was all the invitation he needed. Igor and his testicle-wash be damned.

Chapter 34

It was a beautiful Wednesday afternoon, and this time they both had the day off. Ginger was watching the boys, who were out for Christmas break, and Roland was taking them all to a movie. They drove by his place first to pick up his niece and for the group to play with Rollo. After meeting the pit bull the previous Sunday, the boys were wild about the dog, who bounced around like a ping-pong ball. They played in the backyard together with Kelsey for an hour before leaving to catch the matinee.

As Roland bought the tickets, Ginger waited with the boys at the concession stand. The teen who scooped the popcorn stared at Ginger with round glassy eyes. "Do you know who you look like?"

Ginger's heart thudded in her chest. Luckily, the kids were eyeing the candy counter and not paying attention to the conversation going on overhead. Ginger tried to ignore the question. "How about two large popcorns, extra butter and whatever candy they want?" She pointed to the four kids standing in a row with their eyes glued to the chocolate-covered treats.

The girl behind the counter persisted, calling her friend from the next register. "Darla, come look! Tell me who her movie star look-alike is."

Ginger looked over her shoulder, watching Roland as he walked toward them, waving the tickets. "Emma Stone," Ginger had quickly interjected, trying to dissuade any further guessing.

"Oh my God!" Darla blurted out with a teenage squeal. "Tonya, she's a dead ringer for Dallas in *Seducing Saturn!*"

Shit, shit, shit! Ginger needed to think fast. Turning to the kids, she pointed to Roland. "You guys go grab Roland and get the best seats before all the other kids snap them up. I'll get the candy and drinks." To her relief, the kids told her their drink order and candy preferences, then darted toward Roland, pulling him away to the usher, who was taking tickets.

Ginger gave the girls a blank look. "I don't know that show. Sorry. Can I get a—"

She was interrupted by Kelsey, who tugged on her cardigan. "Ginger, you need a ticket to get in." Ginger smiled at Roland's niece and thanked her for the ticket before watching her run back to the group.

Turning her focus back to the two star-struck teens, Ginger said, "Sorry, I'm really in a hurry, girls, so if we could just fill this order?" She gave them a brilliant smile to soften her request.

Darla snorted and waved her hand as she went back to her register. "If this was anyplace but Magnolia, I would swear it was her, but who'd want to hang out here, even if the world was clamoring over some stupid video. The boyfriend said it was an accident anyway. Not like it was her fault."

Tonya returned with the popcorn and tossed the candy and drinks in a big plastic crate. Popcorn toppled onto the counter, and the girl's bright fingernails flicked it away. Ginger handed her cash for the items and scurried to find Roland and the kids.

As they walked out of the theater, she heard the two girls who worked the concession call out, "Bye, Dallas!"

Roland looked at her quizzically. "Who's that?"

Ginger ignored the girls and hurried to the exit.

"Hm?" she asked innocently.

"Back there. The girls behind the counter. I think they were trying to say something to you. Someone you know from Dallas?"

Ginger shrugged her shoulders. "Sorry, I wasn't paying attention." Her phone vibrated in her purse, giving her the perfect distraction. She fished it out to look. It was a text from Melvina that the diner was slammed, and Maria was sick.

It was hard to say goodbye to Roland when he dropped them off at the ranch, but the boys were getting picked up by their grandmother, and Ginger didn't mind filling in for an extra shift. She could use the money. The night manager was having terrible morning sickness, even at night, and her oldest kid, Maurice, was doing everything he could to fill in the gaps. He worked at the diner and at Melvina's brother's place around his school schedule. Fresh Start was as busy as the diner most days, keeping the teen on the go.

Maurice was busy busing tables when she entered the diner. She waved at him as he called out. "Hey, Ginger."

"Hi, Maurice. Working again?" She smiled. "What do you plan to do with all that money? So many shifts!" she teased.

His face shone with pride and excitement. "I'm saving to buy a crib for the new baby. I'm hoping it's a boy. One sister is enough."

Ginger admired Maurice's maturity and dedication to helping his family. It was obvious that the people who worked at the diner were more than employees to the Nashes. They were one big, happy family. They looked out for each other, and that made Ginger feel warm and fuzzy inside when she thought of being a part of it. The community atmosphere made her rethink her life up until now. Sure, she had regrets, but didn't everyone? Acting had been her passion, but what had fame really done for her? All the money she'd saved was gone—spent on a pricy PR firm to battle the bad publicity and her mother's care. At the end of the day, she had nothing to show for all her success except memories stained by the sex tape's debut on the internet.

She had planned to return to acting after the media flare-up died down. But did she really need to go back? Maybe she didn't want to bake or cook for the rest of her life, but she could do other things that might make her happy. She'd have to think about what, but she was sure other opportunities existed. With all the shifts she was putting in at the diner, plus the wage that Lexi was paying her, it wouldn't be any time at all before her nest egg was big enough to move on. She'd never lived without the nagging responsibility of rent and utilities. Living at Lexi's had so many perks, and it would be hard to give up hanging out with her and laughing with the boys.

Ginger's mind swung back and forth from her career in L.A. to Lexi's ranch and the boys, to the free room and board at the cottage, to Roland's perfect body lying in her full-size bed. His fit form had looked massive against the crisp white sheets, and he was too masculine for the lacy dust ruffle and patchwork quilt, but she'd never get tired of waking up to that sort of perfection. She chuckled to herself as she thought of Igor's mischievous adventure last week that sent Roland jumping from her bed.

The night waitress, Roberta, popped up in the cook's window as she attached a ticket to the wheel and spun it to Ginger. "What's so funny?"

Ginger laughed harder at the memory of the look on Roland's face, then gained control of herself as she looked at the ticket. "Nothing. Just something with my pet, Igor. He's so funny."

"Dog or cat?" Roberta blew a bubble, then popped it back in her mouth.

"Iguana." Ginger laughed again as Roberta's mouth dropped open, almost losing her gum.

"Ew!" Not waiting to hear more, the waitress left to attend another table.

As she filled the order for Roberta, Ginger let her mind wander back to the movie with Roland, his niece and the boys. What had the concession girl meant by "the boyfriend said it was an accident?" Had Kirk made a public statement?

She'd stopped searching online after the tape went viral, and she hadn't checked in with her lawyer in weeks. It would be humiliating to stand up in court and tell her side of the story. Laws against leaking sex tapes carried little jail time and a laughably small fine. Plus, she figured courts didn't hold a lot of empathy for celebrities, especially not ones who already had sex-symbol personas. Sure, Kirk was an idiot, but she didn't want to be the one to put him behind bars. It sucked to lose her career, and he deserved to make amends for what he'd done, but she didn't want to prosecute him. A civil suit would almost certainly be tossed since she hadn't reported him to the police.

Still, karma had a way of coming back around. Kirk would pay for his misdeed some other way, but not through her.

Chapter 35

Lexi was relieved when Noah called to ask her out again. Their schedules had been busy, with her Christmas shopping and his work at the bar. She wasn't sure about her decision to say yes, since he'd invited her to a Wednesday night of classical music at Bubbles. It sounded relaxing, but the whole town would be tongue-wagging about them before breakfast.

She didn't think she was ready for her family to know yet, especially Ran, who had been with her the night she found out Noah was married. Her other brother, Raphe, had been watching the boys at her house when Hank drove her home and kissed her in the driveway. In the weeks following the incident, her big brother Riley had given her the "if you need someone to talk to speech". Lexi's parents had heard from all three of her big brothers about the heartbreak, and they'd quietly let her know they were there for her if she needed them. She never did speak about it directly, but the gossip was sure to have made its way to their ears, leaving them with a bad opinion of Noah for leaving Magnolia and breaking her heart.

Lexi was a mature woman with three half-grown boys. She could make her own decisions, and she shouldn't be ashamed to be seen with Noah. There was nothing wrong with being friends, and so far, their relationship had been strictly platonic, except for the kissing.

As she rummaged through her closet, looking for her little black cocktail dress that would fit the occasion, her hand touched the emerald-green dress she'd worn to the opening of Bubbles. The night she'd secretly hoped to see Noah but had run into Hank instead. It was that same night Hank asked her to take the letter to Dallas, and apparently, the trip had made an impact on Noah. Should she wear it again? The color was perfect, and it was almost Christmas. As she pulled the dress from her closet, she snagged a pair of neutral-colored strappy heels. Platonic or not. There wasn't any reason she couldn't look her best.

The phone rang, and Lexi would have avoided the call from her mother, but she had already picked up the boys for the night, and she might need something. "Hey, Mom, what's up?"

"I wanted to tell you about a new listing. I got a call from Rhonda Fitzgerald. She owns that empty shop at the end of Main Street's plaza. I know it's not in the center, but it's right next to the parking area, which means people would have to pass your store to get to the antique shop and Yarn Barn."

Lexi groaned. She'd already told her mom she wasn't ready, but apparently, her mom wasn't listening. "Mom. Now's not the time."

Maybe this summer when the boys are out of school, she thought, or better yet, next year when the boys go back to school.

"Christmas will be over in a few weeks, and you know people are broke after the holidays. If I open a shop and it tanks, I'll lose money I have earmarked for the ranch."

"Darling, you have got to spend money to make money, and if you need some funds to get started, you know your father and I would be more than—."

Lexi cut her off. "I gotta go, Mom. I'm late. Can we talk about this later?"

"Where are you going?"

It was an innocent enough question. When Ginger dropped off the boys at the ranch and her mom picked them up earlier, Lexi had been wearing yoga pants and a t-shirt. It was before she'd rushed to take a shower and blow-dry her hair. She'd purposely not mentioned that she had a date tonight because she didn't want to go through the twenty questions her mother would ask. She didn't want to lie, either, and her hesitation to answer created an awkward silence. "I um, I'm going out for a bit with a friend."

"Oh." Her mother paused as if she didn't want to spook Lexi from finally going on a date. "I didn't realize. Well, don't let me keep you from going out with…." She let her words trail off, waiting for Lexi to supply the name of said friend.

She wasn't playing that game with her mother tonight. "If the boys are all good, I'll see you tomorrow. Night, Mom." Guilt squeezed her heart a little as she hung up. Her parents were everything to her. They'd been supportive, understanding and the best drop-in babysitters whenever she asked. Lexi knew they wanted to see her get back out there and live her life. They'd often hinted that the boys would benefit by seeing her happy and that it wouldn't hurt having a male role model around. She should have said it was only a second date and given her mom a small thrill of hope. After all, there might actually be something thrilling that would come from time spent with Noah. Lexi assured herself that she would tell her family soon after she was sure where this thing was going.

Walking into Bubbles with Lexi on his arm made Noah feel like he was soaring. He'd been worrying about tonight, wondering if the visit would make him regret the past. He loved what the new Hank's Honky-Tonk had become, and it was the largest bar with a decent menu in the southern half of the state. But Bubbles had been his first dream, and having to give it away had been emotionally tough.

Moving with Lexi through the lounge behind the hostess made his heart swell with pride. All heads turned as they passed, appreciating how beautiful Lexi looked tonight in her emerald cocktail dress. The past evaporated when she was by his side. He couldn't wait to show her how important she was to him and how he wanted to share a life with her.

Noah had bought a ring before ever leaving Dallas, but he knew it was too soon to pop the question when he first got back to Magnolia. But was it still too soon? Undoubtedly, she'd say no if he went too fast. Noah was itching to put the diamond on her finger and tell everyone she was his, that he was hers, and that there would never be another woman for him to love besides Lexi. All he wanted in the world was her and her boys in his life, and God help him, he wanted to have more children with her. The time he'd spent with his sister and her girls had shown him kids could be a pleasure. He wanted to love Lexi and build a family together.

Noah ordered a bottle of the best champagne, and it wasn't long before people were dropping by to say hello. After the third visitor to their table left, she gave him a look of distress. He squeezed her hand and gave her a reassuring smile. "I swear, you won't regret being seen with me."

Lexi gave him a weak smile and a nod as she took a sip of champagne. Her hand shook a little, giving away her discomfort. It occurred to him that his need to have her by his side as he confronted the ghosts from his past might have been a selfish maneuver. He wanted to kick himself for not thinking it through.

"Hey, Lexi. I'm sorry. If this makes you uncomfortable, we can go. Hank asked me to come by so many times, I thought it would be great for us to come here together. Let's go somewhere else. Back to the Grand in The Woodlands? Or, I'll take you to dinner in Houston, instead—anywhere you want to go. Just name the place. I don't care where we end up. I only want to be with you."

The scrape of metal against the hard floor made them both look up at their new visitor. "You better say all the right things, Noah Harding, after hiding out in Dallas. I didn't know who you were the other night, but my niece told me about you tucking tail and running away from this gal. You should be ashamed, and you almost lost this beautiful young lady to that lousy gutter-snipe cousin of yours. He may look like a young version of Elvis, but that ego of his is bigger than Santa's three-X britches!"

Noah tried not to spit out the champagne he'd just sipped. He hadn't met the infamous Ms. Rosie until the other night at Hank's. From what Lexi told him, the woman had a reputation for speaking her mind and tonight, she lived up to the stories. He tried to swallow the tail-tucking insult and focus on her deeper concern. With a calm voice, he held up his glass of champagne. "Cheers to that, Ms. Bush."

The flaming red hair, combed upward in a spiky cut, looked like that famous chef he'd seen on the cooking channel while TV surfing. The style made the older woman look formidable with her matching color flame lipstick that went well outside the lines of her lips. "It's Rosie. Ms. Bush sounds too presidential and a little too private if you get my drift."

Rosie stared directly at Noah's crotch, making him wilt a little into the booth. "Okay, Ms. Rosie. I appreciate your honest observation, and I agree. I'm a lucky man to have the company of such a wonderful lady tonight."

"Tonight?" Rosie inched her walker closer with a shake and rattle of the metal frame. "You better get your head out of your ass and pucker those lips of yours with a promise that will matter. This pretty lady is too old to wait on your less-than-silver tongue. Step up to bat, man, before another player comes along and steals home!"

A pretty blonde he recognized from Hank's appeared behind Rosie and grabbed the walker, turning it around. "Aunt Rosie! If you don't get your butt back at our table right now, I'm going to ground you from ladies' night for three months!"

Rosie muttered a salty curse beneath her breath then turned back to Noah, giving him a two-finger pointing motion from her eyes to his that said she would be watching him. He would have laughed, but she probably had a pistol in that little fanny pack strapped to her hips like The Duke.

Rosie's brow furrowed, and it was obvious she was weighing out her prospects, then finally, she harumphed, grabbed the handles of her walker, and began to scoot back to her table. The niece mouthed an, "I am so sorry," before quickly following behind the older woman. Noah wasn't sure if it was the way Rosie usually walked or if she was half-lit, but she tilted precariously to one side, catching herself with the walker and swung back to the opposite hip. There were three empty glasses sitting at her table where she sat down, so he figured alcohol must have loosened her tongue and her swagger.

Lexi giggled, making a small snort behind her champagne flute. Eyes glittering with humor, she offered, "Don't worry. As I told you before, Ms. Rosie is full of advice. She's the town's...." Lexi stopped suddenly, glanced around, then leaned in. "Well, I would say gossip, but that's not really the word I'm looking for. Let's just say she has a license to tell it like it is, and no one disputes her candor, except maybe her niece. Of course, there was that time when Mona got after her for pulling a shotgun on Eli's wife."

Noah's mouth opened in shock. "Are you serious?"

"As a heart attack. Be glad Ms. Rosie was only giving you a slight set down."

"You don't think I have a silver tongue?"

Lexi rolled her eyes. "Out of all that, questioning your tongue is all you care about?"

Noah laughed, then sobered as he looked at her with more than comical banter. "I don't think my tongue is to be questioned. At least not by you." He dipped his head toward her neck and kissed her earlobe. Lexi shuddered as his warm lips touched the sensitive area below her lobe. With a quick intake of breath, she moved back. "Not here, Noah. Please."

He berated himself for misbehaving. Lexi was already nervous about being seen together as a couple, and here he was, mauling her at the table. But dammit, he found it hard to keep his hands off her. She was gorgeous. Noah could feel the presence of another visitor at the edge of his peripheral vision. *Damn.*

"I'm really glad you could make it, Cuz." Hank nodded to Lexi. "And you, too."

Noah noticed Hank hadn't used Lexi's name. Was there something to that? He remained seated but shook Hank's proffered hand. The booth inhibited him from standing, and the effect of kissing Lexi a few moments ago was enough to keep him in his seat until his mind and body could cool off. "Glad to finally see the place."

Hank tilted his head. "Is it everything you imagined?"

Noah wondered if Hank was still talking about Bubbles, or if he referred to the three of them sitting in such close proximity without Noah killing Hank for kissing Lexi three years earlier. His pulse raced and his jaw muscle worked, but he reminded himself that a lot of water had passed under the bridge since that night. Hank had moved mountains to make things right, and Lexi said they were friends and no more. Noah needed to trust her. Correction, he did trust her. Taking a deep breath, he looked around, admiring the chandeliers, blue silk curtains, plush velvet booths and crystal stemware. "The place is really nice, Hank. You did a great job."

Hank smiled and requested a drink from the waitress, who topped off their glasses. "This round's on me, Maxine."

The blonde waitress nodded and gave Noah and Lexi a beaming smile. "Okie-dokie, Hank."

Seeing that Hank was planning on having his drink delivered to the table, Noah waved his hand in invitation for his cousin to sit. It was a relief that Hank did so without moving too far from the opening edge of the large semi-circular booth. Noah wanted to wrap his arm around Lexi's shoulder and pull her closer, away from Hank, but tension emanated from her stiff posture.

"I'm glad you like it, Noah, and I'm really glad you came with Lexi. Would you like a tour?"

Noah looked at Lexi, who shook her head. "No thanks. I already had a tour when Bubbles opened."

Hank's drink arrived, and he took a sip before standing. "Come on, Noah. You can't pass up the tour. You're an investor, now."

Lexi's head shot up in question.

Noah gave her a reassuring nod. "Will you be okay for a few minutes?"

Lexi held up her champagne. "I'll be fine."

Hank gave her a wink. "No doubt about that." Redirecting his attention to the waitress, Hank ordered, "Maxine, keep a special eye on this table, and don't let any cowboys move in on my cousin's guest."

Noah might have been happy with Hank ordering the staff to look after Lexi, but in typical Hank fashion, there were always strings attached. Why hadn't he called Lexi Noah's date? More important, why had he winked at her? Hank was southern-gentleman-flirt all the way but generally polite.

He'd always bordered on cheesy by Noah's standards, but he reasoned that the wink didn't mean Hank was after Lexi.

The little devil that sat on Noah's shoulder pricked him with a nagging pitchfork. Hank may have stepped up to make things right between them, but that didn't mean he'd been through an exorcism. He was still a man, and Lexi was a gorgeous woman. His core personality was still inside, and if that was the case, Noah could never truly relax when his cousin was around. Hank had always been an advocate for getting what he wanted. Did he bring Noah here as part of some plan to make a play for Lexi? Maybe he was testing the waters to see if Noah had made his move. At the new Hank's, his cousin had warned him that if Noah didn't go after Lexi, he would.

Noah stared at the back of Hank's head as he followed him into the kitchen and down the corridor to his office. Maybe it was time to get it all out in the open.

"So, what do you think, cuz?"

Hank had already asked him that question at the table, so Noah assumed he was asking about the office or the tour. "Like I said, it's great. Just like I imagined it." Noah hoped he sounded sincere and not bitter. The disappointment of letting Bubbles go had vanished when he opened the new Hank's, and he now owned a part of Bubbles, too. He gave his cousin a genuine smile. "You know, you didn't have to cut me in on this place. You paid for it, fair and square."

Hank motioned to the two overstuffed cowhide chairs, and Noah sat. Taking the stopper out of a bottle, Hank poured two fingers worth of amber liquid from a crystal decanter. "Fifty-year-old Macallan," he informed Noah as he brought the glass to his nose, swirling it beneath.

"Good stuff."

"Yeah, and in response to cutting you in on the place… yes, I did have to." Hank paused. "It's not easy for me to look at the past and not cringe a little. But, thank God, I'm not much for lookin' at the past."

He sat in the other chair and took a swig of the whiskey from his rocks glass. "A few years ago, I didn't have any vision for what Hank's could be, for what this town could be, or even—hell, what I could be." Reclining in the deep-seated chair, he propped a boot up on one knee. "When you got in that car accident because I pulled a stupid stunt...." Hank shook his head as his words lodged in his throat.

Noah cut in. "You didn't cause the accident, Hank. You can't blame yourself for my actions. I was looking at my damn phone while I was driving. I'm lucky I didn't kill someone."

Hank seemed to struggle with his emotions for a moment, then finally cleared his throat. "That might be, but I put the plan in motion to take advantage of a situation, and it wasn't my finest hour. I know I was an ass. All of my life, I've been self-centered, and not many people will hear me say it, but I owe you. I owe Bubbles to you. I didn't know that it was what I needed, but I love this place, and after all that's passed between us, I want to work together as family. As partners, again."

Noah hesitated. He felt Hank was being sincere but trusting him was still going to take time. "Well, I appreciate it, Hank. I'm not sure if I have any time to give to this place if that's what we're talking about. As I said before, the new Hank's is killing my free time."

Hank put a hand up and stood. "Naw. I'm not asking for any more of your time. I've been wanting to talk to you, but this is probably not the best time. Let's get you back out there to that pretty little gal of yours. We can talk shop later."

As Noah stood up and walked to the door, Hank clapped him on the shoulder with familiar camaraderie. "Glad to see you two together. You and Lexi deserve to be happy."

Hank's smile was overlarge, and Noah found himself analyzing the comment. Was Hank being genuine? Was it regret in the depths of his eyes, and if so, was it regret for past transgressions or missing out on being with Lexi? Noah shook off his negative thoughts. When had he started overthinking simple conversations? Deciding to leave it alone for now, he said, "Thanks again, Hank, for the tour and the whiskey."

Chapter 36

Lexi's palms were wet, among other things. Noah's light kiss beneath her earlobe had made her pulse flutter, and butterflies zing in the pit of her stomach. She'd been fantasizing about their first night together ever since she'd seen him back in Magnolia. After sending him home the other night, she couldn't stop thinking of what it would be like when she finally let him take her to bed again. Lexi promised herself she'd go slow this time. It wouldn't last if he didn't understand what he was getting into. The possibility of rejection loomed over her, and she wanted to build a little fortress around her heart so that it didn't get crushed this time. Especially if he couldn't handle the commitment.

It was awkward being in the presence of both Noah and Hank. It was unnerving that they were all three probably thinking of Hank kissing her in her driveway. Noah had asked her if she had feelings for Hank, and she'd answered honestly, saying they were just friends. She'd forgotten to mention to Noah that she'd asked Hank to the Blossoms Charity Ball. It was months ago, and it hadn't turned into anything. Hank had dropped her off without so much as a hug. They'd been friends, and he'd treated her politely, if not a little cheesy. She'd asked Hank because she wanted to get back out there and stop hiding away on the ranch. She thought maybe they might share some sort of chemistry and going out might help her get over Noah. Of course, that didn't happen. She could never get over her feelings for him.

Lexi hadn't done anything wrong, and it wasn't like she'd grilled Noah about who he spent time with in Dallas. So, why did she still have this needling thought that she should tell him about the Blossoms dinner with Hank?

A tall, gorgeous man with honey blond hair and a muscular physique entered the lounge with a pretty brunette on his arm. Lexi smiled. Eli and his new wife weren't seen around town much since they returned from their honeymoon. The new healthy fast-food joint they'd opened together was probably taking all their energy, but the glow on their faces said they were enjoying their time at home in each other's arms as well. Eli waved at Lexi, and they started in her direction, but Tabby, his wife, was detained by Mona and the mayor. Eli managed to break away, motioning to the group that he would be a minute.

"Eli!" Lexi beamed, trying to scoot around the booth to get out and hug him. He was her sister-in-law's brother, so he was family to Lexi. "How's married life?"

His eyes spoke volumes. Lexi watched his Adam's apple dip with a gulp as he looked back at Tabitha.

He stopped her from having to wrestle with her dress clinging to the velvet booth and slid in to give her one of his all-comforting bear hugs. "It's great! We couldn't be happier."

She beamed up at him, feeling like a small plush toy next to his solidly built, massive form. Looks could be deceiving. He might be all cut muscle, but Eli was the biggest teddy bear in the world. His sister, Melvina, was a sweetheart, too. Lexi felt lucky to have such amazing people in her life. As Eli hugged her, she had a clear view of Hank and Noah coming out of the kitchen door.

Their waitress, Maxine, was two tables away but managed to break away from her guest and give Lexi a wide-eyed look of warning as she made a bee-line approach to the table. She smiled at Eli and filled Lexi's glass. The waitress didn't ask him if he wanted a drink.

Lexi knew Eli had plans to be with his wife but she asked him anyway, "Would you and Tabitha like some champagne?"

After Lexi mentioned Tabitha, Maxine's brow smoothed and she waited for Eli to confirm.

Hank and Noah arrived, and Lexi introduced everyone.

Eli and Noah shook hands. "Nice to meet you," Eli said. He shook hands with Hank as well. "I think we've already met," Eli said, with a lift of his brow. He gave Lexi a quizzical glance and she remembered that Eli had met Hank the night of the ball. Hank had been less than his most charming self. It had been what sealed it for her, that they could only be friends and that she would never feel otherwise.

Hank's forehead furrowed. "I own Bubbles, so I'm not surprised, but excuse me if I can't remember. There are so many guests in and out of—"

Eli shook his head, pressing his lips together. "No, it was the Blossoms Ball. It's been some months, but I remember you were there with Lexi." He gave her a brief look of what could only be described as disappointment.

Noah glanced at Hank and then Lexi. His eyes narrowed, and his jaw tightened.

Lexi felt her face drain of color. This was not the way she wanted to tell Noah about that night. Not that there was anything to tell. Plus, she definitely didn't want Eli thinking she was here with Hank.

"Hank is my friend and Noah's cousin. Noah is my date this evening." Lexi wanted to crawl under the table for having to toss it out like that, but Eli looked relieved. Tabitha approached the group, saying a quick hello to Lexi, then taking Eli's hand in hers and pulling him away with an apology. "I'm so sorry to drag my husband away." She smiled back at the table then looked at Eli with all the hope and love of a new bride. Lexi could hear the excitement in her voice as she confessed, "The mayor and Mona are asking for the details of your Fresh Start Franchise plans, and I think they might want to invest!"

After Eli and Tabitha left, Hank tipped his glass and drained the contents, then looked at Noah with a sober expression. "Cousin, I know where your mind is at, and let me say, it's not what you're thinking." His eyes darted to Lexi then back to Noah, who looked ready to deck Hank.

Lexi slid around to exit the booth, standing between the two men. "Noah, it was months ago, and I asked Hank to take me to the charity event so I wouldn't have to go alone. Hank never touched me. We're just friends."

Noah stood stiff and unyielding, and it made Lexi nervous to feel the eyes of so many people staring at them. They weren't loud, but the atmosphere felt charged with electricity and even tables halfway across the room stared.

Noah's eyes were cold as he addressed Hank. "The bar wasn't enough? Hell, my ex-wife wasn't enough? I know you, Hank. There isn't anything friendly about your intentions toward Lexi. She is one more thing of mine that you have to have."

Hank glowered back at Noah. "You're a dumbass. You know that?" Hank would have continued, but the resounding crack of Noah's fist against Hank's jaw was a showstopper.

Eli rushed back to their table and was already holding Noah back, while the mayor, who came with him, had a firm hand on Hank's shoulder.

Lexi had had enough. She wasn't going to be the damsel in distress while two grown men acted like preschoolers tussling over a toy. She already had three young boys at home who settled their differences in a more mature manner than embarrassing her in public like this. Making her way to the exit, she kept her eyes focused on the door. She didn't know what came next, but it was a short walk to the diner, and Ginger could give her a ride home from there.

Chapter 37

Ginger rang the bell for Roberta to pick up the order for a second time. Where was the other waitress? It was like everyone had disappeared, and it wasn't that busy in the diner. The dinner rush was over, and business crawled. Hanging her apron on a hook, she grabbed the hamburger order while it was still hot and put it on a tray with the proper condiments. She knew the table numbers, and number five was right by the front door. The customer was seated with his back to her, and according to the ticket, he was dining alone. As she slid the plate onto the table, she asked the guy if she could get him anything else.

"Yeah." He looked up as he started to make his request but froze. "Dallas."

Ginger dropped the round tray she was holding as she stared back at the very man she'd been thinking about. "Kirk." Her feet started to walk backward as she tried to think of what to do next. Should she run before he could tell everyone who she was, exposing her past to all of Magnolia, or should she pick up the tray and crack him over the head with it?

Kirk reached out to her. His tousled dark hair fell across his forehead in that male model look that made his bright smile look so toothpaste-ad perfect. "Dallas, I'm so sorry. It wasn't on purpose. I promise. Please, give me a chance to explain."

Ginger kept backing away, holding her hands up. "Don't! Don't touch me. If you want to explain, tell it to my lawyer."

She was halfway to the swinging kitchen door when she heard him call out, "Dallas," again. Spinning on her heel, she marched back to the table and dumped his full soda in his lap. "Don't call me that! My name is Ginger, and to me, your name will always be Asshole!"

All eyes in the diner were on them now, including Roberta and the other new waitress.

Ginger threw her arms up. "Shit!" Where did she go from here? She'd thought Magnolia was her last hope, and she was starting to like her simple life. As she marched through the kitchen to grab her keys and purse, she continued out the back door and to her car without so much as an "I'm outta here." Later, she would feel bad for leaving Melvina and the other staff hanging, but for now, she needed to get away—far, far away from the man who'd ruined her life.

She put the rental car in reverse, glad that she hadn't returned it. Her recent plan to buy a used car from the Magnolia Car Depot vanished along with her small-town hideout. Ginger didn't know where she'd go, and she couldn't afford to keep the rental forever, but the cost of monthly insurance payments and repairs on a car would be too much without a job. If Kirk knew she was here, then it wouldn't be long until rag reporters and gossip columnists were ordering cupcakes and malts, trying to get the dirty scoop on the illicit video. Maybe she could hide out at Lexi's for eternity.

Oh no! What will Lexi say when she finds out her nanny has a past?

In the words of Gussy, Bert and Damien, "Double donkey doo!"

As Ginger rounded the diner toward the exit, it started pouring rain. Kirk stood in the middle of the parking lot with a menu over his perfect hair, holding one hand out for her to stop. The headlights of the little red rental car pierced his tan complexion, designer skinny jeans and Polo pullover. She could see his mouth moving as he stepped toward the car. As he stood at the front of her hood, she revved the engine. Ginger knew she wouldn't go so far as to mow him down, but she enjoyed the look on his face as she edged forward, physically pushing him back. As he rounded the car, beating on her window, she held up her middle finger in the timeless, go-fuck-yourself salute.

It made her feel good to leave him standing in a puddle of diner sludge as she drove home in the warmth and dry comfort of her car. Tears rolled down her cheeks, and she swiped them away, but the drops kept coming as if it were raining inside the vehicle. When Ginger was far enough away from the diner, she pulled to the side of the road to have a good cry. After finding a few fast-food napkins in her glove box, she blew her nose and breathed out a shaky sigh. *First things first. Go back to the ranch, tell Lexi about what happened and then pack your shit. For better or for worse, it's time to blow this cupcake joint.*

When Lexi reached the diner, Ginger's car wasn't in the parking lot, but as luck would have it, Mona and Manny pulled up in their sedan. With rain running in rivulets down her face, Lexi accepted their offer to drive her home, apologizing as she dripped on their leather seats.

Mona waved a hand over the headrest. "*Psht.* Don't worry about it. We're trading it in next week. There's a clean towel in the seat pocket behind Manny. Help yourself."

Lexi didn't want to talk to anyone right now, but the mayor and his wife were friends. Though they'd witnessed the altercation, Mona said nothing about the exchange between Noah and Hank and instead, rattled on about the upcoming Snowflake Gala as they drove. Lexi's cell phone lit up with texts. One was from Noah, apologizing and saying they needed to talk. He was right, and they would, but now wasn't a good time, so she ignored it. Another text was from Hank, saying he'd talk to Noah when he cooled down and make things right. Eli had called and left a voice mail asking if she was okay and that he and Tabitha were still up if she needed anything.

The night had been worse than she could've ever imagined, and she had played as much a part of it as Noah and Hank. They might have been acting like children, but why hadn't she told Noah about the date with Hank before this? It would have been better to put it all out on the table from the beginning. She had nothing to hide, so why withhold that tidbit from the past?

After thanking Mona and Manny for coming to the rescue, Lexi clattered up the steps to the porch and walked inside the dark, empty house. She made her way to the kitchen and turned on the lights, filling a pot with water, then headed to the bedroom to change. The phone dinged again, and she reached for it. It was Ginger, letting her know she was on the way home.

A deep sigh escaped Lexi as the tea kettle whistled, and she shoved her feet into bunny slippers and headed back to the kitchen. It was late enough to go to bed, but she knew sleep would be elusive after the events of the night. Pulling two cups out of the cupboard and a selection of herbal tea bags, she crossed the kitchen to the table. Car lights lit up the front window of the house, announcing Ginger's arrival. It would be nice to chat with someone who might understand. Ginger was so good about listening and not giving unsolicited advice.

There was a light knock and then Ginger entered. The red eyes and blotchy complexion were a dead giveaway.

Lexi rushed toward her. "Oh, my. What happened? I went to the diner, but your car wasn't there. I was worried when I got home before you."

Ginger teared up again. "I had to leave early. I drove around for a while." Her words broke as Ginger tried sucking in air to speak between sobs. "I don't know what to do. He ruined my life, and now I have to leave. I don't know where I'm going to go."

Lexi wrapped Ginger in a hug. A low moan escaped her troubled friend as Lexi patted her on the back. She could feel Ginger's body shake.

And I thought I'd had a bad night. "Oh my, darlin'. Let's get you out of your wet jacket, and I have tea made for us in the kitchen. Maybe after you're settled, you can tell me more about this man who's ruined your life. No matter what has happened, you know you always have a home here, so don't worry. We'll find a solution."

Lexi didn't know much about Ginger's past, but she knew that there must have been a bad relationship. Why else would she be off men? Though the constable had seemed to melt that particular sheet of ice. Maybe her ex had called her, threatened her, or who only knew, but one thing Lexi was sure of was that if Ginger stayed here, Roland would make sure she was safe.

Another knock on the door startled them both. Had Noah come after her because she hadn't responded to his text? *Men!*

She gently pushed Ginger toward the kitchen. "It's probably Noah. Give me a minute, and I'll get rid of him so we can talk."

Ginger shuffled to the kitchen, looking back over her shoulder like a forlorn child. Lexi's heart squeezed. Her friend looked like she'd been put through the ringer. That was exactly how Lexi had felt on that lonesome drive back from Dallas when Noah had sent her away.

In the doorway, stood a drenched, good-looking man who appraised her with stunning blue eyes. "Can I help you?" Lexi asked. It wasn't often that a person got so turned around that they ended up at her doorstep, but it had happened before.

The stranger looked at her through thick, wet lashes. The dimple in his cheek winked at her as he fidgeted with indecision. He looked back to his car and then at her again, finally choosing to speak. "Uh, is Dallas here?"

She felt her eyebrows knit together before answering. "You're closer to Houston, mister. Dallas is almost four hours north."

He shook his head, and beads of water landed on his wet shirt. A shiver ran through him. "No, I'm looking for Dallas Derringer."

Chapter 38

Noah had made an ass out of himself, and he knew it. Forty was too old to brawl in public, especially with the mayor and other prominent Magnolia residents looking on.

Even as kids, Hank and Noah had never gotten on well. Hank always aroused Noah's sense of competition, and Noah had never been able to let sleeping dogs lie. After he'd come back from Afghanistan, he'd thought he turned over a new leaf from his hot-headed past, and he'd put up with Hank's lazy antics and pilfering the cash drawer of the old Hank's because they'd both inherited it. Noah hadn't wanted to rock the boat by trying to sell his half of the bar and open Bubbles, but Hank's actions forced his hand. He'd seen the sale as a threat and the new bar as competition. Things had spiraled out of control, and Lexi was part of the fallout. Now, three years later, they were back to square one. After the accident, Noah thought he could keep his cool through anything, but Hank moving in on Lexi was too much.

As Noah drove down the gravel road leading to Lexi's ranch, he assured himself that it wasn't going to be a repeat of that fateful night. He was sure he wouldn't find Lexi kissing Hank in her driveway, but what he hadn't counted on was another man entering Lexi's home. He turned his lights off and sat in the drive as the man went inside. They stood visible in the front window. The kitchen light illuminated their figures as they stood talking. It wasn't a romantic interlude, or at least it wasn't at the moment. Noah reminded himself it could be one of Lexi's brothers. It was too far away to tell in the rain.

Noah shook his head as he shut off the engine and got out. *No more secrets!* If her family saw him at her door, so what? He'd taken her on a date in front of half of Magnolia, so she had to be ready for them to know. The gossip about his jealousy and the fight with Hank would be around town and back before dawn. It might not be the best time to make amends, but if Lexi really cared for him, she would find it in her heart to work this out.

He knocked on her door and waited. As footsteps approached, he heard, "Jesus Christ!"

Noah was surprised to see Ginger open the door, brow furrowed and tears in her eyes.

"Out!" she demanded.

Noah raised his hands and took a step back to show he meant no harm. "Excuse me?"

Surely, Lexi hadn't asked her new tenant to send him away.

Ginger turned back to the living area and repeated to the man lumbering behind her. "Out!"

Noah's soldier persona and role of protector slid into place, making his muscles contract and his shoulders set. "Is there a problem?"

Like Noah, the younger man raised his open hands to show he was not a threat. "No, sir. I came to talk to Ginger."

Ginger shrieked for him to leave again, and the guy stuttered, "O—Okay. I'm leaving. I wanted to say I'm sorry and explain."

Noah stepped back and held open the door with a stern look. "Well, the lady has asked you to leave, so I think you better go."

The man stepped out into the rain, digging in his pocket. He turned back, leaving a white square of paper on the porch rail. "Please, Dallas. When you calm down, call me. We need to talk."

Lexi wasn't shocked to see Noah in her living room, but to see him look at the stranger with such a feral glare made her heart leap. She didn't know what this stranger had done to Ginger to make her so angry, but it heartened her to have Noah present. The guy Ginger called Kirk hadn't seemed like any real threat, but he upset Ginger, and that was enough to ask him to leave. Lexi wanted to kick herself for letting him in in the first place, but she really hadn't. When the guy started asking for Dallas, Ginger rounded the corner of the kitchen like a witch on a turbo-broom, and he stepped past Lexi into the living room.

Now that the guy was gone, Lexi sighed with relief. Noah put a protective arm around her as he reached for Ginger's shoulder. He gave her a reassuring squeeze. "It's okay now. You're both safe."

Lexi nodded, patting Ginger's arm. She stepped out of Noah's embrace and walked toward the kitchen. "How about we all sit down and have a relaxing cup of tea?"

Ginger shook her head. "I appreciate it, Lexi, but I think I want to go to bed. Can we talk about this in the morning? I promise I'll tell you everything then. Right now," she sighed with a slight shudder, "I only want to sleep."

Lexi felt torn. Her friend was in some sort of trouble, and she wanted to help, but Ginger clearly didn't want to talk about it right now. Lexi nodded. "If you're sure you're okay. Do you want to stay here tonight? I don't want to worry about you down there by the creek all alone."

Ginger shook her head. "Kirk is my ex-boyfriend. He's not dangerous, and I doubt he'll come back this evening." She gripped the front door handle, looking back over her shoulder. Her bottom lip trembled. "I'll explain everything tomorrow."

It would be hard to let her go home alone in the cold dark. As she looked at Noah with pleading eyes, he nodded. Lexi called out to Ginger. "Let Noah escort you to the cabin."

He didn't wait for her answer. "I promise to get you there safe and sound, then I will leave you alone to rest."

Ginger sniffed and swiped at a tear. "Okay."

Noah looked back at Lexi as he reached the door. "Will you be up when I get back?" His voice sounded full of hope.

"Yes," she replied. They needed to talk about tonight, the date with Hank, and the accident that had kept Noah away for so long. A lot of unanswered questions stood between them, and she obviously wasn't the only one feeling insecure. It was time to talk, but it was also time to listen and make a decision on how to move forward.

When Noah entered the front door, Lexi was pouring water from the kettle into a cup. "Is she okay?"

"Yeah. She seemed sad. I guess this guy must have broken her heart or something."

"She didn't say?" Lexi's eyes searched his face.

Noah shook his head. "No. She thanked me for the ride and went inside. I came back here to see if you still wanted to talk."

She nodded. "Want a cup of tea?"

Noah waited as Lexi refilled her cup and poured hot water into his mug. Not really caring what flavor, he tore open a package and dropped the tea bag into the mug. "I came over to apologize."

She looked at him with tired eyes.

"I know it was childish. I'm sorry I embarrassed you." He stared at the bag steeping in his cup. "Hell, I embarrassed myself. I can't tell you the last time I was in a brawl."

Lexi gave an indignant snort. "I find that hard to believe. You own a bar in Texas." They both chuckled.

"I usually let the bartenders take care of the rough stuff, but since Hank's was rebuilt, there's never been much trouble." He took a sip, liking the smooth taste of black tea with cinnamon. "Um. That's pretty good."

Lexi smiled, picking up a honey bear bottle and holding it over his cup. "It's better with a little sweetness."

Noah nodded. "I remember how much of a sweet tooth you have."

Lexi squeezed a generous amount of honey into his cup and then took a small spoon from the napkin and swirled the hot liquid. "Only Dr. Icing would know that." Her pupils dilated as she stared up at him. Her pink tongue darted out, and she caught her bottom lip between her perfect white teeth. The dimple in her cheek deepened as she tried to suppress a smile.

"I'm sorry we never got the chance to play out that particular fantasy. I remember that icing almost got me into trouble."

Lexi frowned. "How so?"

Noah chuckled as he leaned back in the kitchen chair, remembering how her finger had tasted in his mouth as he'd licked off all the icing. She'd called him Doctor Icing, and he'd promised to finish the job when he saw her next. "Mac Green and the boys came in, and after you left, I couldn't come out from behind the bar for half the day. Every time I thought of you, I imagined you wearing one of those cute little nurse's outfits holding a tray of cupcakes. I still have fantasies of licking the frosting off every inch of your body."

He couldn't stop the shiver of excitement that made him shake his shoulders out. He sat straighter in his chair. Noah reminded himself that he was there to apologize to Lexi, not seduce her.

"I didn't mean to blow up at Hank in Bubbles. I don't know what came over me." He reached out, touching her hand. "I mean the things I've been saying. I want you and me to work things out, and more than Bubbles, Hank's Honky-Tonk or anything else in my life, I want to be with you, only you, Lexi. I promise. If you give me a chance, I'll make things right, and you won't be embarrassed to be seen with me."

"I'm not embarrassed to be seen with you—usually."

When he groaned, she grinned. "I want to be with you, too, Noah. I don't want people to look at us and remember how I moped around for months after you left." She shook her head. "Hell, for almost three years. I'm still not over you."

He leaned forward, brushing his lips against hers. "Then it's settled. You'll give me a chance to prove how much I love you and want you in my life?"

Her eyes sparkled with mischief as she stood and went into the kitchen. She came back with a fancy glass cake stand with an assortment of cupcakes. Her tongue darted across her bottom lip as she presented it to him. "I went to the diner earlier. Before the melt-down, I thought we might end up here together tonight." She paused as she set the plate down and took the glass dome off.

Noah gulped. He'd done his best to behave. To do the right thing by taking his time to get to know her. He'd made a blunder of their date night at Bubbles, and this was the last thing he expected of Lexi. He knew he didn't deserve her flirty forgiveness. Was this a test?

Lexi dipped her finger into the strawberry icing like she had so long ago, before things fell apart. He still remembered how she had tasted, and how that day in the bar, he'd lingered over thoughts of his tongue touching every part of her body. The memory of the sweet offer had haunted him over the past few years. And now she was offering him another chance.

Noah had no doubt what he would do next, but braving the moment, he had to ask. "Are you sure?"

She nodded, and Noah grasped her fingers, kissing them in the same way he wanted to kiss every inch of her. He pulled Lexi down onto his lap, wrapping her in his arms. His hands wound their way through her golden hair as he tasted her lips and tongue. The smell of strawberries drifted between them as her breath caught, and his teeth grazed the sensitive skin at the base of her throat.

She shifted, straddling his lap, pulling the snaps of his shirt open with urgency. As she arched into his erection, he pushed her t-shirt up, and she helped him by lifting her arms. The sight of her breasts cupped in the thin lace bra was heaven to his eyes. He pushed the gauzy material down, taking one erect nipple between his lips. She moaned and grasped his hair, pulling gently at the tendrils with ecstasy written on her face. He felt her looping her feet through the chair rungs as she lifted up enough to undo his jeans. The rough material folded away from his cock, and he felt his erection lift to meet her as she slid her silky pajama bottoms down his shaft. The heat of her body enveloped him through the thin fabric, and his breath caught in his throat.

"For the love of God, please take them off," he rasped, trying to push at the tied waistband that would reveal the rest of her naked flesh. She stood, pushing her bottoms off, taking her matching lace panties with them. He kicked off his boots, shed his jeans and socks, and let the unsnapped shirt trailed down his naked torso. Lexi didn't return to his lap but took his hand in hers, pulling him up to follow her. As she began to lead him away, he snagged the strawberry cupcake from the dish. He would live up to Doctor Icing if it was the last thing he did tonight.

Chapter 39

It was like the worst hangover Ginger ever had, but the feeling wasn't going away. The pounding in her head became audible as she pulled the pillow tighter over her ears to muffle the sound.

"Ginger?" Roland's voice reverberated through the door.

Crap! It wasn't a nightmare. Roland was really banging on her door. The whole town probably knew who she was by now, and it wouldn't be long until reporters were filling up the front lawn.

She'd promised to tell Lexi the whole story today. How could she not? Kirk had all but blurted it out when he called her Dallas last night. Lexi might not have had time to watch TV, but the gossip mill in Magnolia would eventually make its way to her ear. Ginger couldn't stand to think of the look in her friend's eyes when she found out her famous identity. Somehow, she didn't think Lexi would be angry at her, but Ginger couldn't stand to think of the pity either. She already felt pitiful enough.

Roland's knock and bellow sounded again. "Ginger! Open up. Talk to me, please."

He knows. She thought about grabbing her keys and purse and sliding out the back door. If he was on foot, she could beat him back to Lexi's to grab her car and make a quick escape. She had her keys in hand when she noticed Igor staring back at her through the glass terrarium. "Double donkey doo." Ginger set the keys back on the table. "You're too big to make a run for it. I swear Kirk should have told me you were going to be as big as an alligator."

With resignation, Ginger let her feet shuffle to the door. She hadn't even looked in the mirror. She must be a hot mess. It didn't really matter at this point. Roland had already seen her morning hair, and he probably was here to arrest her for impersonating a normal person. As he pounded on the door again, she flung it open. Roland stood tall, his uniform pressed and outlining his perfect physique. *Dang, he was hot.*

"Did you come to arrest me?"

He stepped in without an invitation, massaging the back of his head like someone had hit him. "What? No. Ginger, what's this all about? Half of Magnolia was at the diner this morning. Plus, half of—wherever the hell those reporters came from—showed up for breakfast. You want to tell me what's going on?"

Ginger scowled at him. Why should she have to explain? That's what had gotten her from the start—on her descent from stardom to tabloid tombstone. "This isn't my fault! I'm not the one who needs to be arrested. If you're looking for answers, go find Kirk!"

Roland looked perplexed. "I'm not here to arrest you. I'm here to protect you. Half the town is asking about Ginger Harding, AKA Dallas somebody-or-another. I need you to get in my car before the five o'clock news team comes screeching down Lexi's drive, blocking our exit."

His hands were in the air, gesticulating as he spoke. *He doesn't know!* Or at least he didn't know who Dallas Derringer was or why everyone wanted to find her. That was good. She could work with that. Ginger started shoving clothes in an overnight duffle and dropped her toothbrush, comb and deodorant on top of the contents, spilling over the top zipper compartment. Shoving the bag at Roland, she grabbed Igor's crate. She needed to leave town and fast.

"What are you doing?" Roland looked out of the window nervously, as if he expected a lynch mob to arrive.

Ginger shut the door on Igor's crate and put it on the bed. Hopping around, she shoved her feet into canvas-style tennis shoes. "I'm not leaving him here."

Roland nodded. "Of course not. I mean, but do you think Rollo will eat him?"

If the situation wasn't so dire, she would have laughed. "I can't go to your place, Roland. They'll just find me again, and I'll have to keep running. I'm going to New York. It's the one place I can hide in plain sight. People there leave people like me alone. They've got enough of their own problems to worry about." She stood up and went to look beneath the bed. The tea tin filled with cash was right where she'd left it. "Can you give Igor and me a ride to the bus station?"

Roland's face fell then his brows knitted together. "Get Igor and get in the car. We'll talk about it on the way."

212

Chapter 40

Morning rays of light showered Lexi's bedroom through the wall of windows that looked out toward the creek and the line of trees that framed the open field. She remembered waking up with Noah this way before. Confronted by the wedding photo on the hall table outside her bedroom, she'd been awash with guilt, but this time was different. John was in charge of the farm, and he would feed the animals. The boys were with her parents, giving her all morning to bask in the afterglow of their night.

Noah's light brown hair fell against his forehead as he slept, making him appear years younger. His lips were parted against the white of his almost perfect teeth. One eyetooth had a slight twist, which made him even more appealing. As he slumbered, the lines around his eyes and forehead dissipated. She reached up to run a finger along the shallow crow's feet that emphasized his sincerity when he smiled.

His eyes fluttered open, blinking in the morning light. His voice held quiet pleasure as he whispered, "You're really here."

That made her smile. "I'm as real as the bed we're lying in."

Noah reached for Lexi, pulling her to him and kissing her neck. "I want to wake up this way every day for the rest of my life, with you in my arms and the promise of all that's good in the world at my doorstep."

Lexi thought she might swoon. "Where in the world did you get that silver tongue, Noah Harding? Ms. Rosie doesn't know what she's talking about." She giggled as he rolled on top of her.

"I say what I mean." He ran his fingers down the side of her face, looking like he was about to kiss her.

She put a hand over her mouth, pushing at his chest. "Noah, I haven't brushed my teeth."

He moved her hand and dipped his lips to hers, giving her a chaste kiss. "I don't care, but if it bothers you, let's both go wash up. Then we can come back here, and I can lay in bed with you all day."

Lexi groaned. "Oh, I want to so bad, but Ginger may stop by soon, remember?"

He sighed, rolling to his side, but still pinning her with one thigh. He touched her arm softly with his strong fingers. "Okay, but when she's gone—"

Lexi nodded, looking up at him with half-fascination, half-love. Until Noah left Magnolia, she hadn't known she was in love, and she still felt that beautiful pulse beating inside of her now. It would be impossible to hold back any part of herself from him because, for her, any other option would break her heart. But, what about him? Noah still had secrets, and in order to fully give yourself to someone, you had to know their past. She wondered if Noah might be ready to share all of himself with her.

"You know, you never told me what happened to you when you left Magnolia."

Noah looked beyond her to the pasture outside the bedroom window. He seemed far away as his eyes scanned the landscape. After a few minutes, he scrubbed a hand over his face.

"I was stupid, running off to Dallas in the middle of the night. I didn't plan it, but when I passed Hank's on the highway, I kept on going. I was halfway to my sister, Callie, before I even knew it. Hank was an ass for trying to steal you away, and I knew it wasn't a coincidence that Petra appeared out of thin air."

He eased back into the pillow as Lexi's fingers made lazy circles over his chest. Her head rested against his shoulder as he held her in one arm.

"My ex-wife was never happy with what I had to offer, and I got hurt when she initially left me for a higher-ranking officer with a bigger bank account."

He breathed out a long sigh. "You know about the cancer and her coming back for treatment, but then, when things were good again, she ran off with another soldier. I finally learned to quit giving my heart." He paused, looking down at Lexi. Noah's face was tender, and his lips grazed her forehead. "Until I met you."

He dipped his head to kiss her, pulling her up in his arms to meet his lips, but she sat up, pushing him away. "No, tell me the whole story. I want to know how you were injured." She needed to hear what happened.

Noah blew out another long sigh as he pushed against the pillow.

"I couldn't handle losing again. I didn't want to see you and Hank coming into the bar together, rubbing it all in my face. I figured you'd never forgive me for whatever it was Hank told you about Petra, and without your trust, I figured we were over. Without you, Bubbles didn't mean anything. I had gotten an offer from an investor to buy the land, the building plans and everything, but I'd turned it down.

"So, as I was driving to Dallas and digging for the buyer's business card, I looked away at my phone. I didn't see the deer until it was too late—my SUV crashed into a ditch. I couldn't move, and by some miracle, a military guy showed up and pulled me out right before the whole thing burst into flames. I shattered my femur, ruptured a disc in my spine, and I'm damn well lucky to be alive."

Lexi felt cold fingers grip her heart. He could have died. "I'm so thankful you were saved." She couldn't help one hand from fluttering to her chest while the other hovered at her mouth. "I can't imagine what you've gone through."

"Three surgeries, years of physical therapy, and a doctor who said I'd never walk again."

Lexi frowned. "Well, you proved him wrong."

Noah chuckled. "*Her*, and she was probably right. If it had been anyone less stubborn than me, they would likely still be in that chair."

His smile turned sweet as he looked into her eyes. His fingers grazed the side of her cheek, and she felt him studying her. There were a million things she wanted to say, but she waited to hear him out.

Lexi watched his throat move as he swallowed, adjusting to the memories.

"You know, if you hadn't come to Dallas, I might have sat there feeling sorry for myself for the rest of my life. Knowing you still cared and that there was a chance to have something together was what made me strong again. I thought to myself, there is no way I'll let Hank have what's mine."

It was Lexi's turn to chuckle and roll her eyes. "Yours?" she challenged. "I belong to myself, thank you very much, and Hank never had a chance with me. I know I kissed him in the driveway that night, but you know why. The night he took me to the ball, I'll admit I was ready to move on. I couldn't wait on you forever, you know."

She gave him a small slap on his bicep. "But Hank is seriously not my type, and if I ever had any notion of romance between us, that night at the Blossoms shindig sealed the deal. With or without you coming back to Magnolia, Hank and I would never be more than friends."

Noah nodded, pulling her closer as his index finger tapped her nose. "Glad to hear it because I have other plans for you, lady."

"Wait! I want to hear more about the guy who saved you. Did you stay in touch? Was he surprised by your recovery?"

Noah was silent for a moment. "That's the odd thing. He saved me, and then he was gone before I could thank him. The police thought I was hallucinating when they arrived on the scene, and I told them how I got out of the burning car. I said the guy was military because he was in fatigues, but later I thought about it. His hair was too long, and his beard was unkempt. Maybe he was a hunter going out to his deer stand, but the boots were standard military issue. That's not what most men wear to hunt. Maybe he'd been drinking. It's the only reason I can think of that he disappeared so fast."

Lexi sighed. "It's a shame you can't tell him thanks, but I'm so glad you made it out alive. We have so much to be thankful for."

Noah enjoyed making love to Lexi in the light of day. Every part of her body was imprinted in his mind. He loved the way her smooth skin felt against his rough, calloused fingers and the length of her thighs as he nudged them apart with his knee. She was everything he'd remembered and more. Soft lips, silky hair, toned body and a warmth of spirit that forgave him for leaving her alone. All that was over now, and he'd never desert her again. It was too soon to ask her for anything permanent, but knowing that didn't stop him.

Lexi went to the kitchen to put on a kettle of water for tea. Noah had always been a coffee drinker, but he'd get his standard cup when they went into town later to pick up the boys. He was elated she'd invited him to meet her parents and her kids, all at once, and he admitted he was nervous. Would they like him?

When he searched for her in the kitchen, she wasn't there. He heard the shower running and knew without a doubt where he was going next. As he slipped in beside her, Noah remembered the last time they'd been in the tub together. *It won't end like that this time. I will never give her a reason to doubt me again.*

Her silky blonde hair cascaded down her back as water sluiced over her naked form. Her eyes were closed, and she moved her hands over her wet hair, rinsing the conditioner from the thick mass. He stepped into the shower, his hands cupping her breasts, feeling the weight of each globe as he drank water from her erect nipples. Her head fell back, and her hands came between them. She explored his chest and lower. He kissed her neck and pulled her into his embrace for support. Noah let his hands find her molten hot center, where he massaged her into submission. His pulse raced as she came for him, biting into his shoulder as she found her release.

Lexi kissed him fiercely, and her hand pumped his erection. Her eyes were open and inviting as she encouraged him to let go. He loved the way she caught her bottom lip between her teeth as she let her hands work their magic over his cock, and he loved the way she touched him, but he wanted to be inside of her. His hand reached for the nozzle, and he turned the water off. The hooks on the shower curtain zinged as he slid them back. Noah lifted Lexi's wet form into his arms and started toward the bedroom.

"Noah," she protested. "Ginger might be here any minute."

He continued a wet path to the bed. "She can wait."

Noah lay next to Lexi and made a grab for his pants, shoving his hand in the pocket before returning to the position between her thighs. She wrapped her legs around his waist and gave him a seductive grin. "What are you waiting for, cowboy? I'm ready."

Noah held his body firm, hovering above her beautiful, naked form. "Ready to say yes?"

Lexi looked at him, nodding. "I've come a long way since our last shower together. I'm free of guilt or worry. All I want is you, Noah."

He wiggled the diamond ring on the tip of his pinkie. "I'm glad to hear that. All I've ever wanted is you—more than anything in the world. I'm serious this time, and I know you probably think it's too soon, but I know what I want, and I promise if you say yes, you'll never regret it. I don't want to wait to make it official. Lexi, will you be my wife?"

Her jaw dropped as her eyes fixated on the glittering diamond. "Are you serious?" Her legs shifted as she sat up against the thick down pillows.

Noah nodded with a grin. He couldn't help but smile, even though there was the possibility that she might say no. It was probably way too soon for anyone she knew to accept them getting married. They'd think it was a shotgun wedding, and damn if the idea of Lexi having his baby didn't make his smile widen.

"Noah, I don't know what to say. You haven't met my family yet—my boys. You've never been a father."

He understood her worry, and he kissed her gently to show her he wanted this. "I'm ready, and I can't wait to meet them. Even if the boys are more rascally than Hank and I were as kids, I promise to love them and be a great dad, no matter what."

He brushed back a lock of her long blonde hair as he settled closer to her, letting his hips rest against hers. She wasn't pulling away. His erection flexed against her thigh as he waited for her answer.

Lexi looked at him with glowing eyes. In the reflection of her gaze, he saw the love he felt for her. He sensed it, even though she hadn't said the words yet. "I—I don't know. It's so sudden."

Noah took her hand and slid the ring onto her finger. "Well, I bought this for you, and I'm not giving it to anyone else. I want you to say yes because I want to start forever right now. I don't want either of us second-guessing where we want to be. I'm making a promise to be here for you for the rest of my life. When you're ready, you can let me know your answer, but the ring is yours, Lex. I love you, and I want you to wear it."

Wordlessly, she parted her thighs, letting him enter her slowly, tenderly, and with all the emotion pooling inside his heart pouring into her. He hadn't sheathed himself in the condom that lay on the nightstand, and she didn't protest as they both found their way to climax together.

Afterward, as Lexi lay in his arms, both of them skirting the edges of slumber, she turned her pert face up to look at him. "You know I'm not on birth control."

Noah shrugged. "I'm glad. I want to fill the ranch with a herd of our children. More siblings for our boys to grow up with."

"Lord help me, Noah, you do say all the right things, but do you know what it's like to raise children? Gussy, Burt and Damien mean the world to me, but they are a handful and a half."

Noah brushed a tendril of her hair away from her forehead. "I will love them every minute we spend together as a family and will welcome any new children with open arms. I think bringing kids into the world and helping them discover the best parts of living is one of the greatest purposes in life. I want to do that with you."

Her lashes hid her beautiful eyes from him, but her lips turned up at the corners, and he could see a warm flush across her cheeks. Her hand stroked the hair on his chest, and she sat up, propping herself on one elbow, giving him a daring look. "Well, if that's the way you feel, let's do it again."

Chapter 41

Roland thought it was great to come home to an empty house without family. He felt confident Ginger would be comfortable there for now since Luke, Maddie, and Kelsey were away. Luke had gone back to New Mexico for a couple of days to sign the papers for the sale of his art gallery. He would meet with the lawyers about the separation of assets, but he promised to be home before Christmas Eve. Luke and Charlotte had never married, but according to the state, they were a common-law marriage and needed to divide things fifty-fifty. Maddie and Kelsey were out Christmas shopping, and it was likely they'd be gone all day. Right now, it was just Ginger, Igor, Rollo and himself.

"Will the bathtub be okay for now? I can go back and get his fish tank later."

Ginger nodded as Rollo's back end tapped a happy dance that was moving at a separate beat than the front of his massive chest. Drool dripped from the silvery jowls of the pit bull, making Roland a little worried about Igor's stay.

He closed the door as he and Ginger entered the bathroom with the crate, separating Rollo from his new interest. "I think he's curious, but let's play it safe and keep the bathroom door shut for now."

Ginger leaned against the edge of the sink. "Thanks for coming to my rescue, but I really think you should take me to the bus station before your sister and niece come back, and we have to explain." She slapped a hand to her forehead.

Roland looked at her with concern. "What?"

"I have to return my rental car first. I did text Lexi when we left that I'd call her later. She hasn't answered her phone yet, and I can only imagine what she'll think when strangers start parking in her driveway. Thank God the boys are at her parents' house. She said she was going to get them today. Maybe she's already left."

Roland put the crate in the tub and unlatched the door. Igor stayed inside. "I don't blame you, buddy. I'm not good with change, either."

He sighed and stood. "I'll let you figure out how to best make Igor comfortable, and I'll wait for you in the kitchen. Does coffee sound good? I'll make some, and then you can fill me in on the mob situation and why all these people are chasing you."

Ginger gave him a sad nod, taking Igor out of his crate. She sat on the edge of the tub, holding him to her chest.

Roland's heart ached for her. Even Igor's little reptile eyes seemed to feel her sadness as his tongue darted out, touching Ginger's cheek.

Ginger knew there was a list of people she needed to contact, and she would, but right now, she needed to face Roland with the truth. It wasn't like she'd lied to him. She *was* Ginger Lynn Harding, who worked at the diner and lived on the ranch as Lexi's tenant and employee. Did it really matter that she had skipped over her famous actress past? None of this was her fault, except that she'd depended on prescription medication to dull her fear of flying.

Maybe when she found out about the tape, she should have confronted the problem instead of running away, but there was no way she could afford to stay in L.A. without a job. Hollywood was a cold-blooded lady with a fickle attitude. If the entertainment industry felt your desperation, you might never make it out alive. Though she'd made it this far in life without relying on anyone or having any close friends, living in Magnolia for the past few weeks had made her see possibilities.

Ginger made her way to the kitchen and sat down at the table. Roland set a cup of steaming coffee in front of her, and Rollo draped himself over her feet. "Thanks," she murmured as she leaned down to scratch the pit bull's ears. *Forget the artificial crap.* She scooped a good dose of sugar from the cute porcelain bowl into her cup and stirred. She was officially off her diet and didn't care anymore.

Roland sat across from her. "Who is Dallas, and why was this bozo in the diner harassing you about her last night?"

Ginger shook her head in confusion. "You weren't even there. How do you know anything about it?" She tried not to think about the kitchen light hanging overhead like a scene in an interrogation room.

Roland took a deep breath. "Roberta told Darcey, who called Melvina right away. Melvina called the station and gave the chief the license plate of the guy who was in the diner. Maurice wrote it down. The station put out an APB on a Mr. Kirk McNeil, who was picked up leaving Lexi Nash's ranch last night.

"For now, we're holding McNeil on a technicality for a moving violation, which I'm pretty sure his lawyer will call bogus on as soon as he gets to the station. So, I really need you to tell me why this guy is stalking you at the diner and why a hundred people showed up this morning asking for someone named Dallas."

Ginger held both hands over her mouth. "You're really holding Kirk in jail?"

Roland shrugged. "He's not behind bars or anything. He's probably drinking stale coffee and looking at the ceiling of the interrogation room."

Ginger started with a snort and a giggle, which quickly erupted into laughter, which dissolved into her hunching over and laugh-crying on the table. "Serves him right, the asshole," she managed to bite out between guffaws and tears.

Roland looked at her with round eyes, patting her hand as he waited for the momentary breakdown to finish.

Ginger finally gulped a big breath and sighed. "Kirk is my ex-boyfriend. He is harmless, at least physically, but he's also an idiot and a perv. While we were dating, I had to fly to Hawaii for a shoot. I'm terrified of flying, and November is a turbulent month for traveling across the Pacific. I asked my doctor to call in a prescription and took some Xanax to fly home. It made me loopy and gave me the munchies.

"After making my way through the strip mall of fast-food joints in the airport, falling asleep in the car on the ride home, and drooling on Kirk's shoulder, I never noticed the red blinking light in the corner of our bedroom that night. He recorded us—." She broke off, unable to actually say the words to the man she was having sexual relations with now. Their relationship was too new, and though they hadn't known each other long, she valued his respect.

"Filmed?" he asked in a calm voice.

Ginger looked him in the eye. He may not know who she was, but it was time that he learned. "I'm Dallas Derringer. I lived in L.A. before coming to Magnolia, and I was the star of a TV show called *Seducing Saturn*. That lasted until my a-hole ex decided to release the video he took, without my consent, of us having sex. Kirk plastered it all over the internet, and my life was ruined."

Her elbows dug into the kitchen table, and she let her forehead fall into her hands. She wanted the earth to swallow her whole. Ginger felt a wet tongue washing her arm. It worked its way up her armpit to her tear-streaked face.

"Rollo, down!" Roland commanded. He grabbed the dog by the collar and pulled him away from Ginger.

"Sorry," he said as he guided Rollo to his dog bed. "Like me, he's a sucker for a damsel in distress."

Roland sat down next to her, placing his hand on her shoulder. "Ginger, there are laws against revenge pornography. It's a crime. Why is that guy even allowed within a hundred feet of you? You need to press charges if you haven't already and file for a restraining order."

Ginger shook her head. "I have a lawyer, but the media was hounding my heels, and after losing my career and leaving L.A.... it's all been too much. I don't want to stand in front of a jury while people are watching me have consensual sex with Kirk, even if I didn't know I was being recorded. It's too personal. I don't want or need their judgment."

"Why did he go to the diner last night? What did he want? Did he threaten you?" Roland's tone was gentle, but the red creeping up his neck and the vein that throbbed there were firm indicators he was angry. "You are the victim here, Ginger, and you have no reason to run away from L.A., Magnolia, or any place."

Ginger pointed arbitrarily to the outside world. "I have hundreds of reasons to hide. Have you read the gossip columns, celebrity magazines, social media troll posts?"

He shook his head.

She looked at him in wonder. It was blissful that he knew nothing about modern media, but he had no idea how out of control the information machine could get. "When I sold my condo in L.A., reporters sat outside of the office after the closing of the sale, asking where I planned to go, how would I ever get a job again, or if I planned on doing professional porn!" She swiped at a fresh stream of tears.

Roland closed the gap and took her in his arms, squeezing her with comfort. She supposed he didn't know what else to do. She didn't either.

Ginger let him hold her for a while as she let herself cry out her anger and humiliation in his arms. When the tears settled, she pulled away from him.

Roland still rubbed her arms as if he was trying to ward off the negative memories and repair her discontent. "What do you want to do?"

She looked at him with sudden clarity. "Take me to the station. I need to see Kirk."

Roland tried to contain his anger as he drove Ginger to the station to meet her ex. *The nerve of the guy.* As a constable, he'd dealt with victims of battery, abuse, and a plethora of domestic cases, but he'd never felt a bit of empathy for a man who would take advantage of a woman. As small as Magnolia was, he still saw problems of all kinds—spousal abuse, drug abuse, prostitution, sex trafficking and more. He didn't see it daily, but he ran across all types of criminals.

He'd tried to help several women who were victims of crimes committed by partners who were close to them. The problem was that the psychological trauma sometimes went deeper than the physical damage. Men like Kirk were the scum of the earth, using a woman who trusted him to make money by exploiting them. He didn't know much about *Seducing Saturn* or who Dallas Derringer was, but none of that mattered because to him, Ginger was a person first. A woman with rights that deserved protection. The scum she'd trusted to enter her bedroom had betrayed her, and for that, he would have to pay.

The chief didn't take these instances lightly, and if Roland could convince Ginger to prosecute, they could put this guy away. Even if it needed to be done in L.A., Roland would fly there and ensure she had the support to make the charges stick. He knew the procedures to a successful prosecution, and he knew the way perps worked the system. If it was the last thing Roland did, he would see this guy pay for hurting Ginger.

A small zing of jealousy wormed its way into his stomach, and he felt his gut churn. The thought of someone else touching Ginger and then betraying her trust was torture. It bothered him that she wanted to see McNeil now. Roland knew he needed to prioritize his emotions. Ginger was a victim of a terrible crime. He needed to be there for her and make sure she left whatever she was walking into whole.

He parked the car and turned to her as she unclicked the seatbelt. "Are you sure you want to do this? We can call your lawyer. You don't have to see this guy in person. In fact, I'm not sure I recommend it. Losers like this have a way of twisting their victim's thoughts, and it gets hard to pin them down for their crimes."

Ginger's brows furrowed, and her shoulders straightened. "I may be the victim of a crime, but I will not continue to be beaten by this. It ends here, today. I'm sick of the shame and the drama. My life needs to go on."

With that, she stepped out of the car and slammed the door. He didn't think her anger was meant for him. She was obviously steeling herself against what was to come. He got out of the car and reached for the door as she entered the station.

Before she could cross the threshold, Roland caught her shoulder, making her pause as he squeezed it with reassurance. "I'll be here for you no matter what. Remember, I'm here for *you*," he repeated with emphasis.

Ginger entered the station with Roland by her side. His colleagues moved out of their way as he led her down several corridors to the room where Kirk was being held.

As they entered, Kirk looked up in surprise. "What are you doing here?" Then with more accusation, "Did you have them arrest me? Geeze, Dallas. I said I was sorry."

Roland gripped Kirk by the collar of his t-shirt. "Do you know what we do to sick little twerps like you in this town? This isn't Hollywood, buddy, so you better settle down and show some respect. The lady wants to ask you some questions, and you are going to be on your best behavior. Understood?"

Kirk couldn't really move in the position that Roland was holding him, but he managed to squeak out, "Yes, sir."

Roland dropped Kirk back into the chair. His eyes roved over Ginger, in silent question.

Ginger nodded to him. "I'll be alright."

Roland frowned and, with a sigh, opened the door. "I'll be right outside if you need me."

Kirk kept his eyes on the table between them as if he were too afraid to look at her. She decided to be the one to start. "Why did you do it?"

Red splotches colored his perfect complexion. Kirk's head lifted, and as his gaze finally met hers, she could see the sorrow in his hollow blue eyes. Ginger wondered if he was sorry that he'd released it because of what it had done to her career or sorry that he was dealing with the repercussions of his stupid actions.

"I'm an idiot, Dallas. I didn't mean for it to happen. I swear on my life. I uploaded it to my computer, you know, so I could watch it. The original was on a zip drive, and it was encrypted, but then my computer had an issue, and I took it to one of those geeky tech places. They said my computer had been hacked and there was spyware or something on it. I tossed the computer in the trash, and I promise, I never even thought about that video. After we broke up, I never looked at it again. I swear it." He put his hand up like he was testifying to the court. "I don't know if it was the spyware, the geeky guy who checked out my computer or someone who found it in the dumpster...." He rubbed his forehead with the palms of his hands. "I just know that I didn't do it."

Ginger didn't know if she should believe him, but from what she did know about Kirk, he'd never been malicious. Sure, he'd cheated on her, and she had been so caught up in her new role in *Seducing Saturn* that she hadn't really cared about his infidelity. Kirk wasn't exactly a man of substance, and she'd never fancied herself in love with him. They had been together out of convenience and were hardly more than bed partners and an occasional dinner date. He was her "something to make life off the set less lonely" guy. She hadn't harbored any ill will toward him over the breakup. Ginger knew she'd checked out of the relationship long before he found an aspiring actress to warm his bed.

"I thought you did it because they didn't contact you for the show after the pilot."

Kirk shook his head. "I was pissed," he confirmed. "It was like the show dumped me, and you didn't want me anymore, either. But I would never try to get back at you like that. Sleeping with Anna was an attempt to get you to notice me again. You quit talking to me, sleeping with me and eventually, you barely even came home."

He reached across to touch her hand, but she snagged it away. "I know I look guilty, but you aren't the only victim here. That's my naked body on the film too. If I were trying to get back at you for leaving me behind, I would have released the video of you in the shower instead."

Ginger stood, her chair scraping against the tiles. "What video of me in the shower?"

Kirk put both hands up in front of him. "I deleted that one. I really did!"

She shook her head, cursing as she sat back down. "Why should I believe anything you say?"

Kirk rubbed the knees of his tailored jeans. "I got rid of all the equipment. I promise. After I got hacked, and all this stuff came out, I realized how serious it was. Please, Ginger. Don't press charges against me. I know now that I should have never taped us. The video getting out was an accident, but in the end, you have to admit, you're more popular than ever." His eyes lit with hope.

"Really, I did you a favor. I even got you another gig. Johnny from the studio is here to talk business. He wants to meet you back at the hotel."

"Favor? Are you nuts? Of all the ridiculous excuses and…."

Ginger was fuming with anger at Kirk's immature activities and his inability to see what had become of her popularity. He was an idiot, and he probably wasn't lying about not meaning for the videos to get out, but they had, and actions had consequences. Her stupidity was trusting Kirk and ever sleeping with him in the first place. Her hands massaged her temples as she thought of where she wanted this to go. Kirk was a jerk and a loser, but she didn't want to put anyone in jail.

"Before you arrived, I had already decided to call my lawyer and forget about having you charged."

Kirk stood as if he were about to hug her.

Ginger's arm shot out to stop his approach, and he sat back down. "But—you will still have to sign a confession—notarized—about taking the videos without my knowledge or consent and state that you never intended their release. I'll hold onto it, and if it is ever revealed that you did this on purpose, I will use it to prosecute you to the full extent of the law. I feel it's my personal duty to protect other women from any future abuse by you. Do anything like this again, and *you* will pay the price." She gave him a moment to process the information.

"That means jail time, pretty boy." Ginger's eyebrows raised as she pierced him with a challenging glare. Kirk had little money past rent and groceries, and garnisheeing his wages wouldn't help her get back on track. She wanted to put this behind her once and for all. "I have your address from the card you left at the ranch. My lawyer will be in touch."

Kirk nodded, smiling with what could only be relief. It made her glad to know he'd been agonizing over the possibility of going to prison. She hadn't thought of the secret taping as a criminal offense when it happened, but after it went viral, her lawyer had encouraged her to press charges.

When Ginger stood, Kirk did, too. "So, you want to go talk to Johnny?" Ginger shook her head. "No."

He reached out, grasping her arm. "Ginger." It was one of the few times he'd used her given name. "This is the chance of a lifetime. They've already written three seasons, and they expect at least five. He's ready to give the contract to you today. It's a big role with lots of money. Don't say no. Rumor has it that Kari Blake is going to take it if you don't. You're first pick."

Ginger pondered his proposition. Kari Blake was younger, prettier and probably more famous than Ginger before the video started circulating.

"So why wait for me? Why doesn't Johnny sign Kari?"

Kirk let go of her arm. His eyes studied the laces on his tennis shoes. He didn't have to say it.

She scowled. "Because the sex tape you released has everyone clamoring to see more of Dallas Derringer. Not that I can reveal any more, right? Thanks to you, everyone has seen me in my birthday suit, immortalized forever on the internet."

Kirk dared to give her a half-grin. "The tape was really hot. You have to admit, we looked great together."

Her hands balled into fists, and it was all she could do not to deck him. "You ruined my life. Isn't that enough?"

"Please!" Kirk begged. "I need this break, Ginger. The only way they'll take me is if I can get you. I got a signing bonus." He dug in his breast pocket and handed her an envelope. "It's ten thousand dollars, and it's yours, but you're going to get way more, probably a hundred thousand more."

Torn between throwing the envelope in his face and telling him how ten grand couldn't repair her life or pocketing the money and calling a truce, she froze. Mouth open, hands balled into fists and tears threatening to pour down her face, what she wanted to do finally dawned on her. She had a plan. Plucking the envelope from Kirk's tight fingers, she shoved it in her purse, then walked out the door.

As Roland met her in the hall, she kept walking. His voice was low and conspiratorial. "What do you want me to do?"

"Take me home, please." Then she added. "Let him go. I'm not pressing charges." She'd had her chance to do that before leaving L.A. She supposed they could hold him on harassment for following her to the diner and then to Lexi's ranch. She was tired of hiding, and she was tired of arguing and defending herself over past decisions. Hindsight was always twenty-twenty, and for once, she had perfect clarity. Kirk, Johnny and Hollywood could kiss her ass.

Chapter 42

"You can stay with me. You don't have to leave."

Ginger sighed as she sat on the edge of the tub and picked up Igor, running her painted nails down the scales of his back. "I appreciate the offer, but now that the world knows where I'm hiding out, there won't be any peace in Magnolia."

Roland leaned against the frame of the bathroom door, chewing at the inside of his cheek as he tried to think of an angle that would convince Ginger to stay in his life. "It will all die down in a week or two. They'll all get bored soon enough and go back to L.A. Besides, Magnolia doesn't have sushi."

She laughed. "Nice try, but I found a place in The Woodlands. Granted, it's not the best, but enough to keep them thriving until they get their fill of Dallas's dirty laundry."

Roland shook his head. "Dallas Derringer. What made you pick that name?"

Ginger stroked Igor and looked up at him with a mischievous grin. "It was my laser-tag name when I was a kid. I lived in Dallas, and the whole gunslinger thing was big at the time. Besides, I liked the alliteration, and Ginger Lynn Harding sounds too much like a porn star." She gave him a knowing grin.

He was guilty of thinking stripper name, but he'd never said the thought out loud. Her look said that she'd probably heard similar thoughts over the years. Roland shook his head. "I don't think so. Ginger is a beautiful name, and I know a lot of Hardings around Magnolia."

She winced at the reminder. "Me too. My cousin, Hank, and his cousin, Noah. By the way, I saw Noah again at Lexi's last night. Lexi didn't look all that surprised when he showed up to escort Kirk off the property. He drove

me to the cottage, and I'm pretty sure he went back to see Lexi afterward."
She raised her eyebrows as she turned her face to give him a side-eye look.
The stare said she was aware he could tell her more about that story.

Roland grinned. "I'm glad to hear it. Lexi needs a hero. It's about time
Noah got his head out of his ass."

Ginger put a hand to her mouth in mock surprise. "I've never heard
you curse."

He approached her, taking Igor carefully from her and putting him back
in the tub. Her hand was pliant as he pulled her to her feet. "You think you
know me, but I promise you, I am full of surprises." His head dipped to
find her lips parted and ready for his kiss. Embracing her waist and pulling
her into his hard torso was the easy part. Not ripping her clothes off and
having his way with her on the bathroom counter was the difficult part. He
was rock-hard, and he couldn't stand the thought of her leaving. Maybe he
could give her a firm reason to stay.

What an incredible night and a definite high note to leave Magnolia on.
Ginger doubted she would ever forget the moments she'd shared with Roland,
even if they'd never made it through the complete book of *The Kama Sutra*.

It was early when Roland showered and put on his uniform. He sat on
the edge of the bed, brushing her hair back. "I have to go to work. Kelsey's
at a friend's, and Maddie went to the diner, so it's just you, Igor and Rollo."

As if on cue, the big silvery pit bull jumped up beside her and stretched
himself out on the bed with a muffled snort and a thump of his tail. "I
can't take off today, but I'll see if I can sneak away at noon to check on you.
There's plenty of food in the fridge, and coffee is next to the pot. Call me if
you need anything. I'm just five minutes down the road."

Ginger stretched and yawned, sitting up to kiss him goodbye.

Roland stroked her hair once more, holding a lock between his fingers,
studying it. "Will you go back to your natural color now?"

Ginger nodded. "Probably. I miss being me."

Roland's lips brushed hers in a slow, chaste kiss. "Please don't go anywhere. Get some rest, and we'll talk more tonight."

Ginger felt a twinge of guilt as she agreed, knowing full well she
wouldn't be there when he got home. He lived with his sister and niece,

and Ginger wouldn't let the media make their quiet home a living circus. Kelsey was too young to understand the things people would say, and this time, it was Ginger's job to protect Roland and his family. He hadn't said anything about his future career, but Mona had mentioned he would be the next mayoral candidate. Before the shit hit the fan and half of the gossip columnists descended upon Magnolia, Ginger hadn't thought too much about being seen together, except for that first night at the hotel. She supposed that had been selfish on her part, but she really liked being with him.

Besides avoiding the unwanted publicity, she owed it to Roland to disappear. Wouldn't that be best for him, his career and his family? There wasn't room for him to run for mayor and to keep a tainted lady hanging on his arm. Leaving was something she had to do—for Roland.

An hour later, a car pulled up in front of the house, and Ginger grabbed her things, including Igor in his crate. She gave Rollo a scratch behind the ears and a big kiss that left a red lipstick print on his forehead. "You take care of them, okay, big guy?"

Rollo's whip of a tail thumped as if to say, "Absolutely. I got this."

The diner was off-limits, but she'd call Melvina from the road and explain once she picked up her car from Lexi's.

When she arrived at the ranch, Lexi was out front, waiting for her on the porch swing. Ginger took Igor from the car, paid and thanked the driver. Slow steps carried her to join Lexi, where she sat next to her and let the story unravel. For all the worry Ginger had suffered, thinking Lexi would freak when she found out who she really was, the single mom of three boys reacted in the most rational manner.

"You don't have to go," Lexi insisted. "You didn't do anything wrong."

Ginger nodded. "I know, and I'm glad you see it that way, but you have three boys to protect, and if I stay, things will be said that they won't understand." She turned to Lexi, stopping the swinging motion of the bench. Ginger put her hand on Lexi's shoulder as she met her worried gaze.

"I'll be okay. I promise. You're a good mom, and you know I am right on this one, so please, let's say good-bye, and hopefully, we can see each other when I get settled and come back to see my mom in Plano." Ginger sniffed, not expecting to shed tears.

Lexi's eyes pooled with moisture, too. "It's not fair. You shouldn't have to leave us so soon. What about the diner, the gingerbread competition? The boys are going to be so heartbroken."

Ginger brushed away a tear as she forced a smile. "I'll really miss those little rascals. Tell them I'll be back one day, and besides," she looked down at Lexi's ring finger. "I think they are going to be excited to have a new stepdad to get to know. The family will need some alone time together."

"You are family, Ginger. Don't go running off because I'm getting married." Lexi beamed as she put one hand over her mouth and splayed the other out to admire the ring. "I can't believe Noah asked me to marry him so soon." After a pause, she added, "I can't believe I said yes. We barely know each other. He just met my parents and the boys."

Ginger gave her friend a knowing hug. "You'll be great together. I know it. What is it they say? Love conquers all."

Lexi nodded. "I do love him. I never thought I could love anyone again after Jack, but when Noah and I met, I knew right away how I felt about him. Of course, I felt so guilty back then and screwed it all up, but…."

Ginger sat back, assessing her friend. For the first time in a long time, she really felt like she had a true confidante in Lexi. It was hard leaving, but it was partly because of their friendship that Ginger didn't want to stay and drag everyone down. She squeezed Lexi's arm. "But you don't feel guilty anymore, do you?"

Lexi shook her head. "No. Not anymore. I feel like I'm living in one of those chick-flick movies where everyone is happy and dancing at the end." Her cheeks flushed pink, and her eyes shimmered with joy this time.

Ginger felt something she hadn't felt in a long time, happiness for someone else's good fortune. Maybe there was hope for her yet. Lexi Nash, soon to be Harding, was finally a happy woman.

Together, they hooked up a little wagon to the four-wheeler and drove down the trail to pack the rest of Ginger's things. She hadn't brought much, so there wasn't a lot left to cart back to the rental car. Ginger returned to the porch and picked up the crate with Igor in it, looking nervously at the trees for any reporters who might jump out. "I'm so happy for you. I truly am, and I'm sorry about the commotion I've caused."

Lexi had filled her in on the dozens of paparazzi who appeared as she and Noah went to pick up the boys. Laughter rolled out as she described Noah almost decking one of the men who shoved a microphone too close.

"Roland assured me they will keep people off your property so that you and the boys won't be bothered again." She hugged Lexi one last time.

"Ginger, where will you go?"

"I'm going to New York."

Lexi frowned. "What about the diner and the gingerbread bake-off?" she asked again.

Ginger shrugged. "I'll call Melvina. I'm sure she'll understand under the circumstances. Roland said the café was full of reporters and out-of-town people. Sounds like business is booming, even without my gingerbread cookies."

"I guess that means you'll miss the Snowflake Ball, too." Lexi gave her a wan smile.

Ginger knew the questions weren't about missing the cookie contest or the ball, but missing her, and Ginger felt the same. "There will be plenty of parties in New York. Maybe you can come out and visit me when I get settled, and we'll paint the town red."

Lexi nodded. "I'd like that, but I don't know what a country gal like me would do in New York." Her smile didn't quite reach her eyes. She was stalling. "What about the contract in L.A.? You said you love acting, and it sounds like a lot of money. Don't you think they would get tired of hounding you once you've moved on to another project?"

Ginger felt her brows knit together as she thought about the generous offer and the ten thousand she'd snagged from Kirk's fingers. He owed her that much. She'd lost more on her condo and getting out of her car payment than what was in that envelope, all because of his actions. Sighing, she said, "It was tempting, but I was never happy in L.A. I love acting, but there are other places to do that, and if I don't make it there, well," she paused, trying to beat down the feeling of defeat before she even attempted the challenge, "I can find other things to do in life."

"Like Roland Karr? I thought you guys kinda had a thing."

Ginger hadn't wanted to talk about Roland. He would be upset when he got back, and she wasn't there. "I really like Roland, but it's better this way for him and his family, too. He has Maddie and Kelsey to think of." Taking a deep breath, she pressed her lips together in a tight smile. "I better get going." She made her way down the porch steps and toward her car, glancing back at her friend one last time.

Lexi shook her head, calling after her. "You're ready to sacrifice everything for everybody, but what about you, Ginger? What about what you want?"

One step and then another, she told herself. Keep walking. This life isn't possible. It isn't what you wanted a few weeks ago, and you should be thankful to get away. Get in your car and start the engine.

Lexi followed her. "You don't have to disappear."

Ginger needed to leave, but Lexi had been so generous with her home and kindness, she wouldn't shut her out now. She rolled down the rental car window as her friend approached with sorrowful, imploring eyes.

Lexi gripped the leather edge of the opening. "You know I had my own lonely, sad ending a few years ago, and I thought that was it for me. I was down for a while, trying to accept that it was life throwing me another curveball." Lexi leaned in a little for emphasis, giving Ginger another sad smile. "You never know where life will take you. Be kind to yourself, Ginger. You deserve better." She patted the door and let out a long sigh, waving goodbye as Ginger backed away.

She listened to the crunch of gravel under her tires as she drove down the lane out to the paved highway. The large live oaks and pines blew in the breeze as if they were waving goodbye, too. Swiping at her eyes, she donned her baseball cap and fished for her sunglasses in the console. It was a long drive to New York, and it was best she stay in disguise until she got there. Admittedly, she had enjoyed her time in Magnolia, but if someone had asked Dallas Derringer what life would be like after *Seducing Saturn*, she wouldn't have dreamed of saying, "Like baking gingerbread cookies in a small Texas town with a hot law enforcement officer steaming up my sheets." At least she'd have the hot memories to keep her warm in New York.

He wasn't surprised when he returned to a mostly empty house. It was vacant of any living thing, except for Rollo drooling on the entryway rug, thumping his tail in greeting. Roland patted him on the head as he made his way to the kitchen. A scribbled note lay on the counter, anchored by a warm Shiner longneck. Did she think a hot beer would take away the sting, or was it spit in his eye? He let out a bitter hiss as he read the message, chuffing at the last line.

Thanks for your hospitality and all those…positions.

Ginger might be a lot of things, but he knew she wasn't spiteful. The L.A. chump she let off the hook was a testament to the fact. Roland thought about how irritated she'd been the day he pulled her over. Now he understood why. The internet had plenty of links to the Dallas Derringer scandal, and he'd spent his morning fishing through the terrible posts.

Ginger had given him the brief once-over, but the articles in the gossip columns were endless. It was awful that people could get away with printing anything they wanted and presenting everything in the worst possible light. The original video had been officially removed, but there were cuts of it all over the internet, with fuzzy dots blurring the faces and covering the naked parts of the couple on film. He didn't watch for more than a few seconds. It turned his stomach to see how humanity could find entertainment at someone else's expense. Seeing Ginger naked or with the loser from the police station wasn't what needled him, but the fact that someone could do this to an innocent human being. Ginger didn't deserve it, and it infuriated him to know what she'd been dealing with all by herself. If they hadn't let Kirk McNeil go, he would be back at the station pulverizing him now.

Roland put the warm longneck back in the fridge and closed the door. He wasn't hungry, and he didn't feel like sitting in his house alone. Maybe Ginger had gone to the diner before she left. It was a long shot, but he'd try to catch her there.

"Come on, Rollo. It's lunchtime!"

The silvery-blue pit bull bounced to Roland's heel and followed him to the cruiser. He didn't give the dog a hard time for letting Ginger go. "She probably tricked you with those cat-green eyes, didn't she, boy?" The dog's tail thumped against the seat in response. "Yep. She tricked me, too."

Maddie greeted him with a menu and a hug as he entered the diner. His sister was always sunshine when he needed it most. She gave his arm a squeeze as she walked him to his usual spot. "I'm sorry about Ginger. She was very nice, and Kelsey really liked her."

Roland nodded. "So did I. Did she come by here before she left?"

Maddie shook her head. "She called and talked to Melvina. Mel didn't share much, only that she wasn't coming back for the gingerbread competition, and we'd have to kick butt on our own."

Roland nodded. "Yeah, her note said she was going to New York. I guess she knows someone out there, but don't say anything to anybody. We don't want to be the reason that she can't find peace."

Maddie looked around at the full dining room. "It's been great for business. We're understaffed, but the tips have been double the usual. These

Californians have money, but I feel bad for poor Ginger. Tell her that her secret is safe with us. No one here will give her up to these city slickers." She filled his coffee cup and set it in front of him. The door dinged, and she tapped the counter twice. "I got another table. Be right back."

Roland heard the scrape of the walker before he was nudged by the massive purse covered in plastic white daisies. "Sorry to hear about your actress girlfriend leaving."

Roland bit his bottom lip to contain what he was thinking. Did someone send out a mass text alert to everyone in town? Hell, he'd just found out Ginger left town twenty minutes ago.

Ms. Rosie settled herself in the seat next to him. "Well, aren't you gonna go after her skinny ass? Magnolia folks don't care if she's all over the intra-net in her birthday suit, doing the hide-the-sausage pony ride. It wasn't her fault that she was too famous for her Frederick's of Hollywood britches. We like her, and we don't care if she's a hoochie mama. Now go get her back so we can win this gingerbread competition!"

Ms. Rosie's determined look and age were the only things keeping Roland in his seat.

She cleared her throat and said in a theatrical whisper. "I had one of her practice cookies here at the diner, and I hate to say it, but they were better than Melvina's." Rosie looked over her shoulder to see if anyone had heard her blasphemy.

It was common knowledge that no one ever challenged Melvina's baked goods. They were the best, with the exception of Ginger's gingerbread, according to Rosie. Roland wished he'd had the chance to taste a practice cookie. "I never got to try one, but Lexi's boys couldn't quit talking about them."

"See, kids know a good treat better than anyone. The older we get, the more taste buds we lose. They should make the Nash kids the judges. They know what's what!" Rosie grasped her walker so hard her knuckles turned white. "We need her to put Magnolia on the map. Now go get her, copper!"

Roland forced a chuckle, but he didn't feel all that amused. "Ms. Rosie, I know you mean well, but Ginger is a grown woman, and she made her decision to go elsewhere. I can't do anything about that."

Rosie stood. The wheels of her walker squeaked forward, nearly touching his arm. "Can't or won't?" She made a harumph and scooted away. Roland could hear her as she continued while crossing the diner. "What's the use of having a badge if you can't make people do what you want?"

Melvina came by with an order pad. "Maddie's got another table. Can I put in an order for you?"

Roland liked Melvina. She and her family were salt of the earth, and they'd treated his sister well since she started working there. "I'm having just coffee today."

Melvina scribbled something on a check, then tore it off and set it face down on the table. Tucking the order pad into her back pocket and the pen behind her ear, she gave him a meaningful look. "Don't listen to Ms. Rosie. She gets attached to people rather quickly, and I think she took a shine to Ginger. No one expects you to bring her back, but if you do talk to her, make sure she knows she's welcome here anytime. She left me this." Melvina paused, holding her finger on top of the check. "I'm supposed to mail her last check."

Chapter 43

Ginger landed a role within days of her first audition. She'd researched the Broadway listings and spoke with her agent back in L.A., who'd gotten her in touch with the right contacts in New York. Even though the sex tape had temporarily ruined her career in L.A. and got her fired from *Seducing Saturn*, now both sides of the country were clamoring to sign her on the dotted line. She guessed it was like her agent had told her from the beginning, "All publicity is good publicity."

Ginger had never imagined herself on Broadway when she was growing up. She'd only had aspirations for Hollywood and movie roles that would make her famous. Granted, Broadway successes weren't as well-known or appreciated by the broader public, but anyone who knew Broadway knew she'd hit it big. The role was in a new production with an established playwright who had won multiple awards. It was expected to be the next rave, and she was playing the leading role opposite Hugh Grantham, the best leading man on the Broadway circuit.

So why did it all feel so lackluster? The contract she'd signed offered a huge advance. Her bank account was full of money to live very comfortably for a long while. The media wasn't knocking down her door, but they would be when the play opened, and for an entirely different reason. Ginger would start rehearsals right after the New Year, which gave her a much-needed vacation…alone…in New York…with nothing to do.

Ginger ran her toe along the edge of the coffee table, flipping closed the magazine she'd been reading. As she gazed toward the window, she pondered her predicament. The apartment was small but furnished and above a noodle shop. The sandwich place across the street and the Italian restaurant on the corner meant she'd never have to cook unless she wanted to. She should be thrilled. So, why did it feel like she'd lost her best friend?

Because I have.

She hadn't answered Roland's calls for fear of hearing his voice. Her only text to him was to ask him not to contact her. It was better to rip the bandage off all at once, wasn't it? Roland hadn't seemed upset by the sex tape leak, but she'd worried how it might affect his job in a small town, being affiliated with her. What would his colleagues think? What would voters think? How could she stand in the way of it all? She couldn't see Roland in some city like L.A. or New York. And he had Maddie and Kelsey to think of. Besides, everyone knew long-distance relationships didn't work.

Ginger stood stretching and staring out the window at the expanse of urban blight. She hadn't known it would be so easy to get a job when she'd signed the six-month lease for the apartment near Chinatown. The dumpster, a brick wall and metal fire-escape were her new view—for the many months ahead. A stray cat strolled past her window on the second-floor metal landing and hissed as Igor stared back at it. His reptile hunting stance reminded her that he was getting bigger by the day, and she would need to get him a bigger terrarium soon or let him roam free. Roland had asked her about iguanas and their lifespan. It surprised her that she didn't know much about her pet besides what to feed him. She'd gulped when she searched the internet, finding two-year-old iguanas as large as their owners. She hadn't told the landlord about Igor and hoped that she could find a reptile-friendly place before her time was up.

Time. She had two weeks free before she started rehearsals. What did she want to do with it? Images flashed through her mind of the few weeks she'd spent in Magnolia. She remembered Roland giving her a stern, reprimanding glare as he wrote her a warning ticket on her first day in town, then she'd seen him in Hank's and he'd been polite, offering to drive her home. During her turtle rescue, Roland assessed her with interest as he asked her on a date. The muscle in his jaw had worked, revealing he was unsure she would accept. Ginger shivered as she remembered how he'd massaged her feet in the hotel room and how he'd tried to ignore her slipping robe. He'd made an effort to do the right thing by not taking her to bed that night, and for some reason, his conservative appreciation had appealed to her.

It was hard not to smile as she thought of his intelligent, amber eyes or his trimmed dark hair and how it felt when she ran her fingers through it, trying to mess it up. He was so…*right* all the time. It should have infuriated her to be with someone so good and true and always looking out for others.

Ginger looked down at the rumpled t-shirt she wore, admitting that she was by no means perfect. It was Roland's soft cotton t-shirt with the Magnolia emblem on it. She had borrowed it to sleep in but had purposely packed it when she'd left. It was something to remember him by. Wrapping her fist in the stretchy material, she brought it to her nose. The scent of him still clung to it.

Ginger had been in New York a week, and now everything was going to be okay. She would survive the mistakes of her past and maybe even enjoy fame again. As she showered and brushed her teeth, her mind sorted through endless possibilities. She was finally free. There was nothing in her contract that said she couldn't leave New York until rehearsals started. It was only a fraction of a second that she contemplated laying in the sun in the Maldives, flying to Paris, or going to see the opera in Vienna. The places on her bucket list were longer than her imagination, but there was only one place she could think of that she wanted to be right now, and people were counting on her. One place that was worth braving her fear of flying.

Roland wasn't in the mood for the Galleria, and he sure as hell wasn't in the mood for a Christmas party after, but there he was, with everyone else he knew. All of them were dressed in white—Maddie, Kelsey, Luke and their father by his side. The second-level plaza in the mall had been cleared for The Galleria Gingerbread Extravaganza, and everyone who was anyone in Magnolia was there to support The Cupcake Diner and Dive's team.

Luke nudged him. "Why the long face, Roland? You look like someone pissed in your coffee this morning."

Roland tried not to roll his eyes at his brother's jab. Instead, he let out a calm breath, looked at his watch and turned to Maddie. "How long does this thing last?" It was almost five in the evening, and they'd been there since three.

Maddie gave him a knowing grin. "You look like you're ten years old again, having to dress up and go to Aunt Marge's wedding. It's a Christmas cookie event, Roland. Try to enjoy yourself. Honestly, if you continue that attitude, it's gonna be a long night, and Santa will leave coal in your stocking. The Snowflake Ball is after this, and we need to help Melvina pack up before driving out to The Woodlands."

Roland rolled his shoulders and shifted his head from side to side, trying to let the tension out of his tight muscles. "I know about the party tonight. That's why we're all wearing white. I wanted to know how long it would be until they announce the winners."

Kelsey pointed at the elf walking to the stage. "I think it's now, Uncle Roland!"

The elf talked for some time about the spirit of Christmas and even invited Santa up to the stage for another uplifting talk to the children. He droned on about what signs to look for if they wanted to spot reindeer and what his favorite cookie was—no surprise that it was gingerbread. That led to a person dressed like a mouse who read a Christmas poem and did a theatrical jig. Afterward, an award was given out to the top three high school students who'd submitted creative writing for the event.

Roland suppressed another yawn as he rocked on his heels with boredom. Through the fog of his brain, he finally recognized the mayor's voice next to him. "She did it! Melvina finally won!"

Luke nudged Roland's side again. "Yeah, buddy!" He was clapping hard with the rest of the Magnolia gang.

Roland joined in the clapping, muttering, "Thank God. It's over," as Melvina took the stage and the trophy.

Holding up the golden tower of metal gingerbread men for all to see, she looked back over her shoulder where her father, husband, brother and sister-in-law stood. "Thank you," she said to everyone, but her gaze flashed back to her husband, Riley. "I couldn't have done this without the support of my family, but especially the diner staff." She paused a moment as if to catch her breath.

Scanning the many Galleria shoppers and onlookers at the cookie event, she took a deep breath and blew out a, "Whew," as she swiped her forehead. "We finally did it. I can proudly say that the diner has won a lot of cooking contests, and we have tried to win this for a few years now and came really close. That being said, this year, we couldn't have done it without the help of a friend."

Roland's heart beat harder in his chest as his blood rushed with excitement through his veins. Had Ginger come back? His eyes scanned the stage and the surrounding area. Marching in that direction, his ears were deaf to his siblings' calls as he made his way to the front.

Melvina made eye contact with him, and for a moment, he thought she looked nervous like she'd given away the surprise. "She couldn't be with us today, but we want to thank her for teaching us her grandmother's special recipe. It will remain the official diner recipe every season from here on out. Or, until I can find a way to beat it." Melvina chuckled as Riley laughed heartily behind her. "So, if you want more of these delicious cookies, make your way over to The Cupcake Diner and Dive. We'll be happy to load you up and make your Christmas extra special!" She lifted the trophy above her head as the locals cheered.

Participants and onlookers started to dissipate as Roland stood immobilized for several moments.

Luke's hand squeezed his shoulder. "You ready to help load up?"

Roland nodded. "That's what we came for. Let's get this done."

They took the display apart and loaded what they could into Luke's new truck. He'd bought it upon returning from New Mexico. The rest of the décor from the cookie event would go into other volunteers' vehicles. Roland was careful not to soil his all-white attire, but Luke wasn't so lucky. He sported a smudge of green frosting on his white tie and the edge of his left shirt sleeve.

It was dark outside already, though it wasn't quite six o'clock. Roland loved Christmas, but nightfall coming so early made him weary when he was alone.

They had agreed to take the display setup to the diner's storage facility on their way to The Woodlands. Maddie would meet them at the hotel after she dropped off Kelsey at a kids' Christmas party with Lexi's boys. Their dad's senior apartment was on the way, so Maddie would take him home, too. The complex was throwing their own shindig for the residents, and their father seemed anxious to attend. Roland had a sneaking suspicion that he had a special interest in someone there. Maddie had tried to use the logistics as an excuse to get out of going to the Snowflake Ball, but Roland and Luke had insisted she come. It was important for their sister to get out and enjoy herself as an adult.

The hotel was beautiful, and the ballroom was filled with guests dressed entirely in white. Some, Roland knew, and others he didn't recognize. The sea of strangers must be from The Woodlands or Houston. He went to the bar with Luke. They'd seen no sign of Maddie yet, but he decided to get a drink as they waited. Noah and Lexi were already in line. As Noah handed Lexi a glass of champagne, her diamond ring flashed in the glow cast by the chandeliers above.

"Congrats, you guys! Have you set a date?" Luke asked without greeting.

It was Roland's turn to elbow his brother. "Hello, Lexi." He nodded. "Noah."

Lexi beamed at them, turning and wiggling her hand. "It's okay, Roland. We've told most everyone already. I was too excited to keep it a secret."

"Congratulations," Roland and Luke said in unison, taking turns shaking Noah's hand, hugging Lexi, then grabbing one of the many glasses of champagne from the bar ledge. The four of them clinked glasses and took a sip.

Roland was happy for Lexi and Noah. If anyone deserved to be together, they did, but an empty feeling pierced his heart. He wasn't one to give envy a place in his conscience, but he recognized the emotion pumping through his thoughts. Noah had finally gotten the woman he loved, and Lexi was going to marry the man of her dreams. *Good for them.*

Roland had wanted Ginger to walk out on that stage tonight so badly, and when she hadn't, he couldn't shake off the disappointment. He tried to school his face as everyone around him chatted happily but wasn't sure he was successful. The vise squeezing his heart was suffocating, and he tugged at his tie to let in air. Relieved to see Maddie coming through the door, he broke away from the cheery group.

"Excuse me." He brushed past Luke to greet their sister, but she was walking arm in arm with someone else. The white satin gown floated through the crowd as if on the wings of an angel. Its wispy bottom brushed the floor in her wake like an elegant bridal gown. The guest's flame-colored hair was styled like Lauren Bacall, but he knew the vintage star couldn't hold a candle to the beauty making her way toward him. Roland recognized the actress from the many pictures he'd seen online.

He couldn't erase the glossy images or the blurry video snippets of Dallas Derringer in the arms of her lover. There hadn't been any anger at her for the tape or the media bomb hitting Magnolia, even though it took days to get it under control. Roland was upset that Ginger had left. She'd refused to return his calls and had only sent him one straightforward text.

I think it's better you don't try to contact me.

And he hadn't.

Uncertainty crowded her searching eyes. It looked like she was about to say something, but nothing sprang from her gloss-covered lips.

Roland waited.

"Ginger came to help win the cookie competition." Maddie gripped the elbow of his white jacket, giving him a solid pinch on the back of his arm. "She flew all the way from New York just for us."

He understood his sister was begging him to be polite. "Yes, well, it seems to have paid off. Congratulations." He lifted his champagne glass, then realized he was the only one with a drink.

"Forgive me. Let me fetch you ladies a glass of champagne to celebrate." It would give him a moment to gain composure. An hour ago, he'd been dying for Ginger to walk out on that stage, and now, here she was, and all he could think about was that one ominous text.

Roland had to shake himself mentally. He was acting like a disgruntled, besotted teen. Ginger had never committed herself to him. In fact, she had done the exact opposite, keeping things light and very sexy.

As he grabbed the glasses from the open bar, Luke, Lexi and Noah engaged in greetings and hugs with the new arrivals. Lexi seemed as surprised as Roland was to see Ginger. The switch back to her signature red hair was a hot topic of conversation, and he admitted to himself that it was hard to take his eyes off her. She might as well have been walking down the red carpet at a Hollywood premiere. Every eye in the ballroom was on her. She was gorgeous and way out of his league.

If he'd known that she was Dallas Derringer, Hollywood celebrity when he'd met her, would he have asked her out? Without a doubt, he knew the answer. Roland loved movies, and though he was terribly intrigued, he would have written her off as too fast-lane for his slow-town personality.

As he watched everyone fawn over Ginger's hair, gown and everything about her sparkling presentation, he also considered that the whole time she was in Magnolia, she'd known exactly who he was, and she'd chosen to spend her free time with him. Maybe she didn't tell him about her past right away, but why should she? Ginger didn't owe him or anyone else anything. Her business was her business, but he couldn't help being upset. When she left, a raw feeling had lodged in his throat that had nearly choked him, and there hadn't been a damn thing he could do about it. That kind of emotion was new to him, and he didn't like the thought of it burning inside forever without release.

Roland touched the crumpled paper in his breast pocket. Melvina had written down Ginger's address in New York and given it to him. He had been carrying it around since the day Ginger left, along with an airline ticket reserved for the day after Christmas. He'd been determined to find her, but here she was, right in front of him, every dazzling inch.

Chapter 44

Ginger hadn't thought past getting in touch with Melvina and telling her she was flying in to help win the contest. Melvina had been ecstatic and offered her a place to stay, but Ginger remembered the Snowflake Ball and told Melvina she would stay at the hotel. Everyone would be there after the contest anyway.

On the phone, Melvina had chuckled, "I won't breathe a word, but I can assure you that the coast is clear. Someone started a rumor that you were hiding out in New Mexico with Roland's brother's ex-girlfriend."

Ginger gasped. "Poor woman. Luke must be really mad at her."

"I think it was Ms. Rosie who started it."

Now that she was here, Ginger wondered if her rash decision to return was a good idea. She hadn't wanted to tell anyone, even Lexi. She'd wanted to surprise Roland, but now that he was looking at her with a crease in his forehead and cool assessing eyes, she wondered if he'd changed his mind about her recent past. Had he watched the videos? Of course he had. Half of Magnolia had probably seen the tape. She pushed her shoulders back and held her head high.

Ginger had been seeing a counselor in New York, and though she'd only been twice in the short time she'd been there, the therapist really helped her to visualize the whole event like a movie. She'd taken Kirk out of the evil villain role and saw the whole thing as a sequence of unfortunate events.

Sure, she still thought of her ex as an empty casing of a man-boy who only cared about childish pranks and shallow ornaments to decorate his life, but she realized that was all he'd ever been capable of. She had to take responsibility for choosing Kirk as a means to her own end. Loneliness had prompted her to use him, and that wasn't fair either. Taking the video without consent, then thinking it would never leave his computer was wrong.

Kirk had his own lessons to learn, but Ginger knew she wasn't totally blameless for her own choices. Be that as it may, she wouldn't let the incident ruin the way she felt about all men forever. She refused to be a victim. So what if the world had seen her in her birthday suit, having sex in a consensual relationship? Everyone came into this world naked, and they generally had sex sometime before they died. She wouldn't be ashamed of something that was natural, even if it was on the internet, which wasn't natural at all. The people who treated her differently could be damned. She didn't need them.

As she broke away from the group, she approached Roland, who seemed to be holding up the bar. "Are you going to be mad at me all night?"

He pressed his lips together as if holding back what he really wanted to say. Looking at his glass, he pushed away from the ledge he'd been leaning on. Roland stared down at the golden liquid fizzing upward in a double helix. Finally, his eyes met hers.

"I'm not mad. I was disappointed when you left and maybe a little hurt when you sent that *one* text."

It was her turn to study the bubbles in her glass. "I moved halfway across the country in a day, Roland. It didn't seem likely that we would see each other again. I thought it was for the best."

He stepped toward her. She could smell his amazing cologne and the champagne on his breath. Heat radiated from his fingers as they took her glass, setting it on the bar. "And now?"

Ginger gulped. She knew this would be difficult, but it was harder than she'd imagined. The sizzle of emotion running up and down her spine made her shiver. He was still waiting for her answer, and she wasn't sure what to say. New York was her home now. Her job was there, and baking gingerbread cookies didn't pay the rent.

"I couldn't stop thinking of you." It was the one truth she could cling to. With all the doubts and what-ifs floating around in her head, she truly couldn't forget the way he kissed her, the way he held her in his arms, and the way he moved inside her when they'd made love. Being with Roland was different than the relationships of her past. He was unlike the men she'd known before—in bed and out. Maybe that was the distinction. Roland was a good guy, and she'd always chosen badly. Could she sacrifice her dreams to have him?

Ginger hadn't expected him to take her hand and lead her to the dance floor. He moved with her gently as they worked their way among the crowded couples, and she looked up at him with wonder. "Seriously, you want to dance right now?"

He grinned. "Why not? It fixed our night the first time."

She couldn't help but smile, feeling the heat of memories flood her with a tingling sensation. He was flirting with her, and it felt amazing, like being in his arms always did.

"Besides," he nodded toward the bar. "I heard the scrape of Ms. Rosie's walker."

Ginger fanned herself theatrically. "My hero," she exclaimed, holding onto him tighter as the tempo of the music picked up.

Roland twirled them around, pushing her in the opposite direction, but holding her close. He looked at her with longing in his eyes. "I admit, I want you all to myself. I'm not really good at sharing, and I—" His voice hitched. "I've missed you, Ginger."

She hugged him as they swayed, placing her cheek on his shoulder. "I've missed you, too."

Someone tapped Roland on the shoulder. Half expecting Luke, he wanted to say, "piss off," but it wasn't Luke.

It was Manny Owens, the mayor. "Can I cut in? I haven't gotten the chance to officially meet our lovely visitor, and I want to thank her for bringing home the win for the diner. Trust me when I say, young lady, that for Melvina to give credit to someone else's baking, it's a wonder in itself. You must be something special."

Roland didn't have a choice but to be polite. Manny was a good friend, and Roland hadn't forgotten about the offer that was waiting in the wings. "I'll see if I can find Mona."

The chief looked through the crowd. "She's at the bar, Roland, but be careful." Manny chuckled. "That woman is a Tasmanian devil on the dance floor."

Mona was chatting with Melvina and Rosie when he approached the trio. The walker immediately inched toward him, and Rosie looped her arm through his. Roland looked heavenward. There was no getting away from Rosie's clutches.

"Good evening, ladies."

Mona pushed an imaginary lock of hair into place and pursed her overlined lips at him. "It was so nice of you to let my dear Manny dance with Ginger. We all thought it would make things more…" She paused as if seeing the need to redirect her words.

Roland didn't miss Melvina's grip on her best friend's arm.

"Well, being seen with the mayor on your arm does anyone good." Mona nodded toward the dance floor, emphasizing the truth of her statement.

Roland smiled congenially. He knew the ladies liked Ginger and wanted her to feel accepted by the community. They were all on his team, including Ms. Rosie, who currently had one hand on her walker and the other on his ass. He took a step toward the bar and swapped out everyone's champagne to get away from her bony, groping fingers. Luckily, her niece Bonnie had joined them and inserted herself between Roland and her aunt. He handed Bonnie a glass and clinked it with a grin of thanks.

Rosie frowned at her niece and leaned forward, looking around Bonnie's sparkly dress to Roland. "So, is she moving back? Did you get a room here tonight?" Her hips wiggled a figure eight.

Bonnie scowled at her aunt. "You might as well ask him if you can watch. Seriously, what is wrong with you? I don't see how you and my mother could have ever been related. She must be rolling over in her grave hearing what comes out of your mouth!"

Bonnie looked up at Roland, wincing. "I'm so sorry. She doesn't mean to be so brash." Bonnie sighed, rolling her eyes and brandishing her glass. "Then again, maybe she does."

Roland would have laughed, but Rosie piped back in. "There's no reason to ask to watch. The whole town's seen it already."

Bonnie's eyes widened in horror, but it was Mona who cut in. "Rosie, you and I are going to the ladies' room." Grabbing hold of Rosie's walker, Mona pointed it toward the outer doors of the ballroom. She marched behind Rosie and could be heard lecturing as they walked away. "For the love of God…."

Rosie's voice carried, "What? I thought they were hot. I played it over and over. That guy with the big—."

"Rosie!"

"I was going to say blue eyes. Geesh, Mona. Get your mind out of the gutter."

Bonnie gave Melvina and Roland a sorrowful look. Melvina patted her shoulder. "It's not your fault. I'm sure Roland doesn't hold it against you or Rosie. Some people don't think before they squawk."

Roland nodded, not knowing what else to do. If Rosie had been a man, he would have decked her. "Try to keep her away from Ginger tonight. I don't want her feelings hurt, however unintentional it might be." He gave Bonnie a meaningful look.

Melvina nodded in agreement as she squeezed Bonnie's hand in support. "I think Mona's got it covered, but we'll put Riley and Ran on interference duty. I'd ask Raphe and Nina, too, but they're back in San Fran visiting her brother."

As Manny and Ginger returned to the fold, a photographer snapped a picture. First of Ginger on the mayor's arm and then of Ginger with Roland. Roland grabbed the camera, about to throw it when Mona pinched it out of his hand. Her firm grip on his bicep said she had it under control.

"It's okay, Roland. The picture is for the Blossom Banter!"

He realized the older woman who'd been holding the camera was a Blossom. "Sorry, Addy."

Melvina's father was at Addy's side, scowling at Roland. "Don't think I'm too old to stand up for a lady, Constable." Pop's chest was puffed up like a rooster at sunrise. His fist balled at his sides.

Roland tugged at his collar, nodding. "Dutifully noted, Pop. Again, I apologize. After all those reporters swarmed on Magnolia, I've been a little on edge."

Pop made a begrudging nod, then placed a protective arm around Addy's shoulders. He guided her away to take pictures of other guests in their finery. Roland felt like an ass, but Ginger looped her arm through his, smiling at him.

Maurice and his date wedged into the spot vacated by Pop and Addy. He beamed at the group.

The teen's arrival took the heat off Roland's overreaction with the camera. "Hi, Maurice. Who's your lovely date tonight? Did the truck come back from Mac's okay?"

"Hey, everybody. This is Megan, she goes to A&M." He paused as everyone welcomed her to the party and then he added, "The truck is great. Thanks for taking care of the bill, Constable."

Roland smiled. There had barely been a scratch on Maurice's truck, but Roland had asked Mac to do something to spruce up the kid's ride. Mac had replaced the old front grill with a shiny chrome bumper. The truck was still missing the one in the back, but Roland had plans to see if Maurice wanted to do some odd jobs at the station to pay for fixing the rear.

Ginger hugged Maurice, identifying him to everyone as her right-hand man in the kitchen when she'd worked at the diner. Maurice's young date stared at Ginger with wide eyes.

Roland didn't know if it was because of Ginger's celebrity status, her Hollywood past or the sheer beauty of Ginger in her white evening attire, but it was time to move things forward. "How's your mom? I'm sure you're excited about having a baby brother or sister?"

Maurice nodded as he chuckled, "I feel more like an uncle. I'll be at college by the time he's born."

Roland nodded. "Well, babies need big brothers and wise uncles to be positive role models. I'm sure you'll be just that."

Maurice's smile grew wider. The twinkle in his eye and the flush in his cheeks spoke volumes about his mood. "We're going to go dance, y'all. I just wanted to say hi to Ginger. Glad you're back."

Before the conversation could sway to Ginger again and her reasons for being here or how long, Roland grasped her hand, nodding to the group as he excused them both. He needed to put some space between Ginger and the Magnolia contingent. "There's a buffet on the other side, and we could sit over there." He pointed across the ballroom and gave her a sly wink. "Far, far away from the rest of the crowd."

Ginger chuckled, then leaned toward him to whisper. "I am hungry, but not for buffet food. What do you think if you meet me upstairs? We can order room service—later."

He felt her slip her room key into his pocket.

"Four-twenty-one." She sashayed away, never looking back to see if he followed.

Oh, but he would, right after he found Luke or Maddie and told them not to wait up.

Chapter 45

Ginger opened the door, but this time she stayed in her dress. She hadn't wanted to assume things would play out the same way they had last time. So much had happened since that night a few short weeks ago. He would certainly sleep with her if she asked him to, but she wasn't sure she could handle never seeing him again afterward. Maybe they really would order room service this time. They could talk over a quiet dinner, maybe part on better terms.

Roland leaned on the door frame, eyes sparkling with mischief and something else. "What, no robe?"

Ginger smiled, turned and walked to the bed where she sat down. It wasn't a suite this time, and besides the small table with one chair, there wasn't anywhere else to sit. The hotel was posh and modern but sparse. "That can be arranged, but you didn't give me much time."

Roland followed her in, shutting the door behind him and removing his jacket. He strolled to the one chair and draped it over the back. Looking at her, he grinned and shook his head.

"You stole my thunder."

Ginger's mouth opened in surprise. "How? What do you mean? Were you planning on arriving tonight in a white chariot?"

She could see his tongue press against the inside of his cheek as he slowly nodded, looking out the expanse of the large window.

"Melvina gave me your address, and I bought a ticket to New York. It might not have been a white chariot, but I'm sure I could have found a white limousine if it would do the trick." He looked at her with questioning, piercing amber irises. "Would it?"

He loomed over her. Ginger stood. He was so close that she could feel his heat. His hands settled at the waist of her silk gown.

"I don't know, Roland. I've been offered a leading role on Broadway. I've already signed the contract, and let's be honest, I could never have stayed in Magnolia for long. I tried to be truthful from the beginning, but I was afraid to open up too many questions about my past. I didn't mean to hurt you."

He nodded, then brought his lips to hers. The kiss surprised her, as did his embrace. They rocked back and forth as they had in the ballroom. "Did I tell you how beautiful you look tonight?"

Mesmerized, Ginger shook her head. Roland kissed her neck, swaying to the imaginary music.

"I guess love is complicated," he breathed against her cheek.

She pulled back enough to look him in the eye. He looked lost in thought as if he were trying to solve all the mysteries of the world. She asked, "Are you telling me you love me?"

Roland kissed her deeply this time, running his hands down her back and unzipping the strapless gown. It fell with a rush of air to her feet, leaving her clad only in her white lace undergarments. Ginger was glad she'd opted for designer lingerie with garter belt and thigh-high stockings. His intake of breath assured her that he appreciated her effort.

He growled against her neck as he trailed kisses over her skin, "If I had any doubt before, I don't now." He kissed the swell of her breasts over the top crescents of her half bra. The lacy garment didn't quite contain her nipples. He raised his head and looked her in the eye. "I do love you. So now what?"

The ball was back in her court. "I love you too," she volleyed the simple phrase.

Roland lifted her in his arms and walked to the bed. "That's all that matters. The rest is just details."

They made love for hours and ignored the wake-up call, setting the phone back on the cradle when it rang one hour before checkout. "I was only supposed to stay one night, and I'm supposed to drive back to Dallas for my flight this evening. Yesterday, I went to see my mom first in Plano. I needed to see her and make sure she was okay." Ginger had also seen her uncle and tried to pay him back for covering her mother's stay at the memory care facility. She'd explained to him that she was back on her feet, but he wouldn't accept the money and hugged her instead. He told her that he wanted to continue to help care for her mother, since she was also his sister and that he was sorry he hadn't before now. Ginger promised she'd return for a longer visit once she was settled in New York.

Roland rolled toward her, taking her in his arms. "So, I'll pay them for another night, and you can fly out tomorrow. I'm not done yet."

Ginger's skin tingled as his fingers traced their way up her arm and down her breasts, then lower. Damn, the man had magic fingers. She rolled to her back and gave him access to her inner thighs. Arching her head against the pillow, she gasped as he parted her folds and entered her wetness. As she lifted upward, he slipped his arm beneath, grasping her waist as he rolled on top of her. Withdrawing his fingers, he filled her with his erection, lighting up the depths of her being. A sizzling sensation ran from the roots of her hair to the tips of her toes. She wrapped her legs around him, encouraging him to join her in ecstasy.

Back on birth control, Ginger felt safe, knowing she hadn't been with anyone else but Roland for a year now. He'd also assured her he was clean on his last physical and hadn't been sexually active since. In the brief moments they'd spoken during the night, they'd agreed to be monogamous. Even if their relationship was long-distance, they would find a way to manage things from afar. Ginger was looking forward to phone sex, but they both agreed to voice calls and no video chats for those occasions. She'd had enough of sex on camera to last her a lifetime.

"Old-school phone sex will work as long as it's temporary. Besides, I have my first ticket to New York for tomorrow and I already have time off work. Why don't you stay here tonight, and we'll fly to New York together? I'll change my ticket, or you can return your rental car here, and I'll pay the extra fees.

"Maddie, Kelsey, and Luke would love to have you with us for Christmas tonight. And I'll introduce you to my dad. He'll love you. Not to mention, Rollo. He hasn't stopped panting over you yet."

Roland nipped playfully at one of her nipples. He propped himself on his elbows as his hips nestled between her thighs. He studied her as they basked in the afterglow of their lovemaking.

Ginger thought about it. Her ticket could be changed to tomorrow, and the pet hotel could keep Igor a little longer. "I'd like that." She played with the short tendrils of his morning hair as he kissed her stomach. "But Roland, it's Christmas, and I haven't bought any gifts."

Roland peered up at her through his sooty black lashes. "Your flying back to Magnolia was the best gift you could have given."

Epilogue One

Three months later

Snow fell in thick feathers, coating the streets of Manhattan. "Isn't March supposed to be spring?" Roland pulled up the collar of his jacket as he walked beside Ginger down Broadway.

"Spring isn't until the end of the month. People always think December is winter, but really, most of the month is still fall, until winter solstice."

Roland pushed his other gloved hand into his pocket. Shopping wasn't something he usually got excited about, but today was different. Today was going to be spectacular. "Is that right? I never could keep my months in order. I have to look at the calendar on my desk to keep it all straight."

Ginger stopped and looked at him. "Really? You don't know your months in order?"

He scoffed playfully. "Why? It's good memory space that can be used for something else. Besides, all that stuff is on your cell phone."

She laughed. The sound rang out in the cold air around them and the gray clouds above. "I can't believe you. Mr. Dot All-The-I's-And-Cross-All-The-T's. I would think your OCD would go nuts not remembering a detail like that."

"I remember when it's time to see you." He bent to kiss her. Their lips joined tenderly at first, then she arched against him, and he pulled her into his body, warming them both.

She rewarded him with a small moan deep in her throat. "Why are we out in this weather anyway? You have to leave tomorrow, and I have a show tonight. We should be in bed until curtain call."

He groaned, thinking how he would like to accommodate her, but this was important. "There, up ahead."

Ginger stood motionless. "There aren't any shops that way, and I thought we were going to buy a better coat for you?"

Roland grabbed her hand, pulling her along with him. "Humor me."

They were a little way from Times Square, but from here, they could walk to Broadway if they had to, and that's what he liked best about the location. He walked into the front entrance of the high-rise and past the security guard as he flashed a key. The guard waved them on with a knowing smile.

"Do you know someone else who lives in New York?" Ginger asked as they got on the elevator.

"You'll see," Roland assured her as they rode to the eighth floor of the thirty-something-story building. When the doors opened, she saw a long corridor with only a few doors.

Ginger nodded. "The offices must be huge. So much space." She motioned at the distance between suites.

Roland took a key out and opened the unit at the end. The view was grand, with glass windows along every wall that faced the main plaza below. "The apartment is around two-thousand square feet." It was a mansion by New York standards, but he'd managed to make a great deal through some of his police buddy connections. The eighth floor was low enough for the firetruck ladders to reach if a fire should break out, and that was his only real fear of living in a high-rise. "The place is semi-furnished with the basics, but it leaves plenty of room for you to put your own touches on it." He waited. "Do you like it?"

Ginger spun around, taking it all in as she gasped. "Did you rent this place?"

Roland shook his head. "It's a co-op. I had to jump through a thousand hoops, write letters, and get character references from my coworkers and friends." He couldn't believe he'd withstood the stringent interviews, but it had all been worth it. To live here, in the city, with her. To finally feel like he was living the life he was meant to live.

He loved Magnolia, and he always would, but the Roland that had stayed and had done the responsible thing by taking care of his family wasn't needed anymore.

Maddie and Kelsey were staying in his house, and Luke would live with them, for now, to make sure they were safe. Their dad had made new friends at his senior living apartment and seemed to require less attention. Manny understood when Roland passed on the promotion. The mayor agreed to write a reference letter to the New York City Police Department if it was something Roland wanted, but it wasn't. He'd spent his whole life in Magnolia as a law enforcement officer, and he didn't want to walk a beat in the city.

Roland had done some research over the past months and found a wonderful old theater that had been closed for years. He sold some stocks and cashed in a couple of investments and talked to people he knew that would back him. Riley Nash was opening another restaurant in Manhattan, and he was willing to front half the money for the theater if Roland would run it.

It was a lot to take in. There would be so much work and a lot of changes, but it was everything he'd ever wanted. Roland had always loved old movies, and this was his chance to see them every night. There were opportunities in New York that Magnolia could never offer, and he couldn't wait to start his life here with Ginger by his side.

Ginger's face glowed with excitement. "Oh my God, Roland. You're really moving here?"

Roland fished in his coat pocket and sank to one knee. "Only if you agree to live with me. Forever, that is."

Ginger covered her mouth with her mitten-covered hands but then quickly bit the tip of one and yanked it off. Holding out her hand for him to put the diamond on her ring finger, she nodded emphatically. A muffled, "Yes," came through the cashmere mitten still wedged between her teeth.

He laughed, standing to take her in his arms and twirl her around. "I love you. We are going to be great together in New York."

Ginger giggled with delight. "Oh Roland, that was the best shopping trip ever, but one question. What about Igor and Rollo? Does the building accept pets?"

He chuckled. She was already thinking about their future together. "Igor and one dog are allowed. Rollo will ride back with me when I go get Lucille."

Ginger gave him a look of doubt. "Where will you park a car like that? Someone's bound to steal her."

Roland chuckled again, holding her tighter. "She's insured. Besides, I only care about one red-head now." His lips swept across hers and he smiled when she moaned low in her throat with need.

Ginger pulled back, gazing up at him. Her lips still lingered near his. "I know your affinity for old cars, Roland. You would die without Lucille."

Roland smiled. "Nothing will kill me except losing you. Lucille will be okay in New York. Trust me. We'll find her a safe parking spot."

"I do trust you. I'm going to marry you, buddy. No backing out now." Ginger leaned in, kissing him again. Her seductive lips made their way to his neck and started moving lower, trailing kisses down his chest as she unbuttoned his shirt.

Roland liked where this was going. The new bedding purchase and added housekeeping fee was all worth it. Ginger stopped, looking up at him. Her brow furrowed. "Do you think Igor and Rollo will be all right together, in the same apartment?"

Roland smiled. "With the way Igor is growing, he'll be the size of Godzilla next year. I doubt Rollo will want anything to do with him before long."

He kissed Ginger again. His voice turned serious. "I love you, and you love me. Everything will be great."

Ginger's eyes sparkled as she looked up at him. "You and I will be amazing."

He nodded, steering them toward the bedroom. "The rest is just details."

Epilogue Two

Noah watched as the ranch manager picked up a bale of hay and hefted it to him. He caught it, with a muffled, "oof," trying not to flinch. Picking up another bale, John looked at Noah and said with a serious tone, "You know, if you hadn't gotten your shit straight, I would have married her."

Noah sized up John and wondered how a real fight would end between them. After the run-in with Hank at Bubbles, he'd promised Lexi he'd behave. "Is that right? Well, I did get my shit straight, and she married me. Is that going to be a problem for us?"

A slow grin spread across John's face as he tossed Noah another bale of hay, harder this time. "Not as long as you treat her and the boys right."

Noah chuffed. He could have been offended or even fired John for the conversation, but he knew Lexi would be upset. He appreciated that John had looked after the ranch so well. Those slim times for Lexi and the boys had been hard. And John had stuck with the ranch, even after Lexi had chosen Noah over him. Noah would let the gut check slide. If the guy held a candle for Lexi in his heart, he couldn't fault him. She was easy to fall in love with.

Deciding to shuck it off, Noah looked down from the loft, addressing his would-be rival. "Well, if I don't hold up my end of the bargain in this marriage, then I think you will have to get in a very long line to kick my ass." His hand rested on his hip like a gunslinger as he gave John the pistols-at-dawn stare. "Have you met my in-laws?"

John laughed heartily. "I have. Riley hired me. You should have heard the riot-act he read me before letting me step one foot on the Burns Creek Ranch property."

Noah grunted in acknowledgement. He'd gotten a similar sermon from all three of the brothers at his bachelor party, which included him, Hank and

Lexi's brothers. Her father was still giving him the cold shoulder, thinking that the wedding was too soon for his taste.

Noah tried to explain to Lexi's father, but in the end, he hadn't wanted to wait another minute. The boys took a shine to Noah right away, and he made an effort to make things special in their lives every day. Sure, there was homework, chores and an occasional disagreement, but they rode horses together, four-wheelers together, played with Chef and Ann-Margret, who'd somehow managed to get a rat friend named Sponge Bob, and now they had a litter of six rat babies to feed.

It was a rat infestation as far as Noah was concerned, but he promised the boys they could keep the family together as long as Bob and any male offspring were fixed at the vet, and the kids could confine them to one room of the house. No more meetings on the kitchen counter, asking for cheese, no matter how cute the matching pink and blue rhinestone collars were.

Lexi knocked on the side of the barn. "You men getting along out here?" She gave Noah that sassy grin he adored.

He nodded. "Almost done. I was telling John how lucky he was to have slipped out of the marriage noose."

Lexi made a mock look of surprise and put both hands on her hips. "Noah Harding, you did not!"

He clattered down the ladder and met her at the barn door. She was light as a feather, though last night she'd told him she was three months pregnant. It had made him the happiest man on earth, again.

"Naw, I told him if he's lucky in life, he'll find someone as beautiful as you and that when he does, not to wait."

"Well, you aren't any good at waiting, are you, Noah Harding?"

He caressed her stomach with one hand, looking her in the eye. "Not this time. I'm so glad we didn't wait."

Gussy, Damien and Bert burst into the barn. "Momma, Damien put your skirt on Shrek, and he's got it stuck in the fence. He's bucking like crazy!"

Noah and Lexi both laughed. John held his hand up. "Y'all stay here. I got this one."

After John disappeared from the barn to help the boys, Noah took the opportunity to take Lexi into his arms, kissing her with all the passion he felt since leaving their bed this morning. "Should I be jealous that our ranch manager still has the hots for you?"

Lexi batted his shoulder playfully. "John doesn't have the hots for me." Her cheeks turned pink in the cool March air. When Noah's eyes widened with a challenging stare, she added. "Well, if he does, he'll get over it when he finds *The One*."

Noah nodded. "I don't know, darlin'. It will be hard to find someone like you."

Lexi swayed in his arms as she adjusted her hands around his neck, pulling him down to her lips. He would never get tired of their banter, love and playfulness. She was all he'd ever dreamed of, and he knew they were meant to be together. Fate had ordained it when that stranger pulled him from his burning SUV.

Noah hadn't known it then, but later, he'd studied the photograph of Lexi and her late husband. There wasn't a doubt in his mind that Jack was the man in fatigues who rescued him that night. Noah wasn't someone who believed in ghosts, and since he couldn't explain it without feeling hocus-po-cusy, he kept the memory to himself. He knew he would share it with Lexi one day but not now. Noah still had a hard time wrapping his head around the cosmic events that had led to his blissful present. To be chosen, not only by Lexi but by the children's father, was the ultimate approval. Jack trusted him with her and the boys enough to save his life and to give him another chance. That was heaven. Noah knew he was blessed, and he planned to live up to every expectation.

He spun Lexi around in his arms. His hat fell to the barn floor, but he didn't care. He'd get it later. "Lexi Nash Harding, I can't wait to spend all my days loving you and our family."

"Then don't, you silly man. We're all right here, and we will be forever and ever." She chuckled. "Probably a lot more of us and a lot longer than you ever planned."

Noah clasped her hand and pulled her toward the house. Lexi flapped an arm, tugging back. "Where are you taking me? I walked all the way down here to see you."

Noah kept walking. "I know, and I appreciate you reminding me that I needed to get back to the house."

Lexi gave in, falling into step by his side. "Did you forget something?"

Noah grinned from ear to ear. "Yes, and it's in our bedroom."

Lexi slapped playfully at his arm. "Noah, the boys are awake."

He chuckled. "And there are locks on the door. Besides, John is with them taking your skirt off Donkey…or was it Shrek?"

They clattered onto the front porch, and Lexi raced past him to the door. "Last one to the bed has to buy the next box of cupcakes."

Noah smiled. "They're on the counter already."

Lexi spun on her heel and raced to the kitchen. "Noah, you are so amazing!" She grabbed one strawberry iced cake and started toward him, dipping one finger in the icing.

Noah felt himself grow hard as she put the frosting-tipped finger to his lips. He licked off the sugary treat and kissed her with all the passion that had been bottling up inside him since she'd appeared in the barn. Picking her up in his arms, he knew exactly where he was taking her, and she didn't protest. "Dr. Icing aims to please."

The End

A Message From Your Friends in Magnolia, Texas

Thank you for reading *Gingerbread Kisses*, the fourth book in the Hot in Magnolia series. If you enjoyed it, please take a moment to give it a review. You can **CLICK HERE** to leave a review on Amazon. Feel free to give it a mention on **Twitter**. You can also tag me and follow me at **@lauren_minette**. Help Magnolia get even hotter!

If you want to find out about new releases, fun giveaways, free books and other perks, sign up for my newsletter *The Blossom Banter* by visiting my website, **minettelauren.com**. And don't forget to come on back to Magnolia. New friends are always welcome and there's plenty of iced sweet tea and extra treats to go around.

Psst…keep reading for a Sneak Peek of my next book, *Hurricane Kisses*.

Hurricane Kisses

Hot in Magnolia, Book 5

SNEAK PEEK

Cecilia Lockwood grunted as she shimmied backward with the tall parrot cage in her clenched fists. "Of all the good and bad luck in my life, I'm not sure if my inheritance is the best or the worst."

"Shut up!" The blue and gold macaw screeched.

"That's it, you fancy blue chicken, I'm making parrot soup tonight, with a side of cockatiel!"

The green Quaker parrot, who had been out of his cage and resisting capture all morning, stared at her from where he'd perched on top of her computer monitor. "Um—that's good!"

Cecilia blew at a stray lock of hair that escaped her long ponytail. Years ago, she'd worn it at a fashionable length. That was before she'd lost her prestige with the Magnolia Blossoms Ladies League.

An IRS audit revealed some of her extra purchases with the non-profit money she'd earned, but she didn't understand all the fuss. She was the one who raised the money for charity, so why couldn't she enjoy a day at the spa or buy a new pair of shoes? At the time, she hadn't thought she was cheating anyone out of anything, but according to the IRS and the whole flock of biddies in Magnolia, she'd done just that. After moving back to Dallas with her mother and father, Todd and Brenda Lockwood, she thought things would turn around. Celia felt she had better potential in a city like Dallas and was over her big-fish-in-a-little-pond syndrome. She could admit now that being the president of The Magnolia Blossoms wasn't her destiny.

When her father put her in the accounting office of his oil company, she'd felt right at home. Taking up where she'd left off, Celia tallied columns of debits and credits, including a small account for herself to buy whatever she wanted. She worked hard for her father, so in her eyes, she was just rewarding herself with an extra bonus for all her effort. Unbeknownst to Celia, her father's partner hired a spy. A very handsome co-worker named Steve, whom she'd taken out to lunch several times with her petty cash account, and had almost taken to bed once after a few too many martinis. Thank God, she hadn't. It infuriated her that the ratfink ratted her out. She'd trusted him enough to share her secret, and he had sold her down the river for a promotion. When she was fired, Steve took her job and her dignity. She'd cried to her mother without much success.

Barbra Lockwood sipped her mimosa and petted Mimi, the family's black teacup poodle. "Darling, why are you blubbering? You know your father. He loves you, and he wants you to learn important lessons in life, but I say go get your money the old-fashioned way. Find yourself a rich husband, like I did. Then you can visit with your friends and shop until your heart is content."

As Celia pushed the cage into a corner, Chica, the blue and gold macaw, pinched her finger through the bars, letting out another ear-piercing screech.

Celia let out a howl of her own. "Ouch!"

"Shut up!"

Celia gave the sassy parrot a low growl. Macaws weren't usually the big talkers of the parrot world, but this one wouldn't shut up with the few words it knew. Since inheriting her grandfather's exotic bird sanctuary, and it being the only source of income that she had, Cecilia had tried to catch up on understanding parrots and the necessary habitat they needed to survive. The sanctuary ran off regular donations, but it was barely enough to pay the utilities and have enough left over to buy birdseed. She needed more, and if she had to put up with a teenage macaw that hated her, so be it. When she started parrot adoptions, Chica would be the first to go, but before that, she needed to teach the saucy parrot some manners. Besides, repeating her name, *hello*, *shut up* and *pretty girl* were the only other words Chica knew.

Feathers floated in the air as Celia swept the floor. As she pushed the broom around the cages, she noticed Baby, the Quaker parrot, disappear into his cage. Just as Celia snuck close enough to shut the flap to the enclosure, a knock sounded on the door.

"Excuse me, Miss." A man's voice called out, startling her and Baby, who flew back out of his cage.

"Jesus H Christ!" Celia grabbed her chest and spun on her heel. Glancing at the man and then back at the cage, she scowled and then burst into tears. "Stupid asshole," she sobbed.

She heard the door shut and the man's boots on the hard tile as he approached. "Hey, sorry. I didn't mean to interrupt. I closed the door so the bird won't escape. I'll help you catch him." There was a pause as he put his hand on her shoulder.

She felt her body shudder as she tried to gain control of her tears. Celia didn't even know why she was crying. She was tougher than this. A smarty-pants little bird would not, could not, best her.

His steady voice continued. "I promise. I'm not an asshole. I'll make it up to you. Do you have a towel and a ladder?"

That made Celia's tears turn to laughter. She was cursing the parrot who'd teased her all morning, not the man. As she finally looked up at her visitor, she was mesmerized by his clear blue eyes that were as light as Tiffany-blue glass. His features were symmetrical, and his sandy-blond hair was golden in the light pouring in from the window. He was the stuff of Greek God movie actors in those delicious romantic comedies. His smooth southern drawl sent tingles from the pit of her stomach to her toes. Even touching her shoulder, he was tender and stood his distance, careful not to invade her space. His smile was warm and showcased perfect white teeth.

Feathers still floated in the air around his head, giving him an ethereal look. Entranced, she reached out and touched the side of his face. "Are you real?"

He reached in his pocket and pulled out a handkerchief, offering it to her. Who carried a clean hanky in their pocket these days? As she dabbed at her eyes, it occurred to her that there was no guarantee that it was indeed clean, and she must look like a clown in her manic state. She quickly pressed the kerchief back into his palm. Celia stared at him and he seemed to look back at her with the same dazed look. Did he like what he saw as much as she liked looking at him? It was then that she remembered her messy hair that the cockatiel had perched in half of the morning, and the tired old gym clothes she'd been wearing to clean cages. She probably had bird poop in her hair or worse, and he was possibly contemplating how to tell her. Celia brushed at her shirt, as if it would suddenly turn into a beautiful ball gown, and he would sweep her up in his arms and carry her away from the cage she was living in. She snorted at the thought.

His hand shot out again, offering her the hanky.

Oh god. My life has got to get better than this!

I hope you enjoyed the Sneak Peek of *Hurricane Kisses*, the upcoming fifth book in the Hot in Magnolia series. Don't forget you can sign up for my newsletter, *The Blossom Banter*, if you want to find out when *Hurricane Kisses* hits the shelves.

Just visit my website, **minettelauren.com**.

Champagne Kisses

Hot in Magnolia

Minette Lauren

Published Internationally by Minette Lauren
Magnolia, TX USA
minettelauren.com

Copyright © 2020 Minette Lauren

Exclusive cover © 2020 Fiona Jayde Media
Interior Design by Tamara Cribley, The Deliberate Page

Chapter 1

Noah Harding swiped the bar with a towel from the bucket of bleach water, humming to the music playing from the old-time jukebox. The vintage record player still served as a mainstay of entertainment at Hank's Honky-Tonk during the daylight hours. There was only one small TV over the bar that would be considered an antique by today's standards. The clunky box still worked, but it stayed on mute most of the time. The bar was usually quiet until the happy-hour crowd came in around five thirty, then the place was packed until close. It was only noon now, and Noah moved to the window to pull the chains on the neon signs, letting patrons know that the bar was open. He would move through his usual routine and then sit down to eat lunch and work through the daily crossword puzzle from the Sunday paper. It had been a busy afternoon yesterday, and he hadn't had time to even read the news. He was looking forward to his *Magnificent Monday*, as he liked to call it. The bar would be slow, and he could relax. To Noah Harding, that was magnificent.

He pulled the chain on the sign that said OPEN and turned back toward the bar. A horn blared a moment before he heard the crash, felt the floor shake, and saw the front end of a light blue minivan sticking through the window where he'd just been standing. "What the… ?" He'd almost said it, but he'd promised his sister Callie that he'd stop swearing in front of her girls, his nieces, and the only way he could do that was to stop cursing altogether. He would have patted himself on the back for not lapsing on his promise in the commotion, but at the moment, he was wondering how close he'd been to death. Sweat beaded on his forehead before he got it together and peeled himself off the floor. The car was only a small way into the building, so he went outside to see if the driver was okay. Steam rolled up from the crumpled hood, and he looked at the driver's side, but all he could see was the white safety bag where it had deployed on impact. Pink painted fingernails batted at the drooping bag, and he stepped around the car to aid the woman wrestling with it in the driver's seat.

Noah opened the door and pushed the bag aside. "Are you okay?"

A blonde woman with a messy ponytail and sunglasses that sat askew on her nose looked back at him in shock. "Wha—what happened?"

His eyebrows knitted with concern, and he automatically reached for his cell phone. The lady was dazed and probably needed medical help. After all, she was asking *him* what happened. "I don't know. I was going to ask you the same thing. You just landed in the front window of my bar."

The blonde blinked her pretty bluebonnet-colored eyes and reached for her glasses to correct their lopsided tilt. They looked permanently bent. There was a small cut where the frame had perched along the bridge of her nose, but otherwise, she appeared to be intact. She remained silent, staring up at him with a dazed look on her face. She removed her glasses and rubbed the bridge of her nose.

"Can I help you up? Can you stand?"

The lady shook her head, sending her long ponytail swishing from side to side as she looked down at her legs. She moved one and then the other, as if she were trying to see if they still worked. "I—I think so." Turning her torso toward him, she dragged her legs with her. As one, the wedge-heeled sandals hit the pavement. She stared up at him as if waiting for further instruction. "Did you see her? Did she jump out of the car?"

It was Noah's turn to gape. There was no one else around. She was obviously stunned. "I didn't see anyone. Was there another person with you in the van?"

She shook her head. "No. But Gussy will be so upset."

Noah tried to focus on getting her to safety. She stood up and walked with him inside the bar, and he assured himself she was mostly okay. "I should call an EMS or something to make sure you're all right."

She stumbled, leaning onto his arm. "No! No...I'm okay. Really. I just need a few minutes to collect myself."

He showed her to a stool inside the bar. There weren't any booths or fancy chairs. It was a lively watering hole in the evening with two busy pool tables, a couple of dartboards and a small stage for the band. The open area covered in wood flooring was mostly used for dancing. Black upholstered stools were about the only perching spots to give the patrons a rest.

The woman held the thick wood edge of the bar and eased onto the stool. He stood next to her a moment until she steadied herself and nodded that she was okay.

"Can I get you a water or something?" Noah was already putting a hand into the cooler when she said, "I think I'd like a whiskey. Make it a double, please."

Noah paused, wondering if he should serve a woman who'd crashed through the front of his bar—actually, it was only half his bar. His cousin, Hank, had inherited the other half from their grandfather Henry, but everyone had called him Hank. The younger Hank, Noah's cousin, was too high and mighty to get his manicured nails dirty since he'd moved to River Oaks. In fact, he rarely drove to Magnolia except to clean out the till or gripe about bar costs. Noah kept telling Hank that he should be happy enough to get any cut of the profits. Bars had to purchase alcohol to make money, and though Noah ran a tight ship, Hank was a drain on their budget. He helped himself to the profits every week. The last time Noah talked to his cousin, he'd tried to reason with him about renovations, but Hank wouldn't budge. The bar was one hailstorm away from needing a new roof, and there was no way Noah was footing the bill while Hank reaped the rewards. They were stuck in a stalemate, and in the meantime, Magnolia was getting a higher-income population that was willing to spend more money for a classier setting. Noah was saving up, and all he needed was a few more months before he could go through with his plan, with or without his obnoxious cousin.

The pretty lady sitting across the bar from him looked like she needed a drink. He hadn't called the EMS, but he wasn't sure he was doing her any favors by serving her strong liquor at barely noon on a Monday. She wrung her hands and looked up at him with tears brimming in her big blue eyes. Her tongue darted along the edges of her full bottom lip and then she bit it to keep it from trembling. Her delicate hand touched her messy ponytail, then pushed a loose lock of hair back. His heart thumped. *Down boy, she drives a minivan. She's probably married with three kids.*

"I—I'm sorry about your window...." She looked back over her shoulder at the broken glass. Remarkably, only a small bit of the wall beneath was busted. "...and brick." She pointed. "I swear I'm not an alcoholic. Today is a total toilet bomb, and it has barely started."

Noah grinned, nodding with understanding as he reached for a rocks glass. Pausing, he asked her, "Ice?"

She smiled, holding up her index finger. "One cube, please. My friends from Ireland told me that it's just enough to open up the flavor, but it's a sin to drink whiskey over ice."

"Better not tell that to the night-time crowd. I can't imagine how things would get out of hand if the drinks didn't have something in them to water down the Jameson."

Noah loved the dimples in both of her cheeks when she smiled. She looked sweet and wholesome, like the girl next door, but she also looked like Texas perfection. She had smooth skin and a smattering of freckles on her nose from too many days in the sun. Her hair was deep, golden-blonde with honey streaks woven throughout. She was a natural beauty without a stitch of makeup, and something about her disheveled, vulnerable appearance was waking up his chivalrous side. He hadn't seen that side of himself in a long time. Not since Afghanistan. Maybe he should have a drink, too. Again, she was probably married. The simple gold band she wore on her left ring finger looked like a wedding ring, but it didn't include a diamond, and it looked like it came out of a Crackerjack box. The woman was too gorgeous not to have someone who appreciated her beauty. Maybe she was divorced or just liked to wear jewelry, except that he noticed she wasn't wearing any other baubles, not even a pair of earrings. His sister, Callie, wore them even to take out the garbage. He was pretty sure she slept in them.

"What? Is there blood on my face?" Her eyes widened with worry, and she patted her hands over her smooth skin.

Noah realized painfully that he'd been staring as he was pondering her availability. "No. Sorry." He mentally shook himself. "I'm wondering what happened. How you crashed into my front window." He smiled as he looked at the shattered glass that he really should sweep up before other patrons started to enter.

She sighed. "I'm so sorry. I overcompensated when something ran across my foot. It was probably Gussy's pet rat. I felt something, and when I looked down and saw that pink tail...." She shivered. "I guess I pushed the gas instead of the brake." She shook her head as she blew out a shaky breath. "I didn't want to squish her. I—I wasn't looking at the road, so I have no idea how I rolled into the bar, but I'm glad no one is hurt."

"That makes two of us." He smiled, poured himself a whiskey and clinked glasses with her. She nodded and took another large gulp. "I still think we should call an ambulance or something to check you over. You could have a concussion or something that you don't feel now but will feel later."

276

She slid off the stool, wobbled a bit, and shook her head. "Please don't. My brother is a firefighter, and he will freak if he sees the mess, then he'll tell my other brothers, who'll tell my parents and…." She waved one hand as tears welled up. She straightened her shoulders, letting out another long, shaky sigh. "I'm old enough to deal with the repercussions of my actions, and I have insurance. I don't need my whole family butting in."

Noah nodded with understanding. His sister Callie was always telling him how to live his life. After he returned from his first tour of Germany with a foreign bride, who cleaned him out before disappearing, his sister constantly warned him about his bad choices. He couldn't argue. Marrying Petra had been a terrible decision. He'd only known her a month before he readily agreed to her impromptu proposal. But he didn't want to think about Petra right now, not with a gorgeous woman sitting in front of him.

The blonde minivan driver held her whiskey with a shaky hand. She looked like she might be in her early thirties, but it was obvious she feared exposing the accident to her family. Draining the contents of the glass, she set it on the bar. Noah picked it up and tossed it into soapy water. "I totally understand about family. No worries. They won't hear anything from me, but won't you need a ride?"

She looked like she was still in shock. Even if her van started, he wouldn't let her drive, but he couldn't leave the bar unattended with a shattered front window and a safe full of money. The bank drop wasn't scheduled until later today.

As the pretty lady backed away, he held up his hand. "Wait, I don't even know your name. Let me call you a taxi, and Mac Green, who owns the auto shop, can come down to pick up the van."

It was that moment that the front door burst open and his cousin Hank walked in. In his momentary lapse, Noah succumbed to pure emotion. "Shit."

"Noah, what the hell…." Hank stopped dead when he saw the blonde about to barrel over him. "Well, hello, pretty lady." He was the younger cousin, the more polished cousin, and probably the better-looking cousin if a woman liked that kind of city-slick appearance. Noah tensed. He was annoyed on so many levels that Hank should show his face at this very moment, but the main one was the blonde's glorious smile when she looked at Hank. He was a total tool, and he was the kind who wouldn't take no for an answer.

"Hi Hank, I was about to take the lady home since we seem to have had an accident this morning. Can you watch the bar?"

Hank gave him a look that said, are you kidding me? "I'll do better than that, cuz. I'll give the little lady a ride wherever she needs to go. It'll give you time to get this place cleaned up."

Now she'd done it. Half of Magnolia would either think she had a drinking problem or that she was so desperate to meet a man that she drove her van into the most popular bar in town. Not that she'd ever been inside to know, but the parking lot was packed most evenings when she drove by. Besides, it was the only watering hole within twenty miles of Magnolia, and it was hard to miss on her nightly excursions to grab ice cream sundaes for her boys. Alexa Nash shook her head at the man, who introduced himself as Hank as he reached over to pat her knee. She removed his hand and moved her leg closer to the door.

He was oblivious to her pointed look. "It's all gonna be fine, little darlin'. Don't you worry about a thing. Ol' Hank has money to fix everything. In fact, my cousin, Noah, is planning to bring in a crew to remodel my bar soon."

Lexi frowned. "Oh, I thought it was his." She motioned behind them toward the bar.

Hank chuckled. "He owns a small share, but I make all the decisions. The place was passed down to me by our grandfather, Henry, but everyone called him Hank. I'm Hank Harding the third. Grand-daddy would have liked me to make some improvements, and now I guess we'll have a new window." He chuckled, giving her a broad wink. "So don't fret over the incident. It was meant to be…with the remodel starting soon and all."

Lexi smiled for the first time that day, putting a hand over her heart. "Thank goodness. I've never had an accident before. One of my boys left his pet rat in the van this morning, and I about had a heart attack when it ran over my foot."

Hank frowned but didn't say anything. Maybe he was upset about the window but not expressing how he really felt. Some men were like that.

Lexi stammered on, "I—I have insurance, and I'm sure they will cover it. If not, I have money of my own."

Hank smiled at that. "So, I take it you are on your own then? No husband?"

Lexi wanted to roll her eyes. She felt like she was in the eighties' movie, *Working Girl*. He'd called her *little* twice, grabbed her knee, and now he was leering at her and asking about her marital status. He would have been handsome except for his lecherous aura. She really wished Hank's cousin could have driven her home.

The bartender had a warmth about him, and he'd made her feel calm about having a major accident this morning. His soothing voice and gentle touch weren't lecherous at all. She suddenly felt vulnerable in the leather-upholstered luxury car. She didn't know this man, Hank, and she was alone with him. Just because he owned a bar in Magnolia didn't make the man safe. It meant he probably had enough money to pay his way out of any trouble he stirred up. Then again, the guy at the bar was nice, and he hadn't contested her getting in the car with his cousin. Surely, it would all be okay.

To be safe, Lexi reached in her purse for her cell phone to call her brother Ran. News of the crash would be all over town before dark anyway. She might as well be the one to tell it first. Not leaving time for more conversation, she pointed Hank toward Nichols Sawmill Road. After telling Ran to meet her out at her place, she held her phone firm in one hand. Her brother rode a motorcycle, but there was room for two, and he could still take her up to the rental place after she made reservations.

As she got out of the car, she waved a quick good-bye and started walking away. She heard Hank's door open and the crunch of his shiny boots on gravel before he called out. "I'm here for you if there's anything you ever need."

She glanced back over her shoulder. "I'm good, but thanks for the ride." She pushed the key in the lock and threw open the door, shutting it quickly behind her. Something about that man creeped her out.

Chapter 2

Noah cleaned up the glass and called a contractor to come and fix the window and wall. It'd be an eyesore for a few weeks, but most of the clientele wouldn't mind. Around here, there wasn't any other place to go. He waited for Hank to return, but his cousin never came back. Settling down to the newspaper, he flipped through to the real estate section. Most listings were online now, but he still liked the feel of paper in his hands, and older people who didn't understand the internet still called the paper for local listings. There were only five properties in the section today, and one was across the street. Setting the paper down, he walked to where the window had been and looked out. It was mostly forest until recently. Someone had cleared the land, and he thought they were going to build on it, but apparently, the owners were clearing it for other reasons. They probably sold the timber and now wanted to lease the land. The ad hadn't listed a price, but he'd call and find out.

"Regina Nash. How may I help you?"

"I'm calling about the land across from Hank's Honky-Tonk. Is it for sale or lease?"

"The owner is leasing it, but the price is a steal. Five hundred a month for a twenty-year lease with a ten-year buy-out option of two hundred thousand. That's a full two acres of business-zoned property on a major highway. If you are a Magnolia resident, I don't have to tell you what a deal that is."

Noah smiled. She didn't have to tell him. He saw the growth of this town and knew the potential. If Hank wouldn't listen to him, he would make a go of it all on his own. He could afford the five hundred a month, and he'd sell his half of the business to Hank to get the rest of the capital to build the bar, though Hank was no fool. If he found out Noah was planning to build right across the street, there would be hell to pay. Hank was a hothead, and he knew a lot of people with influence in the county. He could make it hard for Noah if he didn't do this right.

"Hello?" Regina's mature voice was reassuring.

"I'll take it," Noah said without hesitating. He'd saved all his adult life, and now was the time to jump.

"That's wonderful. I told the owner it would move fast, and it's only been on the market two days. I can't wait to tell him. Do you have an agent?"

"No ma'am. Can I just make an offer through you?"

"Sure, I can, as long as you are aware that I represent the seller. I'll draw up the offer and email it over to you. You can fill out the personal information and send it back. If you want, we can have this wrapped up in no time."

Noah's heart thumped with nervous excitement as he smiled. "Wonderful."

He thought about the lady who'd crashed into his bar. He'd assumed it was going to be a bad day when Hank showed up and drove off with her, but now Noah saw her as the catalyst that made him want to search for more. Like a wrecking ball, she'd started the demolition of Hank's and put a detour sign on Noah's old life. He'd buried himself in the bar after his twenty-year career in the military came to an end, and he'd been hiding out in the dusty old dive for too long, waiting for a change that wasn't likely to happen with Hank as his partner. A place to call his own was what he'd always wanted. Now he'd taken the first step. Nervous energy vibrated through him as he moved through the rest of his daily routine. There was so much to do now. Suddenly, Noah felt like he had a purpose, and he hadn't had one of those in a long time. He had been lost as a civilian after spending a lifetime with the military, but now he had a new mission. Noah would find the pretty lady, and when the bar was up and running, he hoped she'd be there to celebrate.

Lexi watched the fancy car drive out of the circular driveway. The wheels caught in the gravel, and rocks flew when Hank hit the gas. She supposed her hasty exit hurt his over-inflated ego, but she didn't care. The man was an ass.

Her brother, Ran, pulled up on his motorcycle, and Lexi sighed with relief, but she didn't know exactly what she would tell him. He was a programmer who could work from his laptop wherever he wanted, and sometimes he sang in a band. Lexi hoped her fiasco wouldn't take too much time from his day. She opened the door, waved, then hustled to grab a pair of leather boots and a thick jacket. The air was cool, and though it would be a short ride back into town, it would be a cold one on a motorcycle.

"You should have called dad. He's been looking for an excuse to get out of the house ever since mom started redecorating their office. He says he can't get any peace and quiet. Besides, I'm not sure if that jacket will keep you warm enough. It's cold." Ran shivered as if to prove his point.

Lexi retrieved her helmet and riding gloves from the entryway closet. She liked to ride with Ran in the summer when she had time, and the pink sparkly helmet she'd found at a garage sale last summer fit better than Ran's spare.

Ran took the helmet from her, turning it over for inspection. "Nice. When did you get this?"

"Treasure hunting with mom and the boys last summer. I didn't think I'd get to try it out so soon, but I need a car before the boys get out of school."

He nodded, understanding. "Okay, let's go. Do you have time to stop and have lunch with me? You can tell me all about it then." He paused as she tried to shove the helmet over her ponytail. She pulled the tie out and then used it to fasten a loose braid. His voice softened. "I mean, if you want to talk, I'm all ears."

Lexi shrugged. She didn't really want to discuss her morning, but Ran was the youngest of her three brothers and the most intuitive of her moods. He might have a cool biker exterior, but inside he was a big warm fuzzy.

"I could eat. Let's get my rental car first and then I'll follow you to the café."

Ran nodded. "Hop on. I'm hungry, and I know just the place."

Lexi had been to Pop's Café a thousand times, but somehow, Ran had just discovered it. Her parents lived closer to The Woodlands, and her brothers Riley and Raphe lived in Houston. Like her, Ran was a local. She'd inherited her grandparents' place after they'd passed. It was before she had three kids and her husband, Jack, had gone off to Afghanistan and gotten himself killed. After the funeral, Ran had found an apartment in Magnolia, saying the cost of living was cheaper than in the city, but she knew it was to watch over her and the kids.

It had been nine years since she'd moved to the ranch, and she'd barely made a dent in getting it in shape. Her family was always trying to help, and she appreciated it, but she was thirty years old, and she needed to stand on her own. Recently, her brother Riley had opened a fancy new restaurant in Houston. He used the excuse that he needed her garden for organic produce so he could help her cultivate the large patch of the farm that backed up to the main house. Things were coming along, and she liked to watch the progress, but her chef brother didn't have time to make the hour drive back and forth as much as the garden needed him. His helping her had actually given her more chores. Ran and Raphe dropped in to help with the horses and donkeys, dropping off hay and getting people to mow the fields. Her boys loved toiling in the garden with their uncles, and it was one of the reasons she hadn't been firm about standing on her own before now. Gus, Bert, and Damien needed good role models around, and her brothers were the best. Fancy chef, fireman, and programmer were all golden when it came to moral strength, hard work, and heart. Their parents had raised them right, and now, she wanted to show everybody she could do it on her own—without Jack, without her parents' financial help, or her brothers picking up all the loose ends. But in order to do that, she needed a job.

"You have got to try the cupcakes. I know that sounds funny coming from your older brother, but I'm manly enough to admit the frosting melts in your mouth. I'm going to take a box to the guys at the fire station when I visit Raphe in Houston tomorrow."

"How will you get them there on your bike without smushing them?"

Ran smiled as he slid into the booth across from her. "I was going to ask if I could borrow your van, but I guess I'll get dad to lend me his truck. I've got to drive into the city to pick up a part for the hog."

Lexi looked out the window where the Harley Davidson was parked. It was beautiful, but she couldn't imagine driving it all the time. "Why don't you buy a small car for rainy days?"

Ran shook his head. "No way. I love ol' Hank."

Ran had named his Harley after Hank Williams Jr. Lexi frowned as she stared at the shiny tailpipes. It made her think of the cheesy guy from the bar, who drove her home. "Well, I don't."

Ran clutched his chest. "Really? Then why'd you buy the helmet?"

She shook her head. Telling him all about Gussy's pet rat, driving the van into the bar, the nice man who'd helped her, and then the pompous Hank who'd driven her home.

Ran's eyebrows furrowed. "Hank…Hank Harding?"

Lexi nodded. "Yes. I accepted the ride home, but something about him creeped me out. I got worried, so I called you. I figured if he heard me talking to someone who'd be there to give me a ride, he'd leave me alone."

"Did he touch you?" Ran's usually calm voice came out low and menacing.

Lexi's eyes darted around, hoping no one thought they were having an argument. "No, no…I mean, he put his hand on my knee, but I think he believed he was reassuring me that everything was going to be okay."

Ran scowled. "Lexi, don't be naïve. Look at you." He motioned a hand at her.

Right now, she was sure she must look a mess, but it warmed her heart that Ran thought she was pretty. "Well, I did get a weird feeling, so I called you."

"Why didn't Noah drive you home? I've met him before. Salt of the earth guy. Just out of the service a few years ago."

"He couldn't leave the bar." Lexi's gut clenched. Noah was in the service. Did he still do the National Guard thing? A lot of men signed up for the supplemental income and benefits. She didn't date military guys. It was her rule. She mentally shook herself. *Noah gave you a drink and made sure you got a ride home. He didn't even ask you out, so relax.* Besides, she hadn't dated anyone since Jack.

"Next time you see Hank, walk the other way. If he touches you again, he'll have me to deal with."

Lexi tried not to giggle at Ran's angry expression. It was like she was a freshman in high school again, and Ran was a senior. She was lucky Jack ever got the nerve to ask her out on a date with her three protective brothers. "Okay, I will," she promised. "Look, don't tell mom and dad about the accident yet. I'll tell them myself, but I need to see what the insurance company says."

"Do you need money, Lex?"

Ran's look of concern made her feel ashamed. She'd let the insurance payment lapse to pay the electric bill that was two months behind and about to be shut off. She wasn't used to being broke. The inheritance she'd gotten helped her to buy out her other siblings when the farm got passed down, then there had been all the repairs, tractors, trailers, feed…the list went on. The life insurance money the Army paid for Jack's death was in a college fund for the boys that she would only touch if they were homeless and starving. Lexi had never attended college, but she was damn sure that her kids would have every opportunity. She had already borrowed money against the farm to pay the taxes, and she hadn't told her parents about any of it. She'd been looking for a job, but outside of waiting tables, what in the world could she do with a high school diploma? When some of the livestock went to market, things would be good again, and she could pay it all back, but for now, she needed to find some way to fill in the gaps.

She hated to confess, but Ran was the one person she could count on to keep a secret. "I think I need to get a job."

Chapter 3

Noah stood in the middle of the cleared land, looking back at Hank's Honky-Tonk. Even though he leased the property without Hank, he'd driven to Houston to talk to his cousin about opening a new place. Hank shut him down before he could barely open his mouth. Noah had ground his teeth and bit back all the things he wanted to say—that Hank was lazy, wanted everything given to him for free, that he tried to cheat their suppliers, and even went so far as to bribe their tax guy into writing off things they hadn't bought.

Noah shook his head as he looked at the boarded-up hole in the wall where Alexa Nash had crashed. It had been a month since the accident, and today he would sign the papers for the land. Contractors were meeting him here, and he thought he had enough investors to actually pull it off. Now, he only needed a catchy name for the upscale watering hole that was going to put Hank's out of business.

Noah spotted Alexa's minivan before it pulled to the side of the road. The hood was still crumpled, and the bumper was held up by what looked like a coat hanger and duct tape. The window glided down, and the pretty blonde smiled at him as she lifted her sunglasses to the top of her head.

"Hi, there! Whatcha doing out here in the grass?" Her eyes darted back to Hank's. "Don't you belong in there?" She pointed a thumb in the direction of the bar.

Noah stepped high as he made his way over a tree stump and across the brown grass to the van. "I'm planning my next move."

Alexa gave him a curious stare, squinting her pretty blue eyes and tilting her head. "Is that right?"

"Yes, ma'am. I'm going to build the nicest lounge Magnolia's ever seen. High-end wine and champagne, small appetizers, lavish ambiance."

Her eyes lit with excitement. "Oh, you're the new owner. My mom is Regina Nash. She told me a new place was coming that would set a precedent of elegance for this town."

Noah couldn't help but share his enthusiasm. Splaying his hands, he described his vision of plush velvet booths, a behemoth of a bar in the center like an island that would serve every kind of champagne, wine, beer and liquor known to man. "Now, if I could think of a fancy name."

"Um, it sounds wonderful. I love champagne. I hardly ever drink, but when I do, I love bubbles."

Noah couldn't suppress his excitement. "That's it! *Bubbles.* The ladies will love it, and it's fancy enough sounding to attract The Woodlands crowd as well."

"Ooh, that sounds fun! I'll be sure to come when it opens." She smiled, then something happened to the light in her eyes. "If I can afford it. I'm sort of living on a beer budget at the moment."

Noah gave her a reassuring smile. "Don't worry, I think I owe you a bottle of champagne for running into my bar."

Alexa's brows knitted together. "Really? How do you figure that? I meant to come by and talk about the cost of repairs. I thought I had insurance, but as it turned out, I didn't pay that bill on time, and they denied the claim, which you probably already know, but I want you to know that I am good for it. Send the bill to my address, and I'll make sure it's taken care of." She rummaged in her purse, finally producing a business card.

"Burns Creek Cattle Company, Alexa Nash Burns, Owner and Operator." He silently pondered the Burns. Everyone he knew who mentioned her called her Lexi Nash. She still wore the small gold band, which prompted him to ask. "Your maiden name is Nash?"

She nodded. The corners of her smile fell a bit as a shadow crossed her features. "Burns was my husband's family name. He was in the service, like you, I'm told. My brother mentioned it when I informed him of the accident."

Noah nodded. *Was…* she was a widow. He'd heard as much, but now she confirmed it. He wanted to pull her into his arms and stroke her silky hair until the sadness left her eyes. But she was in her van, and he didn't know her well enough to offer comfort. He needed to divert the conversation. "You're talking about the brother who came by the bar?"

She looked confused again. "Which brother? I have three, and I'm sure they've all been to Hank's Honky-Tonk."

He didn't like the worry lines marring her smooth forehead. "The one that rides a motorcycle."

She nodded. "Ran."

"Yeah, he took care of everything already. It's paid. I'm not sure why it's taking so long for the contractor to fix it, but my suspicion is that Hank pocketed the insurance money and is trying to whittle down the guy on the repair cost." Noah wasn't sure why he'd said that. Even if it was true that his cousin was a louse, he shouldn't be spreading defaming gossip.

Lexi's jaw dropped. "Ran paid for the accident? Oh no! Why did he do that? I told him I would take care of it."

He tried again to calm her. "The bar's insurance covered it. He only paid the deductible. It wasn't much, I promise."

"Tell me the amount so I can pay him back. He'll never tell me the truth. Ran is a sweetheart, but I can't let him do this."

Noah chuckled. "I think he already did, but the deductible was five hundred if that helps."

"This is really embarrassing. I am so sorry." She shook her head and started the van again. Her pink fingernails tapped a nervous beat on the blue paint of the van door. Without thinking, he put his hand on her forearm.

"Hey, I'm glad you stopped. I felt bad about sending you off with my cousin that day, but I really didn't have a choice. I was worried. When I never saw you again, I figured that Hank probably said something to offend you. He might be part owner and my cousin, but trust me, we're nothing alike. After I sell my share of the bar, I doubt we'll be on speaking terms because Bubbles is going to blow Hank's out of the water." He couldn't resist the brag. After all, Lexi had been the catalyst, and she'd come up with the name.

She pushed back a stray lock of hair, dislodging his light touch. She was blushing, and he wondered if she was embarrassed by the money problems or the physical contact. He stood back, not wanting to impose on her personal space.

"Again, I'm very sorry about the accident." She paused. Her gaze shifted to the windshield like she was about to drive off, but then she turned, giving him a warm smile. "And, thank you for your kindness. I was really out of sorts that day. You helped me to calm down."

Noah fidgeted. He was never comfortable when given praise. It was impossible for him to know what to say, but right now he felt invigorated with new possibilities. The world was a freshly minted gold piece, and his luck seemed endless. "Alexa, let me take you out to dinner." She looked shocked. In her defense, he had more or less blurted it out. "I'd like to talk to you more about the bar. You said you like champagne. Maybe you could help me figure out what labels to buy."

"Uh—I, uh…" she stammered. "I have three boys." She exclaimed with as much eloquence as he had the invitation. "I mean, they're little, and they can't go to bars."

He chuckled at that. Was she being funny, or had he rattled her by asking her out? She was gorgeous, with long blonde hair and blue eyes so deep they bordered on purple. Her skin was creamy-smooth, and her perfect smile was framed by berry-colored lips. He was sure men asked her out all the time. "I'm sorry. I didn't mean to catch you off guard. Would you rather do something that includes your boys?"

The pink returned to her cheeks. "No, I don't usually take them on dates…not that you meant it was a date or anything." She put her hand to her forehead, finally stopping herself.

Noah smiled. "It doesn't have to be a date if you don't want it to be, but I wouldn't mind the company of a beautiful lady, and I really would like your opinion. Will you join me tonight for dinner, with or without your sons? We can go wherever you want."

Lexi gave him a shy smile, but her eyes twinkled with a spark of interest. "Maybe my mom and dad can watch the boys. I think a night out with another adult sounds wonderful."

Lexi wanted more than anything to express her independence, but here she was asking her parents to babysit again. She waved as they said goodbye and drove away with the boys. She sighed and shut the door, missing Captain, their blue heeler's bark. Jack had loved that dog, and she had too, but Captain passed away from old age, and she couldn't bear to get another pup.

She really needed to find a steady sitter, but money was still tight, and catching up on late bills wasn't easy. Now, she needed to find five hundred dollars to pay Ran back and somehow round up enough cash for the vet to vaccinate the cows. A glance in her closet told her she didn't have anything decent to wear. Her wardrobe looked like something out of Farm and Frumpy. Her parents and siblings were well-off, and she was too, on paper, but that didn't pay for groceries. She was currently cash poor and didn't want to run up her credit cards for new dresses. After the boys were born and Jack passed, she'd been the one to impose the strict rule, no gifts over thirty dollars at Christmas. She couldn't afford lavish presents and she wasn't about to accept her family's charity.

Lexi padded to the bathroom to finish her makeup. Thinking about her shabby work clothes, she silently admonished herself, but the truth was that she felt guilty spending money on frivolous things when the boys needed school supplies or new shoes. They were growing up so fast, and little Damien was forever inheriting his brothers' castoffs.

Smearing her eyeshadow to give her blue eyes a smokey look, Lexi shook her head at the results. She looked like a clown. Who was she kidding? A good-looking man like Noah Harding must be crazy to want to have dinner with her. He could probably have any woman he wanted, and he didn't know anything about her, except that she couldn't drive. So why would he ask her out? She thought about it as she assessed her reflection in the mirror. The pink bathrobe she wore was thin and dull from too many washings. The sleeve had a burn mark from catching on fire two months ago when she was frying bacon. Lucky for her, she'd been wearing a nightgown underneath when she threw it off in the middle of the kitchen, stomping on the flames. Her boys had sat wide-eyed along the counter, staring at her as if she were a lion tamer in a three-ring circus.

She'd looked at them with a stern tilt of her chin. "And this is why you don't play with matches!" She'd thought she heard Gussy snort and say, "Yeah, right," with sarcasm to his brothers, but she was too frazzled to reprimand him.

At least her hair was straight and shiny since she'd blown it dry. Long, thick and the color of golden wheat, it was one of her best assets. She unfastened the robe and held it open to do inventory. She'd shaved in the shower. The stretch marks on her breasts had faded well enough. Having her children while she was still young had helped her body bounce back. Her hips weren't as small as they used to be, but the overall package wasn't bad. The farm and the boys kept her daily cardio up. She lifted sacks of feed, hauled buckets of refuse to the compost, and ran the vacuum nearly every night. The ancient Kirby still worked, but it was made of real metal, and it was heavy. Her chores had toned her arms, trimmed her waistline, and sculpted her legs. A while back, her friend Julie had asked her to join Jim's Gym.

Lexi had laughed outright. "Where would I find the time? My entire day is a workout."

Her life was an endless to-do list, and suddenly she felt like she'd added one more chore. *No, Noah Harding is not a chore. The gorgeous hunk of a man is your vacation for the night. A reminder that you are still a desirable woman. Why else would he ask you to dinner? It can't be for your wealth or status.* She snorted at the thought. *Now put on your lipstick and get your fanny ready to have some fun.*

A knock sounded at the door. "Crap on toast!" She threw the robe down and ran into her closet. She grabbed the simple calico dress that she wore to church sometimes. It was the last thing she wanted to wear, but she didn't have time to be choosy. Besides, it was a dress, and if they should go to The Woodlands, it would get her into most places.

Lexi smoothed her hair and tried to calm her breathing as she opened the door. She didn't want to look like she'd been flying around the house on a broom. "Hello."

Noah smiled. His tan face was clean-shaven, and his gray eyes sparkled. His hair was still damp, but she loved the way the drying tendrils feathered above his brow.

"Do you want to come in, or should we get going?" Lexi didn't know the protocol for dating. Her brothers sure did. She should've asked them what was cool or not cool, but she didn't want anyone to know she was going out. She'd told her parents she needed a break, but to confide the truth meant telling people she was leaving Jack's memory behind. Lexi knew it was time, but she wasn't ready to discuss it with anyone yet. Noah didn't know her, and she liked that about him. It left some privacy to her past. He wouldn't be looking at her all night, thinking, "Poor Lexi. Running that ranch all alone, losing the love of her life, and raising three kids without a father…." Well, the last part she'd told him, but still.

"I made reservations for eight, and it's in The Woodlands. We might want to get on the road in case we hit traffic." He held the door open for her. "You should grab a coat, though. It's a little chilly out.

Lexi wanted to die with embarrassment. She was wearing a summer dress in winter. There were better choices in her closet. Why had she grabbed the faded calico? Well, it was too late now. She would look like an idiot if she blazed back in to change, and the only decent coat she had was the jacket she'd worn to ride on Ran's motorcycle. It was army-green Gortex, made for skiing or something more outdoors oriented. "It's okay. I'll be fine. I'm sure the restaurant has heat."

Noah didn't contradict her. He walked her to the passenger side of his shiny black SUV and opened the door. It was new and smelled of leather and cleaning chemicals. She wondered if he had it detailed before picking her up. That made her smile. He'd seen her vehicle. Not only was the exterior a wreck, but the inside smelled like French fries and peanut butter.

As she stepped up into the vehicle, Noah reached for her bottom. She tensed, thinking he might actually use the excuse of giving her a boost to touch her derriere. Was he like his cousin after all? She turned, giving him a raised brow. Noah held both hands up and spoke softly as if she were a skittish colt. "Now, I don't want you to be embarrassed. I'm sure this happens all the time…." His hand glided slowly back to her bottom, but his eyes held hers with honest assurance. Lexi felt a tug as she heard the Velcro-like sound come from the rear of her calico dress. Noah pressed his lips together in an indiscernible expression. Was he holding his breath? Trying not to laugh? What in heaven was stuck to her rump?

He held up a thick, night-time sanitary napkin. "I didn't think you wanted to carry it to the restaurant that way. Maybe it would be better in your purse?"

Lexi wanted to weep. Her eyes began to water, and she thought she might humiliate herself further by crying. The poor man only wanted to go to dinner, and she couldn't even dress appropriately for the occasion. How had she missed the Kotex? The dress had just come out of the wash. She should pour her life out on the table now and save him the trouble of getting to know her before he ran for the hills. She grabbed the pad and stuffed it in her small purse, willing the catch to clasp. "Damien is my youngest, and he's into everything. The doctor has assured me it's a sign of intelligence, and that his curiosity will —"

"These things happen." His words were meant to soothe her, but heat radiated from her neck and face. Noah's smile was probably meant to be comforting, but she still felt like an idiot. To his credit, he got behind the wheel, acting like it had never happened. Lexi decided it was the only polite thing to do, so she tried to push it aside. Maybe one day she would laugh about this, but tonight, she planned on drinking away the awful moment. *Wherever Noah is taking me, I sure hope they serve stiff martinis.*

Chapter 4

The Lamplighter's Steakhouse was cozy, and the food was always great. He'd been there a few times, and he liked the half-moon shaped booths and dim lighting. The establishment didn't serve hard liquor, but they had a nice champagne selection, and Noah ordered the best they had.

"You didn't have to do that." Alexa sounded worried as the sommelier poured them each a glass.

"You like champagne, don't you?"

She eyed the waiter as he walked away. Her cheeks turned pink again and her eyes sparkled in the candlelight. "Yes, but that bottle will cost you a fortune," she said in a hushed tone.

"Alexa, don't worry about it. I think you deserve the best, and I'd like you to relax and enjoy the evening."

She held her champagne glass up to his. "Sorry. That was rude of me, wasn't it? I'm not—I mean, I'm messing this all up. You see, I don't date, so I don't know how to do this." She motioned around them. Letting out a nervous sigh, she added, "And please, call me Lexi. Everyone does."

He gave her a small nod and smiled. He thought it was adorable that she was nervous. "Then cheers, Lexi. To new beginnings and lots of bubbles."

Lexi grinned. "Are you trying to get me drunk, Noah Harding?"

He chuckled. "No ma'am. I'm thinking about the awesome name of my new venture. The one that *you* came up with." He paused, wondering if he should divulge more. He used to be a lot more carefree. In fact, he had pretty much worn his heart on his sleeve when he started his career in the Army twenty plus years ago. His inexperience with women had led him to make a big, impulsive mistake that left him broke and bitter afterward. He reminded himself that he'd been wet behind the ears back then, and he'd done a lot of living since. Lexi wasn't like Petra. She was the All-American girl-next-door, and he didn't think she was hiding much. She'd already told him about the three kids, bills piling up, and she even tried to save him money on the bill tonight. For some reason, she didn't think she was worth the effort, and there couldn't be anything further from the truth. Noah's protective hackles went up, making it his mission to make Lexi comfortable. He wanted to erase the worry lines that wrinkled her forehead and ease the tension around her eyes. She deserved an evening she'd remember, and he wanted to give it to her.

She was so different from his ex-wife. Was that why he felt this pull of attraction? They were both beautiful blondes with blue eyes, but that's where the similarity ended. Petra had wanted to live beyond their means. She'd demanded what he couldn't afford to give, and in the end, she'd left him for someone who outranked him and had a bigger bank account. It was a kick to his ego, but he'd survived it, and no matter how many camp followers he hooked up with over his years in the Army, he never fell for the husband-trap again. Every base had its number of women looking for a way out of their small-town lives. The Military offered great benefits to soldiers and their families. The biggest lure for single women around a base was matrimony, because it meant a free ticket out. It was a chance to see the world, and in Petra's case, a chance to become an American. Lexi was already a legal citizen by birth, and so far, she'd put a lot of honest cards on the table. Taking her at face value, he decided to open up and risk showing his emotions. "That morning, when you busted through the front of Hank's, you saved my life."

Lexi's brow furrowed. "Are you crazy? I almost killed you!"

Noah laughed. "Well, yeah, maybe, but you also got me thinking about my future. My cousin and I inherited Hank's Honky-Tonk from our grandfather. I've been trying for a long time to get him to invest in cleaning it up and turning it into a nicer place. We've both made a good income off of it for the past several years, and we can afford the renovation. The truth is, Magnolia is getting bigger, and the clientele is growing into a high-income status that a place like Hank's won't be able to hold for long. Now, my cousin and I have never seen eye to eye, but reasoning with him about this has had me on hold for too long. When you crashed into the bar, it was like a cannonball careening through my stagnant life. After a career in the Army, I was hiding out from the world at Hank's. I think I was in a funk after Afghanistan, and I was nursing my wounds from the past." He twirled the delicate crystal stem of the champagne glass between two fingers. "I lost a few buddies, and it took a while for the world to make sense." He paused. Willing himself to expose his feelings. "Years. Four years to be exact."

Lexi looked like a land mine had gone off at their table. "Four years? Afghanistan? I heard you were in the Army, but…you were stationed in Afghanistan?"

Noah could have kicked himself. Why had he brought it up? She'd already told him she was a widow. He knew her husband had been in the service, and though he didn't know how long she'd been on her own, it amazed him that such a pretty lady could still be single. She must be shell shocked by whatever had happened to him. Noah put his hand on top of hers. "I'm sorry. I didn't mean to dredge up the past."

Lexi took a big sip from her flute. Her hand was a little shaky. "I don't mind hearing about your service. I guess you know by my reaction that I lost my husband in Afghanistan. Maybe you knew him? Jack Burns. He died four years ago, right after Damien was born."

Noah reached out to her, squeezing her hand as he shook his head. "No, I'm sorry. I didn't know a Burns, but I wish I had. I'm sure he was a great guy."

Lexi nodded, tears brimming in her eyes. She straightened her shoulders, sniffed, and reached for the wine list. "Well, we better look at the menu, hadn't we, if you want to give Hank's a run for the money. That place is rumored to have the best hot wings around, and if Bubbles is going to blow Hank's out of the water, we have our work cut out for us." She reached for her champagne, took a sip, and smiled. "However, it will be easy to top Hank's nonexistent wine list."

Noah scooted closer so he could see the selections as well. They both let the past rest and focused on talking about the future. Lexi told him about the rescue donkeys they'd taken in recently, and that the boys were still searching for names.

"They asked if we could buy them underwear!" Lexi laughed. "I don't know why they thought the donkeys needed underwear, but the cows didn't. Leave it to Gussy to get fixated on something like drawers when he doesn't wear any half of the time. I guarantee by Christmas, those animals will be in my pajamas."

Noah chuckled. "I remember that age. It's a good time in a boy's life. Everything is full of hope, and the world is your playground. Of course, I can't imagine growing up with a cell phone in my bookbag or video games any time I wanted them."

Lexi batted him on the arm playfully. "What makes you think I would let them play video games any time they want? I'll have you know we have strict rules around my house, and games are off-limits until baths are taken, and homework is done." They both laughed and then her face grew serious as she covered her mouth. "Oh lord, all I have done is talk about the farm and the boys. I'm sorry. I must be boring you to tears."

Noah shook his head, admiring her silky hair and continual smile while she talked about her kids. He'd missed out on having a family of his own. His marriage to Petra only lasted a few years before they'd split. He supposed her fidelity issues had developed from his lack of time at home. He'd done three tours back to back, and if he added up the days they spent together, it only equaled a few months. When they had eloped, he hadn't been in the military long enough to know the repercussions of duty versus marriage. After the breakup, he'd put everything he had into being an officer, thinking his career was on a path to the top. That left little time to meet "the one" and fall in love, even if he had thought falling in love was a real thing.

Noah had never thought of himself as a family man, but watching Lexi's infectious grin and hearing about her farm and children made him hunger for something he didn't know he craved. His mind turned over new thoughts in his head. Could he deal with an instant family? The thought hadn't occurred to him when he'd asked her out. She was so damn beautiful, and her shy demeanor and perfect smile touched him in a place long forgotten. Lexi was all woman and yet wholesome, too. She was the perfect mix of stubborn, "I'll do it all on my own and the world can be damned" and yielding, "someone, please save me from my life." She was overwhelmed. He had no doubt about it. Three young boys and a ranch to take care of amounted to a herculean task, but she was proud and tough, and he admired her determination. It sent awareness darting to his lower regions every time her bluebonnet-colored eyes stared over the rim of her glass. The fullness of her bottom lip intoxicated him.

He didn't want to be nosy, but he had to ask. "How do you do it? Keep up with the cattle, the donkeys, the horses, and the farming? Didn't you say you were plowing?"

"We are plowing. My brother started this whole farm-to-table thing at his restaurant, and he is using my land to supplement some of the produce. It's not enough to take care of all the supplies needed yet, but he hopes in a few years that he won't have to rely on his other sources."

"Good. I'm glad you have some help."

Lexi pushed a stray wisp of hair from her forehead, leaning back into the plush velvet booth. "It's a lot to handle. Part of the reason my life is a wreck." She sighed, putting her champagne back on the table. The server came by to refill their glasses, but she put her hand over the top. "I better not." When the waiter left, she looked at Noah with an apologetic smile. "I haven't had much to drink in a long time. If you can't tell, I don't get out much."

She motioned to the flowered dress that did little too complement her figure. He didn't care. It wasn't why he'd asked her out. He wanted *this*—getting to know her, hearing her laugh, watching her relax into a comfortable conversation. It was the best time he'd had in a long while. He loved her stories about the farm and her family. The kids sounded bright, curious, and funny. He couldn't wait to meet them. *Damn. I'm really doing this.* "My life consists of running the bar and my crappy apartment. I can't tell you how much I envy you. The farm sounds like paradise."

She shook her head at him. "Don't go fallin' in love. I have to get up every morning before the crack of dawn to feed the livestock, then get through my list of other chores. I make good money when things go right, but we had a drought a few years back. It set off a string of events that I can't seem to catch up with. Hence falling behind on my car insurance payment, the coat hanger bumper repair, and…." She paused, looking down. "This ugly dress."

He protested as any gentleman would, but she held up her hand and laughed. "It's okay to agree with me on this one, or I'll think you have no taste."

"It's the woman inside that dress that I want to get to know," he began. She looked away, and he waited for her eyes to meet his again. He needed her to hear this. "I enjoy your company, and I'm really glad you came."

Lexi tilted her head, looking at him as if she was trying to figure him out. "We only made it through one bottle of champagne. I don't think I'm going to be much help creating a wine list."

He nodded at the bottle. "It's all right. There will be plenty of time for wine tasting and building the bar. I hope you'll let me take you out again. Maybe we can try something new."

"I do like red wine, and when it's hot out, I enjoy chardonnay, but only if it's chilled properly."

Noah shook his head. "I meant maybe I could take you out for pizza or burgers, and you could bring the boys."

She studied him, giving him a winsome smile. "Noah, I really like you. You seem like a nice guy, but my boys are rambunctious and young. They get into everything. As soon as you see the whole package —"she motioned all around her petite form —"You'll be hightailing it to Houston or somewhere far, far away." She scooted to the other side of the booth and stood. "I need to go to the ladies' room, then I think you better take me home. I've had a great evening, and I appreciate you asking me to come. But, as I've explained, I have an early morning."

Chapter 5

Noah had been a perfect gentleman, and the evening made her feel like a princess at the ball. They didn't go dancing or anything over the top, but the restaurant was warm and inviting. The food was mouth-watering, and the conversation was as casual as the man. Noah Harding was nothing like his letch of a cousin, who'd lied about owning the bar. It turned out that Noah and Hank had inherited it fifty-fifty, and Noah planned to sell his half to build Bubbles.

He said he'd been saving his whole life to start his own business and admitted it was easier to put money aside being single. That concerned Lexi. Had he never had a family? He was forty, and that said something about a man. Was he a player, commitment-phobic, incapable of communicating or sharing emotions? She wanted to laugh at herself. Here she was, dissecting him on her *first* date in the four years since she had become a widow. *Girl, get over yourself.* She was the one with phobias and commitment issues. She had shut down anyone who might be remotely interested in her for years now. It had hurt too much when she lost Jack, and her eldest was heart-broken when his daddy never came home from his tour of duty. Gus had recently stopped asking about him every day, but it had taken four years to get to this point of normalcy. She finally felt like she wouldn't crumble apart at the mention of her previous life. Was that why she'd said yes to Noah's invitation tonight?

Noah parked in front of the house and walked around to open her door. She was already getting out, but he offered his hand to steady her as she stood on three-inch heels. The SUV had oversized tires, and her five-foot-two stature had to slide down to reach the ground. The warmth of his hands on her waist made her tense, but her insides churned with something other than annoyance or nerves. Her stomach flip-flopped, and a sizzle ran down her lower back to her thighs. She recognized the awakening. The champagne might have dulled her defenses and opened her eyes to possibilities, but it was his intense gray-eyed stare that opened the door to something more. Her lips parted as his head dipped toward hers. His arms slowly pulled her into his firm torso, giving her all the time in the world to protest, but she knew she wouldn't. Wrapped in his arms and feeling the warmth of him, she admitted to herself that she wanted his touch. He smelled like warm sunshine, clean aftershave, and something she hadn't been this close to in a long time. *A man.*

Noah's lips brushed over hers in gentle invitation. Her eyes closed as she opened to him, yearning to press her lips to his. Her hands clasped the collar of his shirt and grabbed at the strands of his rich brown hair, silently begging for more. His tongue danced with hers as she sucked in a breath, taking him in with every fiber of her being. Pressing her body against his as his hands splayed across her shoulders and lower back, she wound one leg around his thigh to anchor herself. This intense sexual desire had been coiling inside of her all night as she took in his rugged good looks and masculine allure. Without any warning to herself, she was primed and ready to spring.

How long had it been since she'd been kissed like this? An image of Jack making love to her the night before he was deployed flashed through her mind, splashing her with cold guilt. She pulled back, suddenly embarrassed by the unsuppressed moans of desperation coming from deep in her throat. She hadn't even realized how sexually frustrated she was until now. Breathing heavily, she stepped back, grasping at the SUV's door. It was still open, and she encountered the cool leather of the passenger seat. Torn between her memories of Jack and visions of climbing back in and pulling Noah on top of her, tore at her conscience. As if sensing the tempest of her emotions, Noah stepped back into the crisp night air, giving her the space she needed to move around him. Hesitantly, she took the hand he offered and let him walk her to the door.

What had she started? She couldn't do this. She was so out of touch with dating, sex, or whatever this was. She needed to pump the brakes. "I'd ask you to come in, but it's kind of late, and the boys...."

Noah nodded, looking like he was trying to catch his breath. His eyes flashed silver in the moonlight, and though he backed away, desire still pooled in his gaze. He bit his bottom lip, suppressing what sounded like a groan of regret.

His sexy moan was her undoing. Lexi couldn't contain herself, and memories be damned. The house was empty. The boys wouldn't be home until tomorrow afternoon, and so what if this was their first date? She was thirty years old, and she'd waited four years to get over Jack being gone. He wasn't ever coming back, and, once Noah got a good look at all the baggage she came with, he wouldn't be sticking around for long. So if she wanted to have hot sex with someone, and that someone being drop-dead gorgeous, she needed to open the door and invite him in. Stepping forward, she wrapped her arms around his neck and dragged him to her. Noah didn't need more of an invitation than that. They slammed awkwardly into the front door as she felt for the knob and turned it. Their weight sent them crashing in. The door thumped against the entryway wall, and she yelped from the knob jamming into her back. He wrapped his arms around her, massaging the sore spot, while she tugged at his jacket. She needed to feel his naked skin against her.

He seemed as desperate as she felt, tossing the coat on the hall bench as he took her into another heated embrace. Noah fumbled with the tiny pearl buttons on the front of her calico dress, trying to unloop them through the ribbon holes. She stopped him, grabbed his hand and pulled him behind her to the bedroom, almost tripping on one of Damien's toys in the hall.

"Yum! That's delicious! More please!" The stuffed mouse squealed.

They both chuckled at the toy's timely exclamations. Lexi looked at the rumpled sheets and shoes on the floor of her bedroom. She fussed at the boys all the time over their mess, but now it was her turn to be caught out. Spinning toward him, she tried to apologize. He pulled her against his chest, capturing her in his arms as his lips trailed kisses over her exposed neck. His hands slid to the hem of her dress, tugging it up and over her head. Oh, he was good. He'd figured out that the waistline was stretchy, and the dress was easily taken off from the top. She pushed the dimmer light lever all the way down as he backed her toward the bed. She was confident enough to know she was attractive, but there was no need for him to see every inch of her. Even though she was farm toned and curvy, Lexi assured herself it was better if he felt his way to the important parts.

She moaned as the weight of him pressed down on her. His knee came between her thighs as he caressed and inched his way down her shivering form. She felt like a virgin. Lexi couldn't control her shuddering excitement as his thumb grazed beneath the silky spandex of her panties. Thank God that she wore something bikini shaped and not the usual control-top granny-panty. Shadows danced over his features from the dim light above. He was staring at her as he tugged her underwear down, exposing her whole body to him. His tongue darted across his lower lip, and he bent toward her. Her hands flew to cover herself. She didn't want him to see her most intimate place. That's why she'd turned off the lights. Was he planning to go there?

He gently pushed her hands away, nuzzling his face over the smooth skin of her belly, then lower. "Lexi, you're beautiful. He breathed in deep as he trailed kisses over her sensitive flesh, pushing her panties farther down and over her feet. He glided back up to her, kissing her inner thigh and trailing more kisses over her hip and sides until he reached her breasts. She hadn't worn a bra. Lexi had shoved her dress on so fast when he arrived that there hadn't been time. Her nipples stood erect, waiting for his sweet mouth to devour her.

She wasn't disappointed. He nipped, sucked and swirled his tongue around her peaks like a man who was starving. His hands massaged every inch of her until finally parting her legs and running his fingers over the cleft of her mound. She was more than wet. It was as if a tsunami was sweeping her mind and body away in one big wave of pleasure. She opened for him and arched into his hand, all the while begging him not to torture her by making her wait. She wanted him to enter her now.

Excited by his touch, she couldn't quell her shivering limbs. Lexi had never been with anyone besides Jack. She didn't like being so vulnerable in the dark with someone she barely knew, but the chemistry was off the charts. At this moment, she felt raw and exposed, but she needed to let go—let someone else take over. She laid her responsibilities aside, and she opened her legs farther apart in invitation.

"Please, now. I need you inside me," she begged. Her emotions were centered at the pulsing of her clit, and she couldn't think past reaching a place she hadn't been in so long. Stolen minutes with her shower massager wasn't the same, and it didn't do to have a vibrator in your nightstand with three curious boys romping through the house. She could imagine it would end up tied to a dinosaur as a space jet, or in the bathtub as a submarine.

Noah ignored her plea, instead sliding down to glide his tongue along her slit. The feel of him was hot and wet, and she moaned as the tempo of her pulse sped up to an alarming thump. As his tongue circled the cluster of nerves that writhed with pleasure, the sound of her blood pumping with excitement throbbed in her ears. Oh, God, she was going to come.

"Noah, please. I need to be filled up. I need you inside me." He leaned to the side of the bed, picking up his pants. She heard the tear of the foil wrapper and sighed with relief. Thank God he was thinking straight, and shame on her. She hadn't even thought about protection.

He entered her with one smooth thrust that sent pleasure streaming from her core to all of her extremities. As they rocked back and forth, making more noise than her bedroom had ever heard, she closed her eyes and felt her body coil and release. She moaned as she let go, calling out, "Oh my God, oh my God, oh—my—God!" She sounded like a porn star, and she knew it, but what else could she say? The pleasure seemed endless as it sizzled over her in pulsing waves, making the light golden hair on her arms stand straight with her puckering goose flesh. The aerobic exercise and toe-curling orgasm left her limp with exhaustion. Seconds after her, Noah picked up his thrusts and moaned with his own powerful release. He didn't have to call out to any deity for her to know it was good. He clasped her tightly and shuddered as if he'd been touched by a shockwave. His head tilted back, and his full bottom lip beckoned her to take it between her teeth. She felt his muscles tense and release, then he rolled them both to their sides. She felt the weight of his thigh over hers, and he pulled her closer to his chest.

They lay still for a moment, and she finally found her voice. "Thank you. I really needed that."

Chapter 6

Lexi woke to her usual five o'clock alarm and leaped out of bed to turn it off. The gorgeous, insatiable Noah barely moved. She supposed he was spent since they had run a marathon of sex before dawn. The man was a god. She smiled at the memory of them tangled in the sheets. The temptation to wake him up for a quickie before she started her chores was strong, but she needed to get a few things done, and the lower part of her body was sore from sudden over-use.

The boys wouldn't be home until after school, so maybe Noah would want to go to lunch…or take her back to bed before he left. She smiled at the thought, then her gut clenched. Guilt washed over her as the picture of Jack stared up at her. It had sat on the little hallway table outside of her room since they'd moved into the house. She'd put a lot of the pictures away after the first year he passed, but she kept a few out for the boys to remember him by.

Picking up the wedding photo, Lexi stared back at herself, embraced in Jack's loving arms. He'd been clean shaven when they got married, but afterward, he wore a trimmed beard. Was he looking down on her now? If he was, she knew he wouldn't judge her. Jack was always carefree and had a no-nonsense way of looking at the world. He would probably tell her to go for it with a wink and a slap on her rump. She wanted to. She really did, but in her heart, she knew she wasn't ready. The boys were too young, the ranch needed too much attention, and looking at the photograph, she felt too guilty about the bone-rattling, muscle aching, really great sex she'd had. She shook her head, refusing to go there right now. Why was she obsessing? It was just a fix, right? It was only one night and not likely to be followed up by a second.

She remembered that Noah had said he wanted to meet the boys, but men said anything when liquor was flowing and the head in their jeans was doing all the talking. She'd known that Noah liked the way she looked since she'd crashed into the bar. He could barely take his eyes off of her. Lexi knew what she was getting into as soon as she'd said yes to dinner, and she'd worn her big-girl panties just for the occasion. Though she might deny that she intended to sleep with him, it wasn't a surprise that they had ended the night in her bed. Mother of three, farmer, cattle rancher, or plain old Lexi, she was a woman—a woman who needed to get laid. There shouldn't be any blame or guilt for what they'd done. The boys were with her parents, and nobody had to know anyway, *right*?

Who was she kidding? This was Magnolia, and she'd bet her last dollar someone would get a whiff of the gossip and run it up the flagpole before noon, along with her big-girl panties.

Lexi made her way out to the barn where she ran into John Astor, her ranch hand. The faint light of the barn made his sandy hair look golden. She couldn't afford him, but her brother, Riley, had insisted she let John take care of whatever she couldn't. Riley used the excuse of his little vegetable patch to say he owed her that much, but she knew it was his own way of trying to help her make ends meet. As things were, she couldn't refuse. She needed help, and John minded his own business. She didn't know much about him, but he was around her age, polite, quiet, and never called in sick. Most of the time, she didn't even see him, but this morning he was repairing a horse stall.

"Mornin' John."

"Mornin' Mrs. Burns."

She'd never thought of it before, but he'd always referred to her as Mrs. She was a widow at thirty, and ma'am sounded old. John had been there for two years already, and she'd asked him to call her Lexi, but he was always full of respect, using her married title.

When she thought about the time she'd been with Jack, it wasn't very long. She was a teen when they'd met in high school, and they got married right after graduation. Gus entered the world squalling a few years later, and Bert the year after that. Jack died a few weeks before her twenty-sixth birthday, and their youngest, Damien, was just a newborn. Her relationship with Jack spanned eight years of her life. It wasn't a drop in the bucket, but she'd lived the first seventeen years of her life without him and another four years since he'd died.

There was no doubt about it. She had been lonely for a long time, but the idea of letting a man into her home and around her children seemed impossible. Maybe Noah wasn't looking for any strings attached. It would be nice to go out once in a while and to have adult relations again. Images from their night together flashed through her mind. Damn, the sex had been better than she could ever remember. *Forgive me, Jack.* She looked up at the barn ceiling as she thought about the young, inexperienced sex she'd shared with her husband. He'd been good in bed, and their love made the sex better because of the emotions they shared.

But last night was raw, untamed, and wild. Noah had rolled her onto her stomach and taken her from behind, all the while stroking her most sensitive parts with his strong hands as she fell into submission. Afterward, he rolled her astride him as he bucked with fury beneath her, stretching her body to reach heights of passion she'd never known existed. It was the first time she'd ever climaxed more than once in one night. It made her regret that she hadn't been more forward with Jack in their explorations when they'd been together. She shook her head—the pleasure they'd missed....

"Mrs. Burns? Do you see something up there that needs fixing?" John asked with concern. He walked to where she stood, looking up at the rafters above the hayloft.

Lexi almost laughed. "No, John. Thanks. I think what I was contemplating has already been fixed."

"Uh, we might have a problem." Noah held the towel around his waist as he looked across the kitchen island at Lexi. She'd just walked through the door, wearing pink warmups and what looked like leopard print rain boots.

She smiled at him, but her eyes never reached his. Her focus was on his bare chest. That made his train of thought zigzag back to the bedroom.

Her cheeks turned a pretty pink as she picked up a piece of paper off the kitchen counter that looked like a list. "I know there's not much in the fridge. I am supposed to go to the grocery today. I was thinking —"

Noah held his hand up, almost dislodging his towel. Her eyebrows rose as she studied his hand as it returned to clutching the fabric. She never took her eyes off him as she eased out of her boots. If he wasn't so worried about what he'd done, he would have picked her up and had his way with her on the island. As it was, she was probably about to get upset.

"It's not about food. You weren't here when I woke up, so I thought I'd grab a quick shower." She nodded, encouraging him to go on. "I pulled back the curtain, and a rat fell off the curtain rod onto my head and then into the bathtub. I grabbed the nearest thing to whack it with and…."

"Oh, my God! Did you kill her?" She shrieked.

Noah shook his head in confusion. "Her? No, I missed. It ran out of the shower and straight under your bed. I haven't found it yet, but if you go back outside, I'll get it and take care of the situation."

Her brows knitted together in what appeared to be irritation. "You most certainly won't!" Lexi spouted as she ran toward the bedroom. "Ann-Margret? Are you okay? Here girl. It's Momma. I'll get you a treat."

Noah followed her, perplexed. "The rat has a name?"

"It's Gus's pet rat. The one that ran over my foot and caused me to crash my van into the bar."

Noah remembered she'd said something about a mouse in the car, but Ann-Margret wasn't a cute, cuddly mouse. She was huge, with big beady red eyes and needle-like teeth. He hated to admit it, but he yelped when the fat rat startled him.

Lexi turned, grasping his arm. "Would you mind getting some cheese from the fridge? And shut the bedroom door. If I don't find Ann-Margret, Jumper might eat her."

Noah felt his eyebrows arch. "Jumper?"

"The cat."

He scanned the room, looking around his feet as if the feline would magically appear. He liked animals, but he didn't want to watch the cat eat the rat, so he made a quick path to the kitchen to fetch the requested treat. When he returned, the vision of Lexi's head under the dust ruffle, with her pink warm-up clad derriere in the air, made him think of other things he wanted to capture.

"Do you see her?" Noah asked.

Lexi's bottom swayed as she leaned farther beneath the bed, reaching back for him to put the cheese in her hand. "Yes. Sh! You don't want to scare her again." To the rat, she cooed, "Come here, Ann-Margret. Momma's got you, little girl. How about a nice piece of cheese?"

Noah felt like the cat in the current scenario, watching Lexi disappear beneath the king-size bed. She was petite, and he loved the way she felt in his arms, but she wasn't weak. Her character said she could handle anything. Mother of three, doing it all on her own, and battling everything life threw at her with the courage of a badger. When she low-crawled out from under the bed with the fat white rat wrapped in her hands, he wanted to grab her up in his arms, rat with the pink collar and all. Wait, how had he missed the collar? Were those rhinestones around it? She gave the rat a snuggle, cooing apologetically to her.

Lexi was all woman, and sexy as hell, but the impish grin on her face struck a chord in his loins that made him want to drag her to bed. Her smile faded as she brushed away a stray wisp of hair from her face. "What? Are there dust bunnies in my hair?"

Noah shook his head, approaching her slowly. He looked down at the offending animal, who'd dropped in on his morning. "Is there someplace you can put Ann-Margret so that we can take a shower, and then I can take you to breakfast? I saw the contents of your fridge, and it looks like there's only enough for Ann-Margret and maybe the cat." He leaned down, brushing his lips across hers in a slow, lingering kiss.

"Um," she moaned into his lips. "Sounds good. Go run the water, and I'll put Mischievous Margret back in her cage. Maybe that scrap of cheese will keep her there until I get back from the grocery."

Noah gave her a concerned frown. He didn't like being dropped in on by rodents. "Does she escape often?"

Lexi chuckled, but images of Ann-Margret getting into trouble flashed across his mind—the rat coming out of his boot as he was trying to put it on, or worse, running beneath his boots as he was walking down the hall.

Lexi must have read his concern. As she reached the bedroom door, she turned back, flashing a big smile at him. "Don't worry. Gus probably left Ann-Margret's cage door open. I won't let her get you again."

Noah chuckled. This morning, he thought he was being the man, protecting Lexi from encountering the rodent. "Who's the hero now?"

Chapter 7

Noah didn't shut the door when he entered the master bath, and when he dropped his towel, Lexi's jaw dropped with it. His broad shoulders, muscular torso, and tapered middle were enough to make her bite her bottom lip. His tight, rounded buttocks made her look heavenward. *Thank you, God. I really needed this.*

Was it wrong to thank God for sex? She knew she should feel guilty, but she reminded herself that it had been over four years since she'd been to bed with anyone. After she dumped Ann-Margret back in her holding cell, Lexi scurried to the spare bedroom to grab a new toothbrush and do some preliminary grooming. Noah was Greek God perfect, and she wasn't sure what she could do to hide her imperfections in the glaring bathroom light. There wasn't a dimmer switch she could rely on to camouflage the cellulite or stretch marks, and she wasn't sure she was ready for full-body disclosure. More important, she didn't think Noah was ready to see the reality of a woman who'd had three kids before thirty. The farm work kept her in a size six, but there were other factors at stake. She'd bought a Victoria's Secret push-up bra. It was cheaper than a boob job, and it got the same results—as long as she wore clothes. Somehow, she didn't think she would get away with wearing it in the shower, and she was sure he'd felt the softness of her less than firm breasts last night.

Lexi wrapped a towel around her not-so-perfect form, praying for a miracle. She entered the steamy bathroom and stood outside of the old tub and shower combo. She really needed to remodel this place. *Focus! You are about to have hot shower sex. It's not the time to think about your lack of funds to decorate.*

"I was wondering if Ann-Margret had decided to eat you instead of the cheese."

Lexi giggled. "Trust me. Cheese trumps all with Ann-Margret."

Noah grabbed her hand, pulling her into the shower. Her body slid in next to his drenched form. "Ann-Margret is a rat and a fool." He dipped his head, nipping at her neck and the sensitive lobe of her ear. His soap-covered hands moved down her body, pulling her hips to his. His hardness pushed at her middle. She stretched up to meet his lips in a hungry kiss that sent fire through her bloodstream and down to the pulsing juncture between her thighs. Lexi lifted a leg and wrapped it around the back of his. Hot water sprayed over them and pooled in the crevices where their bodies met. Noah sucked at her bottom lip, biting softly until she moaned. His tongue twirled with hers in a desperate dance to bring them together as one. His hand slid between them, finding the entry to her heat. His fingers traced lazy circles as she rocked her hips into him, begging that he enter her. As Noah pushed his finger inside, she arched against him, moaning. His rhythmic movements shoved her over the edge. The intense orgasm had her spinning out of control as her legs turned to water, and her hands locked in Noah's hair. She cried out, grasping onto him for dear life, but she held nothing back. Sparks of color swirled beneath her eyelids and she thought she would pass out from pure pleasure. With his tender kisses trailing down her neck as he held her tight, a window to her soul glided opened and she beckoned Noah to come inside.

"Oh my God, Noah. I wasn't ready...I mean, I didn't mean to climax so soon." She gasped, trying to catch up with her racing heart.

Noah chuckled, dipping his head to her and taking one of her nipples in his mouth. He suckled and teased it between his teeth, then pulled her hips closer to his. She ran her hand over the edge of his pecs, down the planes of his flat stomach, until she reached his hardened shaft. His lids lowered as she gripped him. Steam billowed around them, and water poured over his cock as she stroked her hand up and down. He sucked in a breath. "I want to be inside of you now."

His words sent a bolt of lightning through Lexi, revitalizing her desire. Her need for him wasn't over yet, and he was ready to give her what she wanted. "Then we need to go back to the bedroom because there aren't any —"

She heard the tear of the foil wrapper and felt the fumbling between them as Noah rolled the condom over his erection. Damn, where had he stashed that? The man wasn't wearing anything but a smile when she entered the shower. Suddenly she was thinking about how smooth he was. He did run a bar for a living, and she was sure he'd been with plenty of women. By his looks alone, she bet Noah had offers every night. Her inexperience and self-doubt needled her, making her feel stupid and frumpy in the wake of her orgasm. She'd been gullible and horny, and she'd opened herself up to get hurt.

"Wait." She held up a hand, but he was already halfway inside her.

To Noah's credit, he stood as still as a marble statue. "What's wrong?" His words were a soft caress, but Lexi made herself pull away.

"This is going too fast." She shook her head, then turned to rush out of the shower. She grabbed the clean towel she'd left on the rack and wrapped it around her torso.

The rings on the shower curtain zinged across the rail as she heard his wet footsteps follow her. "Wait, Lexi. Did I hurt you? Did I do something wrong?"

Tears filled her eyes. She wasn't ready for this. It wasn't something she wanted to talk about, but she had to say something. "This isn't me. I don't do hot sex in the shower. I'm a mom. I have three kids, a farm, a zoo." She motioned to the room where she'd left the rat in her cage. "I'm sure you could have any woman in Magnolia, and I don't know what it is that you see in me, but we better stop things here and now before...." Her voice broke on a sob as she stared at the bathroom door, turning around to look at him. "Trust me, it's better this way."

Noah looked at her with concern in his eyes, but he didn't contradict her. All the more proof that he was there for one thing, and who could blame him? She'd all but laid it out on a silver platter. How desperate she must look. Cringing, she went to her closet and grabbed something to wear, then made her way to the boys' bathroom. She stayed there for a long time, staring at her smeared mascara in the mirror. Maybe he would get the hint and let himself out. She couldn't face him again after the scene she'd made. He must think she was certifiably crazy. First, she begged him to have sex with her, and then she acted like he'd assaulted her in the shower. She really didn't have any idea how to be with a man.

A soft knock came from the other side of the door. "Lexi? Are you okay?" His voice was warm and tender, and she could imagine his strong forearm leaning against the doorframe, his brow knitted with concern.

She swiped at the bottom of both eyes. "I'm—I'm okay. I need to rest. Is it okay if you let yourself out?"

There was a pause and then what sounded like a long sigh. "All right. I don't feel comfortable leaving when you're upset. Are you sure you can't come out? I'm a great listener, and I'm really sorry if I did anything to make you uncomfortable."

Lexi tried to hold back a sob. Finally gaining her composure, she cracked the door and forced a smile. "I'm fine. Really. It's not you. It's me." *The classic cliché.* "I can't talk about this right now. Can you please go?" Awkward didn't begin to describe the moment.

He held his hands up and backed away. "Okay. I'll go, but will you call me later to let me know you are all right?"

Noah picked up his boots from the floor. His shirt dangled casually across one shoulder, the soft cotton collar brushing the crisp hair of his chest. He blew out another long sigh as he walked down the hall.

Lexi closed the door with a soft click. *It's all for the best.*

Chapter 8

Noah drove away from the ranch replaying all the scenes from the morning in his head. He didn't get it. Surely, he'd screwed up somehow. From what little time he'd known Lexi, she was too nice to throw someone out. To be fair, she hadn't thrown him out, but asking him to leave when he had just entered *her* —. He didn't know what to make of it. He wasn't sure if he should be truly worried about her feelings or if maybe he wasn't good enough, and she'd been over the moment. His ego was bruised, but he pushed it aside. He was genuinely worried about her.

She'd been so hot and then cold when things had really heated up. Maybe she was one of those gals who liked to have her orgasm and check out of the game. Noah shook his head. They'd had sex all night long, and whatever it was hadn't been an issue. Maybe it was the light of day. Too much reality? He remembered seeing the wedding photo on the hallway table as he'd exited the bedroom. It was lying down like someone had recently picked it up but had been in a hurry and hadn't set it back the way it belonged. Could Lexi be suffering from grief over the moments they'd shared? She said it had been four years. Could mourning someone be that intense years later? Noah didn't know. His time with Petra was too short and didn't amount to anything more than sexual attraction. Sure, he'd lost buddies in Afghanistan and his grandparents on both sides. He missed them all, but his heart wasn't still aching over them all these years later.

Was that what true love did to you? His gut clenched, and he turned the wheel sharp to pull off the road. The car that had been on his bumper honked. Noah wanted to flip them the bird, but instead he looked behind him at the road. Was she there alone and crying now? He put the truck in reverse, then paused, shaking his head. *She asked you to leave. You left. You didn't do anything wrong. Whatever is going on in her head, you need to give her space. Hell, maybe it's for the best.* He was selling his half of Hank's and opening a new bar. That would take a lot of elbow grease and a lot of money. It wasn't the time to start feeling out a serious relationship and instant fatherhood wasn't Noah's M.O. He'd been single for too long. As things were now, all he had to do was take care of his own problems. Lexi was a decade younger than he was and could start again fresh. He was an old dog, and learning new tricks wasn't easy.

Putting the vehicle back in drive, he peeled out. Back on the road, he headed to Hank's. It was the one place he knew he was welcome. Noah pressed his lips together in a tight smile. His life needed to stay uncomplicated and the old military acronym popped into his mind. "KISS, keep it simple, stupid."

Hank was behind the bar when Noah arrived. "You're late!"

Noah nodded. "Indeed I am, but the bar doesn't open for another two hours, and I did all the stocking yesterday." It irked him that Hank refused to help run the place, but when he was around, it was always to complain.

Hank looked at him with squinted eyes and a furrowed brow as he clasped a toothpick between his teeth. "I heard you had a date."

Noah wasn't going to appease his cousin with the specifics of his night with Lexi. The fact that he was asking meant he already knew who Noah was out with last night. Otherwise, he wouldn't be fishing for details. "That's right."

Hank nodded, hand on hip as he twirled a stack of bar napkins with a rocks glass. The spiraling tower grew as he waited for more information. "Didn't go so well, huh? Well, don't worry. I heard she's a bit of a prude. Doesn't go out much, but I also heard she likes to hang around her work hand from the ranch. I bet he could tell you how to get in those panties."

The guttural laughter made Noah want to jump the bar and punch Hank. Noah knew that his cousin had been snubbed by Lexi the day he drove her home. It was probably what had made Hank fixate on the blonde mother of three. The initial comments he'd made about her had bordered on disrespect—mostly about her assets—but Noah had ignored him. Until now. Hank's tremendous ego was hurt, but Noah wasn't going to listen to his cousin's usual nonsense about women today. He was obviously jealous over the date and looking for trouble. Noah was about to give it to him.

"I'm selling my half of the bar, Hank. It's worth two hundred and fifty thousand. I'll sell it to you for two hundred."

Hank let out a gasp of surprise. Anger lit his eyes as realization set in. "You're serious? Is this why you came to see me in Houston? This place isn't worth the wood holding up the damn ceiling."

Noah shrugged. "Well then, you won't mind that I have another buyer. He's even willing to put money into fixing the place up."

"No way, Noah. You can't do that. Grandaddy left this place to both of us, and if you don't want your half, feel free to walk away, but you're not sellin'!"

Noah smiled. "That's where you're wrong, Hank. I took the deed with the will documents to my lawyer. He said he couldn't find any restrictions in the will about selling the bar or selling my half." Noah walked behind the massive wood bar to where Hank stood, his face was mottled by anger. Noah wasn't backing down. They were going to have it out, here and now.

"Why are you doing this, Noah? Are you out to get me because I slept with Petra?"

Noah's brows knitted in confusion.

Hank looked down at the bar with a sheepish grin. "Ah hell, I guess you didn't know."

Fire blazed through Noah, but he refused to show it. He didn't care who his ex slept with, but why Hank? "You think I give a shit who Petra screws? We've been over with for a long time."

Hank bristled. "Then what is this about? I give you all the freedom to do what you want with the bar. You set your own hours, and I don't butt in. I leave the running of it all to you."

Noah smirked. "Yeah, Hank. You leave all the work to me and eat up all the profits. You won't re-invest, and meanwhile, the value of this place is going down the toilet. If we don't fix a few things, it will soon be worthless. Now Jensen Parker has offered to buy my half, so I'll ask you one more time. Do you want to buy me out for two hundred grand?"

Lexi sat at the diner counter, staring at her pancakes with bacon. She'd imagined being here with Noah for breakfast instead of sitting all alone.

Her appetite was gone, and her day was ruined. It was her own fault for not thanking the man for awesome sex, taking him to the diner for breakfast, and then back to bed for seconds. Who cared if he ever asked her out again, or if they would have a meaningful relationship after? Life was about chances. She was a grown woman and knew she was throwing it all to the wind last night. What had been so different this morning?

A pretty blonde teen with a friendly smile appeared, topping off her coffee, "You want me to wrap it to go?"

Lexi shook her head. "That's okay. I gotta get to the grocery, and it won't taste so good by the time I get home."

The girl gave her a concerned look. "Were the pancakes okay? I could get you some more or something different if you didn't like these."

Lexi shook her head again. "Oh, no! There wasn't anything wrong with them. I'm just not as hungry as I thought I was." She pulled her wallet out to pay her bill.

The blonde with Darcey on her nametag put her hand up. "No ma'am. I'm not letting you pay for something you didn't eat. Now, I am confident enough to tell you that the food here is the best around, and if you're having a bad day, well, let me make it better for you with a few free cupcakes. If that doesn't bring you back to Pop's Diner, nothing will." She held up her hand when Lexi started to protest. "Besides, there is almost nothing in this world that a little frosting won't make better."

Lexi smiled at Darcey. "Thank you so much. My boys will love the treats."

The teenaged waitress beamed. "You have kids? How many?"

Lexi couldn't help but smile with pride. "I have three boys—four, seven, and eight years old."

Darcey filled the box with a variety of cupcakes. She taped the sides and set it in front of Lexi. "Well, it's nice to see you smile. I'll bet those boys are real special. Bring 'em in with you next time. We have a great kid's menu with coloring crayons and everything."

Lexi stood, accepting the box with a, "Thank you again. I appreciate your kindness." She wasn't sure why she felt the need to confide, but something in the diner girl's smile made her want to confess. "I've been a little crazy today. I don't know if cupcakes will fix the problem, but I might have to taste these and find out how potent the power of icing really is."

Lexi looked at herself in the rearview mirror. Her overalls didn't do much for her figure, but she'd blown her hair dry and put on lipstick before she left the house. She hadn't planned on stopping by Hank's on the way to the grocery, but she'd acted like a crazy lady this morning, and maybe Noah would overlook it if she brought him a cupcake. She rolled her eyes at her reflection. *Icing will not fix this. You have to fix it.* It didn't mean she wanted to jump his bones again or start a relationship, but she'd behaved badly, and she wanted to make it up to him.

Noah's shiny black SUV was parked in front of the bar when she passed. There was another fancy car, but she'd never been the brand-name type, so they were all the same to her—shiny paint, shiny wheels, leather interior, and way out of her price range. She opened the door to Hank's, hoping that it was early enough that Noah wouldn't be too busy. When she saw him standing behind the bar with the lecherous cousin who'd driven her home, she wanted to retrace her steps back to her car.

"Lexi," Noah called out.

Damn. Too late. "Hi." She held the box up. "I come bearing gifts." She thought she heard Hank curse, but that was an odd response, considering he didn't really know her, and he was the one who'd made a pass at her. Maybe Noah was telling him the story of how she'd gone bat-shit crazy this morning in the shower and asked him to leave. Heat flamed her cheeks. How humiliating. Would Noah tell everyone? Magnolia was a small town.

Noah hopped the bar and came across the scarred wood floor to meet her. He bent to kiss her cheek. She hadn't expected the intimate greeting, but they had been very intimate only a few hours ago, so maybe she should take a deep breath and not over-think things.

"I'm so glad you stopped by. I was worried about you." His voice was a husky whisper that conveyed his concern.

Hank pushed his Stetson on his head and brushed past them.

"My cousin was on his way out. He has a lot to think about before five o'clock this evening!" Noah said rather loudly as if he wanted to impress the statement on Hank to remember.

Lexi's eyes widened as the door clanked shut. "Did I come at a bad time?"

Noah set the box of cupcakes on the bar, then turned to wrap her in his arms, giving her a breathtaking kiss. His lips moved over hers in slow motion, giving her all the time in the world to pull away, but making her feel wanted in his embrace.

As the kiss stole her breath away, and they both came up for air, she put a hand to his hard chest. God, she would never get tired of touching him. "Wait, full disclaimer. Only one cupcake is for you. Three are for the boys, but if you kiss me again like you just did, I might give you all of mine."

Noah raised a brow and grinned at her. He stepped toward the box, taking her with him in the breadth of his arms. He opened the lid and looked down over the five cupcakes. "*All of yours* does sound tempting."

"The nice lady at the diner said icing makes everything better," she breathed out, still trying to catch her breath, and hoping he didn't let her go. Her knees were weak from their lengthy kiss.

Noah's devilish grin widened as he dipped his finger into one of the cakes with strawberry icing and put it to her mouth. She sucked it off, never looking away from his awe-filled stare. She then stuck her finger in the thick vanilla frosting. It was her favorite. He took it in his mouth and twirled his tongue around the sugary treat. His lips were warm, and the velvet of his kiss sent sparks of desire to her sensitive spots. As he released her finger, he cleared his throat as if trying to find his voice. "Um, I think the diner lady was right. This is definitely making my day better."

It reminded her of the song she liked to sing to her boys when they had to take medicine. She imagined Noah in a white doctor's coat, giving her medicine with sugar. "I'll have to agree with you, Doctor Icing. I'm feeling all better now." Lexi smiled with breathy excitement. The cupcakes had worked, and Noah looked like he had forgiven her early-morning meltdown.

"That somehow sounds naughty, and now I am thinking about you wearing one of those white nurse's uniforms." He growled low in his throat as he nipped her neck below her ear. "Look, I would love to explore this doctor thing a little more, but I'm concerned that Mac Green and the boys will be in soon for their usual first of the month meeting. As much as I would love to cover you in icing and throw you on the bar to lick it off, I'm not sure that Mac and the boys deserve that kind of entertainment." He worked his way back to her lips, giving her one more lingering kiss. "How about I pick you up tonight and take you out to dinner again? We can explore this icing theory further."

Lexi sucked in a breath, feeling like she might faint from the thrill of their banter and his kisses. She finally sighed with regret. "Sorry, I can't tonight. The boys will be home after school, and I have to check all their homework. My parents are pushovers, and the boys really know how to manipulate them."

Noah nodded. "Okay, how about this weekend?"

Lexi smiled. "I'll see if I can find a sitter." She reached in the box and pulled out the strawberry cupcake. Placing it in his hand. "Until then. I think you've earned this."

Noah grinned. The door dinged, and several guys entered the bar in mechanics' jumpsuits. She supposed it was a close call with Mac and the boys. Noah greeted them as he opened the door again for her and waved goodbye.

The diner girl was right. Icing changed her whole day.

Chapter 9

Lexi held the coffee can out to her brother, Ran. "I said, take it! I can't believe you went behind my back, paid for the insurance deductible and didn't tell me!"

Ran looked away from her, not taking the can that she jiggled in front of him. It had twenty dollars in change and four-hundred and eighty dollars in crumpled bills. She'd been saving it for a rainy day, but she hated knowing that Ran had paid a bill behind her back. She had a credit card she could use if there were a true emergency, but this was for something she never had a chance to pay.

She gave him her hardest look and insisted. "I said, take it, and don't ever do that again. Do you know how embarrassing it was when Noah told me you had already paid?"

"Noah? You and Harding are on a first-name basis?" He looked at her with the same look he'd given her when Jack asked her out on a first date. Ran's brotherly teasing was annoying, but she also knew he really cared about her and had only wanted to help.

"Please, let me take care of my own life. That's all I'm asking."

Ran shook his head with a wide grin. "Uh-uh. You are diverting me from my question. Noah? Is there something going on between you and the bartender?"

Lexi tried not to smile. She was supposed to be mad at her brother. He had nosed in on her business, paid the bar insurance deductible for the accident, and now he was nosing into her love life. "Stop it! He owns half of the bar. Of course, I know his name. I owe him money."

"Not anymore." Ran finally took the can from her outstretched hand and held it between his own long fingers. He raised an eyebrow in surprise. "It's heavy."

Lexi couldn't help but grin. Something was always breaking and needed repair, but the plumber finding Gus's Nerf ball in the drain tube made her laugh. *Boys.* "I have a couple rolls of quarters in there from when the washing machine broke."

Ran opened the can and took the cash out, leaving the change. He handed the can back to her. "Consider it my donation for when it happens again. Next time, I hope the clogged washer doesn't involve Ann-Margret."

Lexi grimaced. She hadn't thought of that, but that rat should have been named Houdini. She showed up in the most unlikely places, and even though the boys took her out of the cage regularly, Lexi would never get used to Ann-Margret popping up by surprise, like while she was driving. "God, Ran. Now I'll be double-checking the washer and dryer for every load."

He chuckled. "Not a bad idea." He pocketed the cash and stood to leave. "I gotta get back to my place and finish up some work for a client, and then I'm going out to Hank's. Wanna join me later?"

Lexi cocked her head to the side, studying her brother. A minute ago, he was acting protective. Now, he was trying to hook her up. "I can't. I don't have a sitter."

"Raphe has the night off, and he said he was coming out to see you later. Maybe he could do a little uncle sitting."

She thought about it. Her date with Noah was only a few days away, and tonight was a school night. Raphe wouldn't be much help with homework or baths. "It's probably not a good idea."

Ran looked at her with a warm, knowing smile. "The boys are in grade school, not prepping for college entry exams, and they need time with their Uncle Raphe."

"What about their Uncle Ran?" She teased.

"Uncle Ran needs quality time at the bar with his favorite sister."

Lexi snorted. "I'm your only sister."

"And my favorite. So what do you say we check our responsibilities off the list, and I'll be back to grab you around seven. I'll call Raphe and get it all set up. We won't stay out long. I promise."

She stood with her hand on her hip and blew a stray wisp of hair from her right eye. Since she'd been cleaning house all day, she looked a mess. A hot bath and a book was what she really needed, but she admitted she could use a stiff drink. "All right. But we really can't stay long." Lexi remembered the time she turned twenty-one and Jack had been away on duty. Ran made her stay out until three in the morning, refusing to take her home. It was the days before car apps existed, so she'd been good and stuck. She shook the can at him, making the coins jingle. "And I'll buy my own drinks."

Ran snagged two seats at the bar across from where Noah was leaning down into the cooler, grabbing three longnecks. When he rose, popping the tops off the bottles, he looked startled to see Lexi sitting there. A broad smile stretched across his face, and a warm, skittering sensation danced down her spine. She remembered him licking the icing off her finger. The look he'd given her promised so much more. Images of playing doctor with Noah Harding was almost too much. She squirmed in her seat. *Damn, he was hot!*

The two women next to them tried striking up a conversation, but the place was packed, and Noah had to deliver the beers to the men at the other end of the bar. Skipping over the women who'd been there long before Ran and Lexi arrived, Noah landed in front of them, shaking Ran's hand and asking what they would like. That was right, he'd met Ran when he'd paid the insurance deductible. Thank goodness the constable had been kind when taking down the report. It was another perk for living in a small town where most everyone knew everyone. If she'd lived in Houston, her goose would've been cooked. So far, no one had contacted her from the insurance company. Fingers crossed, she hoped she wouldn't be sued by the bar's insurance due to her lapse of coverage at the time.

After Ran ordered a whiskey, Noah held up a hand and said, "Wait. I got something you're going to love." He went to the back and returned with a whole bottle of champagne in a green glass bottle with painted flowers up the front.

Lexi didn't know much about wine or champagne, but she knew Perrier Jouet, and it wasn't cheap. Anxiety gripped her, making her shake her head too quickly. "No. I can't drink that tonight." She needed to get home at a decent time for the boys, but more important, she couldn't afford champagne on her draft beer budget. "I'll have a pint of the apple cider beer on tap, thanks."

Noah shook his head. "No, ma'am. I happen to know you like champagne, and your brother has his keys in his hand, so I assume he's driving tonight. I have been saving this just for you, though I didn't know if you'd ever come back after…." He got cut off by a younger man who dipped in front of him to retrieve some pint glasses. "Watch out, Brent." The guy beamed a smile at Lexi before looking back at Noah, nodding. Brent zigzagged to the tap to fill the pints.

Lexi looked back at the new window that had been replaced. The sound of the cork popping made her jump slightly and turn back to the bar. Noah poured three glasses, and after they were all half-filled, he held his up for a quick toast. "To the prettiest lady in Magnolia."

She felt the heat creep into her cheeks as her brother stared at them with twinkling eyes. At least she could count on Ran to keep it to himself. He was good that way. They'd had many secrets between them over the years. So far, no one else in the family had heard about her crashing into the bar. Her mother hadn't seen the front of the van the few times she'd picked up the boys. Lexi had parked under the carport for those visits. She wasn't sure why she was still hiding it, except it would draw attention to the fact that she didn't have enough money to fix it yet. After selling some of her barnwood decor on her new eBay account, she was finally able to pay Mac for the tow and for making the van drivable. Cosmetic repairs weren't on the list of must-haves these days.

Ran excused himself to say hello to some guys he knew, and Noah made a few more drinks for other patrons. Lexi looked around the bar at the man-to-woman ratio. There were fewer women, but most of the ladies had eyes for Noah. Tan, muscular and chiseled features like a god, not to mention those sterling-colored eyes. A jolt of jealousy coursed through her as a busty brunette leaned over the bar and put her hand on Noah's chest. A trill of laughter rang out and was followed by a, "You are so funny, Handsome. Stop teasing me."

Lexi looked down at her simple black t-shirt. The presentation of her push-up bra, holding the girls at full mast, was nothing compared to the exposed cleavage of the drop-dead gorgeous woman pawing Noah. The deep V in the woman's silk blouse was probably giving him a solid view to infinity and beyond. Who wore a silk blouse with a ruffle, white linen pants, and four-inch pink stilettos into a place called Hank's Honky-Tonk?

Ran slid back into the vacant space next to her. "Woodlanders."

Lexi's head spun around to look at her brother in confusion. "Say what?"

"Those women are from The Woodlands. They come out to Hank's on nights when their husbands are wining and dining clients in the city. They figure Magnolia is far enough away from their rich society circles that no one will find out about their hookups."

Lexi felt one side of her mouth twitch. She tried not to smile. "And how do you know all this?"

Ran shook his head in denial. Her rock-star-by-night, programmer-by-day brother, with his stylish brown hair and soft brown eyes gave her a sheepish grin. "Oh no, not me, but other family members might have gotten caught with their pants down when a husband came home early."

Lexi covered her open mouth with her hand. "Was that the time that Raphe showed up at my place asking for pants? He said he'd been out in the pasture and landed in a cow patty."

Ran threw his head back and laughed. "I don't know about that particular night, but let's say whoever it was, they don't troll for women around Hank's on a weekday anymore."

Lexi joined him, laughing hard, imagining Raphe jumping out of a second-story window without his pants, but she wouldn't be able to tease him about it later since the intel came from Ran. They had a secrecy pact that she would never break. Lexi was close to all her brothers, but Ran was nearest her age. They'd had more time at home growing up together than she'd had with Riley and Raphe.

On their second round, Lexi noticed the bar was in full swing. A few of the local firemen that Ran knew through Raphe invited him to a game of pool, and Lexi took a pass when Ran asked her to join them. She didn't care for the sport, but more important, she didn't want to miss the opportunity to see Doctor Icing. He didn't disappoint her.

Noah cleared empty bottles and glasses, filled a few more orders, and slid back to where she was perched on a stool at the bar. "I found a buyer."

Lexi's eyes widened. "You mean, you didn't have one when you purchased the land?" She didn't know his finances, but the declaration shocked her. The thought of building a bar when you hadn't sold the other place to bankroll the investment was like buying a house while you still owned one that you needed to sell. For Lexi, paying two mortgages was unthinkable.

"The initial offer fell through, but this guy has cash, and we close on it Friday." He clinked his champagne glass with hers. "Something for us to celebrate this weekend."

His grin was infectious, and she smiled back at him as he topped off their flutes. "I'm so happy for you, Noah. I truly am. But what will your cousin, Hank, do now?"

"He's decided to sell."

"Will he go in halves on Bubbles?" Lexi's brow furrowed in concern. It wasn't any of her business, but Hank didn't seem like a very good business partner, and she hated to think of him dragging Noah down.

Noah shook his head, sliding his glass around in small circles on the bar as he studied the champagne. "No. According to him, I've ruined his livelihood, and he plans to file a lawsuit against me for forcing him to sell."

"Did you?"

He chuckled. "If I had known that selling my half would have made him sell his, I would have done this years ago." They both grinned, and he shook his head, then clinked his glass with hers. Noah nodded to another patron with his bottle in the air before tossing the champagne down like a shot. "I'm sorry I keep leaving you, but I promise I'll be right back."

Lexi smiled as he darted away. The guy on the stool next to her vacated, and another customer slipped in. Lexi didn't know why, but she turned and said Noah would be right back.

The pretty, blonde woman with perfect makeup and an overwhelming floral scent, looked at her with a smile that was too big to be genuine. "Oh, I'm certain he'll be right back. He's my husband."

Lexi tried not to look as shocked as she felt. Heat rose to her face, but it wasn't from anger. It was as if someone had slapped her hard, and the humiliation of it had her climbing off her stool. She resisted the urge to make a mad dash to the ladies' room, but her tight, jean-clad legs desperately wanted to. Noah was forty, and the lady looked younger than her. Lexi held onto the bar, willing herself to stand strong. She squared her shoulders before asking the woman. "How long have you and Noah been married?"

The woman's lips parted as her eyes roved over Lexi, then she tossed her hair, looking the other way. It was as if she was silently dismissing Lexi as competition, and that riled her. Finally, the catty blonde offered, "We got married eighteen years ago. I was barely seventeen, but things were different back then. Germany was different."

The woman was older than Lexi, but she looked like a model. There wasn't a wrinkle on her face. Lexi heard the woman's accent even before she mentioned Germany. Magnolia was mostly made up of white, black, or Hispanic. There weren't many Europeans straight off the boat. Lexi guessed she must have married him soon after he entered the military. Seventeen and twenty-two weren't so far apart. Tears sprang to her eyes as the woman gave her a look of pity, then laughed. "Why do you look so sad? Has Noah been leading you on? He is a naughty boy. Sometimes my husband roams.

He's a man. They all do, but you can be certain of one thing. He always comes back to me." With that, she gave her back to Lexi and waved at Noah.

Lexi needed a quick getaway, and Ran might as well have been across the Atlantic. His head was bent over his pool cue as he took aim at the corner pocket. Lexi pushed through the growing crowd to the front exit. The door swung open, and Hank grabbed hold of her before she could dash out. She glanced back at the bar, where Noah stood, head low, talking to his wife. As he looked up and spotted her, she clutched Hank's hand in an imploring grip. "Can you give me a ride?"

Chapter 10

Noah saw Petra talking to Lexi and knew it spelled trouble. Like a bad penny, Petra always found her way back into his pocket. The reunion usually ended with his bank account empty and his car stolen.

After two years of marriage, Petra had left him for a colonel. She was drop dead gorgeous back then, but she was still beautiful now. Diagnosed with breast cancer shortly after she'd left Noah, she had no one to care for her. The colonel didn't want to marry a woman losing her hair, amongst other things, and Noah felt sorry for her despite her indiscretions. He'd taken leave while she went through a double mastectomy, and they both agreed not to sign the divorce papers that were drawn up. The medical benefits for military spouses were the best, and she needed the chemo for her condition.

The surgery and treatment were successful, and Petra had been in remission ever since. He'd given her the money to have breast reconstruction, and she'd thanked him by taking off with another guy who was enlisted. Noah had never signed the divorce papers, and neither had she, but it was a technicality. He hadn't seen her in two years, and the last time she'd come around, she'd rumpled his sheets a few days and gave him a sad story. In her usual dramatic fashion with tears running down her cheeks, she'd told him that her cancer had returned and that she needed money. Sucker that he was, Noah had fallen for it. The sex had been good, but he didn't have feelings for her anymore. They had gotten drunk at the bar, and she'd claimed she didn't have anywhere to go. He'd felt sorry for her, after all these years, having to battle cancer again. They'd taken a walk down memory lane, and one thing led to another.

Noah had heard from a friend a few weeks later that she was living it up in some guy's high-rise in Houston, and that her cancer scare had been bogus. He was relieved, but it was then he vowed to quit falling for her bullshit and promised himself he'd never be played by her or any other woman again. Now here Petra sat at the bar, smiling at him as if he were still a clueless loser, while the woman he really wanted had flown out the door with Hank. The same Hank who'd apparently slept with Petra after she'd cleaned out Noah's wallet.

Blonde hair, blue eyes, and beautiful, Petra's exterior wasn't so different from Lexi's, but that was where the similarities ended. He used to love Petra's accent, but now, as she purred his name, it grated on his nerves. He preferred Lexi's Texas drawl and warm southern charm. She was feminine warmth with fiery determination. He didn't want to even compare them. Whatever Petra had said to Lexi set her off, and more than anything right now, he wanted to run after Lexi and soothe her spirit. Petra's intimidation tactics had worked on a few women after the initial breakup, but he hadn't really cared. This time, his inner sanity was chomping at the bit to follow Lexi, but he didn't have anyone to watch the bar. Hank's was a full house tonight.

As he held up a finger to a waiting customer, Noah pulled out his cell phone and turned his back to Petra. He didn't have time to sort out what she was doing at the bar, but with Hank's timely arrival to take Lexi home, he wouldn't be surprised if his cousin had brought his Ex there to mess with his head. Lexi's phone went immediately to voicemail. Noah scanned the room, looking for Ran.

As if he'd been summoned, Ran stood right in front of him. "Hey, man, did you see where Lexi went to?"

Noah felt his brow wrinkle as he pressed his lips together. He didn't want to explain to Lexi's brother that she'd run out of the bar upset—over him. "I saw her with my cousin. They stepped out. Maybe he took her home."

Ran gave him an angry look. So much for making a good impression.

"You mean the tool who made a pass at her?"

Noah felt his own gut clench. He didn't like the idea of Lexi being in Hank's clutches either, but there wasn't a damn thing he could do about it right now. He nodded slowly, hoping that his own concern showed in his expression. "I'd go after her, but there isn't anyone here to close the bar but me...." He scratched his chin as an idea hit him. "Unless you want to stand back here for an hour while I go after Lexi?"

Ran cocked his head, studying Noah. He seemed to be determining if Noah was worthy of his sister or the effort to save the evening. "Sure," was all he said as he grabbed the bar towel from Noah and pointed a thumb toward the door.

Noah didn't need to be told two times. He jumped the bar, scattering a few empty bottles as he slid across and hopped to the floor. Fishing his keys out of his pocket, he didn't look back. After all, Hank's was soon to be someone else's problem to worry about, and Ran looked smart enough to hold the fort down while Noah went after his girl.

The realization slammed him in the chest. *His girl.* The thought of losing Lexi was like losing his ability to breathe. He'd never felt this way about anyone in his life, and he found himself wanting to break Hank's face if he laid a hand on her. When Hank had told him he'd slept with Petra, it was like a fly buzzing around his head, a minor irritation to his ego. The idea that Lexi had left mad and hurt, and that she might be vulnerable to Hank's advances made Noah push down on the gas as he hit the highway that led out to the farm. He needed to get there before anything happened.

Lexi left a text message for her brother so he wouldn't worry about her, but when Noah called, she turned off the phone. *Married!* He was married all this time, and he didn't think to tell her! Maybe he was separated, but still, she deserved to know. The look in the woman's eyes as she said his name was enough to tell anyone that she was still interested in Noah.

Hank had been more than willing to drive Lexi home, and for that, she was grateful. He hadn't touched her, and so far, had acted like the perfect gentleman. Maybe she'd overreacted last time.

He darted a glance at her. His eyes looked sympathetic. "You wanna talk about it?"

Lexi sucked in a deep breath and let out a sigh. She gave him a polite smile to show her appreciation. "Sorry for asking you to drive me home like this, but I needed to get back. I have three boys, and it's past their bedtime." *There, that should calm any further interest.*

Hank smiled. "Three? Aw, that's nice. I have a boy, but I don't get to see him as much as I'd like. He stays with his mama in Florida. What are their names?"

Lexi was surprised. She hadn't thought of Hank as the father type with his thick, black Elvis hair and his perfectly chiseled face. He was very handsome, but a little too polished for her taste, though it was nice of him to ask about her sons. "Gus, Bert, and Damien."

Hank gave her a broad smile. "Good names. If they're like my Allen, I bet they're a handful." He chuckled.

She couldn't help but grin. "They sure are, but I can't imagine my life without them."

"I hope you don't mind me poking my nose into your business tonight, but I heard you and Noah are kind of a *thing*, and when I opened the door to the bar and saw his wife sitting there...." He shook his head. "Well, I hope Petra didn't upset you too much. I mean, those two have been on and off for years. She's like a dog with a bone and, hell, you know Noah."

Lexi looked at him, waiting for what it was she was supposed to know—besides the fact that he was married. But Hank didn't go any further with the conversation.

The tires crunched on the gravel drive, and the car lights bobbed up and down across her living room windows. She hoped the boys were in bed and that Raphe wouldn't look out to see her in Hank's car.

She reached for the door handle, but Hank put a hand on her arm. "Please. Allow me to be a gentleman." He got out of the car and came around to open her door. She accepted his offered hand. It was a nice gesture, and Lexi decided she needed to relax and quit judging. When he had mentioned his son and asked about her boys, his expression was sincere. She wasn't interested in Hank, but there was nothing wrong with being friendly. She didn't have many friends, and after her date with Noah, Lexi realized she was missing adult companionship. It was good to get out once and awhile. Maybe the *thing* with Noah hadn't worked out, but she vowed not to let other opportunities pass her by. Maybe she'd join the Magnolia Blossoms and go to a few of their infamous charity events. Her mom and dad were always talking about the friends they met there. She couldn't afford the golf club, but charity organizations always needed volunteers.

Lexi let go of Hank's hand, but he took it back tenderly. "I know this might seem forward, and maybe it's not the right time, but could we go out to dinner one night or to the diner for coffee?" Immediately, her guard flew up but she tamped it back down. Hadn't she just told herself that she needed to get out and meet people? Hank was acting nice, and he hadn't touched her in any inappropriate way. He was handsome, and he was single.

She smiled, nodding slightly. Still not sure it was the right thing to say, she faltered. "All right, maybe."

After all, he'd given her a ride home without complaint. She turned to the house, but Hank pulled her back. She gave him a wary look, but he slowly tugged her toward him, wrapping his arms around her. He held her against the warmth of his chest, rubbing his hand over the middle of her back. She found that she actually needed a hug. Even though she didn't know Hank, he'd been kind to her when she was upset and felt like a fool. The smell of his cologne was nice, and the feel of his body was firm. As if in slow motion, he dipped his head and kissed her.

Her hurt ego and something that felt like rebellious revenge let him move his lips slowly over hers. Noah had lied to her. She'd opened herself up, and he had taken what she had so blindly offered. She'd slept with a married man! The slight brush of Hank's after-five shadow swept across her cheek. The kiss would have buckled her knees if she'd felt any real attraction for him. The man sure knew how to kiss. It must be an inherited trait, but he was the wrong Harding, and she didn't feel that way about him, no matter how chiseled his pecs were or how strong his arms felt. Coming to her senses, she tried to push away.

The lights of an oncoming vehicle flashed over the house, and Hank released her. He stepped back, making a breathy apology as he wiped her smudged lipstick from his face. "Sorry. I shouldn't have done that, but you're so damn beautiful, and I wanted to see if I could convince you to go out with me."

Lexi's brain was still whirling from the surprise kiss. She hadn't expected it, but she hadn't pulled away. As the porch light flashed on, Lexi whirled around to see Raphe staring back at her and Hank. The SUV came to a halt, but the bright lights stayed on, practically blinding them. She held her hand up to shield her eyes, expecting the driver to get out, but the engine roared as the vehicle reversed down the drive. She recognized Noah's SUV and wondered why he'd come all the way out to the ranch. It was obvious he wasn't pleased with how he found her, but who was he to be angry? He was married.

Raphe now stood at the bottom of the stairs, his shoulders square and ready to go to bat for his kid sister. Lexi knew the look well. All of her brothers had practiced the intimidation pose when she started dating Jack back in high school. "Everything all right, Lex?"

"That's my brother, Raphe. He's watching my boys," she explained to Hank. Lexi was sure that her cheeks were painted crimson.

Hank backed away, giving a small wave to Raphe. "It's all good. I was saying goodnight."

Raphe returned Hank's wave with a stiff nod. He waited for Lexi before going back inside.

She put her purse down on the entryway table and kicked off her boots.

Raphe gave her that concerned look that she was getting so tired of seeing on everyone's face when they looked at Poor-Widowed-Lexi. She held a hand up. "Thank you for watching the boys. I truly appreciate it. I don't want to seem ungrateful, but I'm tired, and I don't want to talk about it tonight. So please, you can go home now. I'll be fine." Without waiting for more questions, she shuffled off to her bathroom to brush her teeth. What was she thinking, letting Hank Harding kiss her?

Chapter II

The neon sign's K flickered then went out as Noah passed Hank's Honkey-Tonk, making it look like Hank's Honey-Tonk. He pushed the accelerator and kept driving. When he stopped to get gas for his vehicle, he was halfway to Dallas. He texted Hank that the bar was unmanned, and that he wasn't going back. Hank would have to figure it out on his own. After all, he was the one who screwed it all up. It wasn't a coincidence that Petra showed up fifteen minutes before Hank. This was revenge for Noah selling the bar. He wouldn't have bothered to text his plans, except it wasn't fair to leave poor Ran there all night. He wondered if Hank had also planned to leave the bar with Lexi, knowing that Noah would of course follow them to her place. The way Hank looked up into the headlight's was too casual, and the corners of his mouth had drawn up in a slow grin. Hank wasn't surprised at Noah's arrival. He was sure of it, but Lexi was like a deer in the headlights with her hair tousled and lipstick smeared. She'd been kissing Hank back, or at least she wasn't struggling to get away. For Noah, who'd been burned before, the whole fiasco was too much.

He didn't know where he was going, but maybe he needed to leave town for a while. Noah had tried to make Magnolia work, and he thought he was onto something he could believe in. Lexi had fueled thoughts of a new business, a new relationship, and maybe a new family with a new life. Whatever feelings he'd been buzzing with, the desire to open Bubbles was gone. He'd leased the land already, but he'd been hit up to sell his idea for the bar and the location to build it. He hadn't even considered it before now, but here he was, flipping through his phone, searching for the message left by the real estate guy. Lexi hadn't waited for him to explain. No matter what crap story Petra had peddled, he deserved a chance to tell his side. Again, he'd lost another woman to someone more connected and affluent, and it didn't take more than a half-hour to flip her switch. He should have known, after the morning they'd had in the shower and how she'd come racing into the bar, later that day, tempting him with icing and other possibilities. His instincts were mistaken. Lexi was like his ex. She was a flake.

Noah shook his head in disgust. How could he have been so wrong—again?

He needed to cool off. He needed to get away, and the one woman he could trust not to screw him over was his sister, Cassie, who lived in Dallas. Noah could take his nieces to the zoo and see the monkeys and feed the giraffes. It had been too long since he'd visited them, and he needed to talk to someone he trusted. Cassie would listen.

Noah saw the deer illuminated by his headlights, but he was going way too fast to slow down in time. His mind had wandered for too long, and like an idiot, he'd looked away at his phone, not focusing on the road ahead. He heard the squeal of the tires on the road, but it was too late. He turned the wheel to the right, hoping to avoid the head-on collision, but a rut in the road sent the vehicle tumbling like tossed dice. He held the wheel in a death grip, thanking God he'd worn his seatbelt, but he wasn't sure it could save him. When the SUV finally settled on its side, he groaned in pain mixed with relief. He was still alive. A flicker of images raced through his mind as he tried to stay conscious—Lexi busting through the wall of Hank's in her blue minivan, talking to him through the window of the beat-up jalopy as he assessed the leased land, smiling over her champagne glass as she talked about her kids, and giggling in his arms as he held her after they'd made love. There wasn't anything about his life he could cling to except the joy he'd found in those moments spent with her. It was crazy that nothing else in the world meant more to him than those recent memories.

The smell of gasoline assailed him, and his heart began to race. Noah had to get out of there. The vehicle had landed on the driver's side door, and he needed to stand up and climb out, but he wasn't sure he was capable. Sheer pain throbbed in his right leg, and he feared it might be broken. The left side of his hip and down to his ankle was numb. He struggled, but he wasn't making much progress. Noah called out for help, but the interstate was empty. It must be after midnight by now. The acrid smell of smoke filled the cabin, and he began to cough. Yellow dots swirled under his eyelids as he tried to focus. Just when he thought he was doomed, a man with a thick beard looked down at him from the passenger side window. The night sky was a cloak of blackness behind him.

"I'm stuck," Noah rasped to the man above. The smoke was thick, and he struggled to stand, but the pain was too much. Through the billowing smog, he felt the man grip his arm hard and pull. Their combined effort helped him to get to his feet, and Noah used his upper body strength to heave himself through the broken glass. Falling from the vehicle onto the grassy side of the highway, he low-crawled a safe distance away. As the SUV burst into flames, he looked around for his rescuer but found no one in sight. Noah wondered if the guy was military. The fatigues looked Army, and he wasn't far from Fort Hood, but the beard and hair were overgrown. Where did he disappear to? Maybe the soldier went for help, or maybe he was late returning to base. Had the guy been drinking? Was he worried about the police showing up? Noah shook his head. The whole experience was odd. The guy looked vaguely familiar, but it was probably the uniform. It was strange that the man never said a word, but that was okay. The soldier had saved Noah's life, and he wouldn't look a gift horse in the mouth. He was alive.

Chapter 12

Lexi watched as the construction crew built the bar across from Hank's. It seemed to go up overnight, but winter turned to spring, and today was the first day of summer, so she guessed it was probably built in the normal amount of time. Hank's had been sold and remodeled in record time and was now a wine bar to rival Bubbles. The new homes around the country club and golf course were going up fast. She was sure that both establishments would have plenty of clientele. It seemed that Magnolia was growing and changing at a speed she couldn't keep up with. Lexi hadn't joined the Blossoms Ladies League, deciding she didn't have time to volunteer. The reclaimed windows she used to create beautiful, pressed wildflower wall-hangings was a big hit on her eBay site. Things had really taken off the past few months, and Lexi was relieved of finding another side gig to pay the bills. She did join her mother's book club, and they were meeting at the grand opening of Bubbles tonight to discuss a mystery thriller they had read.

Lexi was on the fence about going for two reasons. One, she hadn't had time to finish the novel. The serial killer had given her nightmares, and she was anxious every time he stalked a new victim. And, two, she didn't think she could see Noah after all the months had passed since Hank kissed her in her driveway. Noah hadn't tried to call her to explain about his wife, and she hadn't tried to call and tell him why she'd let Hank kiss her, but she knew now.

Hank was a good-looking man, and he'd been nice when she'd felt like Noah had made a fool of her. She wasn't interested in Hank, and she'd told him as much when he sent her flowers with his phone number attached. Her short jaunt into the dating scene had taught her that she wasn't ready for something serious yet, and that was okay. In the process of falling for Noah, she realized there was more to life than being a mother and a rancher.

She needed to get out, make a few friends, go places, and do things. Lexi had her loving boys, her amazing family, the ranch, eBay projects and book club to keep her busy—even if the stories they chose were not usually as enjoyable as the gals who discussed them over martinis. If one day she was ready to try a relationship again, that would be nice, but she wouldn't quit living because Noah wasn't the happy ending she'd hoped for.

Nodding to herself, she made the decision. Just because she went to the opening didn't mean she was there to see Noah. Surely, he would be so busy he wouldn't even notice her presence. A thought occurred to her that his wife might be there. As she pondered it, Lexi decided she probably would be, unless they were on the outs again. She'd keep it in mind in case he tried to make up.

She went to the closet where she'd put the new dress she'd bought months ago for Christmas. It was a pretty spring green and would go nicely with her hair and slight tan. She'd worked in the garden a lot the past weeks, and her arms and calves were golden brown. The deep v neck and capped sleeves were flattering, as was the tight fit of the waist. She rarely got the opportunity to dress up, and Bubbles was supposed to be chic. Lexi was not dressing up for Noah, she told herself, but it wouldn't hurt to look her best to show him what he'd missed.

She dropped the kids off at her parents' house, where her brother, Riley, stood in the driveway. His soft brown hair and winsome smile made her wonder how he had avoided being snatched up by some snazzy Houston gal. He was handsome, successful, and had traveled all over the world to sharpen his culinary skills. His restaurant, Braised, was quickly becoming *the* place to eat in Houston, and anyone who was a foody would know her famous chef brother. The way he played with and teased her boys, tossing Damien into the air, had future father written all over him, but he was in his forties now. If he didn't quit fooling around, he might miss out having a wife and kids, and that would be a shame. Riley would be great at it.

They were late, so she didn't get out to greet him. Her mother hugged the boys and got into the car with Lexi. Pulling the visor down, she checked her makeup and smoothed her hair. "It's grandpa night, so you know that no one is going to do homework or go to sleep at a decent time."

Lexi nodded with a sigh. "I know. The things I sacrifice to have a night out."

Riley approached her window. "You all right?" His voice was warm with concern as he gave a supportive smile.

Lexi wondered if he'd somehow heard about her and Noah. Had Ran told?

Their mother, Regina, waved at him to back up. "Riley honey, we gotta go. Help your father heat up the pizza. The last time that man used the oven was before you were born. Now scooch back. We're late." She smiled, waving again as they drove away. "My, don't you look pretty."

Lexi felt her mother's gaze. "Is it too much? I heard it was supposed to be fancy, and I didn't want to embarrass myself."

Her mother gave her a concerned frown. "Dear heavens, you look great. I was telling you how pretty you are tonight."

Lexi shrugged and gave her a wan smile. "Sorry. I didn't finish the book."

Her mother laughed. "I didn't make it past chapter five of that God awful story, but I want to see what all the hubbub is about at this new place, so I Googled the book and read a few reviews. It's not rocket science. They always catch the thief in the end."

Lexi looked at her mother with concern. "Mom, it's about a serial killer."

Regina waved a hand. "Thief, serial killer, whatever."

They were a few minutes late meeting the group, and the table was already reeling with talk about the thriller. Lexi's gaze darted around the full lounge, taking in the plush booths, tall cocktail tables, and huge oval bar in the middle of the room. Crystal chandeliers, silver champagne buckets and fine glass stemware—Noah had gone all out. Trays of small appetizer plates floated by, and the servers wore smart tuxedo-like shirts with bowties. Lexi fingered one of the leather-bound menus filled with appetizers. Shrimp bisque soup, lobster sliders, truffle French fries, stuffed bacon-wrapped quail. Her mouth was watering. The food list was a mere page, but the wine and champagne list required a small computer tablet like the ones she'd seen at the airport. *Fancy.*

They all ordered and talked about their lives, the book, and how amazing it was to have a chic place like Bubbles in Magnolia. Lexi nodded in agreement, noting nothing was said about the owner. Where was Noah tonight? She couldn't imagine he didn't want to be front and center at his own grand opening. Lexi was relieved she didn't have to fake reading the book. She'd absorbed enough to get by. Her mother sagely stuck to talking about community events and her summer vacation plans.

Lexi tried not to give her away when Barbra Hawthorne looked at her mother and asked, "What did you think about where he stashed the victims?"

It was a fact that hadn't been revealed until late in the story, but her mother was a pro. "Well, that knitting needle of all things…." It was all she had to say before the ladies started to crow about the eye-gouging tool that was used on page five. It had been quite gruesome and was the proper amount of diversion to get her mother past the question.

Lexi took that moment to lean close to her mother. "The deep freezer at the ice cream parlor. There was a trap door."

Regina nodded and gave her a sly smile. "Who in the world are you looking for?"

Lexi choked on her champagne. "Hm? What? No one."

Her mother lifted a fine brow. "You keep looking around like someone is going to bring us a surprise dessert."

Lexi thought about the vanilla icing that Noah had licked off her finger that time at the bar. "Um, no. No one. Just admiring the place. It's nice, isn't it?" She wiped a napkin over the dribble of champagne on her dress, watching the spring-green satin turn to emerald.

"Well, look at all you lovely ladies here tonight. It makes a man want to dust off his tuxedo and bring a red rose to the occasion."

When Lexi looked up, Hank Harding stood in front of her, looking as handsome as The Bachelor himself. It was not who she'd expected or even wanted to see, but the women around the table were ogling him with delight. She'd forgotten what a ladies' man he could be when he turned on the charm. Even her mother smiled at Hank's flirtatious statement, and she gave Lexi an oh-my look with a raised eyebrow that silently chanted, *lucky girl.*

"Hello, Hank," was all Lexi could manage.

He gave her a broad smile. His eyes glimmered with attraction, though she'd made it clear she wasn't interested. A woman came from behind him and put her arm possessively on his shoulder, gaining his attention.

"Hank, the waitress with the red hair—I can never remember her name…."

Lexi recognized the European accent before she saw the woman's beautiful face.

Noah's wife looked at Lexi as she tried to recall the waitress's name. "Oh, it is *you*," she said with her hand on her hip, chin jutting forward. Obviously, she couldn't remember Lexi's name either, and Lexi didn't know how to respond to the ice-blonde's cool remark. Lexi's mother gave her another curious look before darting one of her own icy glares at the European lady.

Hank cut in. "Petra, why don't you go back and see if you can help the bar staff, and I'll find Mitzi in a minute."

"Why would anyone want to be called Mitzi?" Petra waved a hand in the air and turned on her heel, tossing over her shoulder, "Whatever, Hank. It's your bar."

Lexi hadn't understood why Hank was at Noah's grand opening after Noah sold the old bar, and Hank supposedly sued Noah. Petra's parting statement left Lexi with her mouth hanging open. She couldn't help it. "You own Bubbles?"

Hank raised up on his heels and puffed his chest out. One of the ladies at the table practically swooned. He did look good in his slacks and dress shirt, but his ego was still a little too large for Lexi's taste.

"Yes, and I am so glad you made it tonight, Alexa."

She wanted to ask how it was possible that Hank owned the bar when it was Noah who had set the whole thing in motion. She remembered Noah saying Hank planned to sue him for selling his share of the bar, but there was no way the suit could have gone to court and settled already. But something must have happened, because, according to Petra and Hank, Bubbles belonged to Hank Harding and Noah was nowhere around to dispute it.

Lexi sat straighter in her chair. She didn't really want to congratulate Hank, not knowing the circumstances. She wished Noah would pop out of the woodwork and tell her it was all a hoax. Maybe things hadn't worked out between them, but she didn't want it to be true. Bubbles had been *his* dream. How could he have lost it?

"You look really pretty tonight, Alexa. Why don't you come up to the bar with me, and I'll give you a tour of the place."

Every woman at the table was staring at Lexi, waiting for her to say yes. She nodded with a slight smile. "Sure." Maybe if she went with Hank, she could find out what happened to Noah's dream. Though Hank had originally told her he owned Hank's Honky-Tonk, so how would she know if he was telling the truth?

Her mother gave her a look that asked, do you know what you're doing? She must have the same instincts Lexi originally had when she met Hank. He might be handsome, but he also had a slickness about his character that kept her on guard. She wouldn't have put it past him to have stolen the rights to Bubbles right out from under Noah's nose.

She kept her posture straight and her tummy tucked in as she approached the bar. Petra was talking to one of the bartenders but never took her eyes off Lexi and Hank. Lexi wanted to ask if they were an item. Otherwise, why would Petra care if Hank was showing her around? She was Noah's wife, anyway…or was she? Had they gotten a divorce? The sparkly rock of a diamond on Petra's left ring finger said she was still spoken for.

Hank tilted his head to the massive oval bar and said, "This is the main bar." He then gave Petra a wink and a grin before grabbing Lexi's hand and pulling her toward the kitchen area. Because it made Petra scowl, Lexi let him hold her hand. Something about the cold, prickly blonde made her feel defensive. Other than Petra's lack of politeness, Lexi knew she didn't have a real reason to dislike the woman. *She* was the interloper. Petra was married to Noah, and Lexi had slept with him. Noah's wife had a right to show disdain. Lexi pulled her hand from Hank's as he swung open a door bearing an "Employees Only" sign.

"I don't really need a tour of the back."

Hank ignored her, holding the door and waving her through. He pointed out a few details of the prep area, coolers, and dishwashing area before leading her into a luxurious office. It seemed out of character for a restaurant and lounge. She'd worked as a waitress before and had seen many offices for management, but this was like none of those. There were plush leather upholstered chairs, a couch along one wall, a large antique walnut desk, built-in cabinets with thick crown molding, and several crystal decanters sitting on a silver tray with four delicate cognac snifters.

"Have a seat. I want to talk to you." His tone was different now that they were behind closed doors. He didn't sound cheesy-charming anymore. Maybe the whole thing was all for show. His no-nonsense tone now said he had something to tell her.

He moved to the decanters and poured two fingers worth of amber liquid into two glasses and handed her one. She accepted, knowing her mother was drinking iced tea and could drive if Lexi needed her to. The subtle bouquet was tinged with toasted oak, honey, and a hint of citrus. She closed her eyes as she inhaled.

Hank placed a small plate of chocolate in front of her. A strawberry garnished the edge. "Try one. The orange peel in the chocolate brings out the flavor of the Kentucky bourbon."

Lexi sat in one of the massive leather chairs, staying far from the sofa. She was too interested to hear what he had to say to decline his hospitality. Taking a small bite of chocolate, she then sipped the bourbon.

"You sent my cousin running for the hills the night we kissed." He paused as his eyes searched hers. "I know Petra and Noah hadn't signed the divorce papers, but that was a technicality so the military insurance would cover

Petra's cancer treatment. Now, I don't like to stick my nose in my cousin's business, but I feel like I owe him for forcing me to change. I should have gotten my head out of my ass long before he wanted to sell his half of the bar, but I wouldn't listen to him."

Lexi was more than confused. She looked over her shoulder, thinking maybe she was on one of those reality shows where they play pranks and secretly film your reaction. She turned to Hank, ready to ask where he was going with this revelation, but he held a hand up, stopping her.

"I have my faults. We all do, and mine was greed. I didn't give Noah his due. After that night in your driveway, Noah hightailed it to Dallas, and I haven't seen or heard from him since, except his lawyer, who asked me if I wanted to lease the land from the previous owner and said that to sweeten the deal, Noah would throw in the plans for Bubbles as an incentive."

Hank stood up and walked to the decanter, refilling his glass. She'd barely touched hers, but he held the carafe up in a silent offer. She shook her head, taking a sip to show that she was still enjoying hers. "So I feel like I owe Noah for giving me a swift kick in the ass and waking me up to something that I should have listened to in the beginning, but he won't answer my calls. Hell, he won't even answer my attorney's phone calls. And you're probably asking yourself why I'm telling you all about it." He flashed a knowing grin and walked around the desk. Leaning against the hardwood edge, he looked down at her.

She nodded as she looked up at him, waiting for the encore. Her pulse beat rhythmically in her neck, and she felt a nerve jump in her lip. She hoped it wasn't visible. Hank loomed over her, but that wasn't what made her nervous. She was worried about whatever he was going to say.

"I was an ass coming on to you, Alexa. I'm not sorry I tried. If you'd been interested, you're the kind of gal I'd put a ring on. I knew you had an interest in Noah, and I know my cousin, though we haven't much seen eye to eye. He's never looked at any woman the way he looked at you. I brought Petra there that night to spoil his plans to sell his half of Hank's. For an ungodly sum, she'd agreed to threaten to divorce him and take half of his money from the sale. I couldn't believe how lucky I was that you snagged me coming out of the bar. The look on Noah's face said he was coming after you. I wanted him to see me kissing you that night. I'm ashamed to say that I wanted to put the final nail in his coffin, and I'm regretful for two reasons. One, Noah is a good guy, and I hurt him. He is my family. Two, I see you're still single, and I think in a roundabout way I had a hand in breaking your heart, too."

Lexi stood up, swiping at one eye. She didn't know why she was on the verge of crying. Anger filled her heart toward this arrogant man, but she knew it took a lot for a person to admit he was wrong. However, his words about his cousin and Noah's feelings for her touched an emotion that she'd buried after that night. Lexi had spent weeks crying and moping over what felt like being widowed all over again. She'd been angry at herself because she hadn't known Noah that long, and he didn't deserve the time she spent mourning lost opportunities. He'd been married, for God's sake.

"I have to go. My mother's waiting." She tried to brush past him, but he grabbed her arm, not in a harsh or aggressive way, but in the desperation of a man who needed to be heard.

He held onto her, assessing her with imploring eyes. "There's something else...." He paused as if searching for the right words. Shaking his head, he started again. "I want to give you some money —."

Lexi's jaw dropped in shock, and a different emotion roiled through her. Who did he think she was, or what? "I don't want your money, Hank!" She tugged her arm out of his grasp.

He rushed to go on, putting his hand on the door to keep her from flying out. "Please. Will you hear me out?" His eyes appealed to her to listen. She crossed her arms and tapped a foot but conceded to hear what he needed to say. "I want to give you money to travel up to Dallas, that's all. I want you to take a letter to Noah and make sure he opens it. I'll pay your gas, airfare, hotel, babysitter, time off work, or another ranch hand to help. I'm begging you. I need to fix this rift between Noah and me."

Lexi relaxed. The man did seem anguished. Maybe he really had turned a new leaf. But if he was sorry for real, why was Noah's ex-wife there with her hands and eyes on Hank? She shook the thought from her head. It was none of her business, and she didn't want to get involved. "Surely someone else could go to Dallas. Why don't you go? Don't you think this is a matter best solved in person between cousins? Noah is a good guy, and I'm sure he would accept your apology if you really meant it."

Hank released the door, looking forlorn. "I have my reasons. I'm sorry I bothered you with your mom and lady friends tonight." He studied his boots for a moment before he looked back up at her. Lexi opened the door and briskly walked away, but he called out to her once more. "If you change your mind, please call. It'd mean the world to me."

Lexi didn't turn back. She wanted to leave. All this talk of that night so many months ago, and in that time, Noah had been in Dallas. It hit her hard. She hadn't a clue he'd left Magnolia and his dream to open Bubbles. Was it all because she had kissed Hank? For the second time that night, she remembered her last kiss with Noah at Hank's Honky-Tonk, when he'd licked the icing off her finger. The memory was tarnished by the kiss Hank had given her afterward. The two moments weren't comparable. Hank admitted to bringing Petra there to destroy Noah's dream, and Lexi had fallen right into his scheme. Maybe she did need to drive to Dallas, at least to clear her own conscience with Noah.

Chapter 13

The phone app showed one hundred degrees in Magnolia and one hundred and five in Dallas. Her tank top was sticking to her, and Lexi wished she'd worn a long sundress to drive her mother's Lincoln. The leather seats were hot, and she stuck to them until the air conditioning cooled the car to a breathable temperature. She looked at the envelope on the seat next to her. It had taken some time to make the decision to visit Noah.

She'd tried to forget the conversation with Hank, but her conscience had nagged her in the barn, feeding the horses, driving the truck for the guys who bailed the hay, digging up root vegetables in her garden, or making dinner for the boys. Maybe Noah hadn't wanted anything serious with her to begin with, and maybe the whole affair had been intended as a fling, but the thought that he might have meant more, and that he might have given up everything to get away from what happened, was too much for her to bear. She had to clear the slate and tell him that the kiss with Hank had meant nothing. She'd thought he lied to her about being married, but regardless, he sure hadn't told her he was still legally married. Lexi knew that everyone was responsible for their own choices and that she wasn't the reason he'd lost his dream. Those were decisions he'd made when selling Bubbles to Hank. However, she wanted him to know the truth about her feelings, and she couldn't live with herself thinking, *what if.*

The apartment complex was new, and the road around the buildings was a simple circle. The addressed envelope had the number two-zero-one on it. She found building number two and parked in front. A pretty brunette pushed a man in a wheelchair down the walkway toward the apartments. Lexi followed behind them, looking for the door with the right number. The woman pushed the man to a unit and opened it with a key. He sounded irritated as he admonished the woman for trying to help as he hefted himself over the threshold. The young brunette followed him in and turned to shut the door. Lexi stood with her jaw slack and her heart in hand. It was the right number, and though she couldn't believe it, it was the right man.

"Noah," she called out. She wasn't sure he heard her. The door clicked shut. Torn between knocking on the apartment or running back to the car, she lingered in the sun, sweating through her summer clothes. Slowly, the door opened, and Noah looked out. She heard the soft curse before the door opened all the way.

"What do you want?"

Lexi hadn't been prepared to see Noah like this or hear the anger in his voice. It had been almost nine months since they'd parted. It wasn't like they'd had a real relationship. Obviously, she cared, or she wouldn't be there, but it was plain to see he didn't want any part of her visit. She held Hank's envelope in her hand.

"I brought you a letter." It sounded lame to her own ears, but it had been the catalyst that brought her to Dallas.

He made a snort of disbelief, cocking his head to the side. "The postman still delivers."

Lexi shrugged. "I know, but Hank asked me to bring it to you personally."

Again, he made another sound of disbelief. "I think Hank has said and done enough, don't you?" He looked down at his tennis-shoe-clad feet. Lexi wondered what had happened. Was he paralyzed?

She shrugged her shoulders, not knowing exactly what to say. "I'm not really here for Hank. He asked me to come a while ago, but I was still upset with you."

Noah's brows knitted together in confusion. "Mad at me? You were the one who kissed Hank!"

"I had just met your wife in the bar!" She shot back at him. He might be in a wheelchair, but the man had nerve. This wasn't all on her. And who was the brunette he was with now? She didn't look like a therapist or a lonely old relative. The woman was much younger and very pretty.

"Petra hasn't been my wife in almost twenty years!"

"And exactly when did you get divorced?"

He pressed his lips together as contemplative wrinkles sprouted around his eyes and mouth. He looked pained. "Why did you come here, Lexi?"

"Hank told me why you were still married. I don't know what's in that letter or if you've read his previous messages, but he told me that he brought Petra there to make you rethink selling your part of Hank's. I know now that he paid her to do it, but I didn't know all this then, because you never told me you were still legally married." She paused.

He nodded slowly, looking out somewhere in the distance.

"I really liked you, Noah. I was hoping we might have had something together, but I was hurt. When Hank took me home, he kissed me. I wasn't expecting it, but I admit that I let him. I don't know where my head was at, but it didn't really matter in the end. You never reached out to tell me the truth, and I have never been the kind of gal to chase after a married man."

Noah held his hand out to her. She closed the distance, handing him the letter.

"I'm sorry I didn't tell you about Petra. There hadn't been enough time to delve into life complications, and not all women would have understood or accepted the reasons I hadn't finalized the divorce." He paused as he clasped her wrist. "But you did deserve the truth. I'm really sorry I didn't stay to tell you."

His eyes shimmered with emotion as they held hers. He seemed to be locked in indecision, but finally he nodded, backing up his manual chair. Noah's biceps were ripped with the muscle he'd gained from his injury. She wanted to ask what had happened, but she could tell by his demeanor, inquiries weren't welcome. "Thanks for delivering this. Tell Hank I got it."

Lexi didn't know what else to say, but she wasn't ready to let him go. "Are you happy, with her?" She motioned to the apartment. The pain of her own words gripped her heart. She knew she seemed desperate to ask. *He is with someone else, Lexi. Get a hold of yourself!*

Noah paused, biting his bottom lip before saying, "They're what I need right now."

They're? Were there more women inside? She heard children laughing in the distance, and the realization dawned on her. Like Lexi, the pretty lady had kids. Not being able to take any more, she looked away in defeat. Too much time had passed. It was too late. Not knowing what to say, she started backing away. "Okay. I guess that's it then." She took her time, waiting for him to call her back, to explain, but he didn't. After a few moments, he shut the door unceremoniously, leaving Lexi dripping in the heat of the blistering sun. She wanted to curl up and cry. Why had she driven all the way to Dallas to torture herself?

She didn't know what to do, but clearly, he didn't have any other words to say to her. The letter was in his hands, and she'd said her piece. There was nothing more to say if he wasn't interested in seeing her. He made that clear when he shut the door in her face. It was his choice, and she had to accept that he'd moved on. A memory rang in her head, of an argument she'd had with Jack before he'd left on his last tour. She'd been angry at him for leaving again. They had children and responsibilities, and she'd begged him not to go, but those responsibilities were the reason he had reenlisted. Jack had looked at her and said, "There is a time and a place for everything, Lex, and this isn't it. Our day to be together will come, but you can't force a man to yield before he's ready."

Memories of Noah flashed through her mind, of how they'd met, his smile when he asked her to dinner the first time, the way he'd held her through the night after they'd made love, and how he'd named the bar Bubbles because she liked champagne. Taking a deep breath, she steadied herself. Life wasn't like champagne, filled with bubbles and tickling your nose pleasantly as you sipped from its golden nectar. It was an intoxicating martini world and there were so many different ways to shake it. She'd tried to avoid the onions in her life, hoping for rich Godiva chocolate or sweet watermelon to nourish her soul. Lexi tried not to ask for more than what was in her glass. She didn't like to tempt fate, but she'd done just that with Noah, wanting him too much. One sip hadn't been enough, and now, the hangover was a bitch.

Noah wasn't ready, and she didn't intend to plead with him to sign up for anything he didn't want. Apparently, he was committed elsewhere, but maybe it was a temporary fling. She wondered if he would read Hank's letter and come back to Magnolia one day. She couldn't guess what was written inside Hank's missive, but she knew Noah needed space. Lexi had come this far to make things right, and it had been painful for too many reasons to ponder right now. If she had learned one thing in her thirty years, it was that the love of a lifetime took two hearts that wanted to be tethered together as one. She knew for a fact that she deserved the chance at love again, and that one day she'd find it, with or without Noah Harding. Her heart skipped a beat at the thought of never seeing him again.

She gripped the steering wheel hard and sped up to enter the freeway. The Lincoln headed southbound down the I-35, and she let out a small sigh as the tears finally fell. The comfort of the ranch and the three boys that she loved more than anything beckoned her home. There was much to keep her busy while her wounds healed. As she knew so well, time was the best balm for an aching heart. She clicked on the radio to her favorite station and tapped a hand on the wheel. The singer crooned about lost love and regret, and Lexi forced a smile. "Don't fret, Lexi Louise, life might be like a country-western song right now, but there will be other hot days in Magnolia."

The End

Books by
Minette Lauren

HOT IN MAGNOLIA SERIES

Champagne Kisses
Prequel (Free!)
(Lexi Nash and Noah Harding—Part 1)

A recipe for hot dates in Magnolia...
*A beautiful widow with a farm, three wild little
boys, and too much work to handle.*
A bar owner armed with chivalry and a dream.
An accident that seems destined to happen.
And a summer too hot to cool things down.

Cupcakes and Kisses
Book 1
(Melvina Banks and Riley Nash)
and (Mona Calhoun and Manny Owens)

What does it take to make it Hot in Magnolia?
One cup of sexy,
Two tablespoons of sizzle,
And a whole lot of heart.

Five-Alarm Kisses
Book 2
(Nina Salas and Raphe Nash)
and (Bonnie Bush and Ran Nash)

What does it take to keep your cool in Magnolia?
**Don't watch over loose ladies, especially if she's your
sister-in-law's wayward basset hound.*
**Do take cream with your coffee at the diner because
it's as hot as the waitress who serves it.*
*Don't bet on love unless you're prepared to risk it all.

Double Trouble Kisses
Book 3
(Tabitha Graham and Eli Banks)

A Recipe for Double Trouble in Magnolia
* One pair of sexy high heels,
* Two identical women,
* One handsome hero,
* And a passel of mischievous pups.

Gingerbread Kisses
Book 4
(Ginger Lynn Harding and Roland Karr)
and (Lexi Nash and Noah Harding—Part 2)

A recipe to lie low in Magnolia
*Take one big secret and bury it in a small town.
* Add a too-handsome, do-good constable hot to find the truth.
**Mix in a sassy redhead who is depending on her
grandma's recipe to save her bacon.*
* Fold in a five-star attraction and watch sparks fly.

THE GUARDIAN SERIES
Chase the Moon
Book 1

The past and the future both exist in the in-between, but fate is never what you think… In the midst of the rocking 1980s, with glamorous pop stars and unlimited possibilities, Regan Hope Landry knows her destiny has got to be better than working at the Piggly Wiggly like her mother, Rona.

THE SOUL WATCHER SERIES
Race for the Sun
Book 1

A reckless act won't change the past, but will it cement the future? Soledad drowns herself in a storm off Key West. Sentenced to an afterlife as a soul watcher, she guards and guides her ward to find answers. Burned by a toxic marriage and struggling to heal the rift with her sister, it won't be easy to help this soul trust and love again.

BOOKS written as Zari Reede (Zoe Tasia and Minette Lauren)

Sins of the Sister

Lana Madison is a private investigator who is searching for the men who abducted her identical twin. Lana suffers from flashbacks and realizes there are gaps in her own memory from the day of the disappearance. She has given up on the police and is determined to find her sister on her own. Now her own life—as well as her sanity—is on the line…

Blinked

It's 1975 in the Big Easy where Mardi Gras floats and strangely dressed people are in abundance. Mindy Nichols, an agent of the Inner Space Monitoring Alliance Team "ISMAT," is about to set the Crescent City on its ear.

Daisy Dukes and Cowboy Boots

When big-city lawyer Nolan Anderson rolls into her small West Texas town, Ferina Kincaid goes into a tailspin of worry over losing her family's ranch.

Sign up for Minette Lauren's newsletter at minettelauren.com
Follow Minette on BookBub and Amazon

About the Author

As soon as Minette Lauren was old enough to write, she composed a play in one act about the love of Seth and Beth, inspired by the movie, *Gone with the Wind*. Not deterred by the play's questionable success, she has been in love with writing ever since. Growing up in a small town outside of New Orleans, Louisiana, has fueled a lot of her creative endeavors. She travels often and takes advantage of any place with a view that inspires her to write. Minette now resides in Texas, where she loves to write outdoors by her pool with her six furry writing muses. Besides her menagerie of tail-wagging pooches, she also has a loving husband, three turtles, and four sassy parrots to keep her company. Together, they make all of her dreams come true.

To learn more about the author or to find other great books written by Minette Lauren, visit www.minettelauren.com

Follow Minette on Twitter: @lauren_minette

www.ingramcontent.com/pod-product-compliance
Lightning Source LLC
Chambersburg PA
CBHW061310170626
46817CB00001B/125